The Guardian's Wildchild

Feather Stone

Feather Stone

OMNIFIC PUBLISHING

DALLAS

Omnific Publishing
P.O. Box 793871, Dallas, TX 75379
www.omnificpublishing.com

First Omnific eBook edition, September 2011
First Omnific trade paperback edition, September 2011

The characters and events in this book are fictitious.
Any similarity to real persons, living or dead,
is coincidental and not intended by the author.

Library of Congress Cataloguing-in-Publication Data

Stone, Feather.
   The Guardian's Wild Child / Feather Stone — 1st ed.
   ISBN 978-1-936305-88-9
   1. Paranormal — Romance. 2. Mysticism — Fiction.
   3. Romance — Fiction. 4. Action Adventure — Fiction.
   I. Title

10 9 8 7 6 5 4 3 2 1

Cover Design by Micha Stone and Amy Browkaw
Interior Book Design by Coreen Montagna

Printed in the United States of America

This story is dedicated to Scotty, a Shetland Sheepdog who came into my life in February of 1994. He quite simply and thoroughly changed my life. Through his need for healing of physical and emotional pain, I found ways of healing myself beyond conventional means. Through Scotty I learned more about unconditional love and the higher good during the past thirteen years than I had in my previous sixty something years. Scotty propelled me forward to discover I had a power that most would not dare to acknowledge.

Table of Contents

Prologue...1

1. The Guardians...3

2. Madame...10

3. The Seduction of the Rule Book........................13

4. Celeste and Sidney...22

5. Stepping Into the Darkness.................................31

6. Captain Waterhouse's Prisoner...........................41

7. Surrender of the Captain.....................................54

8. An Old Mexican's Crystal....................................63

9. Blurry Line Between Friend and Foe..................72

10. Sidney's Escape..88

11. Rules for Sidney..97

12. Hanging on to Secrets and the Sacred.............108

13. A Witch's Magic..122

14. Sam's Dark Prison...133

15. Sidney's Execution..144

16. Revealing the Crystal's Power..........................157

17. The Betrayal and the Kiss.................................170

18. The Missing Prisoner..176

19. The Slow Dance...184

20. Drowning an Admiral..195

21. Savannah's Gift..204

22. Madame's Spy..213

23. Madness and Clarity...222

24. Admiral Garland's Awakening..........................236

25. Guardians of Light and Dark Duel...................246

26. The Admiral's Guardian....................................255

27. Madame's Revenge..262

Epilogue...272

Prologue

Year 2020

The year 2020 was one long, terrifying nightmare. The planet trembled violently for months as if desperately trying to shed its skin. Land masses fell into the oceans or were consumed by the water's thirst for new territory. Tsunamis followed the Earth's devastating quakes, swallowing great ships and sweeping shorelines, sucking debris and bodies into oblivion. In one year, the world's maps became as useless as the rudimentary drawings of ancient explorers.

Governments worldwide activated martial law. Extreme measures were deemed necessary to maintain law and order. There was zero tolerance for anyone threatening the stability of the social order and security of the United States of America. Those arrested were quickly tried and given a life sentence. Over the next twenty years, rigid controls were somewhat relaxed, but not to the satisfaction of many. Protests fell on deaf ears.

Underground rebellion movements became lethal. Intolerant of the continued harsh controls and closed-door leadership, they aimed to destroy governments. Highways were no longer safe for government officials—many were hijacked, executed, and dumped by the roadside.

The government began to implement new tactics. Prisoners convicted of terrorism disappeared without a trace. Within twenty-four hours of arrest, they were quietly tried, then disappeared. No record, no witnesses, no media to voice the underground's grievances, no chance of a hearing, no escape. There was no acknowledgement that terrorist activity had occurred. Fear escalated among the followers of the underground. Their morale dropped, along with the frequency of their activities.

Admiral Garland followed government policy to the letter, and took advantage of the hold he had over Sam Waterhouse, Captain of the USS

Nonnah, a naval supply ship. Prisoners were executed on the *Nonnah*, well away from the public view. Blood was never spilled on the admiral's New Seattle Naval Base. To the outside world, his base's security had never been breached. No one would ever discover his secret.

1. The Guardians

Year 2028

The winter of 2028 arrived early on Hawk's Island. The Stone Clan was long accustomed to the temperamental nature of their island, located a mere twenty miles west of Vancouver Island. They had arrived thousands of years ago during their escape from certain genocide, one of a dozen similar clans fleeing from autocratic leaders who feared the Guardians' challenge to their supreme authority if they were allowed to remain among the people. When the Guardian clans fled, they found refuge in seclusion and carefully concealed their locations across the planet. Hawk's Island had never appeared on maps, and only those who sought the higher good in their deeds and thoughts would see its magnificent towering cliffs and lush, boreal forests. Resources were few, but the fresh water and grazing meadows would provide their sustenance—along with some help from their powerful sun crystals.

Wind moaned outside the Guardian Elders' meditation lodge. In the summer, two window openings would let in the sun and songs of birds from the surrounding forest. But today, shutters sealed the openings, protecting the eight Elders from the drifting snow. Inside, they prepared for another day of meditation.

Greystone, the youngest of the Elders, gathered his wool blanket around his shoulders and up over this head. Even though the blue threads had lost their lustre and the edges were badly frayed, he considered it a treasure. It was all that remained from his past when, lost at sea five hundred years ago, he'd been rescued by the Guardians. His long, dark brown hair was braided behind his ears and lay on his rust-colored, wool shirt. In spite of his great age, he appeared no more than thirty, his stature tall and robust. Merging with the Guardian sacred truths had slowed his ageing nearly to a standstill.

He sat down on another blanket on the lodge's worn wooden floor. For hundreds of years, he and his fellow Elders had meditated daily while seated on this floor. It had absorbed their murmurs, heard their calls to their spirit guides, and echoed their joy. The meditation room was small and spare. Candles, a kettle, and a teapot rested on a table.

There were enough cups for each of the Elders plus a few more, though many were often missing. Some cups could be found beside computers in the children's classroom, others in the fifteen cabins where the Guardians performed their artistic talents, creating their legendary paintings and sculptures. All of these were sold on the continents and provided financial support to maintain the community and its helicopter. The missing cups were a minor irritant, especially for Livingstone, the newest Elder, who was now searching for his favorite.

Gazing into the small fire in the center of the room, Greystone searched for its comforting warmth. It wasn't the chill in the air from which he was seeking refuge. His heart was deeply touched by the coldness of the times. His power of clairvoyance allowed him to witness all that took place on the planet.

He saw people searching for clean water. Medicine was scarce. Poorer coastal countries resorted to piracy in order to acquire scarce resources. Greystone watched the United States claw its way back from the overwhelming loss of land and naval strength during the Great Quake of 2020. Nearly 350 million people had been confirmed dead and another 50 million people were missing. Countless resources had been lost worldwide. Recently, martial law had eased, though only somewhat. The search for answers to the energy crisis had been replaced by the frantic efforts to rebuild lost cities and replace submerged farmland.

Even so, the common citizens continued to raise their families, work in their offices and construction sites, find joy in their sand dune playgrounds, sail their ships, and hold on to their vision of a new order of humanity. Away from the madness in government halls and military bases, there was an underlying current of calm. Greystone heard people question their leaders' motives. "Will the higher good be served?" they often asked.

He saw a dark future for the planet Earth. Traveling forward in time, Greystone stood on a lifeless plain with no clouds, no wind or sun. He saw a planet void of light and sound. Greystone's vision revealed that hope rested on the shoulders of his ten-year-old student, Sidney Davenport.

His fellow Elders, dressed in their simple cotton and wool clothes, sat with him in a circle around the fire—a focal point for their meditation. Birthstone was believed to be the eldest. Greystone thought she appeared to be Light itself with her bright blue eyes; her long white hair, braided and wrapped like a crown on her head; her fair and smooth complexion; small, gentle hands; and soft calming voice. Sometimes he found himself gazing at her, transfixed by her beauty.

Taking their customary seats in the room, the Elders spoke the spiritual truths of the Guardians in unison.

"Our path's burden is equal to our strength. We won't suffer failure if we remember the Creator's love is the source of our power. If we seek the Light and Truth, the higher good will be served. Our actions and thoughts are energies that return to us tenfold in the same manner as we delivered them into the universe. As you believe, so shall it be. We are one. We are eternal."

Livingstone and Lightstone began to beat their drums at a rhythmic tempo. Pockets of Guardian Elders around the planet joined in with the chant, "Let our Light be seen. Let our Light be received. Let our Light be healing. Let our Light be joyful. Let our Light be love." Greystone heard the voice of Paulo, his mentor in Acapulco, and gave him a thumbs-up salute. For thirty minutes they continued until Birthstone raised her hands for the chanting to cease.

For the remainder of the morning, the Elders telepathically shared their thoughts as the fire cast dancing shadows onto the log walls. They sent universal life energy around Earth and to its people, giving powerful healing to all who were open to receiving their gift.

The air was filled with the warm, pungent smell of burning spruce and poplar in the fire pit. The branches sizzled and snapped. The meditation went on. Candles flickered. Hour after hour, the Elders held their trance, focused only on their task of urging all humanity to return to its Guardian heritage. They sent their spiritual messages to all, including the merciless souls orchestrating their destructive storm.

Quietly, Terri Davenport and her ten-year-old daughter, Sidney, opened the door of the Elder's meditation lodge and entered the sacred space. It was time for lunch. They had brought biscuits, jam, cheese, and dried fruit. Without disturbing the Elders, they placed more wood on the fire and set a kettle over it. While they waited for the water to boil, they joined the circle and meditated.

Sidney chose to sit beside Greystone, her mentor. Greystone adored Sidney, or Wild Child, as he liked to call her. He felt her small hand take his. He smiled. He'd have to remind her during their next session together not to interrupt another's meditation.

Terri heard the water boiling and proceeded to make the tea. Gradually, the others returned to the present. While the food and tea were served, each Elder took an opportunity to tease the youngest Davenport. They loved the sound of her giggles. Her long, curly, auburn hair bounced as she skipped from one to another, flashing her beautiful, pale green eyes as she offered her tray of treats. Never shy, she returned the teasing with zeal.

Sipping on her tea, Birthstone beckoned Sidney to sit beside her. The girl was speechless at the invitation. Seldom did she even see Birthstone; to be invited to sit with her was a high honor. Birthstone gestured again, patting the floor where she wanted Sidney to sit. She also beckoned Terri to come sit beside her daughter. Together the three formed a small circle. Sidney gazed into Birthstone's blue eyes.

"We thank you very much for providing this wonderful meal," said the great lady. "I'd like to do something for both of you in return. Would you like to go on a journey with me?"

Sidney expected Birthstone to tell a story. Instead, the Elder held out her hands, palms turned toward the ceiling. "I'll take both of you to a most beautiful place, a place where the Guardians used to live many thousands of years ago. And we'll go to a place in the future."

As Sidney looked into Birthstone's smiling face, the ancient woman wondered if she truly understood what she was saying. The Davenport family had only recently joined the Guardian community, and Sidney was still a novice in the more advanced Guardian powers. She quickly became embarrassed and glanced at her mom.

Terri patted her daughter's hand. "Sidney, you can do this, my girl. I'll be right beside you. Remember your experience with Greystone on the mountain ledge just a few months ago? You told me that at first you were frightened. But only for a moment, right?"

Sidney brought her hands up to her mouth to stiffle to giggle. She nodded.

"Sounds like you have a story, Sidney." Birthstone chuckled while Greystone rolled his eyes and shook his head. "Would you first tell me your story?"

It took no urging. Sidney loved to tell stories. "Well, you see, Greystone and me, we were up on Blueberry Ridge, sitting on that ledge that overlooks the valley. You know the one where Celeste flies around?"

Sidney stopped briefly enough for Birthstone to nod. "Well, Greystone's body became, like, transparent and, you know, shimmery. You know what I mean? Then, he was, like, gone. Greystone vanished right there." Sidney sprung up on her feet and threw her arms up in the air. "Gone!" she shouted. She put her hands on her hips and opened her mouth wide as if in disbelief.

Birthstone was amused.

"Well, I tried to see if he was still there, you know, if I could touch him. There was nothing. I was pretty scared, at least for a little bit. Then I called him. 'Greystone, you come back here, right now!' And he did. He was even laughing. Can you believe that?"

Birthstone laughed. "Yes, Sidney, I can believe Greystone did that. Now are you ready to try something new?"

Sidney sat down again. "You mean, I can travel with you, Birthstone. I can do this? Really?"

"Yes, Sidney, and return in less than a blink of an eye." Birthstone winked at her. "Remember, you can return here anytime you wish with just a thought."

"Okay, I'll try it." She shuffled her bottom along the floor to get a little closer to Birthstone. Without any further hesitation, Sidney and her mother followed Birthstone's instructions, placing the palms of their hands on each other's palms. Immediately, the Elders were no longer around. Sidney was aware of her mother and Birthstone still beside her. Being free of the three-dimensional world's limitations, she could see their auras with greater clarity than through her physical eyes. Light glowed from them, combining energies with that of the universal life force.

Sidney saw that her physical body was diminutive compared to her ethereal body—which possessed a brilliant radiance and a passionate vibration. It reminded her of the dancing lights of the aurora borealis. It was the ultimate freedom. She recalled sensing this energy on other occasions. It was the same exquisite feeling she got when she communicated with her spirit guide, Seamus.

Just for a moment, Sidney created the thought to return to the Elder's lodge. In a flash she was back seated on the floor with her mother and Birthstone.

Birthstone opened her eyes and softly inquired, "Were you frightened, Sidney?"

"Nope, just testing." She giggled. "Let's go for real this time."

She heard the chuckles of the Elders.

In the same instant the lodge disappeared, the trio arrived at their destination. The meadow in which they found themselves took Sidney's breath away. Never had she seen anything so perfect. It was much like the Guardians' island, but in some ways even better. She felt surrounded by a healing energy. Then she saw them—two people walking along a river, a man and a woman.

The man lifted his hand toward a grove of trees, and a bird flew onto his outstretched palm. Sidney was certain he and the bird were communicating. The man nodded, and the bird returned to the skies. A moment later, the couple disappeared. Sidney became aware that she was standing with her mouth wide open in awe.

Sidney reached for her mother. "Mommy! Did you see that? I mean, did you really see?" Sidney became speechless.

Terri kneeled down and held her daughter close. "Yes, Sidney. This is how things were in the beginning. All of humanity were Guardians and lived like this until nearly everyone broke away from the sacred truths. They lost their powers and became servants of their physical nature. We call them the sleeping Guardians."

Sidney glanced toward the meadow. A spray of tiny yellow flowers could be seen here and there between tall grasses waving in a soft breeze. She wound a lock of her mother's brown hair in her fingers. "So they just forgot, right?"

Terri nodded. "Unfortunately, the sleeping Guardians may not have time to realize their true nature. The Darkness of fear is stronger than ever among those in power." Terri turned back to her daughter. "Some Guardians step out into the Darkness, like your father, in the hopes of waking the sleeping Guardians. It's not an easy task. Great care must be taken with sleeping Guardians. Their fear is easily triggered and often escalates to anger and violence, and some Guardians have been lost. That's why the outside world must never know about us."

Sidney groaned. "I know, I know." She leaned into her mother's shoulder. "It would be so much more fun if they all remembered; wouldn't it?"

"Yes," Terri said, chuckling and tweaking her daughter's nose. "Some are beginning to remember, like you in a previous life. Your return to the sacred truths is a tremendous gift to humanity."

"Especially for Greystone, I think," said Birthstone, laughing.

Then her face became somber as she closed her eyes and lifted her hands toward the sky. Suddenly, Birthstone and Sidney's mother disappeared. Darkness surrounded Sidney. Her heart raced. She could vaguely sense dark shapes moving beside her.

"Mommy, I can't see you. Where are you?"

Terri stroked the top of Sidney's head. "I'm right beside you, Sidney. We're fine, nothing to fear, my girl. We've traveled into the future on Earth, a dead planet. This is what may happen if we can't change the forces of Darkness. Darkness will rule. It's time we returned to the lodge, Birthstone."

For the first time, Sidney had seen the truth with her own eyes. The Earth had been a paradise. She understood more than ever why the Elders believed the Earth was dying. In the next moment, the three were again seated on the floor of the lodge.

Sidney sat quietly pondering her experience. She looked into Birthstone's kind face and sighed. "Birthstone, that was awesome. But, well, except for that last part. That was awful. Was that for real?"

Birthstone placed her hand under Sidney's chin and lifted the child's face up for a moment. She saw Sidney's fearless spirit. "Sidney, our tomorrows are shaped by the choices we make today. The Dark place we saw may never come to pass if humanity chooses to embrace the Light. As Guardians, it's our desire to help humanity return to the sacred truths. When you're old enough, you may choose to cultivate a path of Light for others to follow. It will be dangerous, and you may fail. The choice will be yours."

It was a lot for a young girl to consider. "Birthstone, how long will I have to wait, you know, till I can do some cultivating?" Then, tired of the tension, she teased her audience. "My brother, Danik, he'll help. I know he will. Have you seen him dig Mom's garden for her?"

If Darkness had found a niche in the meditation room in which to hide, it was promptly evicted. Laughter sent waves of joy and Light into the shadows and traveled through time to the Dark planet.

2. Madame

In hushed voices, the six scientists debated the lunacy of Madame's outlandish claim. They were waiting for her in the basement of the administration building on Admiral Garland's naval base. Two armed military personnel stood guard outside the door. The walls were as gray as the sinking mood of the six men and women who'd accepted the million dollar annual salary in exchange for an opportunity to resolve the planet's energy crisis.

Madame was an enigma. It was understood that she was highly intelligent and had unlimited wealth. She called no place home. She owned a highly trained militia, which was positioned in strategic locations across the planet. She had become a "person of interest" in the national security offices of many governments. Some believed she was an evil omen and had evolved out of the terror that had gripped humanity during the Great Quake.

Some might have liked to explain to this "ice woman," who no one ever dared address as anything less respectful or more personal than "Madame," that they were unavailable to assist with her project. Two scientists experienced with Madame and her reputation had revealed that working for her meant both wealth and personal risk. Anyone accepting a position with her was hers to do with as she pleased until the project was successfully completed. Then again, opportunities for research work since the Great Quake of 2020 were rare. Survival and rebuilding had taken precedence over research.

When Madame entered the room, the waiting scientists nodded and offered mumbled greetings. She ignored their approach and marched to the table. Two men dressed in dark suits shadowed her every move. With a swift stroke of her hand, Madame motioned for all to sit.

One refused. The woman stood fidgeting with her hands. "Madame, I've changed my mind. I'd like to leave. Now, please."

Madame turned to the female and casually stepped toward her. With uncharacteristic softness, Madame said, "Of course, my dear. I appreciate your change of heart. What area was, er, is your expertise? So that we may find a replacement, you understand."

"Physics, Madame."

"Ah, yes. You're Katherine Turner." Madame patted the scientist's arm. "Goodnight, my dear." Madame then placed a brief kiss on the scientist's cheek. "Mr. Smith will obtain transportation for you."

Miss Turner walked to the door, flushed almost as bright as the red lipstick stain on her face, and left, never to be seen again. As the door closed behind her, two of the other scientists turned pale and glanced nervously at each other.

There was nothing soft about Madame. From her short gray hair and chiseled features to her clenched fists and rigid stance, she exuded self-control and mastery over all. Her feminine qualities were carefully cloaked. Pretty blue eyes were barely visible behind shaded lenses, and her slim frame was concealed under a man's black business suit. Speaking in her monotone voice, she reminded those remaining in the room of the requirement for strict confidentiality.

They nodded.

"Zero tolerance. Is that clear? Any breach of your silence will be fatal." She enunciated each word, and then paused briefly. The men and women shifted in their chairs, avoiding eye contact with her. "You've received the information package. Any questions?"

The scientist least experienced with Madame replied. "Yes, Madame. I presume, however, that this *information* is just rumor. It's quite bizarre, really. No evidence. At least none that's—"

"It's no rumor." Madame smiled. "I personally witnessed the events," she said in almost a whisper. She paused, and her gaze drifted away from the group, not fixed on anything in particular. Her mind traveled to a jungle village in South America. "I saw primitive people perform miracles using crystals, sun crystals, they called them. These sun crystals responded to their touch. Whatever was commanded materialized instantly. Perhaps a type of psychic connection."

Madame turned her back on the scientists, her face grimacing from the frustration of having to admit her failure. Glancing at each other, the scientists' smirks betrayed a reluctance to indulge in the woman's fantasy. She turned, thrust her hand into her pants pocket and tossed a brilliant object into the air. Shards of light danced, illuminating the corners of the room.

A rainbow of colors played on the faces of the startled scientists. Before it fell to the table, Madame grabbed it and displayed it in her open hand.

"There you have it—the sun crystal," she said.

It was magnificent—a multifaceted blue green crystal encased within a clear crystal.

"It will power our machinery, grant unending summers, and transform water to wine. And you, my dear scientists, with the assistance of Admiral Garland, are going to unleash the crystal's power." She paused and snorted. "Too bad that miserable tribe died with their secrets." Tossing the crystal across the table, she announced, "Ladies and gentlemen, the kingdom of the gods is within our grasp."

One year later, on a cold spring evening, the scientists stood in breathless silence. Deep within the admiral's New Seattle Base, their laboratory still glowed from the light which had emanated from the crystal. The glass of water resting on the counter was now sweet red wine. Captain Butchart smiled and slipped away.

3. Seduction of the Rule Book

August 7, 2040

Samaru Waterhouse held his young wife's hand and wondered if she was aware that he was terminating her life. Brain dead, she'd never wake to speak the name of the man who had struck her down with his vehicle at a crosswalk, then dragged her body for nearly a block. With the flick of a switch the hissing of the machine stopped. The rise and fall of Joy's chest stopped. For a long, breathless, eternal moment, time stopped. He watched intently for any sign of a struggle from Joy—any movement at all. There was none. He realized he'd forgotten to say goodbye to the woman who was the wind in his sails while she still could have heard him.

"Joy!"

Throughout the sterile intensive care unit, down the shadowed hallway, and out beyond the windows to the empty night sky they heard him cry out. Someone dropped a tray; then a quiet fell upon the entire ward. For a moment it was all a part of his exploding, inconsolable grief.

Waterhouse couldn't bear to look upon his wife's lifeless face. He turned away and stiffened his posture in a hopeless effort to dam the flood of tears. He stumbled to the waiting room and let his grief flow. It took nearly an hour before he was composed enough to make his way out of the ward. He glanced around, watching medical staff continued their routine, ambling down the hallways, chatting with visitors, moving equipment from one room to another. He heard the sounds of a couple sharing a laugh, saw them touching. A janitor removed some trash and carried on without lifting his head to make eye contact with Sam, as though he wasn't there.

Life continued on. It did a dance around him but didn't invite him to enter its rhythm or pleasure. As grief took root, his connection with his higher wisdom began to detach itself. In place of his Japanese mother's

Buddhist mantras, his military training set up a protective barrier and the door to his heart slammed shut.

His military code of conduct provided a measure of comfort. It gave him motivation to sustain his control. He had Joy's murderer to capture, two sons to protect, schedules to keep, and, above all, the decorum of a high-ranking naval officer to maintain.

Waterhouse needed answers. The day after Joy's death, he went to the naval base administration office. The staff fell silent when he arrived at the admiral's reception floor. Entering Captain Butchart's office, he approached the officer, who was seated at his desk.

"Lieutenant Commander Waterhouse reporting, sir."

Captain Frank Butchart, Chief of Internal Affairs and Security, glanced up and began to rise from his chair.

"At ease, Lieutenant Commander. Did you say Waterhouse?"

Waterhouse relaxed slightly. He'd never met Captain Butchart before but had heard about him, enough to know they had little in common.

"Yes, sir. You probably knew my wife, Joy. I've come to pick up her personal items."

Butchart continued to simply gaze at him as if transfixed by some new thought. He nodded. "My condolences, Lieutenant Commander," he said with the appropriate amount of sincerity and began to walk away. "I'm due for a meeting with the admiral. See Celine with your request."

Waterhouse followed him. "Sir, Detective Flanders from the police station believes Joy was deliberately struck down, perhaps by someone from this base."

"Yes, I've heard that's his theory." The muscles in Butchart's jaw flexed. "Quite impertinent to question me." Again, Butchart believed the discussion was over and turned away.

Waterhouse was becoming annoyed with the captain's obvious arrogance. "Sir, if I can assist you in this investigation…"

"Not necessary, Commander. I've reviewed your wife's personnel file and other related files. There's nothing out of the ordinary. No indication that anyone was threatening her life."

Waterhouse used his six-foot body to hinder the captain's turn into another hallway. It was an aggressive move, but he wasn't going to let Butchart off the hook. The captain, seven years older than Waterhouse, must have known Joy in the ten years she'd worked for the admiral.

Surely, Waterhouse thought, *a man with that maturity would have more personal regard for someone who'd assisted both him and the admiral.* "What other investigations are being conducted? Interviews? Who was away from the base at the same time?"

"Captain Butchart," roared the admiral, standing at the door of his office. "I expected you five minutes ago."

Lieutenant Commander Waterhouse and Captain Butchart snapped to attention.

"Yes, sir," replied the captain, unmoved by the admiral's impatience. "Lieutenant Commander Waterhouse was inquiring about the investigation, sir."

The admiral turned to Waterhouse. "At ease," he ordered. "Frank, see to it that Mrs. Waterhouse's personal belongings are boxed and given to the Lieutenant Commander. Commander, you'll be provided with a copy of our report at the conclusion of our investigation. Is there anything we can do to help you and your boys?"

The offer sounded genuine. Waterhouse gave the standard reply. "Sir, your offer is appreciated, but we're going to be fine, sir."

"Good. Captain Butchart, let's get on with it."

The next day, Sam searched for options as to where he could place his sons while he was on duty in the Pacific as the operations commander of an aircraft carrier. The U.S. naval forces, still suffering shortage of manpower since the Great Quake, wouldn't release him from his contract for another four years. With no relatives or close friends, he kept running into empty options and brick walls.

On the third day, Waterhouse and his sons returned home from the funeral to find an envelope on their doorstep. After sending his boys to visit their friends, he opened the envelope. The message on the single page was clear. He was in grave danger.

The following morning, Waterhouse arrived at the New Seattle Police Station and waited for Detective Clay Flanders. The threatening letter was tucked inside his breast pocket. During the investigation of the "accident," he'd gained a trust in the detective's "good old fashioned horse sense" approach to getting to the truth. He'd told the detective that Joy had inadvertently accessed a confidential file belonging to Admiral Garland. But he'd carefully omitted information about her involvement with underground civil rights efforts.

"Hi, sailor. Doing okay?" said Detective Flanders, approaching from behind.

"Oh, hello, Clay. Got any news from your investigation at the base?"

"Just enough to make my skin itch." Clay spotted an empty table in a corner of the station's cafeteria, and the two men sat down with their simulated coffee. Clay shook his head. "God, I swear I've never seen a more nervous bunch of people. Like a bunch of rats in a science lab. When I asked to talk to security staff about Joy Waterhouse, they just plain disappeared, clean out of sight." He waved his hand up above his head. "A secretary said the Chief of Internal Affairs and Security wasn't available, and then she disappeared."

Clay leaned back in his chair and considered the value of his findings. "I talked with the admiral's staff. Military personnel are the worst, no disrespect intended. They clam up tighter than a bullfrog's ass. I decided to nose around a little. I could tell the security staff was hoping I'd leave. Made a real pain of myself. Finally got word this Captain Butchart fella would give me a few minutes. Sure the hell didn't like being questioned about the base activities. Quite arrogant. Is he that way normally?"

"Can't say. He basically refused to discuss the case."

"Right, right. Apparently on the day of the 'accident' the admiral had sent Joy downtown to pick up a present for his grandson. I told the captain he'd have to produce Joy's records—everything from her work records, computer access records, grievances, complaints, and such."

"Is he going to cooperate?"

Clay smiled. "The murder took place on my turf. He *has* to cooperate. Shit did he ever turn six shades of purple when I explained that to him. Well, Butchart doesn't agree that it was deliberate. If he and his staff are clean, I'll get all her records. If not, I might spot some tampering with her files."

Waterhouse handed the mysterious envelope to Clay.

The detective took out the sheet of paper, which had an imprint of a kiss in red lipstick. "Sam, I suspected this. Smells of underground stuff, specifically an ice woman who goes by the name of Madame. If I were you, I'd pack up the boys and disappear."

"Not the sort to run, Clay."

"Uh huh. I didn't think so. Well, Sam, this file will remain open, but I can't spend much more official time on it. From now on, watch your back." He waved his finger at Waterhouse. "You let me handle this. Understand? Don't go and get deeper in this shit. If the culprit makes a mistake, I'll get him. Agreed?"

"Sure, Clay. Keep in touch."

Waterhouse left the police station frustrated. The idea that his wife's murderer might not be punished tormented him. But there was one man who'd certainly know more than the police—Joy's underground contact, Badger. Even though most civilians, as well as many military personnel, had dealings with the underground to some extent, Sam never thought he'd personally contact them. Joy, on the other hand, had long been active with the organization's more mainstream, benevolent activities that sought change in government policy regarding children's rights and educational access. Though Sam didn't necessarily like her involvement, he'd let her follow her own path.

He'd never met Badger, but Joy had commented once that he was a cold and calculating man, always looking over his shoulder. Finding a public comlink, he gave in to the temptation and keyed in Badger's numbers. It gave him an uneasy feeling, as though he was sailing into uncharted waters.

The tone of Badger's voice was uninviting. "Yes?"

"Gypsy's down." Waterhouse used Joy's code name.

"So I hear." There was no expression of concern.

After a moment of silence, Waterhouse asked in code, "Any info on the market?"

Badger hesitated before giving a short, coded response. "Rat's in the bunker. Bonds are flawed. Watch for the gold shield and dive."

Waterhouse understood. "What's the risk?"

"*Thy Kingdom.*" The connection was suddenly gone.

Waterhouse understood the coded message. People were painfully aware of the government's practice of listening in on private conversations. Nothing was considered sacred. Many adjusted by talking in code. Joy had created a game with the boys using the code words she'd learned. It helped her remember the secret codes so she'd never make a mistake.

The brief conversation with Badger indicated trouble in the underground. Their ranks had been infiltrated by someone with power. Badger's advice to Waterhouse was to disappear. Badger had even dared to mention *Thy Kingdom*, the confidential file Joy had discovered, and implied significant danger in connection with it.

Sam was overwhelmed. Apparently his wife had provided Badger with the admiral's secret file. Driving home, Waterhouse considered his options. Twice he'd been advised to run. *What were the implications of that damn file Joy gave to Badger? Why had it led to her murder?*

For a decade Badger and his sort had fought the government's closed door policies. They were particularly lethal when it came to the military leaders' often violent protection of social order and national security. Now Sam found he was almost dead center between the two adversaries. He had the feeling that if he made any sudden moves, regardless of the direction, a bullet would be fired into his brain.

He envisioned grabbing his sons and disappearing. It was an unrealistic option. Detailed identification was required for everything, even the purchase of an apple. People like this Madame would find him. It would be a lifetime on the run. He wouldn't put his sons through that. And to desert Simon and Nathan was inconceivable.

For the time being, Waterhouse felt he was safe so long as he kept a low profile. He needed to find Joy's killer, but that would take time. He could be patient. His fellow officers had commended him on his skills as a brilliant strategist. He knew how to set up alliances, keep tuned into the flow of information whispered in dark places, and set the trap for the killer. No, he wouldn't run.

Five days after Joy's death, Waterhouse was in the process of acquiring temporary lodging for Nathan and Simon when he received a call from the admiral's office. He was required to meet with Admiral Garland at three that afternoon. When he arrived, the admiral's demeanor was his usual — direct and abrupt. He motioned for Waterhouse to sit down. A leather bound portfolio containing papers was placed in front of him.

"Waterhouse, we have business concerning your assignment. Your service contract ends in four years, July of 2044. Correct?"

"Yes, sir."

The admiral stiffened in his chair. "I, er, the navy has undertaken a few unusual ventures. As you must already know, with the severe cutbacks in air transport, most supplies must be transported using merchant ships. Fortunately, at least for us, most of the cruise companies have gone bankrupt. We've taken over these ships, far more economical than building new ones."

"Yes, I know. It's been twenty years since the disaster, and our scientists haven't resolved our energy crisis enough to make transport by air economical. How do the cruise ships hold up to the pirate problem?"

"These ships are now converted to carry cargo and are armed. I've refitted a small cruise ship, the USS *Nonnah*. It'll carry sensitive explosive devices and weapons. It's armed, has two helicopter landing pads, and one chopper. Our sub, the *Chameleon*, will shadow her as a back-up. Can't risk those pirates getting their hands on the cargo."

"Quite resourceful, sir. She'll still need a sharp crew to fight off the pirates."

"The crew is top drawer. Captain Norton has been putting the ship through testing to make sure she's seaworthy after the modifications. I'm satisfied with his reports. You, Waterhouse, are now the *Nonnah*'s captain."

It was unheard of for an admiral to discuss a lieutenant commander's reassignment or promotion directly with that officer. Waterhouse began to wonder if there was a lot more to this than what the admiral was revealing. He resisted the urge to challenge the admiral, although he was certain there were officers with more experience and seniority who should be considered for this assignment.

"You'll report to the *Nonnah* in one hour."

Waterhouse felt a growing threat in his gut and struggled to give a rational response. "Admiral, I have yet to find an acceptable home for my boys. My leave has been extended for another two weeks. I can't leave today, sir."

The admiral got up and gazed out his office window. "Let me be succinct, Waterhouse. You have a choice. Follow my orders, or—" He turned to face him. "Or you can spend the rest of your days in prison." Contempt was smeared across the admiral's face.

Waterhouse bolted up out of his chair. His body trembled as he struggled to inhale. "Prison! On what charge?"

The admiral marched over. Although slightly shorter than the junior officer's six-foot height, the admiral's shoulders were square with Waterhouse's, and his confidence made up for any difference between their frames.

"I know about your wife's clandestine activity. You're as guilty as she."

"Sir, I knew she opened some document in your files, accidentally. Beyond that, I..."

The admiral raised his fist to Waterhouse's face. "I'm not interested in your lies. You could have stopped her. You certainly can't be trusted. What I propose should work out nicely for the both of us. Sit down!"

Waterhouse hesitated. His instincts told him to grab the boys and run. He weighed the possibility of being shot. He sat down.

"Your kids will stay in my home." A victorious grin spread across the admiral's face. "You'll continue doing what you do best—captain a ship. You'll have some unique responsibilities. My helicopter will transfer you to the ship within the hour. The *Nonnah* is waiting for you just a few miles out from this base."

Waterhouse gritted his teeth. He'd allowed Joy to follow her own set of rules, a choice he now vehemently regretted. Rage began to rise above his normally orderly and controlled demeanour. He struggled to shift back into his military posture.

"What are the unique responsibilities?" He deliberately omitted the standard "sir." It was his first experience in removing himself from the military rule book, and he regretted it immediately. He added, "Sir."

"At South American ports, secured cases will be waiting for loading onto the *Nonnah*. These are not to be tampered with. You are to ensure their safe delivery to me each time you return to this port. Understood?"

"What is in the cases? Is there any risk to the crew or the ship?"

"That's classified information, and as long as the packages aren't opened, there should be no risk to the crew, ship...or you and your sons."

Waterhouse felt the blood drain from his head. He clenched onto his military officer's training. "What else, sir?"

"I don't have time to go into the details. You'll be provided with the codes to open a confidential file on your computer aboard the *Nonnah*. For now, just sign these papers agreeing to the promotion and assignment."

"My boys, I'd better talk to them, sir."

"Fine. Celine will arrange a phone call to the school."

While the call to his sons' school was being placed, he considered the alternative of prison. He had the feeling that what lay ahead for him as captain of the *Nonnah* would only be another kind of prison. But he doubted his case would be heard in any authentic judicial arena. The admiral wouldn't risk exposing the fact that confidential documents had been leaked to the underground. He wondered if the admiral was truly desperate enough to ensure the record would describe how Waterhouse had become so distraught over his wife's death that he committed suicide. For the sake of his sons, Waterhouse signed official documents agreeing to his new assignment.

He reported the promotion to his boys. Not for a second did he reveal his grave concern for their future as a family. Everything that mattered to him was now gone or held at arm's length from him. All that remained was his trust in his own military code of conduct, a sense of order and discipline.

When Waterhouse arrived on the *Nonnah* an hour later, Captain Norton immediately turned command over to him. He was given a quick tour. The ship still appeared more like a small luxury cruise ship than a navy vessel, except for the one helicopter and four guns mounted port and starboard. Thirty-five staterooms were being used as naval personnel quarters and two as prison cells. The rest had been converted into cargo holding rooms. The infirmary had only the basics.

The ship's senior officers were introduced. Waterhouse's first officer, Commander Everett Moon, was meticulous and stiff in his manner. Dr. Duncan was just the opposite, disheveled and nervous. The doctor's medical assistant, Lieutenant Lorna Paddles, had the nerve to wink as she saluted. On the other hand, the navigator, Lieutenant Commander Carla Smart, was obviously confident, striking just the right combination of being friendly and respectful. Then there was Lieutenant Robert John, in charge of the ship's engines and power systems. He was the only officer taller than Waterhouse.

Finally in his office alone, Captain Waterhouse retrieved the code to the confidential file in his computer. The documents were concerning the admiral's special directive—the directive on handling executions. Waterhouse sank into his chair. The walls of his prison began to close in.

During the year that followed, Waterhouse was the epitome of a naval officer, never straying from his duties, and never revealing to his fellow officers the anguish that festered within. He delivered the supplies to the American naval ports, picked up the mysterious packages at the South American docks, and executed Admiral Garland's terrorist prisoners.

The officers appreciated Captain Waterhouse's style of leadership. It was rigid but lacked harshness. Orders were clearly articulated and reprimands delivered appropriately to those in non-compliance. No one had ever observed Waterhouse out of uniform, heard him speak of family, or known him to indulge in activity unbecoming of an officer.

He remained in contact with the New Seattle Police Detective, but there had been no further developments in finding Joy's killer. He had his spies and informants, but there remained no opportunities to escape from Admiral Garland's grip.

With each execution on his ship, his mood plummeted further into an abyss of dark thoughts. Visions of destroying the admiral began to bring him pleasure. Day by day, the essence of the good man that was once Samaru Waterhouse was being replaced with something dark. In defiance of the admiral's tight rein, he allowed himself one avenue of rebellion: he let his hair grow long.

4. Celeste and Sidney

June 22, 2041

Resting on a mountain ridge, the red-tailed hawk stretched her magnificent wings to greet the rising sun. The autumn breeze lifted her into the air. Effortlessly, she glided between the canyon walls. Her domain stretched from the Pacific Ocean's seashore to deep into the valley where the Guardians lived.

There was only one other, a twenty-three-year-old Guardian, who was allowed to share the hawk's sanctuary above Blueberry Ridge—Sidney Davenport. Thirteen years ago, Sidney had boldly introduced herself.

"My name is Sidney, though sometimes I'm called Wild Child." She giggled. "I think your name should be Celeste. You're always up there, in space." She pointed to the sky. The hawk had accepted the name and was grateful at being acknowledged for her superior flying skills.

Celeste recalled her exasperation with young Sidney's sense of humor. On one occasion, the child had offered a gift of food, laid plainly in view on the rocky cliff. As Celeste was about to accept the generous offering, it disappeared and instantly reappeared several feet away. The infernal giggling that followed had annoyed Celeste more than the lapse in the child's respect. When Celeste could no longer tolerate the indignity, she'd telepathically scolded Sidney for using her telekinesis inappropriately, certainly not for the higher good.

Sidney had blossomed into a tall, slim woman with the same long, auburn, curly hair and pale green eyes. Her smile, warm and infectious, was one reason she was able to get away with stretching the Guardian community rules to the limit. Celeste offered guidance, though her advice was often tweaked when Sidney felt the rules were too confining. Continuously arriving late for school, using her telekinesis during meals, and teasing the Elders telepathically had prompted the Guardians to continue calling her Wild Child. So far, the worst punishments that had ever come to her were extra chores and disapproving looks from her cherished mentor, Greystone.

A slight shift in the wind brought Celeste back from her reverie. The sun's rays were beginning to cascade over Blueberry Ridge down into the folds and crevasses, drifting down to the meadows of the valley floor. The excitement of a new day was beginning to stir.

The mist in the valley receded into the distance, surrendering to the keeper of the day. The evergreens and moss released their fragrance into the warmth of the heavens. Morning songs of the forest had replaced the quiet stillness of the night, and currents of air rose, twisted, and tumbled near the canyon walls.

Ah, morning exercise, thought Celeste. Adjusting her wings, the bird called out her warning cry and began her descent.

Rapidly building speed, she descended to the valley. The ochre and rust boulders blended with the ridges of the canyon. Treetops and shadows became a blur of green and blue. The roar of the wind in her ears replaced the songs of the Earth birds. Just for fun, she careened through a grove of poplar trees and felt the flutter of wings madly dashing out of her path. At top speed, Celeste skimmed just above the meadow grasses toward the cliff wall. It took immense concentration to control each feather, the curve of her wings and tail, reaching for the right instant to catch the current of air that would sweep her up within inches of the face of the cliff.

Trusting eons of instinct and her higher wisdom, Celeste began her vertical climb. Her shadow followed her, silently gliding along the surface of the granite, sandstone, trees—and Sidney. And by the look of her aura, Sidney was in more trouble than usual.

Sidney waved to Celeste as the hawk continued flying out toward the ocean, drawing the Guardian's attention out beyond the valley toward the reef. The young woman missed watching the sailboat that used to approach the sheltered shore so often. It had been a year since she'd last seen the ship with its tangerine sails tossed about in the angry waves. She could barely see its captain struggle to keep from being thrown against the jagged rocks. It was unusual to see anything but whales near the reef. The Elders allowed only those humans who sought the higher good in their deeds and thoughts to see the island.

The memory reminded her that she was about to be thrown against jagged rocks of her own doing. She closed her eyes and winced at the thought that if she was killed, it would be a consequence of her choice last year to help the underground organization plant spy devices. Following that adventure, the Elders had expressed their disappointment in the Davenport brother-sister duo.

Birthstone's wise words echoed in her mind: *Our tomorrows are shaped by the choices we make today. Whatever energy you create will return to you. The Dark place you create for another, becomes your Dark place. It is the law of the universe. It is beyond man's law, and it is inescapable.* Birthstone had advised the siblings there were *ways* to make amends with the universal law. The *way* would be revealed if one became committed to the higher good.

Sidney and Danik had been expelled from the Guardian community for up to one year, though not as punishment. They had to make a choice—either prove they could live by the sacred truths and return to the Guardian community, or remain in the outside world with the unenlightened sleeping Guardians. Their work as Lanterns during the year would help them make that choice. As Lanterns, they scheduled singing appearances throughout North America. Their songs were powerful, not to control, but to enlighten those who sought truth. For anyone who was waking from their sleep, it was vital that a Guardian be there to guide their faltering steps. The warmth and reassuring light given by a Guardian would ward off the fears of the unknown, of the forgotten. It had been difficult for Sidney and Danik to live without the guidance of their mentors, though. In less than a year, they had been allowed to return to the safety of Hawk's Island and their family's old log home.

She'd even begun to trust that last year's impulsive action wouldn't return to haunt her. But as of yesterday, her life had changed. She could no longer be the naïve young Guardian. In the next few weeks she'd have to grow up and face a terror from which she'd always been shielded.

She and Danik had continued performances on the mainland even after returning to their island home. The previous day, while performing for her audience, the future had come in the form of Badger and his men. She'd stood, eyes closed, before her hushed audience at the Texas Horizon Theatre. Alone on the candle lit stage, she'd filled the auditorium with her loving energy. The two hundred and fifty people eagerly awaited her closing number. The musicians began. The slow rhythmic drumming of soldiers marching far away cast the spell. Sidney stepped forward and raised her arms as if reaching toward the people. A sweet sound drifted toward the audience. Musical notes surrounded the people like a soothing embrace. At first it was only a hum, then grew to a chant. Her lyrics were passionately sung and spoke of an enduring spirit.

Three men in dark clothes waited in the shadows near the stage exit. Standing behind the curtain, Danik observed them. One of the men indicated with his hands that he wanted to meet with him and Sidney. Danik motioned back that in five minutes the show would be over.

For the year they'd been performing in small theatres, at every performance, there had been someone trying to get into the theater with a weapon. Danik's trademark sense of humor became non-existent the first time someone fired a gun in Sidney's direction. The bullet had narrowly missed her but did wound one of the musicians. There had been several more attempts to silence the singer.

Sidney's audiences were moved by her messages about a grand power all of them possessed. She dared to tell them they no longer needed to follow the harsh and self-serving government restrictions, but could instead follow some "damned inner guidance," as many U.S. Senators had phrased it while protesting her messages. People were listening to her lyrics, it appeared. Now that the crisis of the Great Quake was more a memory than a part of current daily life, the government's hold on the masses was failing, even while it was still enforcing portions of martial law.

Once the curtain was lowered, Danik and a security officer quickly ushered Sidney off the stage. "We got company, Sid. They want to talk to us. Don't like the way they part their hair, if you know what I mean."

Sidney gave him a playful hip check. "Come along. There's a comb in my room, and you can fix them up real nice."

"Sid!" retorted Danik.

"Andy," he said, turning to the security officer outside her dressing room, "three men will be arriving shortly to meet with us. Give us five minutes before you let them in."

Danik slammed the door shut. "Sid, you're way too lax about this business. You go milling about in the crowd during your performances, hugging anyone who greets you … "

Sidney collapsed into a chair, exhausted from the evening's four-hour performance. "We're Lanterns, Dan. This is our path."

Danik grabbed another chair and sat in front of her. "Look, we've just been accepted back into the community on the island. Maybe we should take a break. There's tension building up across this country. I can feel it. Then we come along and stir up the pot. One of these days, someone will pull a knife and — "

"Remember, only fear can harm. And I do see if a person has hostile intentions. I'm not blind."

Irritated, Danik sprung from his chair. "Damn it, you take way too many chances. You're not playing by the rules again." He pounded his fist onto a table.

"I know, I know. So what else is new? I'm tired. Let's see what these guys want."

The door to her room swung open, and three men pushed their way past the security guard and quickly shut the door.

Danik stood like a wall between the men and Sidney. "I don't appreciate your lack of manners, gentlemen!"

The men showed no emotion. Their confidence was unnerving. The older man stepped forward. "Relax. We're not here to cause trouble. Your friend, Ryan, said you two might help."

Sidney gasped. Though she'd never let on, Ryan had been the only man who might have won her heart. He was also a waking Guardian. He joked that he still had his training wheels on. Danik had been looking for a flight instructor in Vancouver and, as the universe does, like attracted like. Meeting him at the Hawk's Flight Training and Rescue Service, Ryan was a match for Danik's easy going manner and daring bravado. Ryan had trained Danik how to fly a helicopter, and in exchange, the Davenports had helped him spy on Admiral Garland.

"Ryan? How do you know him?" Sidney asked.

"Not important. You helped him plant some listening devices a year ago. Yes?"

Sidney paused. "There's no denying that, Mister…"

"Call me Badger. Sit down, shall we?" Badger placed a chair near a table and motioned for Sidney to sit.

Sidney glanced at Danik, standing with his fists clenched. She smiled. "Relax. Let's see how many more rules I can break today."

Danik escorted her to the chair but remained standing while Badger sat down across the table from Sidney and folded his arms across his chest. The other two men remained at the door.

"Well, let's hear it," Danik demanded.

Badger carefully chose his words, revealing nothing of where he was from or whom he represented. "Like I said, we need your help. It concerns a file known as *Thy Kingdom Come*."

Sidney frowned. "Yes, Ryan said that file had to do with Admiral Garland discovering a new source of energy. Sounded routine except that he was hoping to have full control."

"Do you know what that energy source is?"

"No. I figured it was some new technology."

The man shook his head. "Ryan never told you?"

"No, and actually, I wanted nothing more to do with his underground activity." She leaned toward Badger. "And I still don't."

Badger was unmoved by Sidney's defiance. "You must! If we don't stop Admiral Garland, we can all forget about singing, or dancing, or, or breathing. You see, this new energy source is sun crystals."

Sidney looked up a Danik. "How could he … that is, how would the admiral know?"

Danik turned to Badger. "Just what do *you* know about sun crystals?"

"I know that most people can't make them work. People have said they're evil and will cause ruin. Ryan says certain people called Guardians use the crystals to create whatever they wish. That means if the admiral has just one Guardian in his back pocket, the consequences could be devastating globally." Badger shook his head. "Would you agree with that assessment, Danik?"

Danik took a deep breath and sat down beside Sidney. "The power of a sun crystal, well, it doesn't differentiate between good and evil. It only does the bidding of the one who's able to connect with its energy source. Its power is limited only by the clarity of the user's communication. Even Guardians seldom use them without the Elders' approval." Danik looked back at Sidney. "Badger's right. This admiral has to be persuaded to give up the project."

Badger snorted. "The admiral is only one player, and we suspect he is not the one pulling the strings. Listen, most of what we know is from the evening you and Ryan bugged the meeting between Admiral Garland and his scientists. And a few weeks later, a woman who worked with the admiral presented us with some coded information. She was killed shortly afterward. We've sent three men in and, well, they've all disappeared. We suspect they've been executed."

Sidney stood up and backed away from the table. "Okay, Badger, out with it." She was more angry than frightened. "Why have you come to us?"

Badger stood up and hesitated momentarily to respond. "Ryan says you and your brother have special abilities and that you're in with this so-called Guardian cult. You, in particular, can get into places and do stuff that normal people can't do. Is this so?"

Sidney considered denying the truth of her Guardian skills. However, it would mean that Ryan's testimony would be considered a lie and that might cause him trouble with Badger and his men.

"I have some telepathic abilities and a sensitivity to energy. If conditions are right, I can manipulate energy a little, unlock doors. That's about it," she said, downplaying her powers. "Just exactly what is it you're hoping I'll do for you?"

Badger approached and stared into her eyes. "You can get the complete *Thy Kingdom Come* file from Admiral Garland's office."

Sidney laughed, backing away. "You're crazy if you think I'll—"

"I'm not crazy! Just desperate enough to risk revealing our plan to someone not in our ranks," Badger barked.

Unmoved by Badger's belligerence, she asked, "Just how desperate?"

"We've learned that Admiral Garland is planning a demonstration next month, probably something dramatic to prove the authentic power of these crystals. Global authorities will be suspicious of the admiral's intent, and I doubt he's prepared for the chaos and paranoia that'll follow. Then mass hysteria, and then, dear Sidney, what do you think happens when a planet goes insane?"

The image shook Sidney. She brought her hand up to her chest, a habit she had when seeking a connection with her spirit guide, Seamus.

Badger went on. "Much of what we know is only fragments of information. We need to see that file. If you can get it for us, we can find out who all the players are. We can put the right roadblocks up in the right places. We believe Garland is a small fry in this project. Someone bigger is at the head of this insanity."

Sidney nodded. "I understand that. You want me to get into the admiral's computer and send the file to you."

"No, no. You'll have to download it onto a memory rod. We can't risk any electronic files being traced to us. He can't know we're on to him. He needs to continue on as though nothing is wrong."

"That's the real problem, isn't it? Getting in the base is probably easy enough, and making a copy of the file will tax my knowledge of computers, but getting out with a memory rod through the security scans? It's impossible."

"You'll hide the memory rod on the base. Someone will then enter the base with special equipment and retrieve it. If you're arrested, you'll telepathically tell Danik where you hid the rod. The admiral must not discover that you got his file, and we can't help you escape. Is that clear?"

Sidney only nodded.

Badger continued on as though he was merely communicating a grocery list. "You'll perform another task. In case you're arrested trying to leave the base, the admiral must believe your target was something relatively benign. But it must be enough to keep him from digging deeper."

"A diversion? Just what kind of diversion?"

"He's got a small warehouse of old nuclear missiles on his base. You'll get into the warehouse and defuse them."

Sidney threw up her hands. "Oh, sure, no problem. Aside from the fact that I know nothing about weapons, it should be a breeze." She mockingly slapped Danik's shoulder. "What do you say, Danik? Piece of cake, right?"

Danik wasn't amused and stood up. "Sidney, he's serious."

"I know he's serious. Seriously deluded if he thinks I'm going to touch one of those things!" She turned back to Badger. "Look, this is getting way beyond something I can do. The person you should be talking to is my father. He's far more experienced at this cloak and dagger stuff."

"Already tried him, or should I say, looked for him. He's apparently unavailable. People with your … talents are extremely rare. Ryan says you're the best of the Guardians at manipulating electrical currents and telekinesis."

Sidney shrugged her shoulders. "There are occasions when I fail, you know. I'm just as human as you."

"It's your choice. It's down to the last strokes. If you refuse, well, I hope you have a nice place to hide. Most of humanity doesn't. I'll contact you tomorrow for your answer. Good evening."

Sitting on the mountain ledge, Sidney tried to hang on to her connection with what had been her world—one she knew had its dark side, but not the insanity that Badger had spoken of. His prediction of a world gone mad was real. Birthstone had foretold that humanity would suffer a cataclysmic event that was of their own doing. She had taken Sidney forward in time to when Earth had become a lifeless planet. Sidney had assumed it would be due to greed and hatred. Now it was clearer—the Earth's demise would be caused by an all-consuming fear.

She had believed that price would be paid by a future generation—not that it would be now, and not for a novice Guardian to quell.

Just when her vision of the planet's fate was at its darkest, she felt the presence of her spirit guide, Seamus. Light surrounded her as his gentle energy permeated her physical space. She felt his ethereal hands resting on her shoulders, providing her with a depth of love that physical hands couldn't.

Most often it was Sidney who'd initiate the connection with her spiritual guide. It was almost a golden rule among spiritual entities to touch the three-dimensional world only upon receiving a beckoning call from their charges. Seamus occasionally broke that rule. Continuously aware of Sidney's energy, he was drawn to heal her troubled heart. Understanding her need before it was spoken, Seamus spoke.

"My sweet child, fear clouds your wisdom. Fear draws Darkness to you."

"Seamus, I'm concerned for humanity and the Earth. And yet it may be wrong for me to interfere with the admiral's business."

"Sidney, there's no action which is wrong when done with the higher good in your heart. The truth of your intention is the key. Know too, there's a natural rhythm to all life as there is to the oceans and the seasons. When the winter comes to your land, you discover unique beauty and purpose in the snow and ice. The winter presents special challenges. You grow. In life, you need to explore both summer and winter experiences. Move forward, Sidney, in the Light of the Creator. Know that I'm with you always, even if you fail. I'll be there when you return to me. There's nothing to fear."

Then he was gone.

5. Stepping Into the Darkness

Tuesday, July 2, 2041

After two weeks and several debriefings from Badger's staff, Sidney and Danik arrived at the New Seattle Naval Base on Tuesday morning. Security checks at the first gate took only minutes. Badger's attention to the details of their alias identification proved authentic enough to satisfy the armed guards. At the administration building, Danik grabbed Sidney's arm. He looked into her pale green eyes, which revealed determination to see the mission succeed.

"It's not too late, Sid. We can turn around and head back home." He held her hand firmly in both of his. She looked beautiful in the pale blue business suit. The sun shone in the curls of her warm brown hair resting on her shoulders. Her lips were painted a pale tangerine, something she normally did only for her singing performances.

"Come on, Dan. Walk me up the steps to the door." She grinned and patted his hand.

The heat of the sun encouraged Sidney to remove her blazer. The gentle breeze tugged at her revealing, white silk blouse.

"Maybe you should keep the blazer on, Sid."

"I'm going to be fine, Danik. I'll be out by the deadline, tomorrow noon, and meet you at the café. I'm ready."

"Yeah, so why are you shaking?"

"Hey, wouldn't you be nervous if you were applying for a job here?" She grabbed the flight bag he held. "You'd better have a few dollars when I get to the café tomorrow morning. I'll be quite hungry. See you later." She kissed his cheek and pushed her way through the doors.

On Wednesday morning, Danik arrived at the café long before the morning customers arrived. He'd resisted the temptation to telepathically connect with Sidney. She didn't need the distraction. As the morning sun inched closer to its noon place in the sky, Danik finally had enough of waiting. Sitting up straight in his patio chair, he breathed deeply and visualized his chest open wide to release his energy to the universe and to Sidney. On the waves of this energy, he could sense the physical presence of whatever he focused his mind on. He brought Sidney into his consciousness as gently as the mist envelops the sails of a ship.

He recognized her physical signature. But her Guardian energy was evaporating. He was losing her to a Dark force. She was mute, unable to telepathically communicate with him until the very last moment of his contact. Her message was brief and frightening.

Seated on the cold cement floor of her small cell, Sidney tried to meditate. Her mind's chatter refused to be silenced. Never before had she failed at such an easy Guardian gift. Her Guardian powers were evaporating. Her entire body was trembling, not from the cold, but from fear. And it wasn't fear of punishment; it was the gradual loss of her Guardian nature that was beginning to paralyze her mind.

She'd completed her mission. The memory rod with the file was safely hidden, and the missiles had been disabled. So far, the security personnel were only concerned that she'd been trespassing. If she could convince them that she was simply there because of a dare, she'd be set free — if no one checked the missiles. With each passing minute, she was certain someone would discover the missiles had been sabotaged. It was nearly eleven. She'd considered escaping from her cell using telekinesis, but that option was no longer possible. Her mind wouldn't be silenced enough to focus, and she couldn't understand how she'd lost control.

Suddenly, a guard shouted. "Move to the back wall and put your hands on your head!"

She was handcuffed and escorted to a room where an officer sat rigid in his chair behind a table. The officer's snug navy blue uniform was covered with gold braid and badges. Sidney guessed he was forty, though it was hard to tell. His head was shaved clean, as was his face. His most remarkable features were his large, blue eyes and long, dark eyelashes. The man could have been considered handsome if he smiled.

Something stirred within Sidney. Her most basic gift of seeing into a person's aura was intact. Most times she had to switch that ability off because it was distracting. But even just glancing at this man, she saw it—his body's battle with an imbalance.

She took another step closer to the officer's table and cleared her throat. "I … I'm really sorry, truly sorry about all this trouble." Her voice trembled. "I meant no harm. Just wanted to—"

The officer interrupted her. "Miss, you'll speak only when asked a question. Understood?"

Sidney quickly and obediently responded. "Yes, sir."

"I'm Captain Frank Butchart, Chief of Internal Affairs and Security."

Butchart continued to instruct her on the rules of the interrogation. She didn't hear a word. When he'd said his name, Sidney felt like she'd been struck on the back of her head. Butchart was the name of two Guardian brothers who'd lived on the island, brothers who'd left on a mission twenty years ago and never returned. Greystone had told her Giles Butchart had been murdered, but whenever she asked him about Frank, he'd become silent. It was understood but not discussed. Frank was now a fallen Guardian using his powers for his own purposes, regardless of the Dark consequences.

Sidney wondered if Captain Butchart was the same Guardian her mentor had spoken of. Perhaps Badger's worst fears were founded. Perhaps Admiral Garland did have a Guardian in his back pocket. Butchart glared at Sidney.

"Miss Peters," he said, using the fictitious name on her application form. He spoke slowly as if he knew the name was false. "Normally I'd obtain a statement from you." He rose from his chair. "However, I refuse to waste my time on a liar." Butchart walked around the table and stood in front of Sidney. He towered over her. "Your employment application form is full of lies."

Sidney smiled nervously. "I can explain, sir. This was all just, you know, a dare." It was truthful enough.

"And what was entailed in this dare?"

"Nothing much. Get on the base and stay overnight without getting caught, then get off the base before ten."

Butchart grinned and stepped closer. "It's past ten now. What was your prize supposed to be, Miss Peters?"

He was so close she could feel his breath on her face. "No prize, Captain. It was just an initiation exercise. You know, to prove I'd fit in with the gang."

Butchart sighed. His time was being wasted on this prankster. "Explain how you bypassed the gate security check on Tuesday evening and remained unseen until Wednesday morning."

Sidney felt the captain invade her ethereal body, searching for a disturbance in her energy's web, for traces of lies. At that point, it was clear to her that he was indeed the same fallen Guardian, one who'd been trusted by her people.

She had to be careful. If she used her Guardian powers, he'd recognize that she wasn't an ordinary prisoner. Her chances for survival would be gone. He'd not allow another Guardian to survive, nor anyone else who had the power to stop him.

She made no attempt to put up barriers to his probing. She had to avoid lies. More lies would only raise more suspicion. More suspicion would create more questions. Every second that went by was another second for someone to discover the sabotaged missiles.

She told Butchart the truth. That she'd never left the base Tuesday afternoon, that another woman had been disguised to make it look like she'd left the base after the interview with Admiral Garland's staff. She admitted to finding the storage room and hiding out there. She told them she'd planned to talk to the security officer, Lieutenant Weir, in hopes he'd help her get past the security gate.

Butchart leaned forward. "And why would Lieutenant Weir help you get off the base?"

Sidney shrugged. "Well, guess 'cause he seems really nice and 'cause no harm was done, and well, probably he likes to have a good time."

She felt her face warm when she realized the implication. Her innocence may have saved her—Butchart snickered. Returning to his chair, he took a deep breath and released it slowly. Sidney sensed he was attempting to establish a telepathic link. Soon, he became frustrated and returned to the manuscript in front of him.

"Miss Peters, my decision will be based solely on evidence. My staff is combing this base. If there's any evidence indicating an invasion of secured areas, I intend to charge you with spying. Is that clear?"

Sidney nodded. Butchart activated his comlink, requesting one of his men to report to the interrogation room. Within seconds, the man entered the room and stood at attention before the captain.

"Your report is ready?" he asked.

"Yes, sir."

Butchart ordered the security guards to take Sidney back to the hallway. Standing outside the room, she heard portions of what they said. Butchart became increasingly infuriated. She heard him shout, "Are you absolutely certain?"

Every cell in her body convulsed. It was difficult to breathe. This was it; they'd discovered the defused missiles. She'd never be released. The interrogation room door opened, and the guards were instructed to bring Sidney back into the room. They grabbed her arms and shoved her to stand directly in front of Butchart.

She closed her eyes and saw her Guardian mentor's smiling face. Greystone spoke. "Remember you need only the courage to trust in the Guardian sacred truths." In that moment she surrendered to the wisdom of the universe. No longer shackled by fear, she could summon her powers with simply a thought. She opened her eyes and stood tall. With her head erect, she faced Butchart.

"Miss Peters, in view of the fact that there's no evidence of malicious activity, you aren't being charged with any criminal activity. You'll leave once you've signed the interrogation report."

"Thank you, Captain. I'm truly grateful."

Butchart's cold demeanor was unmoved by Sidney's gratitude. He put his hand on her arm and gripped it tightly. "And," he whispered with contempt, "if I should find proof you were here on some mission of sabotage, I'll find you and bring you back. Understood?"

Sidney nodded. The handcuffs were removed. The transcription of the interrogation session arrived, and Sidney signed it as Heather Peters. Butchart stormed out of the room, leaving the security guards to escort her to the front desk where Lieutenant Weir was waiting. He quickly ushered her out of the administration building to the parking lot.

"I've called a taxi for you. Just wait here by the gate."

Sidney worried it may take too long for a taxi to show up. She had to get off the base now. She shook her head.

"Oh, please don't bother. I need to do some walking and thinking."

An alarm sounded, enveloping the entire base compound. Naval personnel began to scurry and run, forming a line near the gates. Sidney looked at the road leading toward the freeway. It was straight without any buildings or bushes to conceal her flight. Before Lieutenant Weir had time to turn back to her, she was running at fast as she could down the road. He started after her.

"Peters, stop! There's probably a mistake," he shouted to her.

Sidney ignored him. Lieutenant Weir wasn't far behind. Gradually she gained distance from him. Others joined the pursuit, shouting for her to stop or be shot. She mentally braced herself and raced on. Survival instincts and a life of running on mountain trails in high altitude gave her an edge. The ramp onto the freeway was only a few yards away. If she could get that far, the officers would have more difficulty capturing her.

A bullet whizzed by her head. A second bullet hit the ground on the left just ahead of her. She began to run an erratic course. Another bullet passed through her left hand. Blood splattered onto the pavement, and a searing pain traveled the length of her arm. The jolt of pain caused her to trip and fall. A security guard pinned her to the ground with his knees and held her wrists in a tight grip. He raised his right hand to strike her with his fist. Exhausted and in pain, she surrendered.

The security guards pushed Sidney into the back of their vehicle. Lieutenant Weir sat next to her. She stared out her side window and called to her brother telepathically. *Danik.* There was no response. Her mind was too focused on the painful wound and dire circumstances to make the connection. Again she tried to redirect her mind. *Danik, go home. Go home now!*

The telepathic link was brief. But in that one moment, Sidney was able to convey that she'd been arrested. She believed Badger could be a danger to both of them now that she'd failed, and the best way for her brother to help her was to return to Hawk's Island. She felt his attempt to continue the link, but his loving energy was overshadowed by her ordeal.

"Come on." Lieutenant Weir led her into the administration building. "The admiral's waiting. Man is he ticked. I don't believe you're a hostile, so I'll try and look out for you. Can't promise anything. It's going to be rough."

Sidney examined Lieutenant Weir's face. She saw pride in his uniform, but also saw that his uniform didn't define him as a man. He was likely the closest thing to a friend available to her now. The lieutenant guided her through the hallways to the interrogation room.

"My friend, don't put yourself in any danger on my account. I do have other resources."

"Is there anyone I can contact?" he whispered while the others were several feet behind. "Someone with some pull, a lawyer?"

"No, I'm on my own for now."

Walking in silence into the interrogation room, Lieutenant Weir grabbed a first aid kit. He seated her in a chair and inspected her hand. The bullet had passed cleanly through the palm. Her hand had stopped bleeding but was swollen, and any pressure or movement of the fingers made her wince. Kneeling on the floor in front of her, Weir wrapped the gauze around her hand and secured it with a piece of tape.

"Where are they going to take me, Lieutenant?"

He glanced up into her worried eyes. She was tired. Her clothes were dirty and stained with blood, her hair was tangled, and she smelled of sweat—a far cry from the vivacious beauty who'd cheerfully greeted him a day ago.

"If you're found guilty of terrorism, you'll be transferred to a ship under the command of Captain Waterhouse, good guy, mostly. You can trust him, if you get that far. That's all I can tell you."

Admiral Garland arrived with two armed men close behind him. Although still agitated, the admiral had mastered his anger. Lieutenant Weir snapped to attention.

"You're excused, Lieutenant. Make sure no one enters this room. If she makes another escape attempt, shoot her legs off. Is that clear?"

"Yes, sir." He swiftly left.

Butchart, carrying a medical kit, burst into the room. "Sir—"

The admiral interrupted. "Frank, we'll talk about this fiasco later. Who the hell helped her get through the security systems? Get a confession, whatever it takes. Understood?"

Butchart glared at Sidney. He barked orders at the two men to secure her to the chair.

Sidney cooperated and made no complaint as the metal handcuffs tightened around her wrists and ankles. Her Guardian nature could help her if she gained control over her fear. She breathed slowly, and silently repeated the sacred truths.

The admiral slowly paced around her chair, his arms crossed over his chest. His demeanor was that of a man in complete control and pondering his next move.

He stood directly in front of Sidney. "Gentlemen, I believe we have a saboteur. Our missiles have somehow been destroyed. I don't need her confession on that matter. She obviously had someone on the inside get her through secured areas. Who was her accomplice? Frank, choose your weapon, whatever will make her talk. I want her accomplice locked up and eliminated before sundown."

Butchart approached her. Sidney stiffened, anticipating a violent blow or an act of humiliation. "You are hereby charged with spying and the sabotage of American military weapons, a deliberate act of violence against the United States of America. You can save yourself considerable suffering if you tell us who your accomplice was."

Sidney looked into the captain's eyes. "No one, sir."

"Liar!" Butchart opened the medical kit and handed a vial to one of his men. "Jack, prepare the first dose of the serum." Jack pulled out a syringe from the bag and ripped open its packaging. Inserting the needle into the vial, he drew a solution into the syringe.

Butchart grabbed her hair and yanked her head back. "Now, one more time before I inject the drug. Once the drug hits your brain, it'll allow only the truth into your conscious thought. And it'll have a very nasty effect on your body. Who was your accomplice?"

The grip on her hair brought tears to her eyes. "Captain Butchart, I promise there was no accomplice. No one." She closed her eyes and again focused on the solution in the vial and the syringe. Briefly, she connected with its energy, sensing its tart taste in her mouth. She asked that it harmonize its energy with that of that of the Earth and the Creator, that its energy be shifted for the higher good of all. That was the last thought she could recall the next morning.

Thursday, July 4, Early Morning

She was awakened by footsteps approaching her cell. They were pounding, like those of a man strutting and sure of himself. Butchart stopped in front of her cell door, smiling with contempt and satisfaction. With a wave of his hand he dismissed the two security guards.

"Good morning, Miss Davenport. That *is* your name, according to what you told us when the serum went to work." Butchart stood tall, his arms across his chest. "No need for further questioning, my dear. Did you sleep well?" he asked sarcastically.

Sidney mustered up some strength. She wondered just how much she'd revealed. Most of the previous day was a blank. Her mind was so muddled she could barely recall how her hand had been injured. She shuffled to the cell door.

"I've been better, Captain."

Butchart smiled. "So, how is dear old Greystone?"

Sidney was taken aback. "Who?"

"My dear little witch, it became obvious when that bullet wound in your hand was healing so rapidly. Then, too, the serum had minimal effect on your brain, though it just might kill you in a day or so." He paced a few steps back and forth in front of her cell's door. "And another Guardian will be eliminated."

"Frank, Greystone hasn't forgotten you. Someone will soon come to bring you back home to him."

"He can try," he said with a pasted on smile.

Sidney hung onto the metal bars of her cell door. "Tell me, does the admiral know who you really are?"

Butchart pounced at her. "Shut your damn mouth," he hissed. "So far your father has escaped my traps, but you are finished. None of you are going to interfere with my business here." He stepped back and regained his military posture. "You're being transferred to a ship. I'll personally escort you there and provide Captain Waterhouse with orders to have you executed." He stepped up close to the cell door. "And then I'll have the pleasure of witnessing the bullet turn your little Guardian brain into mush. You're in no condition to stop a bullet."

Butchart hauled her outside to the rear of the building and waited as the chopper descended. The captain held a knife against her ribs. "If anything out of the ordinary happens, anything at all, the slightest tremor in the chopper's engines, you're dead. Is that clear?"

Sidney nodded.

Stumbling toward the chopper, she struggled to focus. The drug in her blood was again creating a dense mental fog. She felt her body gradually giving in to its poison. Dust rose and swirled with the force of the blades whipping through the air. Bits of grit stung her face. The captain shoved her through the doorway of the chopper and strapped her into a seat. She closed her eyes and made one last effort to reach her universal powers. Thus, her thoughts were delivered to the Light.

Before she was too ill to access her powers, Sidney placed a protective shield around her Holy Membrane. A Guardian's Holy Membrane was a cocoon of energy that became more powerful over time as the waking Guardian's aura became in sync with the Universal Creator. It responded to the thoughts and intentions of the Guardian. It facilitated rapid healing, telepathy, time travel—all of the Guardians' sacred gifts. But if the host was weak, dominant Dark forces could influence and penetrate the Holy Membrane.

Shielding the Holy Membrane was a last resort, a desperate act. The shield's energy came from beings of Light in higher dimensions, neutralizing and repelling anything that came into contact with the physical host. Nothing could penetrate the shield, not even the forces that would benefit the host.

Rapid healing would decline and connection with the Guardian Elders would be lost. It wouldn't allow another foreign substance to have any effect on her body. The secrets of her Guardian people would not be revealed through another drug assault. Sidney knew her choice could result in her death because the energy would also interfere with medication that could save her life. The shield would remain in place until Sidney either died or became strong enough to remove what she had created. She relaxed and became oblivious to the captain beside her and the jostling of the chopper.

6. Captain Waterhouse's Prisoner

July 4, Mid-Morning, Near New Seattle's Naval Harbor

Sidney felt the helicopter shift altitude and woke to see beneath her the gray Pacific Ocean and what appeared to be a modified cruise ship. At the perimeter of the ship's helipad was an officer and a dozen or so armed seamen. Below the helipad were the ship decks, gun turrets, and the spray of the ocean against the ship's silver hull. The helicopter touched down lightly, and its door swung open.

"Let's go," hollered Butchart.

Sidney's hands were still handcuffed behind her, making it difficult for her to maintain balance. Taking a deep breath, she managed to step down. Butchart clutched her neck to push her head below the rotating blades and led her toward the waiting officer.

The formal military greeting was a blur of salutes and stiff postures. Sidney's gaze stayed fixed on the ocean. She longed for its wetness in her parched mouth. Though she wouldn't have had the strength to stay afloat, the thought of the cool waves washing over her feverish skin was refreshing. No one spoke to her until her knees weakened and she faltered.

The ship's officer grasped her arm and commanded, "Stand up. Put your feet farther apart to keep your balance. Understood?"

The officer's voice was unsympathetic, and yet it didn't carry the hatred of Butchart's. She tried to smile, to convey something along the lines of gratitude rather than indifference to his assistance. The officer looked into Sidney's face.

"Captain Butchart, sir, the prisoner appears sick. Why is she so pale? She seems to have a fever, too. Captain Waterhouse is quite clear on not accepting injured or ill prisoners, sir."

"Lieutenant Bridges, the captain's going to have to make an exception in this case. Special circumstances. Anyway, she's to be executed this evening. No need for him to conduct an interrogation on this one. Let's go."

Inside the captain's office, both men stood at attention on either side of Sidney.

"Captain Butchart reporting with the prisoner, Sidney Davenport, sir," called out Bridges.

Behind a massive desk, the captain sat stiffly in his chair. He glanced at Sidney, then gave an almost imperceptible nod to his lieutenant. His gaze shifted to Butchart. A tense silence followed. It stirred Sidney's reserves. She noticed that Butchart's breathing became shallow and his hand gripping her arm was sweating.

Neither Butchart nor Waterhouse spoke the usual words of greeting. The silence troubled Sidney. Finally, Waterhouse rose from his chair. "At ease," he ordered. His voice was crisp and deep. "*Frank*, it looks like you've been rather busy." He eyed Sidney's tangled hair, filthy clothes, and bare feet. "Who or what have you delivered to the *Nonnah*?"

"Nothing you'll have to be bothered with for long. She's to be executed this evening. The details are on this file." Butchart pulled out a memory rod from his tunic and tossed it onto the desk. "I'll remain on board until after her execution."

Waterhouse walked up to Butchart and smiled. "You want to watch, Frank? You're short of blood on the naval base?"

Butchart snorted. "This is a special case. She's quite dangerous."

Waterhouse raised his eyebrows. "Is that so?"

Sidney sensed that under the military fiber of their equal rank something wanted to be unleashed. She felt it in Butchart's tightening grip and saw it in Waterhouse's dark eyes. But she felt a warmth in him even though he held his mouth in a firm expression of cold indifference. While every cell of the ship's captain screamed authority, she felt the word "safe" when she looked at him. And there was something more behind those eyes, something that reminded her of Greystone. But she had no energy to inspect his aura, was no longer able to focus for more than a few seconds at a time. The room's floor swayed, and her mind began to drift. More and more, an adversary more lethal than Butchart took hold of her body.

Waterhouse walked to a counter behind Sidney. "Coffee, Frank?"

"Coffee would be fine once this prisoner is stowed away in a cell. You'll need to post someone in front of her door continuously. I'll escort her there now."

"She looks pretty sick. Or have you just been hard to please?" Waterhouse chuckled as he returned to stand in front of Sidney.

"Captain Waterhouse, she's tougher than she looks. And I wouldn't trust her."

"Carla Smart," Waterhouse called into the comlink on his tunic. He continued to stare into Sidney's face, studying her.

She tried to speak to him with her aura and telepathic gift. *I surrender, my friend, and place my body in your good wisdom and care.*

In seconds, a reply was heard from the captain's comlink speakers. "Lieutenant Smart here, Captain."

"Carla, commence heading to Acapulco."

"Aye, aye, sir."

"Sam," protested Butchart, "we're to remain near New Seattle Naval Base until after this evening's execution. I need to return immediately after this business is finished."

Sidney slumped toward the floor.

"Put her in a chair, Bridges, before she makes a mess on my floor."

Sidney felt a chair pushed against the back of her knees, and she collapsed into it.

"A storm's brewing out near the California coast. I hope to sail past it before it gets too fired up. Lieutenant Bridges has your room ready for overnight. Will you join my officers and me for dinner at eighteen-hundred hours?"

Butchart hesitated as he sorted his thoughts. "Of course. Perhaps we can discuss the execution protocol in more detail. Lieutenant Bridges, take her to her cell."

Bridges looked to his captain for confirmation.

Addressing the lieutenant, Waterhouse asked, "Did she give you any trouble, Bridges?"

"She just had trouble walking, sir."

"On your way to the cells, have Dr. Duncan look at her. I want a report on her medical condition in twenty minutes. Carry her, if you have to. Understood?"

Butchart frowned. "She's merely reacting to the truth serum. Administered well within protocol, I assure you."

"I'm quite familiar with the protocol on Admiral Garland's home naval base. Procedure on my ship is also strict. I don't tolerate disorder. This prisoner is in obvious disorder."

Waterhouse nodded to the lieutenant, who lifted Sidney to her feet and picked her up as she collapsed into his arms. As he left, Waterhouse motioned toward the two chairs in front of his desk.

"Have a seat, Frank. Tell me about Miss Davenport. How did that little thing outfox your security systems?"

He knew the electronic file provided details—the truths mixed in with whatever was required to arrive at the desired outcome. But he was betting a verbal response from Butchart would reveal fabricated knots that might easily unravel under his scrutiny.

"John and I believe she had an accomplice on the base." Butchart used the admiral's first name to emphasize his casual familiarity with him. "So far, we have no leads there."

Waterhouse returned to his desk and popped the memory rod into his computer. "Computer, download file with security codes." With his back still turned to Butchart, he asked, "Another unsolved mystery?" He threw out the taunt as a stinging reminder that his wife's murder hadn't been solved. "If this woman didn't reveal her accomplice during your interrogation, then none exists." Waterhouse winked and grinned. "I'm aware of your techniques. You know she didn't have an accomplice. Why the smoke screen?"

"Christ, Sam, you're paranoid. There are no more pertinent details. I'll help myself to that coffee now," Butchart said, walking to the coffee machine. "I see you've let your hair grow. Didn't notice until I saw how it was fastened at the back of your neck. Not exactly protocol. How interesting to see there's a bit of a rebel in the meticulous Captain Waterhouse." Butchart chuckled. "It's been nearly a year since we last met. How's life as captain of the *Nonnah*? All the pretty ladies in the ports have broken hearts, Sam?" he asked, deliberately stirring more than just his coffee.

Waterhouse sat down in front of his computer and focused on the reports. "Why the rush to execute the prisoner?"

Butchart waved his free hand in the air. "Why not! Truth serum filled in the blanks. We've found her guilty of committing an attack on the U.S. Navy."

Waterhouse sat back in his chair. "This isn't the admiral's usual style. No, the activities of the previous seven prisoners were well-documented with supporting evidence. Terrorists and ruthless military spies. Lives had been lost or gravely threatened."

His comlink beeped.

"Captain Waterhouse, Dr. Duncan here."

"Yes, go ahead with your report."

"The prisoner is rapidly deteriorating, Captain. She should be immediately returned to the mainland. We don't have the capability to manage her."

"What's your diagnosis?"

"Her kidneys are shutting down. The buildup of poison is causing a cascading collapse of all her organs. Anything on her file to explain this, Captain?"

"She's been interrogated using a potent truth serum. Dosage may have exceeded the recommended limits." He winked at Butchart, who made no attempt to disguise a threatening glare. "Has she said anything?"

"No. She's not coherent."

"Do you what can. I'll get back to you in a few minutes." The comlink was disconnected. "Frank, you heard the doctor. The prisoner has to return to the base."

Butchart slammed his cup down on Waterhouse's desk, spilling the coffee. "She's never to leave this ship alive."

Waterhouse watched Butchart regain his composure as quickly as his anger had flared. He wondered what he was afraid of.

"Computer, initiate standby mode. Security on," Waterhouse said. Ignoring Butchart, he pulled a napkin from a drawer and meticulously mopped up the spilled coffee. Tossing the soiled napkin into a wastebasket, he turned to Butchart. "It's time to see if the prisoner will reveal more of her secrets, Waterhouse style." He grinned.

"Waste of time. You heard the doctor."

Waterhouse was already heading out of the office. Butchart swung around to keep in step with him. "This isn't your business. Just execute the damn bitch."

Waterhouse stopped abruptly. In complete control, he replied. "Everything that occurs on my ship is my business. I alone determine precisely when the execution will occur."

He and Butchart continued to the infirmary in silence. Inside the isolation unit, Dr. Duncan and his three assistants hovered over the unconscious prisoner.

"Frank, stay out of her visual range," Waterhouse ordered.

Butchart momentarily glared at him but had to comply. Waterhouse stepped into the isolation unit and moved to the prisoner's bedside.

"Do you have a more definitive assessment on her condition, Doctor?" he asked.

Dr. Duncan smoothed down his disheveled, thinning brown hair. It was obvious the doctor preferred to maintain as much space as possible between himself and the man who managed to find fault with everything from his untidy office to his incomplete and illegible reports. The doctor anxiously glanced from the scanner unit to the heart and respiratory monitors. He thumped a screen impatiently.

"Damn thing," he muttered.

Waterhouse stepped toward Dr. Duncan. Without saying a word, his body communicated with clarity his impatience. Dr. Duncan placed his hands on his hips and began the report, speaking more to the wall behind Waterhouse rather than making contact with the dark eyes.

"Um, simply put, she's severely dehydrated. Yes, sir, that seems to have been her undoing. Electrolytes are way off kilter. Kidneys are shutting down. No life threatening injuries. Her wrists and ankles are pretty much battered from restraints."

Dr. Duncan hesitated and picked up his patient's file and read over his notes before continuing.

"Yes, and there's a lot of serum residue left in her system. Lethal dose, perhaps. Quite remarkable, really. Should have died last night." He glanced up from the chart records. Seeing the stern expression of the captain, he quickly returned to his notes. "Took a bullet in her left hand. Healing is fairly advanced so she must have been shot at least a week ago. Let's see, yes, that's about it."

"What's her general health? Can you tell where she might've come from?"

"Good muscle tone throughout, probably runs a lot. Perhaps she lives in high altitude, has the lung capacity of an athlete. Maybe she's a climber. Yes, and very little air pollution particles in her tissues, so she probably doesn't live in or near a city. Figure she's in her late teens. Doesn't appear she has any bad habits, such as illegal drugs. She takes good care of herself. Took a sample of blood. Cells appear abnormal."

"Explain."

"There's a luminescence, almost a glow or halo around each red blood cell. Figure it's a reaction to the truth serum. Can't think of any other explanation for it."

"Show me her clothes."

The medical staff retrieved Sidney's clothes and handed them to Waterhouse. He checked for labels and any other identifying markers. There were none. Her panties and bra were simple. The white silk blouse, stained with blood, had been cut in half. Her faded blue jeans were slightly frayed at the cuffs. Her faded denim jacket was also blood stained and frayed at the cuffs.

He pondered the character of the person who owned these clothes. With the exception of the silk blouse, these were not the clothes of a well-to-do person. He smelled the clothes, almost unconsciously searching for the wearer's scent, markers of fear or hatred. There was only the odor of sweat and blood. The sickening sweet smell of the blood reminded him of

Joy's face and her blood soaked dressings. He stood up straight and threw the clothes back into the laundry bag.

"The blood stains still have a strong odor. How old is that wound in her hand, exactly?" he asked Butchart.

"She was shot trying to escape. Nearly got away," Butchart said in an attempt to sidetrack Waterhouse. "Like the doc said, she's pretty fit. Good runner."

Waterhouse merely waited for an answer and held onto Butchart's eyes.

"When?" responded Butchart. "She was shot yesterday, shortly before noon."

"Impossible," retorted Dr. Duncan. "That wound is nearly healed."

Waterhouse stepped closer to Sidney's bed. She was unconscious.

"Her blood pressure is borderline," Dr. Duncan said. "What's really strange is that our drugs and fluid therapy are having no effect on her. I just don't understand it. It's like she completely rejects everything we give her. I can tell you, Captain, she's not following the rules."

"Uh huh. Sounds like that could be a habit of hers." Waterhouse took Sidney's hand into his and studied the bullet wound on her palm. He could see that the bullet had traveled cleanly through. Little swelling remained, and the wound had almost completely healed over. He gently squeezed her hand, not expecting any response.

She responded. Ever so slightly, her fingers wrapped around his.

He bent down to her ear and whispered, "Hope you're not leaving, Sidney. You should see the sun outside. It's a beautiful day. Better stick around."

Sidney took a deep breath and opened her eyes. It shocked everyone. Waterhouse didn't know what had possessed him to say what he had. The words had come tumbling out of his mouth. For a few seconds, Sidney gazed at his face and held onto his hand. Then she closed her eyes.

The comlink badge on Waterhouse's coat sounded an alarm. He let go of Sidney's hand and activated the device.

"Captain Waterhouse."

"Sir, Lieutenant Commander Smart. We're well on our way to Acapulco. Weather report update indicates severe weather heading our way. We'll be in rough seas by thirteen-hundred hours, sir. Gives us two hours to ready the ship and crew. Readings predict gale force winds by twenty-one-hundred hours, sir."

"Any chance of going around the storm?"

"No, sir. It's affecting the entire Pacific, right to Hawaii."

"Notify the on duty officers. I'll meet with you in half an hour. Waterhouse out." He flicked off the voice link and stepped into the main infirmary. "Number one, Captain Butchart, there will be no execution tonight. Number two, you're welcome to remain on board for the duration of the sail to Acapulco. Is there anything you require in the meantime?"

Butchart was momentarily stunned by Waterhouse's decision. He lowered his voice so only Waterhouse could hear. "Careful, Sam. There's more at stake than just that broad."

Waterhouse let the remark go. He waited for Butchart to ramble on, knowing the officer's ego was likely to reveal more than he intended.

Butchart glanced in Sidney's direction momentarily. "Lieutenant Bridges, I'll be disembarking. Notify my pilot. Captain Waterhouse, until notified by myself, you're not to send any communication to the base about this prisoner." He stepped up close to Sidney's room, turning his back to Waterhouse. Watching her through the glass window, he fidgeted with something in his pocket.

Waterhouse casually moved to Butchart's side. Together they stood, watching Sidney. "What's happening on the base?" Waterhouse prodded.

Butchart smirked. "Important visitor." He puckered his mouth as if restraining further explanation. "You may live to regret your decision today, Captain."

"I'll risk it." Waterhouse smiled at the insinuation of a threat.

Butchart remained focused on Sidney's face. "If she survives, she won't tell you a damn thing; I promise you."

It seemed to Waterhouse that Butchart was counting on the prisoner remaining silent.

"You haven't tried my methods." Waterhouse spoke softly. "I plan to be nice, win her confidence. You know what I mean?" He winked and began to leave the infirmary. At the door, he turned to Bridges. "Lieutenant, from now on only Commander Moon, you, medical personnel, and myself have access to the prisoner."

"Yes, sir," called out the lieutenant.

Returning to his office, Waterhouse verbally entered the familiar coded numbers into his comlink.

"Lieutenant Weir here. Who's calling?"

"Sam Waterhouse. Is this still a secure line, Chris?"

"Still private, sir. Things could change. Word is the brass is hunting for a traitor. Today the admiral was strutting around with some civilian woman demonstrating our security systems. Never seen him look so pumped up.

We were ordered not to mention anything about the prisoner. In fact, all records of the incident have been destroyed."

Over the past year, Waterhouse had privately cultivated a relationship with Lieutenant Chris Weir. Lieutenant Weir kept a look out over his sons, and through the lieutenant, he was able to secretly remain in contact with the New Seattle Police Force's attempt to hunt down Joy's killer.

"Interesting. Do you have any *interesting* information about her that I might not find in the official report?"

"Plenty. That night she was here all kinds of strange stuff happened. One of the elevators went to the admiral's floor, then later on it went down to the subbasement when no one was in it. A light had been found on in Admiral Garland's office. There was a major power failure in the missile room. Every computer and security system was shut down. Nowhere else, just in that room. And there were no marks in the dust or fingerprints on the missiles. She'd have had to touch them to open the locked electrical compartment. You explain that one, sir."

"Interesting, Chris. See if you can get Butchart's interrogation staff to talk. Maybe something was said during the interrogation that's not in the report."

"Yes, sir. That shouldn't be a problem with those two."

"Use discretion, Chris. Has Clay got information on Joy's killer?"

"Not exactly. But Captain, you told me Mrs. Waterhouse had known someone who went by the name of Badger, right?"

Waterhouse's gut tightened. "What about him?"

"He's dead. Apparently he was found in his home, shot in the head—same day your prisoner was captured on this base. Had red lipstick on his face. The killer cleared a patch of blood off his face and kissed him. Christ, that's sick. The rest of his troop has vanished, maybe dead or gone into hiding."

"Any clues on the identity of the killer?"

"Not yet. His computers are gone. Clay said that since Joy was probably in his files, the killer will come after you once they decode them. Says you'd better watch your back."

"Use discretion, Chris."

"No problem, Captain. You're still sure the admiral didn't have anything to do with Joy's accident?"

"Quite sure. He wouldn't risk his political career. But he's surely involved in something unusual right now. Perhaps there's a connection with Badger's death and this prisoner. And this guest of the admiral's—a civilian, you say. See if you can find anything more about her."

"Yes, sir. And your boys are doing fine. Watching 'em like a hawk, sir."

"Thank you. I'll contact you when I arrive in Acapulco."

Butchart disembarked without another word to Waterhouse. The officers and seamen were occupied with tending to the ship and preparing for the storm. The ship was now twenty years old, and though kept immaculate and in good repair, Waterhouse believed one more big storm would be more than the engines could handle. They'd been updated to provide speed, but felt the strain of pushing a hull meant for more leisurely travels.

In the evening, Waterhouse returned to the infirmary. As he approached Sidney's bed, he saw she'd been cleaned up. Her hair had been washed and she had a fresh hospital gown on. She no longer needed the respirator and had more color in her face. She was beginning to resemble the photo in Butchart's records of the attractive woman who'd entered the base on Tuesday. "She looks better, Doctor. You think she can make it?"

Dr. Duncan was startled and stood at attention.

"At ease, Doctor."

"We cleaned her up." The doctor shifted from one foot to the other. "She changes from one minute to the next. One moment she seems to be on the verge of taking her last breath, and the next, she seems more stable. I've never seen a case like this in my life."

"Has she been awake? Talked at all?"

"Yes, I mean no, haven't seen any response from her at all."

Waterhouse picked up a chair and brought it over to sit close by her bedside. "Take a quick break, Doctor. I'll watch her. So it doesn't appear there's anything we can do for her?"

"Not that I've found. I'll be just fifteen minutes, Captain."

Waterhouse listened to the sounds of the room after Dr. Duncan left—the hum of the ship's engines, soft grunts and groans from within the ship. The *Nonnah* was feeling the ocean's response to the storm. Everything in the room swayed as the ship rocked in rhythm with the sea.

The room had a peaceful feel to it. Waterhouse never spent much time there. Anything that reminded him of Joy's last days was avoided. He paced aimlessly around the room, thinking of nothing and searching for nothing. Picking up medical instruments, he inspected their structure. The prisoner's imminent death was nearly a replica of his wife's. Were both women victims of the admiral's secrets?

Doctor Duncan returned, and Waterhouse made his way to the navigation room.

Though the sun had nearly disappeared below the horizon, enough light remained to see the storm in the distance was full of wrath. The ocean waves surrounding the *Nonnah* were dark and seething with foam. The clouds were the color of slate with a slight tinge of green — like a vengeful monster moving and twisting, the gale thrusting them into shapes like dragons. The wind sprayed seawater high up onto the ship's upper decks.

As Waterhouse entered the navigation room, the men and women there stood at attention.

"As you were. Any problems?" he asked

"No, sir," replied Smart.

"Any other ships in the vicinity?"

"We have our sub cruising along with us a mile to our starboard. A Canadian freighter is one hundred seventy miles to the south, heading our way on its way north to Vancouver, and one Egyptian cruise ship is eighty miles on our port, heading east toward Mountiago, sir."

"Our ETA to Acapulco?"

"We should arrive at Acapulco shortly after noon tomorrow, depending upon what this storm throws at us."

Just then Commander Moon arrived. "Commander, what's the intensity level of the approaching storm?"

"It's been building up steam, sir. So far the reports don't show signs of hurricane force. It should remain only as a gale. Everything has been fastened down and covered. We're ready for a ride."

Waterhouse nodded. "You have the bridge, number one. I'll see you in the morning."

Evening, July 4

It took Danik one full day to arrive back at Hawk's Island. He'd been able to telepathically contact Ryan, who covertly picked him up on a small mountain near New Seattle and deposited him safely in the haven of the Guardian community. By evening, Danik was seated in the meditation lodge, surrounded by the Elders. He sought their wisdom. What was he to do? He suffered pains of guilt for a mission gone terribly wrong. When attempting to contact Sidney again, he'd encountered a wall he couldn't penetrate. He looked to Sidney's mentor for guidance.

Greystone appeared unmoved by Sidney's circumstances. But then, the Elders' serenity was seldom touched by dark events of the physical world—not for more than a moment or two. Finally, he spoke.

"Why do you fear for Sidney?"

"They're going to kill her!" Danik shouted, more angry than he thought was possible in the meditation lodge. He got up and paced frantically. He tossed a log of spruce into the fire, and the sparks scattered up toward the dark ceiling. "This wasn't supposed to happen. I'm responsible for all this. We, I have to—"

Greystone held up his hand. "Danik, stop. Yes, Sidney may die. But none of us can come to her aid. She's placed a shield surrounding her body's Holy Membrane."

Danik winced.

Greystone continued. "Only Seamus can help her, and, perhaps one other." He glanced toward Birthstone. "But even Seamus may simply allow her to pass from this world to his."

"What other one?" He recalled the spirit child who occasionally visited Sidney. "Savannah?" Danik demanded.

Danik's mentor, Livingstone, called to his pupil. "Danik, come sit beside me."

Danik continued his pacing. "I...I can't. I have to do something, anything!"

"You're right. You have to do something. You have to sit here." Livingstone pointed to the floor. "Now!"

Danik had to look only briefly into his mentor's eyes to realize how far he'd strayed from his Guardian nature and the sacred truths. Still agitated, he slumped down beside Livingstone and crossed his arms over his chest.

"Now, tell me about the sacred truths."

Danik recited, "Our path's burden is equal to our strength. We won't suffer failure if we remember the Creator's love is the source of our power. If we seek the Light and truth, the higher good will be served. Our actions and thoughts are energies that return to us ten fold in the same manner as we delivered them into the universe. As you believe, so shall it be. We are one. We are eternal." He spoke as if reading from a page in a book.

"Again."

Again Danik recited the sacred truths without heart or thought.

"Again."

Again and again, Danik spoke the sacred truths until he paused after reciting, "We are one." He turned to Livingstone as if suddenly waking from his sleep. "We are eternal."

Livingstone nodded. "You'll meditate here with me for the remainder of the night. Tomorrow morning you'll resume your chores with the livestock. You'll also need to maintain the home you share with Sidney. The students will need you in the afternoon to help them with their telepathy exercises. You'll return here after the evening meal for more guidance. We won't lose you to fear. Understood?"

Danik reached for his mentor's hands and grasped them tightly. And so, the meditation began.

7. Surrender of the Captain

Friday, July 5, 0215 Hours

Waterhouse woke to the sound of his comlink's alarm. He jumped out of bed and grabbed his communicator.

"Captain Waterhouse." He glanced at his watch. It was 0215 hours.

"Sir, the prisoner's condition has deteriorated. She may be dying," Dr. Duncan informed him. "Do you want to come to the infirmary?"

"I'll be there in five minutes." Waterhouse pulled on his navy uniform. He tied his long hair back and grabbed his hat. In three minutes he was running down the corridors. As he stepped into the room he noticed Lorna and two of Dr. Duncan's assistants trying to restrain Sidney. The patient was thrashing and flailing at invisible objects.

"Captain, you want to witness her passing or do you have something else in mind?" Dr. Duncan asked.

"She seems to be trying to say something. What have you heard her say so far?"

"Most of it's just mumbling. Can't make out most of it. She did call for someone, though. Someone by the name of Dan or Danny."

Sidney continued to struggle with the medical staff. Waterhouse walked over to her bed and saw she was soaked with perspiration. She let out a scream. Waterhouse took off his hat and tossed it onto the bedside table.

"Let me try." He stroked her forehead tenderly, and his voice became soft, almost a whisper. "Sidney, Dan is here. Everything's okay now. Tell me what's wrong." He wasn't sure she'd understand but hoped she might respond to Dan's name. It worked. Sidney stopped struggling and became quiet. "That's better. I'll stay here with you. Everything's okay."

Sidney's eyes didn't focus on anything or anyone. Her breathing was rapid.

"Dan?"

"Yes, I'm here, Sidney. Everything's okay now."

Her breathing slowed. In another fifteen minutes the monitor showed a slight improvement in her body temperature. Her faced was still flushed, and her entire body was covered with sweat. Her lungs sounded like they were drowning in fluid. Waterhouse noticed the medical gadgets and equipment. They dominated the room. It restricted closeness with the patient. Just like with Joy. Tubing, lines, sensors, and traction equipment had made it impossible to hold her.

He stepped over to Dr. Duncan and spoke in a whisper. "I want you to take her off these machines. She's dying. Make her at least comfortable. I'll stay with her for the rest of the time just in case she gives away information. Everyone else is to leave."

"Okay, Captain. I'll need you to record the time of her death for my records." Dr. Duncan's staff quickly disconnected the scanning monitors and removed all medical equipment from the room. In minutes they were gone and Waterhouse was alone with her.

Sidney began to fuss and mumble again. Again, Waterhouse gently stroked her forehead and called to her.

"Sidney, this is Dan. Calm down. How are you feeling?"

"Can't move. Trapped. Help me, Dan."

Waterhouse could see the panic in Sidney's eyes.

"You're not trapped, Sidney. You're okay, sweetheart."

"No. It's so dark. Where are you?"

"I'm right here." Waterhouse held her hand tightly to his chest as he leaned close. "You're safe, Sidney. Are you ready to go home?"

"Home?" Her voice was a mere whisper. Waterhouse had to listen carefully.

"Yes, home. We should go home."

"Home. Take me home, Dan."

"Back to Canada?"

"No. Home."

Waterhouse had to stop and consider her answer. She'd reported on her application form that she was from Canada. Where else could she be from?

"Back to New Seattle?"

"No. Take me home, Dan."

"Okay, Sidney, we'll go home."

He let her rest. All the while he held onto her hand and stroked her forehead. He listened to her breathing and kept two fingers over the pulse in her wrist, just in case her heart stopped.

"Dan?"

"Yes, Sidney. I'm here."

"Cold. So cold." She became frantic, struggling with the bed covers.

"I'll get another blanket for you." Sidney grabbed his hand and wouldn't let go.

"Hold me, Dan. Hold me. Cold," she whispered.

Waterhouse sat on the bed and shifted his position so his back was against the headboard. He raised her shoulders to rest against his chest and cradled her in his arms. Immediately, she became calm. Waterhouse was certain this wouldn't be considered appropriate action, but in the dim light of the room, there was little need for his rule book. His heart was with Joy, a million miles away from military protocol.

"Hold me, Dan. Please. Don't go."

"I won't leave, Sidney." He had to remember to call her Sidney. His thoughts were of Joy.

"I love you, Dan. Hold … me," she rasped, breathless.

Waterhouse wondered how this man, Dan, could have ever let someone he loved go on a hopeless mission. If he really loved her, why he didn't stop her like he himself should have stopped Joy? Was it his guilt in not protecting Joy that had left him too mute to say goodbye to her?

He placed his fingers again over Sidney's wrist to check her pulse. It was weak. Her body was very warm, her hair and pajamas soaked in sweat. Not much longer, he thought. He clasped her hand in his with the tenderness of a bird sheltering her chicks under her wings. He felt the smallness of her hand. With his palm against hers, he felt a soothing energy wash over him. It seeped into his bones and swam throughout his body, gathering up all his tension. Remembering his meditation practice from years ago, he set aside his need to be in control and silenced the rules that governed Captain Waterhouse. The true essence of Sam emerged and quickly surrendered to a gentle, yet powerful force. In a moment he was asleep.

Friday, July 5, En Route to Acapulco Harbor

A few hours later, Dr. Duncan entered the infirmary looking somber. "Good morning, Captain. What time did she die?"

Until last night, Waterhouse saw himself as only a captain clinging to his rule book to define himself and to dull the pain. Now, he saw that he was, first and foremost, Sam Waterhouse using the rule book to guide his officers. Sam stood with his arms folded across his chest. He grinned and wasn't sure how to tell the doctor that he was going to have to deal with Sidney's peculiar physiology a little longer.

"Take a look, Doctor. She's much better. In another day, she'll be ready for interrogation."

Sam gestured toward Sidney's bed, and Dr. Duncan froze. She was indeed alive.

After leaving the doctor to care for his patient and changing into his exercise clothes, Sam went to the ship's deck for his morning jog. The sun was just lifting its rays over the ocean's horizon. He took in a lungful of crisp, salty air and savored the elation that surged through him, hoping to trap it. For the first time in a long, long time, he was actually looking forward to the day and whatever it brought. He sensed a shift had taken place within himself. It was nothing he could explain rationally. But when he woke, still holding his prisoner, he felt a power that energized his body and mind. No, it was more a clarity. And something else. For some reason, he no longer felt alone. He tried to find an explanation for this new way of being, but then he understood that acceptance was enough.

At 0900 hours, the informal breakfast meeting with his senior officers began. All six of them were waiting when he arrived in the boardroom, and the food and fresh brewed coffee had been delivered. The other officers briefly snapped to attention and then relaxed with Sam's "As you were."

Eagerly, they filled their plates and sat down. As far as they knew, there was only one item on the agenda—the prisoner. But Sam was determined to maintain the routine. He asked each officer to present his or her report. Commander Moon reported the events that had transpired during the stormy night.

"Several nearby ships, including those anchored in Mountiago Bay, were reported to have suffered major damage. The *Nonnah* easily sailed through the storm. In fact, the raging gale had seemed to be all around us, but, as we sailed on, the sea in our path became calmer. It was good fortune."

Sam noted he'd hadn't noticed the storm while he was in the infirmary. He remembered only a sense of peace.

Robert John, the Engineer Officer, gave a brief overview of the recent engine leak. "Nothing to be overly concerned about, Skipper. Replacement parts will be at the Acapulco harbor."

The Communication, Navigation, and Personnel Officers reported on preparations underway for the *Nonnah*'s arrival at Acapulco in the early afternoon. Lastly, Sam asked Dr. Duncan to present his findings on the prisoner. The doctor reported that she was still alive. He described her unusual physiology just as he'd reported to Sam the previous evening.

"Why was the prisoner in such a terrible state, Captain?" asked Casey Cropley, the Communications Officer.

"She tried to escape and was shot. Following that, the interrogation methods resulted in her becoming quite ill. The rest of the information concerning the prisoner is strictly between Admiral Garland and myself."

The officers nodded, with the exception of Casey. He shook his head and was about to respond. Sam raised his hand, an indication that the discussion was over.

Dr. Duncan cleared his throat. He shifted in his chair and tapped the table with a large, brown envelope. He'd brought one more item to the meeting.

"A gift for you, sir, I think," the doctor said.

He shoved the envelope across the table, and it easily skidded across the polished, dark walnut and came to rest in front of Sam. The captain smiled, suspecting the officers were playing a joke.

"So, is this going to blow up or just make a mess of my breakfast?" He grinned.

The men and women laughed. His staff had been known to play the odd prank on each other, and he'd come to appreciate their sense of humor.

"You won't believe your eyes, sir. It's no joke, I promise," said the doctor.

Gingerly, Sam picked up the envelope. It had no weight to indicate anything inside. He opened the flap, taking care that it was pointed away from him. Before continuing, he stopped briefly and checked the expression on the faces of everyone at the table. They appeared to be only eagerly interested in seeing the surprise gift.

Sam cautiously peeked into the envelope. At first glance, it appeared empty. Then he saw it. Handling the envelope as though it contained a fragile piece of porcelain, he allowed the contents to slowly slip out onto the table in front of him. It was a large tail feather, brick red, measuring about fourteen inches long. It was beautiful, with dark brown bands around the red shaft. Murmurs of wonder rumbled around the table. For a moment, everyone gazed at the feather in disbelief.

"What's the connection, Doctor?"

"Actually, I was hoping you could help me with that. You see, my staff found it near the prisoner's bed this morning. It was just lying there on the floor. It wasn't there when we left her with you last night. I'm certain of that."

Moon looked at the feather more closely. "Looks like a hawk's feather. My grandparents used to keep one on the mantle. It was considered sacred. Had a lot of power, or so they said." Commander Moon smiled at Sam. "You got a hawk hiding in your private quarters, Sam?"

Everyone chuckled.

Sam picked up the feather and inspected it closely. Turning it over, he noticed it was in nearly perfect condition.

"So, no one here knows anything about this?" He twirled it in the air.

"No, sir," was the reply from everyone.

Sam was more than just a little concerned. He stood up. The tone of his voice was commanding.

"Does anyone have any theories about how it could've gotten into the infirmary?"

Everyone shook their heads.

"Not a clue, sir" said Carla Smart.

"Are we sure it's real? Nowadays, it's hard to tell the real stuff from the synthetic products," another officer commented.

"Let's put it under our scanner here and see what the computer has to say about it," said Casey Cropley. He positioned the feather carefully on the scanner and activated the unit. The computer issued a light beam onto the feather.

"Feather identified. Red-tailed hawk. Known to have once inhabited a vast range of territory. Breeding territory in Canada's Prairie Provinces ranging from the north to approximately fifty-six degrees latitude in the east, but in the west extended north to western Mackenzie and Yukon. Known to winter in southern states and Central America. Females larger than males. Bird of prey, raptor. Now on endangered species list; sightings are rare and must be reported to local authorities."

The computer played a short video on the wall monitor showing the bird in flight, gliding between mountain peaks and swiftly skimming over a meadow, grabbing a small rodent with its talons. They heard the bird's warning call. They saw close ups of the bird's body, glistening brown feathers, red tail, and the stare of its large yellow eyes.

Sam requested the computer to identify this particular feather's host. The computer sent another scanning beam over the feather.

"Recently removed from living female bird. Age of feather one thousand, five hundred and eleven years."

Everyone in the room gasped. Sam wondered if the computer could be wrong. He walked over to the scanner and, picking up the feather, inspected it again. It didn't appear frayed or damaged. He placed it back on the scanner.

"Computer, verify feather's age. How long ago was the feather shed? Identify bird's age."

Again the computer scanned the feather. "Age of the feather is one thousand, five hundred and eleven years. Feather shed within the last twenty-four hours. Unable to determine age of female bird. Program not compatible with samples older than two thousand years."

The officers looked at each other in shock. All but Sam were speechless.

Sam ordered, "Computer, verify. Is the feather from a bird older than two thousand years?"

"Affirmative."

"Computer, save data to Captain Waterhouse's computer under file 'Prisoner Sidney.'"

"Save complete."

The ship's computer programs were without fault. They had been tested regularly. The officers looked to Sam for his reaction. He paced, silent and deep in thought.

Sam seldom saw birds other than the usual gulls and such that eked out a marginal survival on scraps near fishing communities. Birds of all kinds were rare or had become extinct. Sightings of raptors in particular were almost non-existent since their food sources had disappeared or became contaminated. Still, he had the feeling he'd seen a hawk, a long time ago. The memory returned to him in a flash — the beautiful bird that soared above the cliffs at his mystery island. *That was probably a year ago,* he thought. He felt a chill over his entire body. The hair on his arms stood on end.

Sam had to know without any shadow of a doubt that the computer program wasn't providing foul data. He had to laugh at the unintended pun. It had been a long time since he felt humor rise out of his misery. He turned to his officers.

"There will be no discussion of this outside this room. Cropley, run a check on this computer and all its programs. Find out if there are any glitches."

The meeting was adjourned, but the officers were reluctant to leave the matter up in the air, as one had put it. Even Sam had to chuckle along with his officers. It was rapidly becoming a rather different day. His officers on the *Nonnah* were known to be more relaxed than those he'd worked with on the *Intrepid*. Life on this merchant ship was far removed from that on a heavily armed aircraft carrier.

Sam picked up the feather and carefully placed it back into the envelope. He caught the eyes of Lieutenant Bridges, Commander Moon, and Dr. Duncan and motioned them to follow him into his office. Bridges was the officer who took on a variety of duties on the *Nonnah*. For the most part, he oversaw personnel needs, food, security, loading and unloading of the cargo, scheduled shifts, and generally made sure the personnel followed protocol and orders. He was also the unfortunate officer to have the duty of carrying out Sam's execution orders. The three men stood with Sam and became obviously tense, standing stiffly.

"Captain, is this about the prisoner?" asked Moon.

"Yes, Rhett. All of us here know when a prisoner arrives on this ship what the end result will be. I want to make sure you know this prisoner is no different. Also, my orders are to ensure that the reason the prisoner is on this ship is kept strictly confidential. As a result, yesterday's order of no official communication with the prisoner stands. No one is to speak to her other than the medical staff and yourselves. Is that understood?"

"Yes, sir," they replied simultaneously.

"You're not to interrogate her. Treat her well and with respect. I want her to feel comfortable, even at ease. If she asks you questions concerning her status as a prisoner, simply tell her that I'll answer those questions. Understood?"

"Yes, Captain."

"Bridges, drop by her room a few times a day at random. Make it look like the presence of security. Tell her we're just making sure no one bothers her. I'll interrogate her up to three times a day.

"When you feel the prisoner is ready to leave the infirmary, Doctor, she'll be confined to the usual locked quarters. When she becomes more mobile, Bridges, you'll need to assign security personnel to stand guard at her door. Doctor, let me know when that becomes necessary."

Dr. Duncan frowned. "You plan to wrestle the information out of her, Captain? Drugs don't work on her."

"No. My tactics will be the opposite of Butchart's. In other words, I plan to be nice and conduct myself as a gentleman. I'll sweet talk her if that'll get what I want. After a few details are filled in, we're done with her."

Sam entered a security code on his desk computer panel, and a drawer moved forward. He placed the envelope containing the feather inside and closed the drawer.

"Any questions?"

They had none. The officers left Sam's office much more somber than they'd felt immediately after the breakfast meeting.

Bridges spoke as the door closed behind them. "Hope to hell we get this over with soon!"

8. An Old Mexican's Crystal

Afternoon, July 5, Acapulco

As Acapulco's harbor came into view, Sam went into the navigation room to watch the navigation officer and her crew maneuver the ship beside the others anchored near the docks. It was a busy day. Many of the other ships were under repair as a result of the previous night's storm.

Sam still didn't understand how the *Nonnah* had escaped the violent winds. Again, the hair on his arms stood up. He'd had enough of mystery. He was anxious to disembark and relax in the open-air markets of Acapulco where he planned to buy something for his boys. It would be a welcomed treat to clear his mind of business.

Cargo was offloaded, and Admiral Garland's sealed package was stowed in the vault. Parts arrived for the *Nonnah*'s engine, received by the anxious Robert John. Sam disembarked by 1400 hours and headed toward the streets lined with shops. He went in search of small gifts and a change of pace. Walking leisurely in the hot afternoon sun, Sam found the town almost deserted with the business people taking their traditional siesta during the hottest part of the day.

Shops were closed except for a few tourist markets and cafés near the docks. Colorful Mexican blankets draped over supports, and huge sombreros lazily waved with the passing of a breeze. He heard only an occasional murmur from the few people sitting along the sidewalks. Men and children here and there leaned against a wall or dozed in the shade of their small tourist stands. They were oblivious to the flies buzzing around and unconcerned with strangers passing by.

Sam found an open tourist shop packed full of inconsequential items — every sort of memorabilia was either piled on shelves or hung from rafters. Although the items appeared trivial and cheap, they were what he was looking for. In a reed basket, he found a collection of key rings. Two were just what he knew Simon and Nathan would enjoy. One key ring medallion was embossed with a three mast sailing ship, much like the type of ship Nathan loved to watch in the sailing races. The other medallion was embossed with a replica of the car their mother had driven—the Indigo. Simon loved that car and dearly wanted ownership once he was of age.

Sam had the gifts wrapped, wrote the admiral's address on the package, and paid for the postage. He was satisfied, but reluctant to return to the ship. The Mexican sidewalks invited him to stroll further away from the docks. He didn't resist. After several blocks, he found a small outdoor café where he ordered a cold, refreshing drink of spicy tea and sat down at a table in the shade of a tree.

It was almost 1600 hours, and people were beginning to emerge from the back of the shops. Children started scurrying about. Still, an almost dreamy calmness persisted. There was no rush, no expectation, and no worry of what the next moment would bring.

The shopkeepers, parents, and children simply accepted each moment and were in no hurry to anticipate or prepare for the next. The atmosphere was a continual state of grace. Sam listened and drank his tea. In the quiet afternoon heat, for just a moment, he thought he heard the sound of bells in the distance. Serenity drew him into a place he'd seldom been. It was soothing, tempting him to stay too long. Yet his watch told him it was time to return to duty.

He was about to leave when he noticed an elderly Mexican man slowly making his way down the sidewalk. The man appeared frail, gingerly taking small steps, aided by his weathered, wooden cane. His long gray hair was tied in braids that hung loosely in front of his shoulders. He made his way to the café and asked the waiter for an herbal tea.

The man surveyed the empty tables. He spotted Sam and shuffled his way over.

"May I sit with you, sir?" asked the elderly gent.

Sam was perplexed by the man's request, but stood up and offered a chair. "Your company is welcome, sir."

The waiter had followed him, bringing the herbal tea. "Is there anything else you'd like, Señor Sanchez?"

"No, Señor. Gracias."

"How is Señora Sanchez?" the waiter asked.

"She's well. I'll tell her you were asking of her." The man's face was that of an ancient sage, tanned and creased with lines. The eyes, however, conveyed both wisdom and youth, twinkling with mischief. He smiled at Sam.

"Gracias, my friend. My name is Paulo Sanchez. What's yours?"

"I'm Captain Waterhouse. Please call me Sam. My ship, the USS *Nonnah*, is in the harbor undergoing maintenance."

"Oh, you had trouble in the storm?"

"Actually, we were quite fortunate. The storm was around us but didn't give the *Nonnah* any trouble. It's our engine that's the problem. Rather old and cantankerous."

"Ah," said Paulo, waving his hand in the air. "I know all about old and cantankerous. These damned old bones." He tried to lift one leg up off the ground. "You see that? All my parts are wearing out. Figure it's about time I traded this bag of bones for a whole new set."

"Uh oh, Paulo. And what would your wife say to that?" Sam teased.

Paulo winked and sipped his tea. "Well," he whispered, "I think she'd be pleased. You're married, Sam?"

Sam winced. "My wife died a year ago. Accident. I've got two young boys, twelve and ten, in New Seattle." Sam tried to steer the conversation away from his personal life. "How about you, Paulo. Maybe you have grandkids keeping you busy?"

Sam and Paulo talked on into the evening. Paolo's voice was calming, and Sam forgot about the time. The conversation drifted from Mexican spices to local soccer games, far afield from military structure and obligations. Sam laughed when he tried his Spanish on Paolo and used the wrong words. They munched on Mexican delicacies and savored a growing camaraderie. Paulo was wise and saw the humor in the simplest things. *It was incredible,* thought Sam — right from the very start, he felt at ease with Paulo as though they had known each other for many years.

A thought kept creeping into Sam's mind. *Ask him,* the voice said.

No, was Sam's response to the shadow voice.

Ask him, the voice urged.

No.

Ask him, the voice pleaded.

Why? asked Sam in his mind, still carrying on a separate conversation with Paulo.

Why not? replied the relentless voice.

"Sam, it looks like there's something troubling you. What is it, my friend?"

"It's nothing. I should get back to my ship." Sam reached for his blazer and hat.

"I've been around a long time. Seen and tried most of it. Failed sometimes, too. I have a few regrets laced with many victories. I've enjoyed your company a great deal. Let me do something for you, Sam. What's weighing heavy on your mind?"

"Many things, Paulo. I'm reluctant to spill my troubles and burden you. They're mine to resolve."

"Yes, this is true. I can't take them away from you. But, perhaps I can shed a different light on them. Sometimes we get stuck in seeing things in a certain way. Give me a challenge, Sam. Let me see if I can lighten your load a bit."

"All right, Paulo. In the last twenty-four hours a patient on my ship hasn't been following any rule book as far as her physiology is concerned. She'd been poisoned prior to being brought aboard, and my ship's doctor was unable treat her condition. He expected her to die last night. And yet, she survived. She also had a bullet wound that healed in less than a day."

"She sounds intriguing. What do you know about this woman?"

"Very little. I suspect she's associated with underground activities, perhaps even dangerous."

"Ah, I understand your concern. You have a challenge ahead of you, Sam. I believe the more you understand her and her motives, the more you'll find it difficult to find her guilty of anything, no matter what she did."

"What do you mean?"

"She sounds like those who follow a path of the higher good in all they do and think, guided by spiritual forces. They become closer to the source of all things. They have great power, Sam." Paulo held his hand to his chest. His head bent in reverence to the words he spoke. "There are many legends about these people. Thousands of centuries ago, our ancestors knew them as the Guardians. It was said the people in power began to see the Guardians as a threat to the stability of their economy and the government. Those in power planned to destroy the entire Guardian community. Guided by their wisdom and their connection with higher dimensions, the Guardians fled, leaving no trace of their escape or destination."

"Why were they feared? Did they try to take power?"

"No, Sam. The Guardians had been respected and honored for their gifts of healing, for their wisdom, and for their reverence of all life. Those in power saw the Guardians as a hindrance to acquiring total obedience from the masses. Political leaders wanted to be the gods, to be the ultimate power."

Paulo's story was the most outrageous fantasy Sam had ever heard. "You're not saying these Guardians truly exist?"

"You'll have to decide that for yourself, Sam."

"Okay, suppose your story is true. Have you personally ever met a Guardian?"

Paulo winked. "I've met one or two. If one becomes your friend, it will change your life. I promise you. Chances are you've walked right by one and never knew it. They live in total secrecy. They must. If governments knew of their whereabouts, well, who knows what would happen?"

Sam shook his head. He didn't know if his friend was delusional or if his story was based on fact. If it were fact, it would explain a lot about Sidney. But it was just too incredible to accept.

"Who else knows about these Guardians?" he asked.

"The Guardians have revealed themselves to only a trusted few who are returning to their Guardian path. You see, we were all Guardians once."

"Now you've really tipped the boat over, Paulo. How can I believe that?"

"The truth lies within you, Sam. You're right to question what I've said. It shows your intelligence. What you need to do is to search for the truth within yourself. You'll find it right here." Paulo placed his hand over Sam's heart. "You may even discover your Guardian heritage is closer than you realize."

Sam felt a vibration travel from Paulo's hand into this chest. It took him by surprise. Paulo lowered his hand and reached for his cane. As he stood, he fumbled in his pants pocket and pulled out what appeared to be similar to a quartz crystal. It easily fit in Paulo's hand and was shaped like a main sail with hundreds of facets. As it caught the rays of the sun, it flashed shards of light back with such brilliance that Sam had to shield his eyes. Paulo thrust the crystal into Sam's hand.

"A gift for you, my friend."

Sam studied the gift. The crystal formations were rough but clear. In the center was a small, bright blue and green iridescent crystal—a crystal within a crystal.

"Paulo, this is too much."

"No, it's yours. The crystal has found its way to you. Forgot it was in my pocket until now. I'd been wondering what to do with it. Got a few of my own. Now I know why it was in my pocket. It belongs to you. Crystals do that, you know."

Before Sam could respond, Paulo thanked him for a wonderful evening and said goodbye. He reached for his cane and slowly headed to the café's exit. Sam gathered his belongings and tucked the crystal into his coat pocket. When he looked again to wave to Paulo and say goodbye, the old man had disappeared.

Sam took a deep breath. He felt disoriented and wondered if his time with Paolo had been a dream. Shops were beginning to close. The setting sun cast long shadows across the streets. The time was nearly 2000 hours. He was considerably overdue, and it was going to take another thirty minutes to get back to the *Nonnah*. It annoyed him that he'd been so lax. He wouldn't allow his officers to be so tardy. His disciplined training had been overruled, and for a brief moment he wondered if he'd been under the control of Paulo.

The whole afternoon was becoming a blur, except for Paulo's story. *The Guardian's story—what nonsense!* he thought. He toyed with the crystal in his pants pocket. *Why does it fit in my hand so perfectly, like it belongs there?* He gave himself a rough shake and stepped up his pace, almost to a run.

Sam met Moon as he embarked onto the ship. Moon was obviously tense. After a salute and the standard officer's greeting, Sam walked with the commander to his office in silence. Once there, Sam entered the code for his security drawer and pulled out the envelope containing the feather.

"Rhett, have you learned anything more about this?"

"No, sir. Actually, I'd forgotten about it. We've been busy dodging the admiral's bullets."

"What concerned the admiral?"

"You, sir!"

"Explain, Rhett."

"Apparently he received a report that you were talking to someone in a café in town. After an hour had passed he called to see if you'd returned. He's been calling every hour, and every hour he gets hotter. He called forty minutes ago spitting bullets."

"Who told him I was talking with someone in a café?"

"No one that I know of. Reassured him you were keeping in touch with us."

"Thanks." Sam was relieved the commander had backed him up. "I'll take the rest of your shift tonight."

Coffee arrived just as the commander left. After a minute of contemplation about how to handle the admiral, Sam activated his comlink.

"Call to Admiral Garland, private residence, scramble gold code."

Sam watched his computer monitor for the connection with the admiral's video image. In a few seconds he saw the admiral seated at his home office's desk.

"This is Admiral Garland."

"Admiral Garland, I understand you were calling, sir."

"Goddamn it Sam. You know what time it is? It's goddamn almost twenty-one-hundred hours. Why the hell were you not available?"

Sam resisted being drawn into the admiral's combat zone. "Admiral, sir, have you ever been in Acapulco? The city's on a different time dimension. Things move at half the speed they do anywhere else. You should try it, sir."

Admiral Garland glared at Sam. "Don't get impertinent with me. You live and breathe according to my personal time zone, Sam. What took you so long?"

"In fact, Admiral, I was doing some research on our prisoner. I'll have a report on my findings for you in the morning. Is there anything else I can do for you, sir?" Sam was in the driver's seat and knew he was pushing the admiral's buttons just a hair into the red zone.

"Fine. I want the report by zero-eight-hundred hours. You planning on doing any more research off ship?"

"No, sir. Concerning these reports, sir. I suggest that they're sent directly to you. I recommend Captain Butchart no longer receive information on my interrogation of the prisoner, sir."

The admiral paused. "Explain, Waterhouse."

"Sir, is it possible the prisoner and Captain Butchart have a history?"

"You mean as in they know each other? Nonsense, Waterhouse. I've known Frank for nearly ten years. He's as loyal as they come. You're making a very serious accusation,." The admiral shifted in his chair. "Captain Butchart is by the book, trusted with the safe keeping of all our military confidential material. If you have information to the contrary, let's have it!"

"Sir, Captain Butchart is extremely anxious to have the prisoner executed. What's he afraid of, unless she's a threat to him?"

"Captain Butchart had orders to ensure the woman was punished for terrorism."

"Admiral, we need to learn how she carried out her activities. We need evidence or at least the prisoner's declaration regarding how she accessed the secure areas, sir. How else can we stop another incident? She had no help from the naval personnel on base. Give me a few days, sir. I'll find out how she did it, and you can prevent another like her from putting the base at risk."

The admiral nodded. "Agreed. However, Waterhouse, it's imperative that the base security is known to be tight—no implications of having had any breach."

"You don't want anyone to find out the back door was left unlocked two days ago. Is that it?" Sam sat back in his chair, amused.

The admiral's tension rose a notch higher than before. He looked away, perhaps reassuring himself that no one else was in the room. "I won't tolerate any further insubordination, Waterhouse. If my guest has any concerns about base security…You'll execute the prisoner the second, I repeat, the *second* you find out how she managed to enter our secured areas. And as far as Captain Butchart, leave him out of the information loop, for now. I don't want to hear anything more from the *Nonnah* unless the ship has sunk. Understood?"

Sam smiled. "Yes, sir." Sam was pleased to have created doubt in the admiral's mind about Butchart's loyalty. "One more thing, sir. The engine repairs are taking a little longer than expected. We'll likely not be ready to sail to the next port until after midnight tomorrow. I'll keep you posted."

"Captain Waterhouse."

Sam knew the admiral was about to play his trump card when he referred to him as "Captain Waterhouse."

"Yes, sir."

The admiral's voice became smooth and controlled. "Simon and Nathan were wondering why you hadn't called. Of course, they've gone to bed already. I'll let them know you called late."

Sam knew his boys wouldn't be in bed this early, especially on a Friday night, but he decided to let the admiral have the last dig.

"I appreciate that, sir. I've sent some small gifts to them. They should arrive in a couple of days. I'll talk with them tomorrow."

"Actually, Captain Waterhouse, they'll be away tomorrow. My daughter is taking the kids camping for the weekend. They won't be back until Sunday night. Late Sunday night."

Sam had been duly punished for his rebellion. "Then I'll talk with them Monday evening."

The comlink was disconnected.

Stepping back onto the ship's main deck, Sam found the weather had brought a warm shower. He took off his hat and let the rain wash away the dust from his face and neck. It was invigorating. Standing in the rain, a feeling of harmony swept over him. He wondered how long the feeling would last. It was disturbing to find that the more he tried to hold on to the tranquility, the more it evaporated into the night sky.

Sam went to the infirmary and found Dr. Duncan sleeping on one of the three hospital beds. The lights had been turned down and the room was quiet. He stepped into Sidney's room and found her also sleeping. She appeared childlike. The soft light on her skin revealed increased color in her face, which was framed with the waves of her brown hair.

Paulo had said it would be difficult to find her guilty of anything. Sam wondered what that meant exactly. She was guilty, according to the admiral. Still, given the odd circumstances of the prisoner—her rapid healing and survival of the poisoning—perhaps there was a connection with Paulo's bizarre story. Were her motives the real issue? Sam felt a huge piece of the puzzle was missing. Until Sidney could be interrogated, he saw no purpose in wasting more time pursuing phantom answers.

As he studied her face, he noticed her long eyelashes flutter slightly. She moaned as she tried to shift her position. Her eyes opened.

"Who are you?" she murmured.

"I'm Captain Waterhouse." He extended his right hand to shake hers.

"I'm Sidney," she said, weakly shaking his hand. "Where am I?"

"You're on my ship, the USS *Nonnah*. You were brought here yesterday morning after being arrested on the New Seattle Naval Base. Do you remember?"

Sidney closed her eyes for a moment, and then reopened them. "Vaguely, Captain. You're Captain Waterhouse, did you say?"

"Yes. Right now you're under the care of Dr. Duncan."

"Is it raining outside? Your clothes are wet."

"Yes. Just a shower."

"I thought I could smell the freshness in the air. I love to walk in the rain, too. The world changes, becomes softer in a rainstorm. Everything seems to slow down for a while. It's like before the rain, life raced so fast you could barely see where you were going. When it rains, everything becomes slower and softer. Do you know what I mean?"

Sam felt uncomfortable at the invitation to reveal his personal side. He was glad, though, that she was willing to share her thoughts openly. He pushed further into his plan to present himself as her ally.

"Would you like the porthole opened?" he asked.

"Oh, yes."

Once Sam had the porthole fully open, air filled the room with its cool freshness.

"That's the best medicine, Captain. Thank you so much." Sidney closed her eyes.

"I'll see you in the morning, miss."

Sleepily, Sidney responded, "Okay. But please call me Sidney."

Sam was satisfied. He'd established a good rapport with his prisoner. He hoped that in the morning she'd still remember their pleasant conversation.

9. Blurry Line Between Friend and Foe

Saturday, July 6, 0800 hours, Acapulco

The Saturday morning sun had barely revealed itself when Sam got up for his morning routine of jogging around the ship's deck. After an hour, he walked down to the infirmary to check on his prisoner. Through the glass windows of Sidney's room he saw that Dr. Duncan's medical assistant was straightening up things and getting her ready for her first meal.

Lieutenant Lorna Paddles had been in the military for at least a hundred years, or so the seamen figured. Her short, gray hair was without style except for the wispy curls framing her round face. Large blue eyes told of a time when she'd been a beauty. She was a strong woman with shoulders as wide as those of most of the men on the ship. It was well understood by all that she didn't take any of the seamen's guff.

She stood with her back to Sam, and he could just barely see beyond her shoulders that Sidney was seated in a chair. Lorna tossed used linen onto the floor and snapped fresh sheets into place on the bed. She fluffed pillows into submission so they sat only as her big hands demanded. Lorna turned around and saw Sam standing in the main infirmary. She hustled into the main room and snapped to attention in front of him.

"You caught me working again." She feigned worry. "Damn!"

Lorna had her own military decorum. She respected the rules but usually with a twist. She'd been around long enough to know what she could get away with and with whom. Sam was one of those with whom she, and only she, could push the envelope, just a bit. Not everyone was as successful as she was in getting Sam to "lighten up," as she often advised him to do.

"As you were," he said with as much authority he could muster over his desire to laugh.

Lorna relaxed her stance. "Didn't see you sneaking up behind me, sir."

Sam smiled. "Any problems?"

"No, sir. She's pretty quiet most of the time."

Sam nodded and stepped into Sidney's room where she was now sitting on her bed.

"Good morning, miss. How are you doing?"

"I'd feel better if I could stand up. Dr. Duncan still has me attached to this hose." She pointed to the tubing connected from her urinary catheter to the collection bag hanging at the foot of her bed. "Very effective bag and chain."

Sam was taken aback by her quick wit and humor. Her mind was sharp. He took the opportunity to exercise his plan to gain her trust. He made a deliberate attempt to appear relaxed.

"Yes, we have unique ways of keeping wayward people under control. It would appear you're well enough to have breakfast this morning."

"I'm looking forward to getting some real food. Feel weak as a kitten. Have you had your breakfast?"

The casual conversation with his prisoner made Sam uncomfortable. He was anxious to get down to business.

"Not yet. Do you feel up to a few minutes of questioning?"

Sidney frowned and shifted her eyes toward the porthole. "Someone closed it last night. Would you mind opening it again for me?"

Sam hesitated. Her apparent disregard for his military status as captain almost bordered on insolence. But he nonchalantly moved to the porthole and opened it, becoming absorbed in the scene beyond the ship. The porthole faced the ocean, away from the Acapulco harbor. The sky glowed from the sunrise, illuminating brilliant orange and rose-colored clouds and edging them with gold. Streaks of the sun's rays dipped into the ocean.

"What do you see, Captain?"

He made an effort to sound casual in his response. "Mostly just the ocean and the early morning sun. There are a few sailing ships."

"Sailing ships? Oh, I love to watch them. I've never been on one. Have you?"

Remembering his sailing years, Sam relaxed his military posture. He turned to face her.

"Actually owned one up to a year ago. Used to sail whenever I was on shore leave."

"What's it like?"

"What do you mean exactly?"

Sidney's face glowed as she imagined vivid and wild adventures. "Well, what's it like to move with the ocean and the wind? You, your ship, the wind, and the ocean as one, harmonious. It must be wonderful!"

"It's not always, as you call it, harmony. I've battled a reef while trying to sail into the harbor. The reef won."

"Can you describe what that was like? It must have been exciting."

Sam was wary of her curiosity, but it was his mission to appear benevolent so he began describing his attempt to find access to his mysterious island's shoreline.

Sidney interrupted. "Wait. First tell me about your ship. What did it look like?

Sam described *Tears of Joy*. He felt pride in the ship's beautiful, bright tangerine sails and the royal blue hull with its brass trim. Sidney urged him to paint a more detailed picture. She wanted to know each and every detail of every moment of the day Sam had tried to anchor *Tears of Joy* at that island. What color was the sky? Were there any clouds? Was it warm or cold? How deep were the waves? Were other ships in view? What did the shoreline look like? Were the waves charging at the reef and spraying mist high into the air?

Sam remembered each detail like it had happened just yesterday. He found that the more he thought about his sailing ship and that day, the more he felt himself back there, and the more easily his words flowed. He told her how he had to continually adjust the sails and work the rudder. He described the ship leaning heavily and how he had to work to keep her upright. He recalled glancing at the GPS and realized he had misjudged his ship's speed. Sam felt the wall he was leaning on suddenly lurch and the floor dip. The spray of the waves crashing against the reef fell on him as the *Tears of Joy* slid by. *That was too close*, he thought. He swiftly grabbed the rudder and yanked it to the right. *Tears of Joy*'s bow lurched to the left, and the ship leaned heavily to starboard. Sam could see the jagged rocks just a few feet from his ship's hull. His heart raced, and his muscles began to ache. The salt water stung his eyes. If they were to get out of there in one piece, Sidney would have to quickly adjust the jib sail. He saw her standing near the bow, leaning forward against the railing with her arms raised high. She enjoyed sailing immensely and had no fear.

"Sidney! Take the jib and pull it toward you. That's right. Good." The ship was again upright and moving away from the reef. Sam grabbed a towel and wiped the water from his face. With his ship under control again, he made his way to the bow and stood with Sidney in his arms. "That was close. Want to do it again?"

"Why not? Look, Sam, there's another bay. Let's try it."

Sam peered in the direction she was pointing. He could only see a cliff that rose sharply several hundred feet straight up. Above the tree line, he saw a hawk circling.

"You see a hawk?" asked Sidney.

Sam was puzzled as to why she couldn't see it. He saw her beautiful pale green eyes and ... her sitting in her pajamas. He felt dazed. Where had the vision gone? It had been so real. He could still feel the salt water on his face, the ache in his muscles, and her in his arms.

Sidney continued to stare at him. "I could barely hear you. You seemed so far away for a while. Did you say there's a hawk out there?"

"Huh? Oh no. Don't have time to talk. I'll see you after lunch."

As he turned to leave, she spoke. Her voice was different. It wasn't that of a frail person. It was now clear and strong.

"Captain, I'll reveal all that I remember. I'll only draw the line at risking the safety of my people."

Gone was the impression he had that his prisoner was merely a young, foolish rebel. Sidney was no fool. She was mature and quite ready to face his interrogation sessions.

"I expect nothing less than the truth," he stated.

"You shall have the truth, Captain. In return, I expect the same from you."

Sam returned to her bedside and extended his right hand. "Agreed."

Sidney shook his hand firmly and smiled. Sam was satisfied he'd get the information he wanted. He knew how to set the trap, and before Sidney was aware of the setup, she'd reveal all. It would take a day or two, perhaps, at the most. The execution would be carried out by Monday. Sam abruptly withdrew his hand from Sidney's and left the room.

Sam returned to his office and placed a call to Lieutenant Weir to follow up on his last report. The ring tones stopped, and a recording began: "Lieutenant Weir is no longer available at this number."

Sidney supported her back against the bed's headboard. She began to fully comprehend where she was. The previous few days were a collection of moments merging into the next without any logical sequence, punctuated by hazy glimpses of faces and machines. But she clearly remembered standing beside her body at one point. An officer's hat was on the bedside table. Sitting on her bed was a stranger with his arms around her shoulders. Her hand was tightly enveloped in his.

Then, as the physical world had begun to recede, Seamus' voice had sounded clearer than ever before. He was urging her to return to her body.

"Sidney, my precious, there's more for you to do."

"Seamus," she'd called out to the familiar voice, "the body's state is beyond my ability to heal."

"If the body can be healed, would you choose to return?"

"Have I not completed my work?"

"You've done well. The Light shines brightly along the path you've cultivated. Many are finding their way to the Guardian path, one you tilled and lovingly sowed the seeds of the Creator's Light and unconditional love into. But there's much more. There are those who wait for you in the physical dimension. Will you return?"

Sidney found herself surrounded by mist. It glowed with a Light that shone from beyond its veil. She felt drawn ever higher and faster toward the Light, like she was on a ship approaching the shoreline of her home. The joy of returning was overwhelming. Then she saw him on the sandy shore.

Seamus rode a dusty, black horse. Unable to recall her previous incarnations, Sidney had always imagined him to be like an ancient sage, old and bent.

"Seamus, I … " She fell to her knees, in awe of meeting the spirit that had guided and comforted her throughout her life's challenges. Now she remembered they had shared many past lives.

He sat proud on the mare's back. His dark, long hair framed his chiseled face and brown eyes. He reminded her of Greystone, though perhaps younger. She stood before him, her mind racing back through time, at last remembering when she and Seamus had shared many lives together.

His horse danced and shied away.

"Easy, Dusty." Seamus dismounted and came to Sidney, taking hold of her shoulders. "My precious, stand with me."

Sidney recognized his signature energy. Even if she hadn't seen him or heard his voice, she'd have known it was Seamus who embraced her. She felt strong again.

"You ask me to return. There's more?"

"It's your choice. You're welcome to stay and be with me again. Or you may choose to return to your body. Either way, you serve the higher good."

"Either way, you'll be at my side?"

"Me…and Celeste." He laughed.

Sidney suddenly heard the hawk's call. She couldn't see Celeste, but she knew her childhood companion was near. As she stood with Seamus, Sidney was aware of something calling her back. She could resist. It was *her* choice. The desire to stay with Seamus was powerful. But so was the voice calling her to return. She became aware of a deeper knowing, something she couldn't express—but it longed for her, had been waiting for her in the physical dimension. It filled her with a tender warmth and more.

"I'll return, Seamus."

Seamus's energy swirled and glowed with brilliant, iridescent colors. He drew her into his arms and lifted her face to his. She gazed into the softness of his eyes and became lost in their message of unconditional love for her. Gently, he lifted her and carried her back to the mist. She could no longer see him but felt cradled in his strong arms. Again she had felt the weight and restriction of her body.

She understood from the medical staff that that had been two nights ago, the night they'd all expected her to die. They made no secret of their surprise at the speed with which she was recovering. At the moment, she was alone, the staff busy with other duties in the main infirmary.

Perhaps, she thought, *I'll just slip gently over the side, unhook the bag and chain contraption, and edge my way toward the doorway. See if anyone notices.*

When her bare feet hit the floor, she found her legs wobblier than expected. The lack of food for so many days had taken its toll. Still she persisted. She could see through the glass windows that Lorna and the male nurse in the main infirmary were busy stocking shelves and cleaning equipment. She unhooked the urinary bag from the bed and eased her way to the room's open porthole.

She caught a glimpse of the shoreline and docks toward the far end of the ship's bow and wondered at what city the boat was anchored in. She caught the salty breeze in her nostrils and breathed in, then shuffled toward the room's door, opened it, and peered into the main infirmary.

"Excuse me?" she said.

Lorna dropped the box she was holding and glared at Sidney. "What in the world do you think you're doing! No one said you were allowed to get up! If you wanted help, you could have used the call button. Get back into your room." She waved her hands in the air as if to shoo a dog.

"I just want to make a visit to the bathroom. I don't know where it is."

Lorna stood with her hands on her hips. "Now, why do you need the bathroom?"

"I'd like to clean up a bit. I feel awfully sticky. My hair's a mess. Could I just put some water in the basin and wash myself?"

"Oh, all right. You're sure you can handle it?"

"Just need a little help—a bit dizzy and weak."

Lorna guided Sidney a few yards away to the bathroom. She placed a chair in front of the sink and helped her patient sit down.

"There now," Lorna said as she filled the basin with warm water. The medical assistant's manner was curt and brisk but with a touch of softness. "Here's the soap, towels, and cloths. Toothpaste and toothbrush too. I'll get you fresh pajamas." She waved her finger at Sidney. "For God's sake, call the second you think you need help. Got it?"

"Yes, thanks Lorna. I won't be—"

Lorna dashed out of the room before Sidney could finish. The door was shut and Sidney found the privacy a luxury. She took off her pajamas and began to wash. In a few minutes, the door opened slightly, and Lorna's arm appeared as she hung fresh pajamas on a hook on the wall near the door.

Sidney considered the possibility of escape. If her body had a little more rest and food, perhaps there'd be a chance to get off the boat while it was still anchored, she thought. But she didn't know how much time she'd have before the ship headed out to sea again.

"The sooner, the better," she whispered to herself.

There was just one problem. She wasn't going anywhere while attached to the urinary bag. Her years of volunteering in a palliative care ward in Canada gave her all the knowledge she needed to get rid of the nuisance. All she needed was a syringe. There were no supplies in the bathroom. She was almost desperate enough to give the catheter a good yank. She tugged on it a little. It was firmly in place, and the small balloon inside her bladder didn't give. She noticed the disposal unit on the floor.

Carefully, she felt around the container's contents finding mostly used papers and medical supply containers. Success! There it was—a used syringe at the bottom of the can.

"God bless wonderful people who don't follow all the rules all the time," she whispered.

It was easy to hook the syringe to the catheter's small airline and deflate the balloon. The catheter slipped out easily. She folded the tubing and bag into a small roll and concealed it in the disposal unit.

Just one more good meal and off I go! Tonight, if not sooner.

She planned to find out where the ship was and figure out what direction and how far away her home was. She remembered Seamus saying there were those who were waiting for her. Were they waiting nearby for her to get off the ship, she wondered.

Sidney washed, combed her hair, and put on the clean pajamas. Opening the bathroom door, she peered into the infirmary and saw Lorna waiting for her. She wondered how long it would take for the woman to notice the bag was no longer attached. Perhaps she'd forget about it if Sidney kept her busy with chatter.

It worked. Sidney went on and on about how great she felt. When she and Lorna arrived at her bedside, a pot of tea, two slices of toast, and some cheese were waiting for her.

"Wow, Lorna. This is for me? You're so thoughtful!"

"Hey, don't look at me. Lieutenant John had this delivered. Better finish it before it gets cold again."

Lorna helped Sidney sit down in a chair and moved toward the door. She took two steps and stopped. "Wait a minute!" She turned on her heel. "Where the hell is the damn bag?"

Sidney put her hand up to her mouth to stop a grin, but the smile worked its way through her fingers anyway. "Where's what damn bag, Lorna?" she asked, trying to look innocent.

Lorna's hands were on her hips. When she spoke again, her voice was raised a few decibels. "The damn urinary bag, for Christ's sake. What did you do with it?"

"Um, tucked it inside my pajamas?" She winked at Lorna.

"Yeah? Right! You just stay there while I go get it. If you're lucky, Doc won't make me put the old one back in. Damn it all, anyway," she muttered as she stormed out of Sidney's room, continuing to curse all the way to the bathroom. Sidney heard Lorna tossing garbage out of the disposal. "Ah hah! You thought you could pull a fast one on old Lorna, didn't you?"

When she returned with the tubing and bag, she flung it onto Sidney's bed. "We'll see what Doc has to say about this, missy! Captain Waterhouse ain't going to be pleased either." She waggled her finger at Sidney. "You just sit there and don't try anything more. Understand?"

Sidney decided to face Lorna on equal terms. Grabbing the remains of the offending tubes and bag with her fingertips, Sidney threw them into the garbage container beside her bed.

"Sorry, Lorna. I just couldn't stand that thing anymore. Feels like a damn lump sitting inside my bladder. I know how to remove them, and voilá, the damn thing fell out. Bloody pain in the ass, if you ask me. At least you don't have to keep measuring my output anymore. Right?"

Lorna and Sidney stood toe to toe, each measuring the other's strength.

Lorna shook her head. "You got balls, girl. Got to admit that. Now, you better hope Doc is okay with this." Walking away, she murmured, "God, wait till Sam hears. He's probably got some rule about this too. We're both in trouble. You know that? You cause me any more grief and I'll sit on you!"

Sidney laughed. "Can't be good all the time, Lorna. What's the point if a gal can't make at least one man's day just a tad more complicated than he'd like it?"

Lorna thought for a moment. "You got a point, missy."

Just then, Sam appeared at the doorway. The sweat on his brow and smudges on his shirt indicated he'd been working hard.

"Looks like you two are having an intense conversation. May I join you?" he asked.

"Of course, Captain," said Lorna. "We were discussing the ramifications of someone undoing my work."

Sidney stood up, bracing herself against the side of the bed. The sudden appearance of Captain Waterhouse shook her. Though she'd seen him before, her mind had been in a fog. Now, she saw not only the man, but sensed his power. When his staff acknowledged him with a brisk salute, she couldn't help but notice it was performed with respect. She sensed they would willingly put their lives on the line without a moment's hesitation if he so commanded. It took her breath away.

Sam raised his eyebrows. "Problems, Lorna?"

"Well, no harm done. Sidney took the initiative and removed her catheter."

Sam crossed his arms over his chest. "I see. Isn't that painful?"

"Not if you know what you're doing," Lorna explained.

"Interesting." He paused, studying Sidney's expression. "If you're finished with your discussion, Lorna, I'd like to have a word with the prisoner."

Lorna left.

"It would appear you know more about medical procedures than the average person. Is that correct?" Sam asked.

"I worked as a volunteer in a palliative care ward for a while, Captain. I saw things most people don't. Wasn't trained, just watched a lot of procedures."

"Right. So you know the importance of procedures being properly carried out by the right people. Rules are there for a reason."

Her back straightened, and she lifted her chin higher. "Not necessarily, sir. Rules are made mostly for machines or those who can't be trusted to make decisions using sound judgment for the good of all. I live by only guidelines."

"Well, the rules here on my ship are not simply guidelines. And, they're not just for machines. I expect everyone, including prisoners, to follow procedure." Sam's voice was almost harsh.

He never broke eye contact with her for a second, yet he never made any threatening gestures either. He didn't need to. His authority remained steadfast. And she never shied away from his domineering stance in front of her, though his broad shoulders reached the level of her chin.

"Well, Captain Waterhouse, you're right about some rules. I do have one,"

"Yes?" he retorted.

She stood with her hands on her hips. "I control what goes on or in my own body. I control the what, where, when, why, and the how! If I don't want a catheter, I won't have a catheter. I bet, Captain Waterhouse, that's in *your* rule book too!"

She was so tense she was barely able to take in a breath and began to feel lightheaded. But as long as Sam maintained eye contact, she didn't dare show weakness. For what felt like an eternal minute, he said nothing and stood firm. Eventually, a hint of a smile appeared on his face.

"Touché. I'll give you that one." His smile broadened.

At last she was able to step away and take in a breath.

"Thank you, Captain."

She wanted to hide the fact that she was trembling, but her knees gave way. Reaching for the bed, she felt the floor sway, and her vision blurred. Sam called out for Lorna just before the darkness surrounded her. As she lost consciousness, she felt Sam wrap his arms around her.

When she opened her eyes moments later, she was back on her bed. He was bent over her, trying to unhook a lock of her hair from a button on his shirt. His face was close to hers.

Weakly, she asked, "What happened, Captain?"

"You fainted." He frantically wrestled with his shirt's button entangled with her hair. "I grabbed you just before you hit the floor. Got your hair caught in this button. There!"

He stood up and straightened his shirt. Meanwhile, Lorna fussed with the medical scanner and mumbled to herself, and Dr. Duncan arrived.

Sam stepped aside and reported, "One minute she was talking, and then she collapsed. Caught her before she hit the floor."

Sidney tried to sit up. The room began to swim again.

"Just got dizzy. That's all. Really, I'm okay."

She had the feeling all three people were ignoring her comments. They turned their attention to the machines and gadgets.

"Excuse me, Captain," said Dr. Duncan as he pushed his way between Sam and the bed. "She looks pale. Lorna, what's the scanner saying?"

"Possible hypovolemic shock. Not definite. Her blood pressure's low. She's had a busy day so far. Perhaps she just needs some rest."

"Can't take any chances, Lorna. The spleen could be bleeding, a delayed reaction from the truth serum. Draw up a blood sample. Get her blood count, and start an I.V."

Dr. Duncan unsnapped Sidney's pajama top and flung it open, exposing her chest. Sidney was suddenly well aware that Sam was standing at the foot of her bed. She tried to cover herself with her hands while Dr. Duncan continued to palpate the area around her ribs. She focused on the ceiling and winced with every prod of the doctor's hands on her chest.

She became aware of a towel being flung across her chest. The captain had done it. His dark eyes briefly met hers, and then shifted away. There was little expression on his face, if any. He again maintained his resolute distance, and she chastised herself for being momentarily drawn to those dark brown eyes. "Doctor, perhaps we should ask the patient what she thinks is wrong," said Sam authoritatively. "After all, it's her body."

Dr. Duncan glanced up incredulously at Sam. "I'm going in to do an exploratory. I don't have the equipment here to rule out internal bleeding, and I'm almost certain that's what's happening."

Sidney held the towel to her chest and struggled to sit up. "You mean surgery? No, absolutely not. I'm not bleeding. There's no need for surgery. No!"

Dr. Duncan grabbed Sidney to get her to settle back down onto the bed.

"Be quiet," he demanded.

"Doctor, let her go. She's fine. Lorna said it herself—she's had a busy day and took on too much too fast. If she says no to surgery, then we won't do any surgery on her. Understood?"

Dr. Duncan looked at Sam in disbelief. He let go of Sidney's shoulders. "Captain…"

"We'll talk about this later," Sam said. "Right now, I've got to take this ship out to sea."

He disappeared through the doorway and out of the infirmary, but in Sidney's mind, much of Sam's presence remained in the room. She didn't know what to think exactly. This man, who'd eventually carry out her execution and who seldom showed a hint of any emotion whatsoever, was considerate of her dignity and then came to her defense. She'd never known anyone quite so bizarre.

Lorna fastened Sidney's pajama top and coaxed her to relax. "Get some rest. Old Lorna'll make sure no one gets any scalpels heated up."

The doctor shook his head and asked Lorna to keep him updated on her vitals. Then he stomped out of the room.

Lorna followed him into his office. "Doc, since when have you been in such a fired up rush to cut someone open? That's not your style. What gives?"

Dr. Duncan tossed about some papers on his desk in frustration. "I've got my reasons."

"I think you're just too curious to see what she looks like on the inside." She chuckled and left the office with her head held high and a wiggle of her hips.

Shortly after her supper tray was removed, Sam appeared at Sidney's doorway in his usual indifferent manner. "You've recovered from this afternoon's incident?"

She thought it would be appropriate for her to stand to greet him. "Yes, Captain. I want to thank—"

His raised his hand in the air as he interrupted her. "No need. Stay on your bed, please. All your responses to the next several questions are being recorded. Do you understand?"

"Yes, sir."

Sam was confident she saw him as an ally. He'd defended her and displayed respect for her needs. He'd get all the damn questions answered, and he was certain the mystery would have a rational explanation.

"It's time you received formal notice of the charges laid against you." His serious expression didn't betray hostility or any other emotion. He was simply attending to business.

Sidney would've preferred to stand, thinking that might take away a little of his dominance, but since he'd requested she stay on her bed, she sat up on her heels, raising herself to above his eye level.

"Captain Butchart advised me briefly of what I was accused of."

Sam stood almost at attention and read his dissertation as if a judge was present. "Admiral Garland has charged you with sabotage and spying. You've been transferred to the USS *Nonnah* for interrogation. I'll be carrying out the interrogation sessions. Up to three sessions each day. Is that understood?"

"Yes. I already said I'd tell you what you want to know, at least what I remember."

"I expect your full cooperation. Do you understand the consequences if you're found guilty of these charges?"

The muscles in Sidney's stomach tightened. She took one deep breath and looked back at Sam. "I recall mention of an execution, Captain."

"Correct. I have orders from Admiral Garland to carry out your execution. It will take place within twenty-four hours of confirming your guilt. Two shots at close range to the head with a pistol is the method of the execution. Death is instantaneous. Do you have any questions?"

Sidney's throat tightened and a chill penetrated to her core. She wanted to ask if he'd have the pleasure of personally carrying out those orders. Instead, she held her tongue and looked toward the porthole.

"About a dozen, but I don't think I'm ready for the answers yet. My head still feels like it's in a fog."

Sam paused momentarily. Instead of following a drill, he mentally sorted files and strategy.

"Do you admit that you defused the nuclear missiles on the New Seattle Naval Base?"

Sidney thought for a moment. "I do remember being in a room with the missiles and that my intent was to defuse them. I believe I was successful."

"I'll take that as a yes to my question. Did you have any assistance during the sabotage to gain access to secured facilities?"

"No. No one helped me. I was on my own at all times."

"How did you gain access to the secured areas, such as the missile room?"

"There was no lock on the missile room's door."

"You accessed the subbasement tunnels from the administration building's stairway. Is that correct?"

"Yes."

"The door to the tunnels in the subbasement has a sophisticated locking mechanism. How did you open that door?"

Sidney had to decide if there would be any harm in telling her interrogator of her Guardian telekinetic skills.

"Captain, I can't answer that."

"Why not?" he demanded.

She squared her shoulders and made an attempt to show she could equal his tenacity. "Anything connected with my people is off limits."

"I don't understand. How are your people connected with you getting a locked door open? Did they provide the knowledge on how to open it?"

Sidney respected the captain's intelligence. He refrained from emotional reactions and focused only on the facts and logic. She quickly came to the conclusion that she had to be more careful.

"No, Captain. My people don't have information about that door or its locking mechanism."

"Ah, *that* door. Is it fair to say they have information on how to open a variety of locking mechanisms?"

"Yes."

"Therefore, your people are connected to your ability to open *that* door. They're responsible for you gaining access to the tunnels."

Sidney stared at Sam. He'd successfully cornered her. "Touché, Captain Waterhouse. I'll give you that one. But they have nothing to do with me being on the base."

"Okay, for now, I'll accept that you were able to unlock that door because of whatever training you've received. I'll also assume that you were trained to defuse the missiles using a similar method. They both operate by electronic devices. As a result, your technique on one would work on the other. Is that correct?"

"Yes."

"I'm curious to learn what that method is. For now, we'll move on to other questions. Number one, why did you defuse the missiles?"

"I was hired to defuse them. That's all. What difference does it make why?"

"The motive for defusing the missiles is important. For example, if you were doing something illegal to save a life, that would result in a different outcome. If you were defusing the missiles to put the United States of America at a disadvantage in defending Americans or American allies, that's considered an act of war. Therefore, it's important that I understand, without any doubts, your motives. Who hired you?"

"Someone concerned about the future of this planet. That's all I'll say."

The captain frowned. "I'll accept that for now. But I doubt your employer was interested in some mothballed missiles. That was a diversion. What was your primary mission?"

Sidney endeavored not to change her posture, not so much as to even blink. "You have my confession. You have enough to carry out your execution, do you not?"

"It's not my execution. It's the U.S. Naval Command's directive."

Sidney began to tire but was not going to let this opportunity slide by. She quickly got off the bed and stood close to the captain.

Her eyes narrowed. "I have serious doubts the U.S. Naval Command has any knowledge of me or what I did or that I'm on this ship about to be executed under the U.S. Naval Command's authority at the direction of Frank Butchart. Do you understand that, Captain Waterhouse?" She maintained eye contact with Sam for a moment, and then, before her knees gave out on her again, climbed back up onto her bed and sat in her lotus position. "No disrespect intended, sir."

Sam paused. "None taken." He stood silent for some time and made a mental note of her statement. She'd referred to Butchart—someone she shouldn't know—in the familiar as "Frank Butchart." He found that very odd. He shifted his position away from Sidney and studied the scanner above her bed. It had been turned off.

"I should have figured you were feisty. No one goes through what you have and survives without being rather…spirited."

Sidney was becoming increasingly frustrated with her inability to maintain her mental focus and physical strength. Her body didn't respond as well to her draw of the healing energy as it had usually done. It felt as though a stronger force was sedating her mind. She shook her head, trying to refocus.

"I'm sorry, Captain. I shouldn't take out my anger on you. You've been a gentleman. It's Captain Butchart with whom I have a bone to pick." She began to tremble and leaned forward over her knees, resting her head in her hands.

"You do?"

She immediately regretted revealing that there was more to her story. She had to be more careful. She laid her head down on the pillow.

"I'm sorry. Just too dizzy to sit up. I guess I haven't got the right to ask if we can continue with this interrogation tomorrow."

"You do have rights. I thought by now you'd realize that I'll protect your rights as well as I protect the rights of my staff and superiors. Tomorrow we'll both have clearer heads on our shoulders."

"Captain, I remember something odd about the first night I arrived on the ship. There was someone sitting here beside me on the bed. He was holding my hand. No one else was in here. Just one officer. Do you know who that was?"

"You were in a coma. You must be mixed up from a dream or a hallucination."

"No, Captain. I'm certain. I remember it very clearly. I wish I knew who that was."

Sam looked away and fidgeted with his hat. "Why?"

"Because he's probably the reason I survived. He should know that his simple act of compassion perhaps performed a miracle. All these medical gadgets here in this room will sustain the body for a while. But they won't keep body and soul together. Only something deeper can do that."

"I'll check into who was here and pass along your gratitude to him. Will that be sufficient? People in the military get rather uncomfortable with receiving overt affection. You understand?"

Sidney understood. She also noticed the hat Sam had in his hands—just like the one from her memory of that night.

"Yes, thank you, Captain. Just let him know that perhaps I can return the favor one day."

Sidney pulled the bed covers up to her chin. Staring off into the distance, she spoke almost as if to herself.

"It's seems a little strange. Why would he take the time to sit with me, a prisoner?"

Sam cleared his throat. "In my experience, when one is faced with death, those kinds of issues have little significance. When faced with death, people, even military men, do things they normally wouldn't do."

Sidney didn't respond. He put his hat on and headed for the door, but stopped.

"Miss, do you know Captain Butchart?"

She appeared to have already dozed off, but he saw her head briefly nod and utter a barely audible, "Uh huh."

Sam considered it odd for any civilian to know Butchart. For a short while, he stepped out of his captain's mindset. He became just Sam. His expression softened, and his voice was caring.

"I'll open the porthole. The fresh air will help."

After he opened the porthole, he stood at the foot of the bed for a few minutes, studying his prisoner. He hit the comlink on his shirt and gave the command for the recording to end. Quietly, he left her room.

10. Sidney's Escape

Early Morning, Sunday, July 7

The sound of voices outside Sidney's porthole woke her. The loud banter was in Spanish. Except for small indicator lights blinking on equipment in the main room, the entire infirmary was dark. Quietly, Sidney slid out of her bed and listened more carefully at her porthole. The voices gradually disappeared into the night, and all was quiet again. Something else caught her attention—the ship was still anchored at a dock.

The lights of the port shone into the water and traced the shoreline with their shimmering eyes. They winked at Sidney. *Do I dare?* she thought. Without taking any time to plan, she began her escape. She realized she was wearing pajamas and had no currency. *Small matter. Getting off this boat will be half the battle. I'll deal with the rest later.*

Peeking through the windows of her room into the infirmary, she saw no one. She figured someone must be nearby; there always was at least one medical assistant around. She slowly opened her door and checked to see if anyone was resting on the beds—all three were vacant. Her heart beat rapidly. *Surely someone's just outside the infirmary.*

Ever so silently, she opened the infirmary's door and looked down the corridor. It was completely void of any people, and the lights had been dimmed, inviting her to slip through the doorway. She heard muffled footsteps. This was no time to hesitate. She sprang down the hallway.

She quickly but silently trotted through passages and up stairways. She had to use her intuition to find the deck with the gangplank leading down to the dock. She wondered if anyone had spotted her on the security videos and dared to stop momentarily to listen for footsteps of guards in pursuit. She heard only the sound of her pounding heartbeat. The thought of soon being free was exhilarating. Her weak body received a massive surge of adrenaline, and she sprinted to a doorway through which she could see the harbor lights.

Opening the door just a fraction, she felt a rush of the cool night air. Again she heard no sound of people. The ship was almost motionless, as if waiting for her to make her move. Just beyond the door, she saw the wide expanse of the ship's main deck. She passed through the door and clung to a wall as she scanned for a ramp, inching her way toward the bow until she saw it. She heard voices, the same Spanish speaking ones that had woken her. The men were amusing themselves in some game—perhaps cards, she thought. Between her current position and the ramp, there was no cover to conceal her movement. Still, she had to chance it.

But first, if she were to fool the men, she had to look like she belonged—give them the impression she'd been a "visitor" and was leaving before the sun rose. She rolled up her pajama sleeves and legs in an attempt to make it look like a funky kind of sun outfit. She tied the shirttails of the top into a knot and undid most of the snaps, hoping the men might simply admire her body and not notice the navy insignia on the material. It was her only chance. Finally, she raced to the ramp.

She could see that the men at the bottom weren't concerned with watch duty. They were seated at a card table several feet away from the ramp, and their cheerful banter went on as poker chips were scooped up by the winner. She could have waved at them and she doubted they'd have noticed.

The ramp was long and sturdy. As she stepped onto it, she stood up straight and took in a deep breath. Slowly, she descended. In her mind, she rehearsed the Spanish she'd learned. She casually played with her hair as if she was relaxed and simply attempting to tame it in the breeze.

Then, to her surprise, Seamus appeared before her. Sidney was shocked. Never had he ever shown himself to her in this dimension.

Seamus, is something wrong? she mentally asked.

Her spirit guide remained several feet away from her. His blue tartan cloak and dark hair waved in the night air with the breeze's taunting.

"My precious, there is only the higher good. Your struggle to survive has turned your focus inward to the self. The higher good is beyond the self. Reach for the higher good, Sidney."

Sidney reached for him. The closer she came, the more his form evaporated into the night until she could no longer see him.

Seamus, I want to go home.

"You may go home, Sidney. But you may never be free of this ship and its people. Do you remember how the admiral's secrets followed you?"

Yes. I'd become a part of those secrets. Knowledge of the admiral's plans tormented me at times, like a song that keeps playing in my head.

"So, can you go home and not wonder if your disappearance created hardship, perhaps even death?"

Seamus, I'd never… Sidney suddenly saw the consequences of her escape. *You mean, the admiral would blame, maybe even accuse the ship's officers of… oh no. I couldn't live with that. But, Seamus, oh, please. I want to go home!*

Seamus appeared again briefly and winked. "You were home just the other day, Sidney—with me. Forget not your true home, my precious. Listen to your heart. Know with every beat *that's* where you'll find me … and your home. Your heart will guide you to see choices which lead to the higher good."

As he vanished again, he swept over her body, touching her heart with his love. Sidney stood silent in the night, a statue on the ramp. Unable to move in either direction, up or down, she felt frozen in her mind. Either way, she'd experience pain and regret.

The sound of footsteps approaching from the ship's deck brought her out of her trance. She crouched down against the walls and braced herself for an attack. She glanced up to the top of the ramp. It was Sam.

He was wearing his jogging clothes and was focused only on the deck in front of him. When he neared the ramp, he stopped and grabbed onto the ship's railing. Seeing the guards at the bottom, he called to them greeting them and asking how they'd been.

"*Buenos días, caballeros. ¿Cómo están ustedes?*"

"*Somos bien. ¿Y tus hijos, Capitán Waterhouse?*" called back one of the guards.

"Ah, *es usted, Señor Ben. Ellos son bien, gracias, ¿Y Ricardo, estar mejor?*" said Sam.

Sidney remained crouched in the darkness as low as she could. Sam was only a few yards away from her, off to the side of the ramp, leaning against the railing. She was able to pick up the odd Spanish word or phrase. It was apparent that Sam and the guards knew each other fairly well. Sam had even known the name of one of the guard's children and they asked after his sons.

"*La medicina que dio ha hecho maravillas. Estamos muy agradecidos, señor Capitán. ¿Tiene tiempo de jugar un poker pequeño?*" said the guard, motioning Sam to come down the ramp.

Sidney froze. The guard was inviting Sam to join them. If he moved to the top of the ramp, she'd be caught.

"Ah, *desafortunadamente, no. Debo permanecer en la forma. Mis hijos crecen y pronto no escucharán a su papá.*" Sam laughed.

Sidney understood enough to know that Sam had declined the invitation to join their card game. Something to do with being a good example for his sons. She breathed a quiet sigh of relief.

"*Buen viaje, Capitán Waterhouse.*"

"*Buenos días, caballeros,*" called out Sam, waving as he resumed jogging.

Running on past the ramp, the captain disappeared, and Sidney relaxed. She could still make her way down and begin the charade with the Mexican guards. But she now had serious doubts that they could be easily fooled. They were good friends with Sam and probably knew how he kept to the rule book's written word.

Sidney sat there for several more minutes weighing the risks. Her imminent execution was enough incentive for her to get up and put on the best call girl performance anyone could dream of. She walked down the ramp.

Acapulco's wharf glowed in the brilliant sunrise. Church bells called the devoted to Sunday morning mass. Sailboats tied to piers waved their tall wooden masts in greeting to the morning sky. As Sam began his fifteenth lap, the ship's alarm sounded. Within seconds, his comlink alarm sounded.

Striking its sensor, he responded, "Captain Waterhouse."

Commander Moon replied. "Sir, the prisoner is missing. I'll be giving orders to the search teams on the ship's main deck in five minutes." Sam's momentary euphoria twisted into a cold knot. Thirty seamen ran to the main deck and stood at attention. Moon directed team leaders to search the ship and the harbor.

Sam called out. "Commander, she's not to be killed. Understood?"

"Aye, aye, sir."

Sam ran down to the infirmary. Dr. Duncan was pacing nervously and interrogating his medical staff. As Sam entered the room, all the staff snapped to attention.

"Dr. Duncan, I want a report."

The two men moved into Dr. Duncan's office.

"Sir, from what I've gathered so far, the prisoner slept through the night. Early this morning, medical personnel decided it was safe to go get coffee and a bite to eat. Since the prisoner was sleeping and presumably weak they didn't get someone to watch her. When they got back ten minutes ago, she was gone."

"Damn it all, Doctor. Didn't they realize she'd be plotting to get off this ship? Where's Lieutenant Morton?"

"When Lieutenant Morton returned from shore leave, he met in the infirmary with Roberts, who'd been assigned to watch the prisoner. They discussed a problem with an alarm two doors down the hall from the infirmary. The medical attendant was due back from his break, so they believed Sidney would be unsupervised for only a few minutes. She was sleeping soundly so they left to deal with the alarm problem. The attendant was slow in returning, and they must've been occupied repairing it when the prisoner escaped."

"I'll take this up with Commander Moon. In the meantime, she's had up to an hour head start on us. You know the chances of finding her? Damn it! Did she take anything?"

"Not as far as I can tell. She doesn't have her clothes either. She should be easy to spot if we ask the local people to be on the lookout for someone wearing U.S. Navy pajamas."

Just then, Moon knocked on the doctor's door. Perspiration ran down the sides of his face from racing about the ship, and he was nearly out of breath. Sam motioned for him to enter.

"Rhett, this is one hell of a screw up! How is it no one saw her on the security monitors? How the hell does this woman continually dance around the navy's security systems?" Sam took a breath. He didn't like losing control. Just the thought of behaving like Admiral Garland was enough for him to regain a calmer demeanor. "Were the men attending to their posts?"

"Yes, sir."

Sam realized that the officers tended to be less diligent toward the end of their shifts, and it would take only a few seconds while they looked away from the screens for someone to get to the ramp unnoticed.

"I talked with the security guards on the dock. They report no one came by their post," Moon said.

Sam nodded. He knew he was just as much to blame as anyone else for the disappearance of his prisoner. He'd assumed she was too ill or weak to make an escape.

"Rhett, I think we've all underestimated this … this woman."

Sam turned his back and returned to the ship's deck. He thought back to the last hour when he'd been running there. She might have even seen him. He gritted his teeth in anger. *What a fool I've been!* Grasping the ship's railing, he tightened his grip until his knuckles were white. He looked out at the city's streets and pictured her sneaking through alleys, perhaps stealing food and clothing. *How long will it take her to find refuge?*

Sam couldn't stand the wait. He walked around the ship checking on the search of the ship. His men were thorough, eager to be the first to find the prisoner. Gradually, Sam made his way to the highest deck level. He decided to contact Paulo through the waiter at the outdoor café. If Paulo couldn't—or wouldn't—help, he'd have to call the admiral.

He walked to the bow of the ship near the navigation room. Leaning against the wall, he felt the warmth of the morning sun already on its surface. Gazing out over the docks, everything around him appeared lazy and in its proper place. He walked back to the ship's stern.

"Psst!"

The sound came from above him. He looked up to the roof of the air conditioning housing. Peering over the edge was Sidney.

"It looks like you've misplaced something, Captain Waterhouse." She winked. "I see the seamen exploring every nook and cranny. What are they looking for?"

Sam could scarcely believe his eyes. If he could have reached her, he'd have grabbed her by the shoulders and given her a violent shake. "As if you don't know. Get the hell down from there." Sam activated his comlink to Moon. "Rhett, call off the search. I've found the prisoner. I'll meet you in the infirmary in fifteen minutes."

He saw that she hadn't moved. "Miss, get down here. Now!"

"I can't, Captain. The ladder broke when I climbed up. If it hadn't, I'd have gone back to my room a long time ago. Honest!" She was still smiling nervously.

Sam found the ladder hanging by one bolt on the other side of the building. "All right. I'll steady it. Climb down!"

Sidney carefully stepped onto the top rung as Sam held it. Once she had both feet firmly placed on the floor, he ordered her to stand against the wall. She stood straight but trembled slightly as she held her hands behind her back. Her smile had disappeared.

He barked at her, "Put your hands down by your sides where I can see them." He stepped forward, and she backed against the wall and gasped, bracing for a blow.

"Relax! I don't abuse prisoners. Just don't move. Not so much as one toe. You've disrupted my ship's routine. My entire morning's shot." He glanced at his watch. It was already 0800 hours and he was still out of uniform. "This isn't acceptable."

"Captain?"

He glared at her. "What?"

She tried to smile. "Well, why didn't someone just holler out 'Sidney, where are you?' I would've answered sooner or later." She shrugged her shoulders. "It was getting pretty hot up there. Was hoping someone would come along."

"So why didn't you call for help?"

"Well, truth is, it was the last bit of freedom I'll probably have." She gazed out over the ocean. "Just wanted to hang on to every precious second."

"You're right about the 'last bit of freedom.' I won't be making any more mistakes. Take one last good look at freedom, Miss Davenport. Now, back to the infirmary!"

He grabbed her arm and thrust her forward. During their walk, both Sam and Sidney were quiet—one falling into despair, the other agitated. By the time they were at the infirmary's door, Sam's anger had dissolved into mere annoyance. He was well aware Sidney could have escaped, and his curiosity began to overshadow his hostile feelings toward her.

At the door, he asked, "Why? You could be off this ship and God only knows where by now. You would've been free. Why didn't you go?"

She looked thoughtfully at him. "For the higher good. When I was on the ramp, it occurred to me that Admiral Garland would make sure you suffered a great deal if I escaped."

Sam stood stiffly in his arrogant posture. "Nothing I couldn't handle."

"Maybe so. But I also overheard your conversation with the guards on the dock. You have children. Having tasted the admiral's rage once myself, I know he's capable of great violence. If I'd escaped, he'd have made sure you paid a heavy price. Perhaps your children would never see you again. I couldn't live with that."

Sam's rule book began to dissolve. "Even knowing … "

She looked softly into his eyes. "Yes, Captain. There are many things more important than death."

She reached for the door handle, but Sam gently took hold of her shoulder to stop her. Still trying to maintain his authoritative posture, he asked, "The higher good?"

Sidney nodded. "Yes, Captain."

She opened the door and walked back to her room. Sam stood in the doorway, watching her as she disappeared into her room. Moon was waiting with two seamen.

"Rhett, I want security in front of her door twenty-four hours a day. In the meantime, the holding cell is to be prepared for the prisoner."

Dr. Duncan was just as relieved as Sam that his patient was back. "I'll check her over and let you know if she should stay here."

"Thank you. Rhett, it's time we got this ship out to sea. Notify the port officials that we're heading out. Tell the navigation staff to prepare for our arrival at Lima. Doctor, I want your report on her in thirty minutes. Once we're away from the Acapulco harbor, I'll call a meeting with senior officers. In the meantime, two seamen are to be posted in and outside the infirmary. Any questions?"

There were none.

Dr. Duncan called Sam to say the patient was reasonably healthy, but suggested Sidney remain in the infirmary, locked in the isolation room. He wanted to observe her, study her unusual physiology.

"No," Sam replied. "She'll be moved this afternoon. We'll talk about this rather peculiar prisoner at this morning's meeting in half an hour."

The meeting began promptly at 0930. Sam outlined the importance of maintaining security around Sidney. Without going into detail, he advised that she had a way of getting by security systems unnoticed and undetected. Therefore, he told them, the seamen assigned to watch her had to visually account for her presence every ten minutes. There were to be two seamen assigned to guard her twenty-four hours a day: one at her cell, one at the next doorway. The orders concerning no one but the captain, Commander Moon, and medical staff having official contact with her remained in effect. Bridges would be added to that list as soon as the prisoner was moved to a cell. Sam asked if anyone had observed the prisoner and noticed anything unusual.

Robert John spoke. "No disrespect intended, Captain, but if she's the enemy, and if I was her prisoner, well ... not sure I'd attempt to escape."

A few of the officers laughed until they noticed Sam's eyes narrow. He sat like a corpse in his chair, more rigid and cold than usual. The room became silent. When the captain spoke again, his words were delivered with precision. He exhibited an almost frightening lack of emotion.

"The prisoner may be in collaboration with the underground, Lieutenant John, or she may be involved with other dissident forces. She's to be treated as a hostile enemy of the United States of America. There will be no leniency. Once I'm satisfied all the facts have been revealed, she'll be executed."

He stood up. "You should be aware that she's confessed to the crimes Admiral Garland has levied against her. She did, in fact, invade secured sections of the New Seattle Naval Base and subsequently defused several nuclear missiles."

Moon frowned. "Sounds as though there's enough evidence to carry out the execution now."

"We could if we were sure we had all the facts," Sam explained. "First and foremost, the problem is that she accessed highly secured areas and defused the missiles without the aid of inside help or equipment. No doubt there are others with her ability. If we're going to be successful in preventing any further attacks, we need to know what she knows.

"Secondly, I believe she's hiding something else. Frankly, I suspect the defusing of the missiles was only a diversion. The underground wouldn't take such great risk to defuse a few outdated missiles. I intend to dig deeper to see if there was a greater reason for her presence on the base. So you see I need everyone's full cooperation to keep this prisoner alive and healthy."

Everyone responded, "Aye, aye, sir," and the meeting was adjourned. Most of the officers quickly swallowed the last of their coffee and rushed to the door. The tension of dealing with the prisoner wasn't to their liking, and they were happy to depart to their usual routine. Sam motioned for Robert John, Dave Morton, Dr. Duncan, and the commander to join him in his office.

"Gentlemen, the escape of the prisoner this morning is unacceptable. I hold myself responsible as much as the four of you. There will be no more errors in judgment or communication. That will be all, gentlemen. Dismissed!"

Commander Moon returned to his quarters to rest and check his messages. He hoped for responses to his inquiries. Moon wasn't a man satisfied with driving in the dark on faith alone. Although he trusted and respected Sam, his gut told him Waterhouse was a man headed for destruction—and Moon wasn't going to be standing with him in the midst of the explosion. He needed to know who was going to ignite the bomb and when. The message indicator flashed on his computer, indicating a reply—from Captain Butchart.

11. Rules for Sidney

Mid-Morning, July 7, En Route to Peru

Prior to his prisoner's arrival, Sam had struggled to apply himself to the drudgery of mindless tasks. But the numbing routine had transformed into a state of continuous chaos the day she arrived. He was now tired of the constant barrage of unexplainable events. Mindless tasks were almost appealing now.

Sam was determined to get his ship back on its routine. After reviewing the standard daily crew reports and enjoying lunch with the officers, Sam went to relax on the upper deck near the *Nonnah's* bow. The solitude was as healing as a Buddhist meditation retreat. Recalling his Buddhist roots, he wondered why he'd left his mother's teachings and meditation practices behind. The experiences had been powerful. Perhaps, he thought, they had showed him a truth he hadn't been able to accept, one that often conflicted with his military training. He turned his face toward the sun, feeling its warmth soothe away the morning's tension.

As the *Nonnah* sailed the Pacific Ocean in a southerly direction, her nose surged through the heaving waves. Out in the water, all was in rhythmic harmony — the wind, waves, ship, and him. It was just as Sidney had said when she'd inquired about his sailing. He had to admit she'd been right.

Sidney's mood tumbled and fell toward a dark place. She was painfully aware of the distance between herself and the life she'd once known. Mornings with her people had been filled with quiet solitude. She'd be high above the valley with Celeste nearby, immersing herself in the Guardian sacred truths. Afternoons passed quickly with harvesting vegetables, preparing meals, collecting eggs, and chatting with friends. Evenings were blessed events while seated around the fire with the Guardian Elders, basking in their eternal and unconditional love. All the things that had given Sidney strength and courage were now gone.

Sitting in her lotus position on her bed, she closed her eyes, breathed slowly and deeply, and let her gloom slip away. Gradually, her breathing slowed. She became acutely aware of everything in her room. Even with her eyes closed, she sensed the medical scanner's energy. She knew where dust particles hid in the corners of the room, and she sensed the energy remnants of each person who'd been in the room that day.

So deep was her meditation that her awareness expanded beyond the confines of the isolation room. She mingled with the energy of the ship, old and full of history. Still conscious of the space around her physical body, Sidney traveled in a dimension without time or space. She found herself seated in the circle with her Guardian Elders.

Birthstone was the first to acknowledge her. "We've been waiting for you, my dear Sidney. You've done well, and we're filled with joy that you're here with us."

"Birthstone, I don't feel I've done well. The mission was a failure. I'm to be executed soon."

Greystone got up from the other side of the room and sat down in front of her. He reached out and caressed her face. "Sidney, you haven't failed at anything in your life. All that's required is for you to remain true to your higher self. Have you done this much, my dear?"

"Yes, Greystone. Mostly. Sometimes, I … "

He put up his hands. "Then, you've done well. Nothing more is required." He cocked his head. "You've come here for advice, perhaps?"

"No. I just miss everyone. How's Danik?"

"We have him busy most every day attending to our livestock. Keeping him occupied with herding instead of scheming. He's tempted to charge in to rescue you."

"Oh no. He mustn't. These people would destroy him at first sight. They're a rather angry lot. More concerned about following rules than anything else. Few listen to their inner wisdom."

Greystone nodded. "Hmm. That's military life, I suppose. Sidney, I want you to make a promise to me."

"Yes, anything for you, Greystone."

"Promise me you'll follow your heart."

"I always do."

Greystone waved a finger in the air. "You've put limitations on where you allow your heart to go. Let it be free. Free as you when you decided to swim in the river's current rather than near the safety of the shore. Free as you when you climbed the cliffs instead of taking the pathway to the top of the mountain. Free as—"

"I think we all get the message, Greystone." Livingstone rolled his eyes. "Do you Sidney?"

Sidney shrugged. "I guess so. But my heart belongs to the Guardian people. I don't need to—"

Birthstone interrupted. "True enough, Sidney. You don't need to. But, if your heart should speak to you about being confined and limited, listen. Listen and follow your heart."

Sidney looked back into Greystone's eyes. They shone with love for her. They spoke of his wisdom and patience. Then, they faded away as she returned to her isolation room. The supper tray was still there.

She tested the sides of the teapot. It was still hot. She poured the tea into a cup and pulled the tray of food closer to her bed. Holding her hands palms up, just above the food, she thanked the Creator for the gifts of the Earth, her life, and her lessons. Then, taking a fork into her hand, she scooped up a portion of the cheese and noodles and tasted it. It was hot and delicious.

When her supper was eaten, a feeling of doom still hung over her. She resumed her meditation. She had to consider the promise she'd made to Greystone. She heard her door open, and knew it was a man when the fragrance of aftershave hit her nostrils. Her eyes remained closed.

As Sidney sat cross-legged, ignoring his presence, she felt his tension, even a hint of contempt. She continued to breathe slowly, eyes closed and her hands placed on her thighs, palms up. He stepped closer to her bed. She sent loving kindness to the man, attempting to soften his anger. Quietly, he moved to the side of her bed, careful not to disturb anything.

She opened her eyes. Commander Moon was bent down closely, inspecting the old bullet wound in her left hand. Without warning, she spoke.

"It doesn't hurt anymore."

Moon gasped and bolted up straight. Sidney smiled, amused at having surprised him.

"Excuse me." He grabbed his hat off his head, and then placed it on again. In the next breath he was in command again. "You appear fine." He waited for a response.

It seemed to Sidney as if he expected a report from her—as though she was one of the seamen. She got off the bed on the opposite side from where he was standing and stood up straight.

"Yes, sir. All systems are functioning at optimum performance. Do you require verification, sir?"

His face remained as a stone for a moment before a sneer took shape.

"Very amusing, miss. And, if I asked for verification, what would you do?"

"Well, let me see." Moving around to the end of the bed and toward the door she considered her response. "I know. Swimming is a great workout for the body. Perhaps I should jump into the ocean and see how far I can swim. Would that satisfy you, sir?"

Moon simply glared at her. "If you have any notions of getting off this ship, I suggest you come back to reality."

Sidney had hoped to break through his hard shell, but she discovered it was impenetrable. There was only one other alternative—challenge his beliefs about her. She walked right up and stood toe to boot with him.

"I know more about reality than you can guess."

She stabbed one of her fingers into his breastbone. Moon grabbed her hand, lifted it off his chest and held it painfully tight. For a brief moment, she could see he'd lost command of himself. He regained it quickly once he released her hand.

"You won't give me any trouble. You won't step outside the infirmary doors. You'll do exactly as the medical staff commands. Is that clear, miss?" he snarled.

"I have no wish to be any trouble to you or anyone else."

"That's difficult to believe in view of your attempted escape this morning."

Sidney now realized she'd made a serious mistake in making light of the situation. She'd made her escape attempt during his shift, and it was now obvious he held a grudge against her beyond the fact that she was a prisoner.

Looking directly in his eyes, she declared, "It clearly states in the Prisoner of War manual that a prisoner is duty bound to attempt to escape. So when I found the door unlocked and no one around … well, it occurred to me that perhaps I'd overstayed my welcome. You would've done the same thing, Commander. Except, I think you'd have been more successful than me." She hoped that would be enough to repair some of his damaged ego.

A smug grin emerged on his face. "The captain tells me you claim to have decided not to continue with your escape attempt because you became concerned the admiral would punish the captain's family for your escape. Do you realize that the captain's sons have been well taken care of by Admiral

Garland since the captain's wife died? They live in luxury in the admiral's mansion, attended to by servants and go to the best school in New Seattle. No, Captain Waterhouse's boys wouldn't have suffered any ill fate."

Sidney was initially staggered at the news of the close relationship between Captain Waterhouse and Admiral Garland. It created a new depth of fear and doubt in Sidney's mind. The captain's benevolent manner toward her was truly just pretense, a ruse for a gullible prisoner. Sidney was humiliated and angry.

Moon leaned down to her face and grinned. He went in for the kill. "I want you to think about that. You could be on your way home, right now, had you not been so naïve. Pleasant dreams, miss," he said sarcastically before he strode out of the room.

Sidney paced around her bed. Her anger continued to gain strength and fury. Sam opened the door, and she spun around on her heel and glared at Sam.

He was lacking his usual military stance. There was even a flicker of concern on his face.

"You're upset," he said.

She stood rigid. "Do you have a question, Captain?"

Sam stepped into the room and shut to door behind him. "All right. You have a complaint?"

Sidney narrowed her eyes. "As if that matters."

"What's at the bottom of this?"

Sidney stepped forward. "I have a question of my own, Captain."

"You answer my question, and I'll answer yours. Deal?"

"No deal. I know exactly what would've happened if I'd escaped? Nothing! Apparently, I've been a fool. Your sons are quite safe. In fact, Admiral Garland has taken on the role of protector to your kids. Is that not so? You and Admiral Garland must be great pals!"

"Who's been talking to you?"

Sidney crossed her arms over her chest.

"Come with me," he demanded.

He took Sidney by the arm to lead her out of the room. She tried to pull away.

"I can walk on my own."

Sam tightened his grip on her arm and pulled her through the doorway and into the infirmary.

"Phillip, who's been talking to the prisoner?"

"Commander Moon stopped by. Left just half an hour ago. No one else that I know of, sir."

Sam clenched his teeth. It was disappointing to discover that his first officer had been nosing into his personal life. His actions had seriously jeopardized his relationship with the prisoner.

"I'll be using the Doctor's office for the next while. I don't want to be disturbed. Get her clothes ready. She'll be transferred now."

Sam let go of Sidney's arm and motioned for her to go into Dr. Duncan's office. Still fuming, she complied. Sam followed her and slammed the door shut behind him.

"Sit down!" he demanded.

Sidney hesitated but decided to show some cooperation. She chose a chair farthest away from Sam, who went behind Dr. Duncan's desk and sat down.

"What did Commander Moon say to you?" he asked stiffly.

"Why do think this has anything to do with Commander Moon?"

"Sidney, answer my question and I'll consider answering yours."

"Oh, yes, that's right! We'll all be honest." Sidney's anger was turning into rage. She stood up and shouted, "I've been told once today that I'm naïve. I think he was right. All you want, Captain Waterhouse, is to know how I got into the missile room and how I defused the missiles. Let's get this over with. Now!"

Sidney was trying to hold back the tears. She felt like a fool. Her anger was more with herself than anyone else. How could she have been so stupid as to turn down perhaps her last opportunity to go home?

Sam stood up and ordered her to sit down. She refused. Sam took her by the arm and pushed her back into her chair. Grabbing another chair, he sat in front of her.

"Now, calm down."

"I won't calm down. I'm fed up with your bloody rule book and never knowing what's going to happen next." A tear escaped. Roughly brushing it aside, she continued, "And … "

Sam decided to take extraordinary measures to regain her trust. Bending forward so his face was near hers, he whispered, "Sidney, there's one thing I can say honestly but off the record." He paused. "Admiral Garland is not my friend." He stared intently into her eyes.

She breathed in the warmth of his scent. The tension in her gut gave up its hold. She raised her chin just a bit in an effort to appear defiant.

"Your boys live with him, don't they?" She sniffed.

Sam had never told anyone about his boys living with Admiral Garland. "Commander Moon told you that?"

Sidney nodded. "Yes."

"Thank you for your honesty. I'll continue to be honest with you. For now, all I can say is that things are not as they appear. I'm grateful you decided not to leave the ship this morning."

He resumed his military posture, stood up, and returned to sit behind Dr. Duncan's desk.

"Now, I want to make one thing as clear to you as I have to my officers—there are specific people allowed to speak to you besides myself, Dr. Duncan and his staff, Commander Moon, and Lieutenant Bridges. Commander Moon is in charge during the night, and you must cooperate with him whether he is on duty or not. However—" he brought up his hand with the index finger raised "—at no time is anyone allowed to cause you pain of any kind. Understood?"

She nodded and looked away from the brown eyes. It was impossible to stay angry.

"And, anything even remotely connected with your activity at the base or your status as a prisoner is off limits to everyone. Therefore, you won't provide information to anyone on this ship except to me. Any questions?"

She was still suspicious, but knew there was no point in debating with him. "No."

"Dr. Duncan has advised me that you're well enough to leave the infirmary. Therefore, I'm confining you to a locked room. No one will have access to that room other than Commander Moon and myself. The two seamen posted at your room will be responsible for ensuring you don't wander off."

He gave a hint of a smile, and Sidney found herself once again having to shield herself from his masculine charm. It was a most annoying predicament. Her anger was gone, but trust had jumped overboard. The feeling that he could be orchestrating this whole charade nagged at her, and he certainly had the means to create an illusion of hope. Yet his calm strength stirred her feelings for him. She had to admit that Captain Sam Waterhouse was more than her only hope for survival. He was a man who seemed to have the power to rule out her determination to be solely focused on her mission. She had to remind herself that he'd be pointing a gun at her head in a few days.

"Actually, Captain, I'm eager for some privacy, and I want to apologize for being so angry. I hope we still have an agreement."

Sam stood and motioned for her to go into the infirmary's main room. "Nothing's changed. Now, let's get started. Get your clothes from Phillip."

"Do I need to bring towels and sheets?" she asked.

"No, the room is completely equipped—bathroom, linens, toiletries."

"Does it have a window, er, I mean, a porthole?"

"No."

"Oh."

Phillip handed over her jeans, socks, and jacket, cleaned and folded neatly in military fashion.

"Perhaps if you're more cooperative, you could be moved to a room with a porthole later," Sam said.

"Captain, if I'm more cooperative, I won't need any room for very long."

"Let's just take this one day at a time. Now follow Lieutenant Bridges. Seaman Yarns and I will follow. Do you have everything?"

"Some of my clothes seem to be missing—underwear, blouse, shoes."

"Must have been too badly damaged. You weren't wearing shoes when you arrived."

Sidney looked off into the distance, her eyes wide. "My shoes!"

"What about them?"

Sidney thought for a moment. A memory had flashed, and then it was gone. "Oh, nothing. Just thought I remembered something."

"All right. Let's go, Lieutenant."

Sidney followed Bridges as he led her through hallways and down three flights of stairs. The hint of the evening's daylight rapidly disappeared as she stepped further into the bowels of the ship. The thundering footsteps of the seamen's boots spoke of their power over her. Artificial lighting brightly lit the corridors with a harsh greenish glow as steel rapidly closed in around her.

The few seamen they met along the way stood at attention as Sam walked by. She could hear their murmurs as they returned to their duties. At the end of a hallway, Bridges stood to the side. Sam opened a flap on the security system unit bolted to the wall and entered a code onto the numbered pad.

"Disarm and release," he said

The unit's red light flashed to green and announced, "Code and voice print acknowledged and approved. Open door within eight seconds."

Sam pushed down on the lever and pulled the door open.

He motioned for Sidney to enter the small, austere room. It measured about ten by fifteen feet. A single bed with a gray mattress stood directly opposite the door against the far, white wall. A black metal bedside table and one gray metal folding chair were the sole amenities in the room. At the far corner was a white toilet against the same wall as the bed. Between the bed and the toilet was a gray locker. Next to the toilet on the adjacent wall was a white, pedestal sink with a bar of white soap on its ledge and a simple square mirror on the wall. On the floor beside the sink was a black garbage receptacle.

If it weren't for the neatly folded navy blue linens and blankets on the bed, the room would've looked like a movie set from the era of black and white motion pictures. The room was illuminated by one ceiling fixture that shone so brightly the only shadow noticeable was the dark recess under the bed. Sidney noted a tiny video camera high on the wall above the bed.

Sam stepped into the room close behind her and shut the door. She stepped away from him, and nodded with approval at the space.

"This is good. I've never had a master en suite attached to my bedroom before. It's very clean, too. Who's your housekeeper?"

She wasn't going to let him see her crumble, not for a second. The room wasn't the problem. It was the ceiling, its one, cold, lifeless eye glaring down on her. It grated at her skin like a badly tuned violin. If there were an opening to the outside world, a tiny window, it would have been at least tolerable.

Sam didn't sway from his stiff manner. "You're the housekeeper for this room. You'll be expected to keep it clean and tidy."

"I hope I measure up. I'm not the best housekeeper. Usually there are a few dust bunnies in my humble abode, might keep a spider to two as a pet."

"There are a few more rules you need to know about."

"I should have guessed."

He ignored her comment. "The camera over the bed is monitored by only myself from my office. A record will be kept of who enters and leaves this room twenty-four hours a day. No one can enter this room except by my voice command. I'll release the locking mechanism via my office comlink and observe on my monitor all activity at this doorway. Understood?"

Sidney tilted her head to the side. "Are you more worried about someone getting in, or me getting out?"

He hesitated. "There will always be two personnel guarding the entrance to this hall and your door."

"You're very thorough, Captain."

"Thanks to you, we've found where things were getting slack. The admiral has come to the same conclusion. There will be no civilians allowed on the base from now on."

Sidney held her breath. The news was a shock. The underground would have little chance of retrieving the hidden memory rod if they hadn't already. Now it looked like the mission was all for nothing. Time was running out. The admiral would have his demonstration the following week, and the world would go mad.

Sidney endeavored to hide her alarm. "All because of one lost visitor?"

She thought she saw a hint of a smile on his face. This time, though, she resisted being led into surrendering her trust to a false benevolent master. She moved farther away and turned her back to him. Opening the locker door, she noted fresh towels, an extra blanket, disposable cups, and pajamas. A white plastic box sat on the top shelf.

As she closed the door, she asked, "Are there more rules, sir?"

"You'll be required to be up and dressed for breakfast by oh-seven-hundred hours. You'll be notified via the intercom in this security unit one hour in advance of mealtime. You'll be escorted to my office to pick up your food tray. The same will occur for lunch at noon and dinner at six o'clock. You'll be interrogated after at least one of those meal times every day. You'll be allowed exercise on the ship's main deck for half an hour twice each day—at ten o'clock and at four o'clock. That schedule may vary depending upon what work is being carried out on the ship. Any questions?"

She stepped forward toward Sam, almost shyly, worried about the whimsical nature of her need. "One question. Can I have a candle?"

"No."

"Why not?"

He smiled. "You said you had 'one' question. That's two."

"Touché," she said, not showing the least bit of disappointment. *He's infuriating. Arrogant! Playing his one-sided games at his whim,* she thought.

"You'll find some supplies in the box on the shelf in the locker." He paused just as he grabbed the door's handle and glanced back. "My turn to ask a question. What was it you remembered about your shoes?"

Sidney shrugged. "Being in a cold space."

As he pushed the door open, he again stopped and turned around. "That's all?"

Gotcha, she thought. "That's more than 'a' question."

Sam nodded as if to say, "Ah, yes," stepped out of the room, and shut the door.

Once he'd left, Sidney breathed a sigh of relief. Alone at last. No one to spy on her and probably no unexpected interruptions to her meditation sessions. The bleak room suddenly felt almost like a luxury. She looked forward to the chance to tune in again to the Guardian sacred truths—she'd been slowly slipping away from their harmony and power.

As she made her bed, she thought about Frank Butchart. Time away from the Guardian's protective shield had left him vulnerable to Dark influences. Exposure to corruption, fear, and greed was like being sucked into a spiral of mental anguish. Solitary confinement was actually a blessing.

It would give her the time and space to reconnect with her people and the sacred truths and avoid the same fate as Frank.

Filling the sink with warm water, she washed her body and hair, savoring every precious minute alone. She put on fresh pajamas and used a towel to dry her hair. With her evening chores finished, she took the extra blanket from the locker, set it on the floor, shut off the light, and sat on the blanket in her lotus position. She took time to just be—free in her space and her thoughts. Holding her index fingers to her thumbs, she closed her eyes, breathed, and drifted into a world Captain Samaru Waterhouse couldn't control.

12. Hanging on to Secrets and the Sacred

Monday Morning, July 8, En Route To Peru

Monday morning, Sidney awoke in her cell's black tomb. She immediately assumed her lotus position and breathed deeply, confident her internal alarm clock had stirred her to life to give her this time to prepare for the day's task of survival. After meditating, she made her bed, paying meticulous attention to detail — not something she was in the habit of doing with her own bed at her island home. She considered it worth the effort, just in case Mr. By-the-Book Waterhouse was capable of softening enough to reward her with a candle.

It felt great to slip on her jeans, even as frayed as they were. The jean jacket was too warm in the tropical heat, but it would have to do. With nothing else to wear underneath, she had to keep it zipped up.

A familiar voice came over the intercom. "Miss, you have one hour to report for breakfast. Acknowledge!"

"Yes, Captain. I'll be ready.

She busied herself washing, brushing her teeth, and combing her hair. The mirror reflected back the image of a woman who'd matured much since the previous week. A woman not about to spend her last days groveling for a candle. *Well, maybe it wouldn't hurt to ask once more.* Regardless of whatever he was about to throw at her, she was prepared to stand her ground. She had resources far beyond his understanding. It was a fact she had to keep reminding herself of more often than usual, which caused her concern.

Ever so slightly, day by day, she felt more and more removed from her Guardian nature and the sacred truths. Her commitment to the truths had been challenged before. Especially during the several months she and Danik had spent away from Hawk's Island. Her work as a Guardian Lantern during that time had proved she was capable of avoiding the pitfalls of fear and the ego's demand for power, but now she was surrounded by people whose energy lusted after power, demanded complete obedience to a rule book, and refused to listen to the heartbeat of their higher selves. It was nearly suffocating to be constantly under the weight of their oppressive way of thinking.

Sidney managed to push her anxieties under a camouflage of compulsive behavior, making doubly sure her room was tidy, herself clean and presentable. Still her heart sent shards of doubt and foreboding to her consciousness. *Execution!* There it was again, that word! She swallowed and paced. *The captain did say there was hope,* she reassured herself. *I doubt he's the sort to lie blatantly about something like that.*

She considered Sam's ability to sense her thoughts and read between the lines, even during her momentary silences. It was irritating. He was always in control. In some ways, he reminded her of Greystone. The Elders had rules too. She and her mentor had disagreed on many occasions when it came to adhering to the community routine—what she considered overly protective restriction on her spontaneous and natural instinct to test her physical limits.

"Wild Child," Greystone would call to her as she arrived late for class. "I see you again wish to volunteer to clean the classroom after today's lessons."

After Sam's verbal command, Seaman Moore opened her door and ordered her to stand in front of him. She did so quickly. Without another word, he pulled out handcuffs and placed them on her wrists behind her back.

"All right. Let's go," he ordered. "Follow Lieutenant Bridges outside. No funny stuff, you hear me!"

"Yes, sir." Sidney thought it wise to say as little as possible. Yesterday, her mouth had gotten her into more trouble than she could handle.

Her two escorts appeared smart in their dark blue uniforms, neat and polished from head to toe. They weren't the drones of the ship who wore uniforms more suited to tasks of physical exertion and toil. The officers' movements were exact and in unison, as if responding to one brain. Seaman Moore was behind her. His breath on her neck sent tingling sensations up and down her spine as they progressed down a hallway, up a stairway, through a doorway, down more halls, upstairs, and through doorways. With each step, Sidney found herself subconsciously making an effort to step to the same beat as the men.

Interesting, she thought when she realized she was copying their movement. She felt a sense of power and unity, of belonging and security. *It would be so easy to let go of one's own personal drummer and step to the beat of another's.*

Again Sidney thought of Captain Butchart. He'd been a powerful Guardian, or so she'd heard. He and his brother wouldn't have been sent on a mission if their loyalty was in question. Still, Butchart did abandon his drummer. *Will I?* she wondered. The passing thought frightened her more than the threat of execution.

Sidney's thoughts preoccupied her to the point that she didn't notice where she was going or who was around her. She was still analyzing Butchart's fall from grace when Bridges stopped abruptly at a large, oak door. Engraved in a brass plate on the door was *Captain Samaru Waterhouse*. Bridges opened the door and held it for Sidney and Moore to pass into the reception room.

"The prisoner is here, Captain," Bridges said through a desk comlink.

Sam's voice came through the comlink's speaker. "Bring her in."

Bridges maintained his hold on Sidney's arm as they stepped into Sam's office. His grip was beginning to be uncomfortable, but she made no complaint and willingly moved as he pushed and pulled her.

Inside Sam's office, both men stood on either side of Sidney, slightly behind her. Bridges released her arm as both seamen stood at attention.

"Lieutenant Bridges and Seaman Moore reporting with the prisoner as ordered, sir."

Sam sat up stiffly in his chair. Without saying a word, he got up and stood in front of Sidney.

Turning to Bridges, Sam asked, "Was she giving you trouble?"

"No, sir."

"Moore, remove the handcuffs."

"Yes, sir."

The handcuffs were removed, and Sidney massaged her wrists and arms.

"Miss, sit down in this chair." Sam pointed to the chair in front of his desk.

"Yes, Captain." She walked past Sam and sat down in the designated chair. She sensed trouble. Her heart felt as if it was beating in her throat.

"Miss, I'll be back in a minute. Do not move from that chair. Is that understood?"

"Yes, sir."

Sam motioned to the door on Sidney's right. "Bridges and Moore, step into the conference room." As the three men stepped into the conference room, Sam called out, "Doors lock." Instantly, the conference room door slammed shut and Sidney heard a click in all the office's doors. She was locked in again.

Sidney surveyed Sam's office. As always, order and simplicity ruled. Sam's desk was immediately in front of her, and a credenza stood against the far left wall. In the right corner behind her was a small kitchenette. All the chairs in the room were royal blue leather. There were three doors—one behind her led to the reception room, one to her right adjoined the conference room, and the other, beside the credenza, Sidney presumed connected to Sam's private quarters. A large window behind his desk revealed a bright morning sky that promised a warm, sunny day. The room had taken on Sam's scent. Sidney ignored it.

Sam's desk was a massive, oak, L-shaped piece. It was stained a rich cherry red with its edging carved to resemble rope. The desk's unblemished satin finish was free of any clutter except for the computer keyboard, built-in digital sensors, and the comlink system.

On his credenza was a picture of his family. Forgetting Sam's orders, Sidney got up to take a closer look at the photo. Sam had his arm around a beautiful woman with long, blond hair. Two young, dark haired boys stood in front. The boys resembled Sam, having inherited his Japanese features. The younger boy, however, had his mother's vivacious smile. The other held himself in check, like his dad. In the scene behind the family was the bow of a sailing ship. She could barely see its name, painted across the bow: *Tears of Joy*.

Just moments before Sam returned, Sidney noticed the crystal at the far end of the desk. It had been partially obscured by the comlink unit, but there it was, set upon a short, ornately carved, wooden pedestal. The root of her difficulties. The sun crystal—the ultimate source of power for whomever chose to unleash its energy. There it sat, asleep. She wasn't surprised to see it. Many sleeping Guardians had one, but not knowing its true purpose, used it merely as a pretty ornament.

When the door to the conference room opened, she rushed back to her chair. Sam frowned and stepped to the front of his desk.

"You don't follow orders very well, miss."

"Sorry, sir."

"Step into the boardroom. Your breakfast is ready."

Sidney took a deep breath and moved to the entrance of the conference room, with Sam following close behind. Inside the room she saw a long, walnut table in the wood's natural, warm shade. Windows lined the wall to the left. A dozen royal blue leather chairs were neatly positioned around the conference table. A number of technical gadgets sat in the center of the table. Against a wall at the far end of the room was another, smaller table. Above it was a video screen pulled down from the ceiling.

On the conference table was a tray of food. Forgetting her apprehension, Sidney stepped over to it. "All of this is for me?"

"You'll have twenty minutes. I'll then conduct an interrogation. This first meeting will be a review of all recorded investigations. You'll listen to audio recordings and view all video recordings." Sam was about to step back into his office and close the door behind him. "Oh, the seamen are just outside that door." He motioned to a door that led directly back into the reception room.

After Sam left, Sidney breathed a sigh of relief. *Well, that wasn't too bad so far,* she thought. As she sat down and looked over the breakfast, she considered how it was going to feel listening to the recordings. She couldn't remember much before waking up on the ship. Her memories from the navy base were still distorted. Flashes of anger and fear surfaced and blended into dreams of isolation and darkness.

The breakfast was good. It gave her renewed strength to face the task ahead. According to the clock on the wall, she had a five more minutes. She cupped the mug of hot tea in her hands, sat back, and closed her eyes. Gathering up the universal energy that had always sustained her, she again felt the presence of Seamus. She was ready.

After giving her precisely twenty minutes, Sam reentered the room. Sidney put down the cup and stood up before him.

"I enjoyed my breakfast. Thank you, Captain."

"You're welcome. Have a seat. Dr. Duncan will be joining us in a few minutes. Once he's here, we'll begin reviewing the records."

"Why does Dr. Duncan need to be here?" Sidney asked as she returned to her chair.

Sam sat down at the table directly across from her. "Just a precautionary measure. These images and recordings may trigger your memories to return. Those memories may not be pleasant. I may need his help if you develop any problems, physically or emotionally."

"I see. I appreciate your concern, but I'll be fine."

"It's my rules, miss."

Sidney shook her head. "Oh, yes. I forgot about them." Sidney moved her breakfast tray aside and sat back in her chair. She remained calm and sat perfectly still as she resisted shifting in her chair or fidgeting. The captain seemed to be watching her every move, reading her thoughts. She focused on the equipment sitting on the table, occupying her thoughts with the possibilities of their function. Soon, there was a knock on the door.

"Come in, Doctor," said Sam.

"Good morning, Captain."

Dr. Duncan sat down at the head of the table.

"The following is a partial recording of the first interrogation between you and Captain Butchart. This occurred on Wednesday morning. Do you recall that session, Sidney?" Sam asked.

"Yes, I recall it occurred, but the details are unclear."

"Okay, we'll begin. Computer, begin playback of interrogation session number one."

Sidney listened to the recording. When the thirty-minute recording was finished, Sam asked, "Was there any pertinent information missing from that recording?" He'd accurately determined what was useless data.

Sidney shook her head. "No, nothing important."

"All right. We'll play an audio recording of the interrogation session that took place that same day after your escape attempt. Computer, begin playback interrogation session number two."

Sidney listened intently to the recording. Most of the memories of that session returned to her. She tried to remain calm while remembering the injection of drugs into her arm and the hostility of the officers. Her rapid breathing exposed her anxiety.

Sam stopped the recording. "Do you need to take a break?"

"No. Let's get this over with now."

"Okay. Let's move on to the video recording. Computer, begin playback of video recording number one."

The blinds on the window automatically lowered, and the lights dimmed. The first security gate showed on the screen at the end of the room. It was a recording of when she and Danik arrived at the base. Glancing at Sam, she found he was still intently watching her reactions. Finally, the show was over.

As the blinds opened and the lights came back on, Sam chatted briefly with Dr. Duncan. Her clouded memory was now razor sharp, and the reality of her situation clearer than ever. She was in a situation that was miles beyond her training. She was no match for the military machine. Garland, Butchart, and now Waterhouse were at the controls. The bottom line, she thought, was to not lose sight of the Guardian sacred truths. They wouldn't save her life, but they'd keep her connected to a reality known only to a Guardian.

"Dr. Duncan, you can return to the infirmary," Sam said, and the doctor nodded and left.

Sidney glanced at Sam. He sat in his chair, confident he'd win, eventually. It was just a matter of time.

"Would you like some tea?" he asked.

"No thank you." It was impossible to sit still. She pushed her chair back from the table, stood up, and walked over to the windows. Gazing out to the ocean's horizon, she asked, "What is it you want to know, Captain?"

"Why were you on the base?"

"To defuse the missiles."

"Is that all?"

Sidney focused on the ocean's rhythmic dance with an audience of large white clouds. She decided she wasn't ready to tell the whole truth.

"It's all I remember doing with any clarity," she responded.

"That doesn't answer my question."

Sidney turned toward Sam. "I know. I have to be sure before I say anything more."

"Sure about what?"

"That no one gets hurt if I reveal more."

Sam busied himself with his computer's electronic files. "For now, I'll accept your statement as a partial truth."

He got up and triggered the video monitor to ascend up. As it disappeared into the ceiling, a painting was revealed on the wall above the side table. It drew Sidney to inspect it more closely.

The closer she got, the more the painting felt familiar. It was of an old porch. Droplets of rain merged into puddles on the weathered boards. She got close enough to see the artist's signature on the canvas and gasped, bringing her hands to her chest.

Sam stood beside her. "You admire art, Sidney?"

Momentarily stunned, Sidney simply stared at the painting. "Ah, ah, yes," was all she could say.

"I obtained this quite a while ago, long before my assignment to the *Nonnah*. Have been searching for more ever since. There doesn't seem to be any on the market. Pity. The artist is extremely talented."

"Do you know anything about the artist, Captain?"

"No, not a thing. It all seemed so mysterious when I found it. There was no accompanying pamphlet about the artist like one usually gets along with a painting. No one had any information about this 'Nahonnay.' Strange name, so close to the name of this ship. Have you seen other paintings by this artist?"

Sidney considered revealing a piece of herself—the piece, fractured and heavy with pain, that clung to her in spite of years of attempting to heal the guilt. The piece that tormented her, reminding her that she was responsible for her mother's death. Before she knew it, the words were tumbling out of her mouth. "I know this painting's about nine, ten years old. And I doubt you'll ever find any others."

"How do you know all that?"

Sidney straightened her shoulders, lifted her head and swallowed. "My mother painted it."

Sam exclaimed, "Your mother?"

"Yes. These are the porch steps of our house. It was a very old house. It collapsed about two years ago. We managed to use some of the wood to build another home. Built it mostly of straw bales."

Sidney continued to talk, gazing at the painting. Her chatter eased the painful hollow place in her chest. "I didn't pay much attention to her work. She died a year after this one. Didn't have much time for painting, Mom said, chasing after me all the time." Sidney felt her chin quiver.

She reached out to gently touch the brush strokes on the canvas. "I was thirteen when she died. She was looking for me when I was supposed to be home. She fell off a cliff in a rainstorm. I saw her fall... heard her scream... saw her fall."

Sidney jerked her hand back off the canvas. She realized she was shedding all her pain to a man not predisposed to an appreciation for emotions.

She cleared her throat. "Oh, Captain, I'm sorry. I didn't mean to go on and on."

"Sidney, no apology's necessary. Finally, I know who painted this. The mystery is solved." He had the faintest glimmer of sympathy on his face.

Both Sidney and Sam realized they had momentarily stepped outside the limits of prisoner and captor. Both fell silent for a moment. The spell was broken by a knock on the door. It was the kitchen staff delivering the food for the officer's breakfast meeting.

"Is it oh-nine-hundred hours already?" Sam murmured. "Miss, you'll return to your cell. At ten-hundred hours you'll be allowed to exercise on the ship's deck. Bridges and Moore will advise you what's permitted. Your next interrogation is scheduled at twelve-hundred hours. Any questions?"

"No questions, sir."

Sam called for Bridges and Moore. They arrived and motioned for her to follow. This time, the handcuffs weren't used. The pace felt slow. She'd have preferred to run back to her cell. Once she was there, she stepped into the dark room and collapsed on the bed. A sea of tears flooded into her hands.

At 1000 hours, Bridges and Moore opened Sidney's cell and delivered her to the ship's main deck. The instant the hallway door opened to the outside, warm, fresh air showered over her. Moore told her she could walk around the deck's starboard side from mid ship to the stern and that she was to stay fifteen feet away from the ship's railing. Gone was her rebellious spirit. Her heavy clothes, the hot sun, and low mood pulled her into the shadows of the ship's deck. She considered how much she should reveal to Sam. She still wasn't sure how far Sam's allegiance to the admiral extended.

Her other problem was the hidden memory rod containing the admiral's file. She was reluctant to telepathically communicate its whereabouts to Danik. And yet, if she did nothing, Badger and his people would have no chance to find out who all the players were, and the admiral would have time to carry out his plans, casting a shadow with the power of his crystals. Once the power nations were aware of the crystals' power, there would be debates in the United Nations about who should have control of them. Though there might be promises to use the crystals for the benefit of all, the truth of the matter was that no one could be trusted with that kind of power. The debates would quickly escalate into paranoia. Chaos would erupt.

In her mind's eye, Sidney once again saw the Dark world that Birthstone had shown her so many years ago. It was becoming a reality, after all.

Bridges called to her. It was time to return to her cell. For the duration of the morning, she sat on her bed in the dark void, listening for any sound that might inspire her, any movement that would transport her from her prison. She breathed. Minute by minute, she reached for an understanding. *Was this all a waste?* Then, in a whisper from Seamus, she received her answer.

Her spirit guide was present only as an energy. She felt him and knew exactly where he was, within inches on her left side. His voice was soothing.

"The danger is ever present, Sidney. If you allow the forces of Darkness to cloud your connection with your higher self, all could be lost, including you. You'll suffer the same fate as Captain Butchart."

Losing her gifts was minor compared to that. To become entrenched in fear and Darkness was akin to being trapped in a nightmare for eternity. But Seamus never let his messages end on a dark note.

"You were born in the Light," he told her. "You are of the Light. What's the purpose of the higher self?"

She thought for a moment as tears rolled down her cheeks. She centered her energy within her heart and showered Seamus with her Light.

"To love," she answered and felt Seamus smile.

"And that, my dear one, you do so well when you're not focused on fear. Your incarnate purpose will be revealed to you when you let go of fear."

With a flourish of dancing colors, he was gone.

At lunchtime, Bridges entered her cell and delivered her back to Sam's office. Sam had little to say. He directed her to the conference room and informed her the next interrogation session would begin in thirty minutes. When she'd finished her lunch, Sidney knocked on the door to his office and was directed to sit in the chair in front of the desk.

Sam picked up a comlink badge off his desk and handed it to Sidney. "Put this on your jacket. It will transmit anything you say to my computer, which will transcribe your statements."

Sidney attached the badge and sat back in the chair.

"For the record, this is Monday, July eighth at twelve-thirty-five hours. This is interrogation session number four. Miss, please state your name."

"Sidney Davenport."

"Let's begin. First, please explain how you were able to bypass the security systems. The admiral believes you were assisted by someone on the base."

"Absolutely not, Captain. On the base, I was on my own. Completely on my own."

"All right. Now, tell me what your objective was. Your true objective. The truth, miss."

Sidney's weakness was lies. To be accused of lying was paramount to a slap in the face for her. She sprang out of her chair.

"Are you accusing me of lying?"

Sam remained calm. "Miss, please sit down."

Feeling trapped between telling the truth and protecting her mission, Sidney's rage escalated. Her sacred truths evaporated.

"I'm leaving, Captain. I'm done with this damn charade."

She headed for the door, and Sam rushed to block her exit. Grabbing her by her arms, he pulled her toward him. Sidney regretted her stubborn decision. With a desk between them, she could manage to deal with her attraction to him, but with him so near, it was a different matter. Her heart raced. She stepped back a half step.

His piercing gaze reflected that he'd lost patience.

"Your defusing of the missiles was a diversion tactic. Those missiles are old and barely compatible with our current defense systems. Not worth the risk. Your real mission was something much more significant. You're withholding information on that part of your mission—something vital enough to risk your life for."

Sidney trembled. She knew she had to say something fast—without lying. He'd know if she wasn't being truthful.

"That's an interesting theory. If the mission was that important, don't you think someone more skilled would've been assigned? I have no experience in this, this … stuff!"

"Perhaps. But you do know Captain Butchart."

"I do admit I've heard the name Frank Butchart. A friend had mentioned the name, and I remember thinking it was an odd one."

"Miss, you've stated that you know *Frank* Butchart. Not Captain Butchart, but Frank Butchart. That tells me that you're familiar with the man. Explain how you know him."

"I don't know him! I just know of him."

"You know a hell of a lot more than you're admitting to. Remember our agreement? I know two facts, miss. One, Captain Butchart was very anxious to speed up your execution for a reason I don't yet understand. And two, I know you and Captain Butchart are somehow connected. And when I find out why and how, that's when I'll know what you were doing on the base. We'll continue this conversation another time. It's time you returned to your cell."

Sidney was brought back to her cell, then for more exercise on the ship's deck at 1600 hours. She remained morose. Indeed, everything she believed about her true nature was slipping away. Anger was never acceptable in the sacred truths, yet it seemed like she was giving in to it at every turn. It was a matter of time, perhaps days, before she'd slip further into the Dark world of Captain Butchart.

The prison she was building within was more terrifying than the admiral's punishment. Those who followed the Dark path retained some of their powerful gifts, but they walked alone. There was no sharing of the heart, no offering of compassion, and no companion in the Dark. Eventually, the Dark forces returned to haunt the one who wielded the sword. It wasn't a form of punishment. It was simply the law: as you give, so shall you receive.

At 1800 hours Bridges brought Sidney to Sam's office. In the preceding hours she still hadn't been able to devise a plan to deal with his probing. *Breathe*, she thought. *Just breathe.*

When she arrived, Sam was busy with his computer. After he finished typing, he stood up.

"There will be no interrogation tonight. Do you have any comments about our afternoon meeting?"

He remained preoccupied with shutting down his computer and tidying his office. Determined to show only strength, she walked up to him.

"Just one request, sir."

"The candle thing?"

"No. Would it be okay if I talked with Lorna for a minute or so, after supper?"

He snapped his hat onto his head. "What for?"

Sidney blushed. "It's personal."

Sam was hesitant regarding his next move. He put his hat on his desk and activated his comlink, contacting Lorna.

"Are you available in about half an hour, Lorna? The prisoner wants to see you. She says it's personal." He nodded at Lorna's response and cut the link. "Lieutenant Bridges, you'll bring her to the infirmary after her supper."

Sam turned back toward Sidney. "Be sure you do exactly as Bridges says. Is that clear?"

"Yes. Thank you, Captain."

"You're welcome."

Sam was gone in the next second. Before picking up her meal in the conference room, she gave Sam's crystal a telepathic nudge, knocking it off its pedestal, and placed it a few inches from the far edge of his desk. If nothing else, after a few days—if she had that much time—he might let go of his analytical brain and use his creative brain to consider the crystal's mysteries.

After dinner, Sidney was brought to the infirmary, where she was met by Lorna.

"Well, Sidney. How in the world did you get this privilege?" Lorna asked, chuckling. "Bridges, wait outside."

"I've been behaving like a model prisoner. Make my bed, keep my room clean, and answer all his infernal questions. Besides, when I told Captain Waterhouse it was personal, he didn't seem anxious to get more details. He's such a gentleman."

"Too damn much of a gentleman, if you ask me. What do you want, Sidney?"

"I need your help, if it's not too much trouble. Captain Waterhouse allows me to exercise outside on the deck. But I can't do much wearing this heavy jacket. My blouse was apparently damaged, and I was wondering if you still have it somewhere, and if I could fix it. My bra, too."

Lorna smiled. "Oh, so that's it. You realize I'll have to report to him anything we discuss?"

Sidney grimaced. "Oh. I never thought about that."

"You really aren't an experienced ... subversive, are you?"

"You won't get into any trouble with Captain Waterhouse if you help me, will you?"

"Are you kidding? I think I'm going to enjoy explaining to Sam about your bra. Anything that'll get him to loosen up, put a smile on his face — that's my purpose in life."

"Sounds like you kind of like the man."

"Sam? What's not to like? He's gorgeous." Lorna fluttered her eyelashes and fanned her face. "Actually, the blouse and bra were disposed of right away. Nothing left to save. We really didn't believe you'd survive, so ... well, there wasn't any point in keeping them." Lorna went back to stripping the linen off the beds. "Let's see. What can I do? Seems to me the navy owes you some clothes."

"I just need something to wear that's not so hot, Lorna. Please don't go to any trouble."

"No trouble. I can probably find a t-shirt for you to wear. There are some gals on the ship your size that I can wheel and deal with. The bra's another matter. I'd let you have one of mine, but I'm afraid you're a wee bit too little." She cupped her large breasts and grinned.

"Ah, yes. One gift I didn't receive."

"That's okay, little one. You do have a nice figure. It hasn't gone unnoticed, particularly by some of the officers. I tell you what. Tomorrow we'll be in port. I'll go shopping for you. How's that?"

"But Lorna, I can't pay you. Bras are expensive."

"Never mind. Let's see. You're about a thirty-four B. I think I'm going to enjoy this, trust me. You go back to your cell now. I'll have this fixed by tomorrow night."

Before Sam retired for the evening, he received an urgent call from Admiral Garland. Over the monitor, he could see that the admiral was as tense as ever, pacing and obviously taking great effort to remain in control of his emotions.

"I've captured another saboteur," the admiral informed him. "At the Mountiago Naval Base. The bastard was in the process of planting bombs. Caught him red handed. Goes by the name of Marcus Darby. He's being transported to Lima. You'll receive him at the docks tomorrow afternoon. He's to be executed forthwith—as soon as you leave the port. Is that clear?"

Sam stiffened and held his breath. Immersing himself in military conduct, he responded. "Yes, sir. I trust the reports on his interrogation and hearing will be arriving with him."

"No interrogation necessary. Like I said, he was caught in the act."

Sam had his doubts about that. "How are my boys, Admiral? Haven't been able to talk with them since last week."

"Oh, yes. Forgot to tell you. They were having such a good camping trip that it was extended another day. They'll be home tomorrow night."

"Glad to hear they're getting some experience roughing it a little. I'm requesting a visit with them next weekend, sir."

"Fine."

"I'll book a room at the West Coast Inn. I trust your staff will arrange for the usual air transport for me, sir?"

"I'll notify Celine. How soon will the *Nonnah* be docked at Pearl Harbor?"

"The *Nonnah*'s scheduled to be in Honolulu this Friday about seventeen-hundred hours."

"Celine will arrange for your flight from Honolulu to leave early Saturday morning. She'll send you the details. How many days are you requesting?"

"At least four days. I'll send Celine my itinerary. Of course, I'll pick them up and return them each day at your home, sir."

"Fine."

The comlink was disconnected. Sam leaned forward with his elbows on his desk and massaged his forehead. *Another execution*, he thought. *More blood to clean up off the deck and ever deeper in the admiral's grip.*

13. A Witch's Magic

Tuesday Morning, July 9, Peru

By 0400 hours Tuesday morning, the USS *Nonnah* had arrived at Lima, Peru. Sam and Commander Moon stood together on the bridge monitoring communication between the ship's staff as they carefully guided her into place. Few words were spoken between the two men. An uneasy tension was building. Sam wondered how Moon knew his sons were living with the admiral. He'd never discussed his private life with anyone aboard the *Nonnah*.

"Are you going ashore today?" Moon asked.

"No, but why don't you join some of the officers for some well-deserved R and R?"

"I just might do that. We set sail by fourteen-hundred hours, according to our schedule."

"That may change, Rhett. This morning there are only a few small containers for Admiral Garland to load. We'll leave as soon as the Darby prisoner arrives. I'm expecting him about noon, so ensure you and the shore leave personnel are back before then."

Moon nodded.

"By the way, I'm flying back to New Seattle from Honolulu to spend some time with my boys. You'll be in command during that time."

"And the prisoners, sir?"

"Both prisoners will have been executed before arrival at Pearl Harbor."

For the remainder of the morning, everyone steered clear of Sam's path. It was a sound practice when a prisoner was to be brought on board. The captain's mood dropped, and he was ever more exacting.

After Sidney ate her breakfast, he again ordered her to sit in the chair and place the comlink on her jacket. She sensed the change in his demeanor and quietly complied with his demands.

"Miss—"

Sidney interrupted. "It would help if you'd call me Sidney, sir."

Sam shifted nervously in his chair. "All right. I don't have much time this morning, so I'll get right to the point. Your mission's objective, you'll explain later. Right now you'll explain how you bypassed security and defused the missiles."

She breathed deeply.

"*Now!*" he barked. "And I don't want a long, convoluted answer."

Bringing her hand to her chest, she sought the guidance of her Guardian wisdom. Her eyes darted from Sam to the crystal, and back to Sam. "Captain, normally I'd never discuss my abilities with someone who might not use the information wisely. And I'm trying to search for the words that will make sense."

Sam was relieved by Sidney's desire to cooperate. He also reminded himself that he was trying to gain her confidence and trust, and barking at her wasn't the way. He shifted to a more controlled and softened manner.

"I suppose it's something that's not easily explained. May I suggest a demonstration of your skills? Would that help you?"

Sidney smiled. "Yes, that way is always easier, especially for someone like me who's always been the student, never the teacher."

"You're a student?"

"In a manner of speaking. When it comes to the skill of sensing energy and redirecting it, I'm a novice. My teacher continues to guide my understanding of energy. It's a lifelong study."

Sam resisted reacting to her claim, thinking that perhaps he hadn't heard her correctly. Casually he responded, "It sounds as though your teacher is powerful."

"I suppose that's one way of seeing him. I see him as the most gentle and loving person. But, he's capable of doing things I can only dream about. He's far more disciplined than me. In fact, you and he are much alike. You're not the only one who gets annoyed with my disregard for rules. In fact, I'm known as the 'Wild Child' at home."

Sam chuckled and sat back in his chair. "Wild Child? It suits you."

Sidney blushed. "Over time, he taught me that all things—our bodies, our thoughts, and especially our intentions, are actually energy." Sidney interrupted her explanation. She studied Sam's face to see his reaction. "Are you with me so far?"

Sam was now more intrigued than on a mission to have control of the interrogation. "Yes. It sounds interesting. Please continue."

"When Greystone—"

"Greystone?"

Sidney hadn't meant to reveal the name. "Yes. He's my mentor. Greystone's ability to access the universal energy, or the Creator, combined with his intent to seek the higher good for all and his unconditional love for all, allows him to transcend dimensions, even time and space."

Sam shook his head. "Now you've tipped the boat over. You're saying this fellow, Greystone, is the same thing as a god, are you not?"

"I suppose so. Greystone sees all things, all people as being one with the Creator and thus having the same ability to create and to love unconditionally. We're all equal, or more precisely, we're all from the same source, cut from the same cloth. You, me, and even Admiral Garland. Greystone sees all as being worthy of unconditional love."

Sam put his hands up. "Hold it. This is all very interesting, but we're getting off track. You were going to tell me how you bypassed the security systems. Does any of this have anything to do with that?"

"Sorry, Captain. How about that demonstration? If you lock a door, I'll show you how I unlock it. That would be a start."

Sam was delighted. "Good." He tripped one of the sensors on his desk. "All three doors in this room are now locked."

"Okay. I'll unlock them, one at a time." Sidney got up, standing tall, and closed her eyes.

Sam braced himself to witness bizarre actions. However, he saw no movement. She seemed merely to be in a trance, breathing deeply. It took less than twenty seconds. One by one, the green light over each door came on. Sam dashed to each door. They opened easily. He glanced at Sidney, then the door. His mouth was agape.

"This can't, god, how ... I really never expected you to do this, at least not that easily. I could see no effort on your part. How on Earth?"

Sidney grinned. "Is the boat still tipped over, Captain?"

All his previous anger had washed away. "You can really do it!" He rechecked a door. Turning back to Sidney, he asked, "Can you lock the doors?"

"Yes." Sidney again returned to her meditative state. One by one the red light over each door came on.

Sam again checked the doors. They were indeed locked. He keyed in his security code, and the doors opened. Nothing had changed. Everything still functioned normally.

"Okay, now how far can you go with this? Can you lock and unlock the doors beyond this room?"

"It's possible, Captain, but I wouldn't do it."

"Why not?"

"It may cause harm or frighten someone if they weren't aware of what I was doing. If someone needed to get out of room in a hurry and expected the door to be open, they might suffer injury in having to take time to unlock the door. It's something I won't do."

Sam crossed his arms and grinned. "Hmm. A witch with scruples."

Sidney smiled. "Yes, partly. In truth, though, my skills are conditional. If I were to not have the higher good as my intention each and every day, I'd suffer the consequences. Other things reduce my ability to use my gifts."

Sam's curiosity was at an all-time high. There it was again. That feeling that everything was fine. That he wasn't alone Being in the moment, that was the key, he thought. His interest had gone beyond his official need to learn more.

"Like what?" he asked

"The more fearful or angry I become, the less I'm able to use my gifts. If someone were to attack me suddenly, and I was in fear for my life, chances are I wouldn't be able to unlock anything in time to escape. I must be completely calm before I can access the energy."

Sam moved over to stand in front of Sidney. "You feel safe here, Sidney?"

"Strangely enough, yes. I was angry yesterday. I'm sorry for that. It didn't serve the higher good, nor honor you."

Sam frowned. "The higher good?"

"Yes, Captain."

"The higher good for whom?"

"For all. Always, for all."

"This," he said, waving his hand around his office, "hasn't been exactly for your higher good."

Sidney brought her hand to her chest briefly before walking to the window and becoming lost in the beauty of the morning sky. "Sometimes, Captain, the higher good isn't obvious. I've learned to trust and accept the fact that I can't understand all things right now." She turned to face him. "Doing something for the higher good doesn't necessarily guarantee a long life, Captain. Or a peaceful death."

Sam's curiosity took hold. He moved up to her. "What's the point then, aside from being able to unlock doors with your mind?"

Sidney brought her hands up to lightly rest on his arms, still crossed in front of his chest. "Your life becomes more than just an isolated physical exercise. It becomes deeper and freer of the physical world's limitations. You're no longer restricted to the rules of a three dimensional world. You separate yourself from fear and anger. You discover the essence of *you*, beyond the physical form." She delicately tapped his chest with her fingers. "You discover your essence in a reality beyond your imagination — eternal, powerful, peaceful, joyful."

Sam stared into her eyes for some time. He'd momentarily become comfortable with her closeness. He sensed the room's artificial light softening, and the small space between them was calm, even inviting. When the intensity became too foreign, he stepped away from her, and cleared his throat.

"Remove the comlink, Sidney. That's all for this morning."

Sidney removed the comlink while Sam focused on his computer. Once again she eyed the sun crystal, perched again on its pedestal. While Sam was busy, she gave the pedestal and crystal another telepathic shove. Not much, just enough that he might notice it had been moved, like last time. He wouldn't see the movement itself. The crystal, in a flicker of a second, was now an inch from the far end of the desk.

Once Sidney had left his office, Sam prepared a pot of coffee. More than ever, Sam wanted to learn more about Sidney's peculiar talent. He believed it was significant. While the coffee was brewing, he paced the floor as he considered how much to reveal to the admiral. If Garland believed Sidney's skills were a threat, he might demand her execution immediately.

The aroma of coffee filled the room. Sam poured himself a cup and sipped slowly between dictating to his computer His report was scarcely complete, stating only that the prisoner had admitted she'd been able to unlock the doors through telekinesis. He omitted the demonstration in his office, offering just enough information to grab the admiral's interest so that he might want to dig further and find out how many more Sidneys existed out there. Learning where they lived would be a real coup for the admiral — and perhaps Sam's bargaining chip to get his freedom back and the release of his sons.

Sitting back in his chair, he noticed the crystal had moved, perhaps accidentally shoved by his arm, he thought. Picking it up, he gazed into its beauty and held it to see how it might capture the light coming in from his window. Shards of light danced throughout his office as he twirled the crystal in the air before setting it back on its pedestal.

Sam's comlink beeped. It was Lieutenant Bridges.

"Captain, the Mountiago prisoner is early."

"Bring him aboard. I'll see him in my office right away."

Fifteen minutes later, Lieutenant Morton and three security guards delivered a hostile and handcuffed man, sweating, shaking, and spitting threats. The guards were attempting to keep the prisoner under control, and everyone had been stressed to the limit.

The prisoner was young, no more than thirty years old. He had dark brown hair and the bluest eyes Sam had ever seen.

"Sit down," Sam demanded.

One of the guards pushed the prisoner into a chair while another handed Sam a computer memory rod. Sam plugged it into his computer and briefly scanned the report.

"Your name is Marcus Darby?"

The prisoner refused to answer and avoided eye contact with everyone.

"You have the right to not answer my questions, Mr. Darby. Keep in mind, though, that choosing to remain silent won't help you. You've been charged with attempted mass murder. The report states you were caught planting bombs on a naval base. Perhaps several dozen people would've been killed. What do you have to say about that?"

Again the prisoner remained silent, his eyes not focused on anything in particular.

"The penalty for this crime is death. I've been ordered to carry out your execution as soon as possible. If you have anything to say that would cause me to question the appropriateness of these orders, you better speak up now."

The prisoner stopped clenching his teeth and took a deep breath.

"Guards, remove the handcuffs," Sam ordered. "Has he had anything to drink today?"

"No, sir," said one of the guards.

"Dave, get some water from the fountain and give it to Mr. Darby."

The cuffs were removed, and Marcus massaged his bruised wrists. His hands trembled slightly as he reached for the cup of water and gulped it down. Only then did Marcus look directly at Sam. Contempt filled his expression.

"Guards, wait outside. Dave, I'll speak to Mr. Darby privately for a few minutes."

Everyone but Sam and the prisoner left the room. For a while, the two men allowed silence to soften the tension. After a while, Sam sat forward in his chair with his arms resting on his desk. "What's your version, Mr. Darby?"

Marcus snarled in an Irish accent, "Like the report says. I planted some bombs."

"You intended to kill a lot of people. Why?"

"What the hell difference does it make?"

"Probably none. But lately I've become more interested in the why of things. If we knew the cause, maybe something could be done to prevent it."

"Like bloody hell! You American bastards, you just walk into wherever and take whatever. And if anyone gets in your way—" Marcus slammed one fist into the palm of the other. "Bang, right between the eyes with a thirty eight."

"Can you be more specific, Mr. Darby?"

"I'd rather not waste my breath. Like your government gives a bloody damn! Americans have gotten very good in covering up and disguising their political maneuvering as so-called humanitarian programs. Nothing but lies and deceit. To hell with you all!"

Sam sat back and gave Marcus a few moments to calm down.

"Mr. Darby, if you'd explain yourself, at least that much will go on your record. Your attempt to bring some injustice to the forefront will be documented. Right now, it's assumed you're some kind of lunatic or fanatic. Which do you want on record? The military's suppositions or the truth?"

"You'll record my truth?"

"Word for word, and you can sign it if you wish."

Marcus thought for a moment. "All right. It's a deal."

"Put this comlink onto your shirt. Your report will be directly transcribed word for word. State your name."

Marcus followed Sam's instructions and told his story.

"The American and British armies took over my country. Desperate for more farmland, they said. They killed anyone and anything that got in their way, including my family."

Darby bent over as though he was in pain. He told of the callous way survivors were treated and his single-minded focus in making the aggressors pay. Sam surmised that Darby worked alone in his failed attempt to bomb the naval base.

"There you have it, Captain."

Sam nodded. "Your report is disturbing, but it doesn't change the fact that you've attempted to commit murder. Is there any reason you shouldn't receive the death penalty?"

Marcus sat silent for a while. "Yesterday I was glad to die for the sake of justice. Now, it all seems so pointless. So, what am I in for, Captain?"

"The execution?"

"Aye."

"Tonight you'll be brought to the ship's deck. Death will be quick by firearm, point blank range to the head."

Marcus became pale, like a beaten man. "I'd like to sign that report."

Sam keyed in the print command. While waiting for the report, he poured two cups of coffee and gave one to Marcus. "Take yours black?"

"Aye. Don't normally have the luxury of a cup of coffee. Thank you, Captain."

"Is there anyone who should know about your capture?"

"No, not a bloody soul. Had nothing. Now I got no one, all been killed by those bloody Yanks and Brits. I know farmland is scarce but, Jesus, Mary, and Joseph, why are we being killed for it? We never did have much in Ireland, but now, there's no Ireland. Just territories claimed by whoever has the most gunpowder."

"Marcus, there are better ways to settle such conflicts."

"Like bloody hell, Captain. When was the last time someone killed someone you loved? And no law to bring the culprits to justice?"

Sam remained silent.

Sam was clearly distracted during Sidney's afternoon interrogation and not in any mood to play hide and seek. His first question was direct.

"Explain precisely what happened once you arrived at the base."

"I waited until it was safe to go down the tunnels to the missile room."

"Not so fast, miss. You're taking me down the same path as you did Captain Butchart. I won't accept that answer. I want the truth."

"That is the truth!"

"It was about oh-one-hundred hours in the morning when you reached the missile room. Where were you from the time of the interview with the admiral's staff until arriving in the missile room?"

Sidney shot back her answer. "I waited!"

Sam stood and paced behind his desk. "Where?"

"In the stairwell."

"Why did you need to complete an application form?"

"To get into the building."

He pounced at her. "A goddamned tourist could have gotten a pass to get into naval base administration building, most of it anyway. You needed to see the admiral's office. What were you looking for?"

Sidney had thought she'd made a breakthrough with the captain at the breakfast meeting, but now he was back to the old routine. It was frustrating. She was again losing her battle with anger. She continued to evade the question.

"You really think that man has anything I want?"

Leaning forward, Sam shouted at her. "Glad you're amused, miss. I'm not. This afternoon you'd better consider one thing." He thrust a finger in her face. "If you want someone to help you avoid an execution, I'm it. However, I'm nearly convinced my time's being wasted. Unless you tell me the truth, I can't help you. Is that clear?"

Sidney stood up and put her hands on her hips. She glared at Sam. "You wouldn't believe me anyway. You're so tied up in your precious rule book. Yes, sir, aye, aye, sir, how high, sir?" She gave a mock salute. "You're completely incapable of trusting anything that's not documented in your military code and protocol manual."

Sam was taken aback by her hostility.

She moved toward him, her finger pointing accusingly. "You put on a real good act of being polite and friendly." Her hostility continued to escalate. "You think I'm stupid. You even think I'll fall for some idiotic line that you're going to save me from execution. Well, Captain Waterhouse, maybe *you* better think again."

Sam pushed her back into her chair. "Sit down!"

Sidney became livid. She sprang up again. "Let's get this over with! I'm tired of being your prisoner. Call your executioner."

Sam tried to wrestle her back into her chair. She shifted her balance, and he fell toward the floor, pulling her with him. In one swift move, he used the momentum of her fall to fling her onto her back. She let out a scream as her back hit the floor. In a second, he was on top of her, straddling her as he held onto her thrashing fists.

Bridges burst through the doors. "Heard the commotion, Captain. I'll get my cuffs on her."

"No," Sam barked. "I've got her under control. Wait outside."

Sidney quit struggling and resigned herself to the futility of escaping from Sam's grip. He let her stand up, and Sidney wrapped her arms across her chest and stood facing away from him, toward the credenza — anything but let him see her tears fall. Roughly, she brushed them away.

"You're quite unique, you know," she said.

Sam tucked in his shirt. "What do you mean 'unique'?"

"No one else has been able to get me that angry. As for convincing me of the possibility of avoiding an execution, I'm a lot less naïve since arriving on your ship, sir."

"Look! As far as most everyone else is concerned, you should have been eliminated days ago." He glared at her. "So far, I'm the only one who's willing to sort through all the crap, fall for your trick show, listen to your ramblings—which by all accounts should get you at least a life sentence in a mental institution. Not to mention I've tolerated disrespect and probably will have my service record permanently marred by giving you the benefit of a doubt. And did I mention wasting my time to give a good goddamn?"

The room went silent. Sidney sat down, leaned forward, and rested her elbows on her knees. After a while, she sat up straight, and fidgeting with her hair, pulled it back behind her ears. The captain's anger was valid. If he had simply followed orders, she'd be dead. He'd strayed from the rules, probably more than he'd admit. She owed him her life.

"Captain, you're right. I was sent for more than defusing the missiles, but nothing will come of it. I failed."

Sam sat down behind his desk. "Then why the secrecy?"

"If I reveal all I know, people will be killed. Perhaps you, too. I'm sure of that. I can't live with that."

"Does the name 'Badger' mean anything to you?"

Sidney's eyes opened wide, and her mouth dropped open.

"You knew him, didn't you?" Sam stood up. "What was your relationship with Badger? You tell me the truth and tell me right now!"

Sidney hesitated. "Captain, I can't … "

He marched to her chair, grabbed her by her shoulders, and shook her.

"Tell me. What was your business with Badger?"

Sidney stood up and wrestled free of the Sam's grip. "We—I met him a few weeks ago. He asked me to help him. I met with his staff a few times to be briefed on the base layout and the admin building's floor plan. Then his staff prepared fake ID for me."

"Wait a minute. Who's 'we'? You and Butchart?"

"No. I never met Captain Butchart before I was arrested. That's the absolute truth."

"We'll revisit that later. For now, who are the others that were involved in this mission?"

"Just friends. They brought me to the base. The rest was up to me."

"All right. Now, what did you do for Badger?"

"I've told you. I defused the missiles for him."

Sam increased the pressure. Each question was rapidly fired at her as soon as the previous one had been answered.

"And what else?"

"That's it. Nothing else matters."

"What else?"

"Nothing. I failed."

"Failed at what?"

"Getting off the base."

"Who was to get you off the base?"

"No one."

"Who's Frank Butchart?"

She relented. She had too much respect for the captain to keep evading his questions.

"He's part of the people I protect."

Sam stared at her. "Are you saying that you and Captain Butchart were in this scheme together?"

"No, definitely not!"

"Then why are you protecting Captain Butchart?"

"I can't tell you, sir."

"Listen carefully. I'll tell you what I know. You did more than defuse the missiles. That was a diversion. You were after a secret file in Admiral Garland's office. That was your main target, miss!"

Sidney was dazed. How did he know so much? Her silence was a dead giveaway.

"Bingo!" He pointed his finger at her.

Just then, his comlink beeped. Bridges was reporting that shore leave staff was back and Lieutenant Paddles was mad as hell.

"Tell her to come to my office," Sam instructed.

Sam regained his military posture, but he became eerily dark, his face twisted with hate. "Before you go there's something you should know. Badger was indirectly responsible for my wife's murder. And I've received a report that Badger has been murdered. Fitting! So if you're protecting that bastard, you're wasting your time—and mine. Now go!"

Sidney left with the guard, but not before giving Sam's crystal the customary nudge at the end of the interrogation. This time, however, it landed on the floor.

14. Sam's Dark Prison

Tuesday Afternoon, July 9, Peru

Sam picked up his crystal and wondered why it had fallen. Before he could give it too much thought, Lorna burst into his office.

"What's the problem?" he asked.

"Oh, just that damn Pots. He has some nerve trying to snoop into my package." She threw a bag across Sam's desk. "That's for Sidney."

"What's this about? Since when do we go shopping for a prisoner? Damn it all, Lorna. She certainly isn't going to be around long. You know that. What's so damned important that the navy has to spend what little funds it has on her?"

Lorna sat down and placed her elbows on his desk. "My money, Sam. Never had much of an excuse to go shopping before. It was fun buying stuff I'd never have a reason to wear. Besides, you might get a chuckle out of this, too. What's eatin' you, anyway?"

Sam leaned back in his chair. "Your timing's a bit off. Got an execution tonight."

Lorna sat up straight. "Sidney?"

"No. Not yet. I suppose this bag has something to do with Sidney's meeting with you last night. What was that about?"

"What she said was that she wanted her clothes. You know, the ones we cut off her and threw out—blouse and underwear. Told her they couldn't be fixed. She says that heavy jean jacket is a problem with the heat."

"She could've told me that."

"Well, I doubt she'd want to discuss her bra size with you." Lorna grinned as she watched the color rise in Sam's face. *Thank God he's still human.* "Anyway, I suspect there was more to it than wanting her clothes."

"Such as?"

"A friend, perhaps? Helps having a friend."

"Lorna, keep in mind she's confessed to sabotage on Admiral Garland's base. She willingly committed a hostile act against the United States."

"Oh, hell, if she's a hostile, I'm a ballerina. How would you like to see my performance of *Swan Lake*?"

Sam smiled at the image of Lorna's large frame tiptoeing and twirling around on a stage in a tutu.

"I can arrange it, my friend, if I get anymore disrespect around here from that damn Pots," Lorna threatened. "Anyway, the last time I heard of someone defusing missiles, they just put him away for a long time. Why's Garland so bent on getting rid of Sidney permanently?"

"It's possible she's gotten mixed up in the admiral's secrets. Lethal secrets. If I can get her to talk, maybe…" Sam hesitated. "Anyway, I'm trying to be nice to her. You know, get her to open up."

"Yes, I know about what you call being nice, and your nice needs work, Sam. Anyway, everything should fit her. What do you think?"

Sam opened the bag and saw a lavender blouse and a pair of white shorts. As he pulled out the garments, a blue lace bra and panties fell into his lap.

"Oh Christ, Lorna!"

Lorna laughed as she departed. "Tell Sidney I hope everything fits. She should be a lot cooler, don't you think? My god, it feels warm in here suddenly. Got to run."

"Lorna!" She was out the door and gone before he could utter any further objection. Sam tucked the clothes back into the bag and tossed it aside. He gave orders to the navigation room to set sail for Hawaii's Pearl Harbor.

When Sidney arrived for dinner, Sam handed the package to her.

"Lorna brought this in for you," he said casually.

Sidney took out the blouse and shorts. Her mouth was wide open in disbelief. "I was just hoping to borrow some clothes, Captain. I didn't want her to go to all this trouble."

"She said you were having a problem with the heat. Couldn't take advantage of your exercise time on the deck. Seems you have a friend among us, Sidney." Sam tried to show a casual smile.

"This is too much. How can I repay her?" Sidney looked directly at Sam. Giving a sigh, she glanced away. "Oh, I see. You expect information in payment for these nice things."

Sam could see his strategy backfiring. "If you prefer, I'll give them back to Lorna. She'll be ticked, but it's your choice. Makes no difference to me, one way or the other. Is that clear?"

Sidney relaxed. She looked more closely at the blouse. "I've never had anything this beautiful. Lorna has very good taste."

Sam thought of the soft lace underwear still in the bag. He shifted position in his chair. "Yes. Well, let's get on with business. You'd attempted to carry out some other task on the base. What exactly?"

Sidney placed the clothes back in the bag and set it down beside her chair.

"I wish there was a way to give you the answers you want without endangering anyone else. I just haven't been able to come up with a solution."

"All right, let's take this one step at a time. My guess is you were trying to stop the admiral from doing something. Is that right?"

"Not exactly. Well, yes."

"Badger hired you to do something that would interfere with the admiral's plans?"

"More or less."

Sam stared at her. He recognized the determination he saw in her eyes, and the worry. It was the same expression Joy had when she'd told him of the confidential file she'd accessed.

"Is this related to government strategies to solve the energy crisis?"

Sidney swallowed. "Yes."

He was now convinced that both his wife and Sidney had been on similar missions. "What are the implications if the admiral isn't stopped?"

"If I said, you'd get the straight jacket out."

"Answer the damn question."

"Nothing will be the same once he and whoever he's connected with put their plans into action. They seem to be very near to making a move."

"Please go on."

"I can't. I've said too much already."

Sam got up from his chair and looked out the window. "Trust is a precious thing, especially when lives are at stake. I understand your reluctance to trust me, Sidney. I wish there was more time." He sat back down again and shut off his computer. "Off the record," he stressed, "my gut is telling me that what you were doing is worth my stepping outside the limits of this uniform. What was it?"

Sidney studied him for a moment, weighing his apparent sincerity against the risk of opening up. Finally, she surrendered to trust, albeit hesitantly, revealing small pieces at a time.

"Captain, there would be a total power shift—devastating if placed in the hands of those not well-balanced in spirit."

Sam struggled to remain patient in his approach. "Okay. What's on that base that you, and only you, would be able to retrieve? Evidence of some new weapon?"

Sam detected the slightest change in Sidney's demeanor. She was tense—almost holding her breath.

"Captain, would you trust the admiral if he had full control over a source of energy with limitless power?"

Sam was speechless for a few seconds. "Hell, I wouldn't trust anyone with that much power. In the opinion of the underground, is there any urgency to stopping the admiral soon?"

"Yes."

"How soon?"

"Perhaps a few days, a week at the most." She lifted her hand to her chest. "Then prepare for the world to go mad with fear."

"What?" Sam's comlink indicated Bridges was calling.

"Captain, the prisoner is ready."

"Bring him to the deck. Get a guard to take Sidney back to her cell." His expression had returned to that of the man with a rule book and heavy responsibilities. "That will be all for today, Sidney. Tomorrow morning we have to conclude this business. Perhaps for both our sakes," he muttered. "Is that understood?"

Sidney nodded. She wanted to stay longer with Sam. She hadn't yet revealed the possibility of the destruction of the planet. But what she wanted even more was to forget the troubles for one hour, even just a few minutes, and simply be near him.

The guard arrived to take Sidney back to her cell. She asked Sam if she could spend some time on deck to watch the sun set.

He was gruff again. "No, not now!"

Taking a chance, she promised to be no trouble. "Just a few minutes," she pleaded.

"Just go with the officer. Perhaps tomorrow evening."

A vision came to her in a flash. "The prisoner. Someone is to be executed *now!*"

She blurted it without realizing the impact of her words. Again she felt the anxiety of being placed on deck for her own execution. It all became so much more real.

"That's not your concern," Sam retorted.

"Captain," she replied, "I need to be there. Someone needs my help. And you might learn a little about me at the same time."

"It's not a pretty sight," he cautioned her.

"Death isn't new to me," Sidney said with conviction. "Please let me help the prisoner. I've worked with the dying. Death can be terrifying, or it can be experienced as simply a transformation. I promise you won't regret it."

Sam was curious enough to comply with her wishes. He and Bridges escorted Sidney to the deck where the prisoner was seated. Bridges and Dr. Duncan stood nearby awaiting the captain's orders to carry out the execution.

Sidney stepped into the daylight from the deck's hallway and saw a somber sky. The sun, partially obscured by the clouds, rested on the horizon. Only faint traces of its golden glow trickled along the crest of the waves to the ship's bow. Sidney stretched her awareness beyond the gloom on the sea and the ship. She became calm and quiet in her mind. She found her center—the place where she could become in tune with the sacred truths.

The ocean breeze played with Sidney's long hair, reminding her of her connection with the hawk on the island. Celeste had complete trust in her wings' strength and ability to master the turbulent winds. Lifted by Celeste's courage, Sidney would trust in her ability to resist the Dark forces that could be within the prisoner.

As the trio approached the prisoner, Sidney noticed his shoulders trembling. Trying to hide his fear from the view of his enemies, he turned his head away. His entire body filled with convulsions of terror. No longer fighting, no longer angry—just a man dreading every second.

Sidney asked Sam if she could approach the man alone and spend five minutes with him. She told him she'd put her hand to her chest as a signal that the prisoner was ready and the officer could continue with his duty. Sam agreed to the terms and relayed the orders to Lieutenant Bridges.

Sidney knew there was no possibility of pleading for the prisoner's life. She knew nothing of the prisoner or why he was to be executed. It didn't really matter why. She only hoped that through her, the prisoner's death would be less traumatic.

She walked up to the prisoner and knelt down on the deck directly in front of him. His body and legs were secured to the chair. There was no aging of his face, now pale, no trace of scars from a difficult life behind the frightened blue eyes. His clothes were clean and tidy, and his dark brown hair combed. It was obvious he'd made an attempt to deal with this death sentence with dignity.

When their eyes first met, Sidney simply smiled at him. The prisoner continued to tremble so violently that he was vibrating the chair he sat on.

"Help me," he pleaded. "I don't want to die. Please, I don't deserve this." He was scarcely able to form the words in his mouth.

Sidney reached for his handcuffed hands. Shaking wildly, he tried to grab hers.

"I can help you. My name is Sidney. What's your name?"

"I'm Marcus." He began to sob uncontrollably.

"Marcus, you're going to be fine."

She took his hands firmly in hers. He felt the warmth of her touch and listened to the calming tones of her voice. Sidney believed it wasn't so much what she said that mattered; it was more about letting him know he wasn't alone. His crying slowed, and he searched her face, looking for a hint of something, perhaps something that would indicate this was only a cruel joke. What he saw was compassion. There wasn't a trace of fear on her face.

"Marcus, I want you to look at only my eyes and listen to my voice. I want you to breathe in as deep as you can. Follow me as I breathe." Sidney took a breath, and then slowly exhaled, watching Marcus make a weak attempt to follow her instructions. "Try again, with me. We'll do this together."

She caressed his arms. All the while, Marcus held his gaze on her eyes.

"Again, Marcus, breathe like you've never breathed before. Follow the air into your lungs. Feel its life force throughout your body."

Marcus heard her voice more clearly and the certainty in it. His trembling subsided, and he inhaled more deeply. As he exhaled, Sidney asked him to release all his anger and fear. "Let go of all that stuff. It no longer serves you. Replace it with joy. Tell me about a wonderful memory."

Marcus thought for a while. "I guess it would be the day I met my wife."

"Good. What kind of day was it?"

"Oh, like none other, to be sure. I remember looking up into the blue sky and watching a few birds, swallows, I think. Lord, they flew with such grace. The sun was so bright, I had to look away for a moment. When I did, there she was."

Sidney prompted him to tell her more about that day, and they talked as friends for a while. Marcus was gaining control.

"Now, Marcus, I want you to close your eyes and listen to my voice. Know that I can help you on this journey. I'll place my hand on your chest. You'll receive the guidance you need. Know that the essence of you isn't dying, Marcus. You'll go on. You just need help to get from this place, through a doorway, and on to a greater place. It's that simple."

Marcus began to tremble again.

"Marcus, think of the people who love you, how their love feels, how it has always given you strength and courage."

His trembling eased a little. Sidney lifted her hand, and the sensation of healing energy surged through it into the man's chest. This same flow of energy also connected her to a world the Guardians understood. She closed her eyes. Allowing her mind to become quiet, she saw the hawk soaring above her mountain home. She heard the hawk calling, guiding her to the place of her higher self.

Suddenly, a figure stood before her. It was a stocky woman with graying hair and a round, cheerful face. Smiling, she said her name was Francis and that she was there to take Buddy home. Sidney acknowledged her and returned her attention to Marcus.

"Marcus, who's Francis?"

Marcus opened his eyes with a start. "Francis was my grandmother's name. Why do you ask?"

"She's here. She said that she came to take Buddy home."

Marcus grinned. "She always called me Buddy. We were very close."

Sidney instructed Marcus to close his eyes again and to remember times with his grandmother. He did as she asked. Sidney put her other hand to her chest.

The pistol fired twice. Marcus' body jerked in a spasm and then slumped forward. The bullets had entered the side of his head and passed through his brain, exiting the opposite side of his skull. Blood ran down from his face onto Sidney's hand, still resting on his chest.

The ship was silent. No one spoke, there was no expression of any kind. Even the ship's movement seemed to cease, momentarily suspended in time and space. The officers waited. Sidney's hand continued to rest on the man's chest. She appeared to be almost in union with him, both of their figures surrounded with an air of peace.

At last, Sidney opened her eyes and nodded to the officer standing by Marcus' chair. The doctor examined the prisoner's body and confirmed he was dead. Without a word, the crew untied him, lifted him onto the gurney, and took him away to the morgue.

Still kneeling on the deck, Sidney saw Sam standing a few feet in front of her. He bent down on one knee and simply looked into her eyes. His gaze touched her in a way she'd never known. She found herself seeing beyond his uniform into the eyes of a man who appeared as powerful and gentle as the energy she called upon.

After a few moments of silence, he resumed his detached and direct manner and told her she could remain on deck a few more minutes. He offered his hand to help her up. The setting sun slipped into the horizon, gathering up what remained of its consoling warmth. Darkness enveloped more than the ship.

The seamen had begun cleaning the blood off the deck. Soon, the ship would again appear simply as another armed merchant ship. No trace of any loss of life. Sam's comlink earpiece advised him that the admiral was calling. He grabbed hold of Sidney's arm and swiftly returned to his office with her. He nodded toward his office sink.

"Wash the blood off your hands. Be quick."

When she finished, Sam motioned for her to sit down in the chair farthest from his desk and out of view of his computer monitor's receiver. He motioned for her to be quiet. Activating his office comlink, he looked into the monitor.

"Good evening, Admiral. Sorry for the delay in getting back to you. I was in the middle of the Darby execution."

The admiral paused before saying, "I see. I guess it's too late, then."

Sidney noticed that Sam appeared to be holding his breath. He stood motionless in front of his computer monitor staring at Admiral Garland's face.

"Too late for what, sir?"

"I've just been informed that the bombs Darby planted were harmless. Only duds, but I doubt he knew that."

"Admiral! Do you realize what I just did! I just executed a man that did little more than trespass." Sam used every ounce of strength in his body to keep under control. The muscles in his face were tight from clenching his jaw. Sam began to pace. "God, I just committed murder."

"Like hell, Sam. Don't go overboard. The man committed a terrorist act."

Sam snarled back. "You can paint it any which way you like, Admiral Garland. How many of the others—"

"Captain, watch your step. Need I remind you of your shady past? You could be dead or rotting in a jail and your sons in some foster home.

I gave you the benefit of a doubt—more than any other reasonable man in my position would've done. That can change, Captain Waterhouse. As long as you follow my orders, you'll have your rank and your sons will enjoy a good life."

Sidney couldn't believe what she was hearing. She'd wondered before if Sam was on a path not of his own choosing. Now it was obvious that Admiral Garland had full control of him.

Sam turned his back to the admiral and yelled over his shoulder. "You'll have my usual report in the morning. Waterhouse out!"

Silence took command of the captain's office. Sam went to his window and stared out into the night's void while Sidney waited for the razor sharp tension to soften. Sam crashed into near despair, and even though his back was to Sidney, she sensed his intense regret. He stood motionless and spoke to her only through his aura. It was saturated with pain and hopelessness. It left Sidney confused. She'd never thought of him as anything but in control, unmoved by circumstances, always knowing his next move.

Still gazing out his window, Sam finally spoke. "So, Sidney, do you still believe that man is cut from the same cloth as you?"

She got up from her chair and stood beside him. "Yes, without any doubt. It's not a belief. It's a knowing. Like I know in every plain, hard seed, a beautiful flower lies sleeping, dormant until awakened under the right conditions. It's just a matter of time."

Glancing in her direction, Sam almost smiled. "You sound like a poet."

Sidney felt uncomfortable. She had an impulse to offer more than encouraging words. He was so close and now seemed more human than ever. He needed comforting arms to embrace him. Her hands reached up toward his arms. He stepped away, and his rule book sprung up from out of nowhere.

"I'm interested in discussing your behavior with the prisoner."

"I thought you might be."

"You seemed quite effective in calming him. What were you doing?"

"I gave him some techniques I use in meditation. It brings you more in focus with the present moment and less with the next. And I helped him remember a special moment in his life, something that gave him comfort. The mind is a powerful tool."

"I see. There was more going on that just that. What were you doing with your hands?"

"You mean when I put my hand on his chest?"

"Yes. That looked like it had special meaning."

"It was a transfer of energy. Some people call it *Reiki*. My hand was channeling healing energy from the universe to Marcus. It provided comfort and a connection." Sidney noticed Sam eyebrows raise in surprise. "The best way to understand it is to experience it. May I?"

She lifted one hand toward his chest.

He hesitated, and then reluctantly agreed.

"Here, sit down in your chair." With Sam seated, Sidney knelt down beside him and laid her right hand on his chest. It was her first contact with him on such a personal level. "Close your eyes."

Again he raised his eyebrows.

"Trust, Captain. I won't harm you in any way. I promise."

Sam closed his eyes.

"Now take a few slow, deep breaths. Focus only on your breathing. Follow your breath into your lungs and on to the rest of your body. See your breath as a soothing river that revitalizes and nourishes your entire body." Sam followed her instructions.

Sidney wasn't sure how long this stoic military man would put up with being held in this position. As the seconds passed into minutes, the muscles in his face relaxed and his hands fell to his side. His breathing became slower. Sidney decided to see if Sam would permit her to take him to another level.

"If you wish, this is a time when you can receive a message or even send one."

He briefly opened his eyes. "What kind of message?"

"Whatever's in your heart."

Sam gazed at her thoughtfully for a while. Again his eyes closed.

Sidney rose and stood behind him. She placed both her hands on his shoulders. The universal life force energy surged through her hands. She felt her body become light and filled with surreal calm. Sam's head fell back and rested against her. For over twenty minutes, she stood there, occasionally repositioning her hands on his upper body.

Sam drew in a sudden breath and woke. Sidney slowly lifted her hands and stepped back. She knelt down in front of him again.

"How do you feel?" she asked.

Sam turned away. Speechless, he focused on nothing, his mind still taking in the journey he'd just experienced.

"Fine. Thank you. That was … interesting. Like you say, you have to experience it to understand this energy thing." His mind was becoming focused again. "So, how did you acquire this skill, Sidney?"

"One doesn't need to acquire it. Everyone has this ability to varying degrees. You do, Captain."

Sam sat up straight, regaining his control. "Not likely!"

"Would you like to try?"

"Some other time, perhaps. It's time you returned to your cell. I've had enough of this day."

He activated his comlink and told Bridges to get Sidney. Sidney grabbed the bag of clothes and walked toward the reception room's door.

"Something just occurred to me, Captain."

"What's that?"

"The problem with rules. My mother died, at least in part, because I chose *not* to follow her rules. Marcus died because you chose to follow the admiral's. It would appear as though much of this is out of our hands. Don't you think?"

Sam shut off his computer and got up. "You always this deep?" For a while he just stood near her. "I hope you know you're giving me one hell of a problem here."

She frowned. "What do you mean, Captain?"

Bridges knocked on the door, and instead of answering her question, Sam opened the door and sent Sidney back to her cell.

The demeanor of Sidney's escorts was cold, more like that of machines than men. No words, no contact, no emotion of any kind. Sidney knew they were behind her only through the sound of their boots. They had shut down, trying to not be touched by the death they'd witnessed earlier. Perhaps, too, the executed prisoner's quiet acceptance troubled them.

"Good night, gentlemen," Sidney said as she stepped into the darkness of her cell.

The door shut with a thump.

Inside, Sidney found herself moved by the day's events: the argument with the captain; the revelation that the captain's wife had been involved with, and killed working for, Badger, who was now also murdered; the death of Marcus. In one short day, her growth had propelled her light years forward. She reflected on the past few days and barely recognized herself. With each confrontation she'd given in to fear and anger. Tomorrow, Sidney Iris Davenport would hold the sacred truths as firmly to her chest as Captain Waterhouse held to his rule book. It would surely come to pass that one would have to give up his or her dogma. She hoped it wouldn't be her.

15. Sidney's Execution

Wednesday Morning, July 10, En Route to Pearl Harbor, Hawaii

The next morning Sam awoke early as usual and jogged along the *Nonnah*'s main deck. It had been six days since Sidney had arrived on his ship. He'd planned to be rid of her by now. Sweat began to drip down his chest. With each stride he recalled the unexpected twists and turns of the interrogation sessions — and Sidney.

Her strange ways had often caused him to lose sight of his objective. He'd even discouraged the admiral from initiating the execution order. It annoyed him how his life aboard the *Nonnah* had become unpredictable. Every day something bizarre occurred. The *Nonnah* sailing through storm unscathed, the prisoner's rapid healing, the hawk's feather, the visit with Paulo, the constant changing of his crystal's position. Then there was Sidney's demonstration of her ability to unlock doors. And, the energy thing — *Reiki* she called it.

Perhaps, Sam thought, *if Sidney was eliminated all these disturbing phenomena would end.* He almost craved the monotony of the days before Sidney. Anesthetized by boredom, he could tolerate the admiral's paranoia and the endless string of executions.

On the other hand, the possibility that he could use Sidney as a means of freeing himself from the admiral was too tempting to ignore. He doubted she'd agree to an alliance with the admiral in exchange for Sam's freedom, but a ruse might be possible. If he could gain the admiral's confidence, it would work. He'd have to get rid of Butchart though. The man had too much influence. Somehow, Sam needed to make the admiral question Butchart's loyalty.

Sam thought back to the connection of some type which seemed to be present between Sidney and Butchart. He'd not pursued that query, but now a plan swirled in his mind. He could see at last the possibility of grabbing his sons and disappearing from the admiral's suffocating grasp. A twinge of guilt pricked at him. Sidney would be in the midst of the crossfire. *So be it!*

Sam returned to his office to find the admiral had sent an urgent coded e-mail. It was an order to execute Sidney before midnight that very day. Instead of being intrigued by her telekinesis, the admiral had come to the conclusion that she was too great a risk to keep alive any longer. And perhaps Butchart had been deliberately feeding the admiral's paranoia.

The hope of acquiring his freedom, hazy as it was, vaporized. But his disappointment was mollified by his sense of relief. The awkward pretense of benevolence was over, and so were the endless questions without answers, as well as the disruption of his meticulous routine. When Sidney arrived for her breakfast, Sam was more abrupt than ever.

Briefly making eye contact, he said, "You have fifteen minutes to eat."

He motioned her to go to the boardroom and continued with the business at his desk. When she returned, he ordered her to sit down. Holding the admiral's communiqué in his hand, he hesitated. It wasn't as easy to notify her of the execution plans as he'd thought it would be. She sat anxiously on the edge of her chair, wearing her new clothes.

The lavender blouse and white shorts were a good fit as far as Sam could tell without making an obvious examination of her figure. He tried not to notice her long slender legs or how the color of the lavender blouse complimented her pale green eyes.

Sidney eyed him suspiciously. "There's trouble, isn't there, Captain?"

"Why do you say that?"

"You're way too quiet. That paper in your hand, is it from the admiral?"

"Yes. He's ordered that you be executed before midnight today."

She gasped and braced herself with her hands holding firmly onto the front edge of the chair seat. She took a calming breath and gazed down at her bare feet.

Sam remained silent, waiting for more of a reaction. He expected fear, hostility, or crying, something more than passive acceptance.

She continued to avoid eye contact with him and remained deep in thought. Her face revealed only a solemn expression.

Focused on the paper in Sam's hand, she asked, "Can I see it?"

Sam handed her the decoded communiqué. She read it and nodded. Returning the paper to Sam, she asked, "What are your plans?"

"You'll be executed according the protocol—at sunset."

"Lieutenant Bridges?"

"Yes."

"Will you be there?"

"Of course."

Sidney nodded.

"Do you have any special requests?"

"Two. I'd rather get this over with as soon as possible. Before it gets too hot. Sometime before lunch. Won't feel like eating anyway."

"Yes. And the second?"

"If Lorna doesn't mind, I'd like her to be with me. Just be near. Do you think she'd mind?"

"I'll ask her. Anything else?"

"No."

"Sidney, for the last time. Is there anything you can tell me that would give me enough reason to reject this order? It would have to be significant."

She got up and went to the window. He swiveled his chair to watch her. She gazed at the ocean's horizon.

"No." She glanced back at Sam and grinned. "Unless you resign from the navy."

Sam sat back in his chair and leaned on one arm. Again she'd managed to throw him a curve.

"You mean if I were to step out of this uniform?"

"Please, Captain. You know how easily I blush," she teased.

"How can you make jokes when you're just hours from being executed?"

She returned her focus to the ocean. "Trust me, Captain, I'm not looking forward to it. But I see the death of the body only as a release of my attachment to the physical world. I'll simply return to my true home. The timing seems off, but I trust in the higher power. I thought ... it seems too soon." She turned back to Sam with her arms crossed over her chest and grinned. "So, tell me, Captain, what happens when you step out of your uniform?"

"What I meant was that if your statement was off the record, would that satisfy you?"

"No. Actually, I'm still thinking about you out of your uniform. No disrespect intended." She studied alternatives in her mind. "You have some other clothes, Captain? Just plain street clothes?"

Sam stood up and took a few steps closer to her. "You look like you're conjuring up something, little miss witch. What is it?"

Sidney smiled. "Ever been on a picnic, Captain?"

"Sure, with Joy and the boys."

She straightened her posture. "Captain, I'd like to go on a picnic, but not with Captain Waterhouse. I want to go on a picnic with Sam."

Sam took a deep breath. "You don't go on picnics on a ship, and you can't separate me into two people."

Sidney moved closer to Sam "I know you're not two people. But you can be just Sam, a man with no ties to your rank. Yes?"

"No!"

"No picnic. Pity."

"Why is that a pity?"

"Well, it would be the only way I could tell you so much more."

Sam could tell he was being drawn into something he'd have little or no control over. Still, his intense curiosity urged him to pursue her train of thought.

"So, why can't you do that now?" he asked.

"Well, as captain your behavior and choices are dictated by a rigid set of rules established by Admiral Garland and the government. You've taken an oath to abide by those rules. But as Sam, you're free to weigh the pros and cons, come up with your own set of values and rules. In these things, the Sam part of you is guided by a higher power that I trust with my life. That's why I'll reveal all only to Sam."

"And I suppose I'd be expected not to pass the information on to the admiral."

"I see you as an honorable man. I believe information told to you in confidence might be revealed to others, but with the intentions of the higher good."

"Sidney, you're asking too much. To participate in something like that would be tantamount to … well, almost treason."

"By whose definition—yours or the admiral's?"

For a while, Sam simply studied Sidney and her proposal. It could be done, but it would mean complicating his already difficult situation. The officers started to gather in the boardroom for their breakfast meeting. Time had run out.

"Sidney, what you're suggesting isn't possible. There's nothing more to discuss." Sam activated his comlink and directed Bridges to get Sidney.

"Guess I'm a bit relieved. Wasn't feeling too comfortable with baring my soul, even to Sam. Lord knows you probably think I'm weird enough now without adding more to the heap."

"Why a picnic?"

"Well, because it's fun and it's a million miles away from duty, for both of us."

As Bridges entered his office, Sam directed him to let Sidney have her exercise time on the deck for the rest of the morning. After they'd left he went to the boardroom. The officers stood at attention as he entered the room.

"As you were," he instructed.

Once they had filled their plates, the usual routine began. Robert John reported that the new engine part was a problem. "Going to have to replace the sleeve again in Honolulu. In fact, I'll be grateful just to get there. Damn thing just isn't holding the pressure. Going to have to slow down, Skipper."

"I'll have a replacement ordered."

Moon reported there had been an increase in attacks on merchant ships. "In fact, one small ship was completely ransacked last night, and all twenty-four hands were killed." The officers became quiet.

Sam reassured his staff. "We have our sub shadowing us. It's been more than seven months since any attempt was made on the *Nonnah*. Still, we better initiate a yellow alert until the *Nonnah* arrives at Honolulu. Moon, make sure all personnel carry a weapon. Place a seaman on each of the gun turrets around the clock. Casey and Morton, I want continuous watch, port and starboard. No more problems with the radar equipment, Casey?"

"Other than being antiquated, no, sir."

"Any questions?"

They nodded in agreement that there was little risk. Sam continued. "Admiral Garland has ordered that the prisoner is to be executed today."

The officers fell into silence again. "Lieutenant Bridges, she wants to get this over with as soon as possible—before lunch. Dr. Duncan, she's requested that Lorna be present. Lieutenant Paddles isn't required to do anything. Sidney said she just wanted her nearby. Ask her if she's willing to attend. The execution will be conducted in one hour."

"So, she's guilty as hell, Sam?" asked Robert.

"Always knew she was guilty. There are still a lot of unanswered questions. However, the admiral is finished with her."

The officers were again silent and finished their breakfast quickly. The meeting was adjourned and all returned to their duties.

Sitting at his desk, Sam opened the drawer containing the mysterious hawk's feather. He pulled it out of the envelope and held it in his hand. Trying to get his mind off the execution, he gazed at the red plume. At first glance, the feather appeared rather plain, but the more he studied it, the more he noticed the details of the black bar markings and its softness. In spite of the delicate nature, he noted its strength as he stroked the edges across his hand. He could imagine it still attached to the large bird as it supported her, gliding on the air currents high above the ground. He felt more relaxed than he had in years. His mind calmed and flowed with the bird on the high cliffs.

The buzz of his comlink sounded. It was Bridges advising him that he was preparing for the execution. Sam carefully tucked the feather back into the envelope and locked it in his desk.

His heart began to beat rapidly. He busied himself with shutting off his computer and activating the security systems. The crystal was again moved back into its designated resting place. He barely considered the reasons why he kept finding it in another location. Grabbing his coat and hat, he went to the main deck.

As soon as he left the air-conditioned hallway, the tropical heat hit him. Normally he'd have found it unpleasantly hot. Instead, it was welcome relief from the chill he felt over his entire body. He noticed his hands had become cold and clammy. Bridges, Dr. Duncan, and Lorna waited near the chair placed in the usual spot. Their solemn expressions were rigid, set as if their faces were made of stone. They made no attempt to converse with him.

Sam looked about for the guards and Sidney. Several yards toward the bow, he saw her. Sidney was seated on the floor of the deck several feet beyond the guards. She was in her meditative state. As he stepped up to her, she remained in her trance.

He bent down on one knee, waiting for her to open her eyes. They remained closed. He could barely detect her breathing. He was astonished by the peace evident on her face. She showed no trace of fear. The breeze gently lifted her long hair away from her face. Her body, sitting erect in her lotus position, didn't tremble. Her hands rested on her knees, palms open to the sky, receiving the loving caresses of the sea breeze.

"Shall I pick her up, Captain?" the guard asked.

Sam shook his head. "No." He waited a moment longer. Slowly, Sidney opened her eyes.

"It's time?" she asked.

Sam stood up. "Yes. Stand up," he commanded.

Sidney rose to her feet. For a moment, she gazed out over the horizon.

"This way." Sam said.

She followed him to the chair with the guards close behind her. Standing beside her, Sam asked, "Is there anything you wish to say?"

Sidney thought for a while, and then smiled. "Words alone don't seem to be enough. And anything more than words could bring that rule book of yours to the surface."

Sam looked deeply into Sidney's eyes. It was a mistake. The tightness in his chest made it difficult to breathe. His throat become restricted, as if a hand was squeezing his Adam's apple. Swallowing hard, he flexed the muscles in his back to stand as rigid as the spine on his rule book. Bridges waited with the pistol in its holster on his hip. Finally, Sam was able to breathe again. Stepping back, he began the procedure.

"Sidney Davenport, you've been found guilty of spying and sabotage and sentenced to death. Under the regulations established by the United States of America Naval Authority, you're hereby to be executed forthwith. Lieutenant Bridges, you're commanded to carry out the execution of the prisoner."

Bridges stepped forward and ordered the guards to place Sidney in the chair. Before they could, she knelt down in front of Sam. As the guards were about to hoist her onto the chair, Sam waved them off. "She can remain there."

The guards began to place the handcuffs on her. She slightly resisted.

"Leave the cuffs off." Sam ordered, and the guards stepped a few feet back.

Dr. Duncan and Lorna stood beside Lieutenant Morton. They made no eye contact with Sam. Their gaze remained on the prisoner. "Proceed, Lieutenant," ordered Sam.

Bridges stepped forward. He pulled out his pistol, cocked it, and aimed it toward Sidney's head. She remained very still with her eyes closed although her shoulders trembled slightly. The lieutenant's gun was within two feet of her right temple. As he began to squeeze the trigger, his hand shook. He grabbed that hand with the other to steady it. Still his hand shook. "Captain, I … "

"Step aside."

Bridges handed the gun to Sam. Almost in one motion, Sam swiftly raised the gun to Sidney's temple and pulled the trigger twice.

The gunfire echoed throughout the ship's deck, its noise shattering the awful tension. The pungent smell of the gunpowder blended with the sickening sweet smell of blood splattered on the deck and Sam's uniform.

Dr. Duncan quickly stepped forward. Sidney laid motionless, face down on the deck. Her head was surrounded by a pool of blood that flowed to the edge of the deck. Dr. Duncan bent down to inspect her wound and used his scanner to detect signs of life.

"The prisoner is dead, Captain," he pronounced.

Sam stood motionless. He first stared at her body and then the gun in his hands. Both it and his hand had blood splatters, skull fragments, and traces of Sidney's hair on them. Repulsed, he tossed the gun across the deck. It went skidding along the wood floor. Nausea and dizziness took command of him. The guards were placing Sidney on a stretcher. In another minute, she was out of his sight.

Lorna came forward. "Sam, you didn't have a choice."

He spoke in a strained whisper. "Didn't I?"

Everyone left. Standing alone, he felt as though the breeze could pass right through him. He was certain he'd become transparent, without shape or substance. He tried to find his feet. He couldn't move.

A year of being the admiral's accomplice in the expedient disposal of enemies had finally taken its toll. *God's punishment reserved for the damned*, he thought. The only good thing about his exploding terror was that it gave him the motivation to find his legs again. They were heavy and awkward but carried him to his office where he tore his coat off and tossed it to the floor.

He collapsed into his chair, groaning like a wounded animal. He buried his face in his hands only to find the stench of the blood unbearable. He dashed to the sink and tried to wash it from his skin. The sink became filled with Sidney's blood. It splashed onto the counter and the wall. The more he tried to wipe it off, the more it spread.

Sam felt the slow and terrifying loss of his mind. If he still had the gun with him, at that moment, he'd have placed it in his mouth and fired. Never before, even in his darkest times, had he ever considered suicide. Never before had he regretted so much.

Sam began to sob. He continued to feverishly struggle to clean up the red stain. So intense were his efforts he hadn't heard the knocking on his door.

Lieutenant Bridges stood in front of his desk. "We're ready for you, Captain."

Sam was stunned. He was seated at his desk. He looked at his hands. The blood was gone. In his hand was the red feather.

"Ready?" he murmured.

"Yes, sir. It's eleven-thirty hours. The prisoner is on the main deck. So are Dr. Duncan and Lieutenant Paddles."

Sam dropped the feather onto his desk and ran out to the ship's main deck. As he arrived, he saw his staff just as he'd seen them only moments ago. Sidney, still very much alive, was seated in her meditative state. He bent down on one knee in front of her and breathed a sigh of relief. He reached out and touched her cheek the way one would caress a child's face.

She opened her eyes and asked, "It's time?"

Sam stood up and said to the guards, "Tell Lieutenant Bridges the execution is canceled."

The guards relayed the message, and as Lorna turned to leave, she gave Sam a big thumbs up signal. Sidney stood up and looked toward the horizon, smiling as if a friend was in her field of vision. She turned to Sam.

"Captain, I hope this wasn't a test to see if I'd break under the threat of an execution, was it?"

Sam smiled at her. "No." He was perplexed by her calm demeanor. "For having narrowly escaped certain death, you appear rather calm."

She grinned. "I have my ways, Captain."

"Don't I know that." He motioned for her to follow him to the ship's railing. They stood for a while side by side, not speaking. Not needing to speak. He felt her calm energy. It was a strange sensation, unifying him with something vaguely familiar. More than ever, Sam felt as though he wasn't alone. He chuckled to himself as he considered his list of allies. Since Joy's death there had been Lorna, then Paulo, and now Sidney. And another. Perhaps a hawk. *An odd assortment,* he thought. *A doting-like aunt, an old man, a witch, and a very old bird.*

He studied Sidney, gracefully moving with the ship as it swayed on the waves, the breeze tugging at her auburn hair. Without the usual adornments and paint many women fancied, she still had a natural beauty about her. She could have used her strange power dozens of times to overpower her captors and escape. Perhaps her gods were testing her, challenging her to remain true to what she called the higher good.

Sam wondered if the man in her life truly loved her. He was perhaps going mad with grief, believing she'd been executed. He wondered why the man would let her go on such a risky mission. But then, Sam had let Joy follow her own path too.

Sam directed his gaze at the ocean's horizon. He knew without a doubt that he had to change course. But he was at a crossroads with no directional signals. The only thing he knew with absolute certainty was that he wasn't going to continue along the path he'd been on.

"Sidney, I think I've just been put through a test."

She grinned. "Did you pass?"

"Don't know yet. I don't think the test is over yet." He looked back at her. "Got a few big hurdles ahead, and I think you're going to help me get over them. If I pass the test, I might get my sons back, and if I survive that, you might get to go home. How does that sound?"

"What do you mean, 'get your sons back' and 'if you survive'?"

"That's a long story. You still game for that picnic?"

Sidney stepped closer. "You name the place and time and I'll be there."

Sam's first reaction was to step away, but he resisted the urge and found the closeness with Sidney more comfortable than before.

"'Course, you know, Captain, there are rules."

Sam's eyes opened wide. "Rules? You? That's hard to believe. Okay, what are *your* rules?"

"Well, first of all, no uniform. No hint of your rank or connection with the navy. I want to talk to Samaru, not Captain Waterhouse. Second, unconditional trust—both ways."

"Uh huh. What else?"

Sidney studied him briefly. "You know, I've got this feeling I could ask for almost anything right now and you'd agree to it, even the candle."

Sam knew she was right. He felt so good, he'd agree to almost anything she asked for. The impending insanity had vanished. He'd had a taste of a Darkness he thought only existed in the minds of the criminally insane. He vowed he'd no longer be the admiral's puppet. Sidney was now *his* ace in the hole. She didn't know it, but she was going to get him out from under the admiral's death grip.

He tried to put on an authoritative tone in his voice. It barely qualified. "Don't push your luck, Sidney," he said, playfully tapping her nose. "You're still a prisoner—for the time being anyway." Then, still feeling elated, he teased. "What's your schedule like for tonight? Care for a picnic on my veranda?"

"See—you *can* have a picnic on a ship. Shall I dress up or down?" She grinned.

"My rules are 'come as you are.'"

"Wow! That's a relief. Any other rules?"

Sam thought for a moment. "You'll answer all my questions."

Sidney hesitated. She looked thoughtfully to the horizon. "Yes, Captain. I trust you'll use the information wisely." She looked back at Sam. "I do trust you. I hope you trust me."

"I have to, Sidney. My sons' lives depend on it. You see, there's a method to my apparent madness. It'll be risky. We may both end up dead. You'd better understand that right up front."

Sidney shifted her gaze from Sam's eyes to his forehead and followed his hairline down to folds of his ears, followed his strong jaw line and down his throat to the hollow spot just above his breastbone. She noted how the neatly pressed shirt hugged the muscles of his chest and arms. His left hand rested low on his hip.

"All morning I was preparing to leave this world. Instead, I'm going to a picnic and may eventually return home. Perhaps I'm just too grateful to waste my time worrying about what may or may not happen tomorrow. The present moment, Captain Samaru Waterhouse, is all I need."

Sam wasn't sure if he understood her meaning, but she appeared radiant and quietly joyful just to be alive. He'd never so clearly noticed her beauty until then. He stepped away.

"Come back to my office and have your lunch. When you're done, you can spend the rest of the day on the deck again, if you wish."

After her lunch, Sidney returned to the deck. In the hot afternoon, even the ocean seemed to roll lazily under a cloudless blue sky. The *Nonnah* quietly surged ahead through the waves. The few seamen outside leaned on the ship's railing and watched the endless horizon. Sidney found a shaded area on the deck and sat, under the ever-watchful surveillance of Bridges and Moore. She closed her eyes.

Once again, she clearly heard her mother's scream as her body fell from the cliff, saw her vacant eyes and bloody face. The childhood trauma had followed Sidney and refused to release her from the prison she'd built around her heart—until today. Today, with a touch of Sam's hand, her heart was free of its bonds.

Each day she'd wrestled against the feelings that had begun to grow since the day Sam had told her about sailing *Tears of Joy*. She'd felt his passion and pride for his sailing ship. She'd seen his joy in challenging the tides and wind. She'd admired the way he hadn't felt defeated, even when the island had refused to grant him safe passage to its shore. She'd heard his resolve to one day stand on the island's shore. *Could it have been my island?* she wondered.

Sidney had no illusions. Sam had revealed not a glimmer of love for her. Nevertheless, the love she felt for him surged with a longing to be near him. She immersed herself in this new energy that swirled around and through her. It carried her effortlessly higher and higher to a dimension Greystone had talked of but had never been able to describe as vividly as she felt it now. She understood why.

She shifted her consciousness and searched for Danik. Telepathically, she called out to him, inviting him to join her. In a flash, he appeared before her in their cosmic dimension, grinning like a puppy who'd just buried a bone and was proud of his accomplishment.

"Danik! Pay attention. Sam, I mean, Captain Waterhouse, is in some kind of trouble. All I know for sure is that he's no friend of Admiral Garland. His kids are involved somehow. We might be able to help him."

Danik fought for control of his impetuous nature. "So it's 'Sam' now?"

He stepped away and paced around her once before drawing near again. Offering his hands to her in the Guardian's symbol of unconditional trust, she placed her palms on his. All barriers of their telepathic world evaporated.

Their spiritual energies merged. The union was brief, but it was all that was necessary for Danik to receive the details of Sidney's dilemma.

"I'm going to New Seattle," he stated.

"No, Danik. It's much too dangerous for you. You'll be recognized. Badger's people will be on the watch for you. You mustn't. Let Ryan and the underground handle it."

Danik's boyish demeanor gave way to his underlying tenacious warrior spirit. "Sidney, that ship you're on is bound to return to New Seattle, and you'll be on it. When it arrives, I'm getting you off of it. Besides, Greystone's decided that Frank Butchart has to come back to the island. I'm the lucky one who gets to deliver that package."

Sidney opened her mouth to speak, but Danik held up his hand to silence her.

"I'll be there, Sid. In New Seattle. Me and Ryan and whoever else we can dig up."

Sidney knew it was no use arguing with him. She reached out and touched his face. "I love you, Danik."

Sidney returned her consciousness the ship's deck. It was late in the afternoon, and she told Bridges she'd like to return to her cell. It was time to prepare for her picnic with Sam.

Moon reported to the captain before he began his shift.

Sam, sat at his desk. "Have a seat, Rhett."

"Sir, I understand the prisoner's execution has been postponed. Has the admiral changed his mind?"

Sam thought for a moment. Just how much should he reveal to Commander Moon? It still rankled him that he had information about his personal life, information that Butchart would've been privy to. It was disappointing to discover that Moon may have been collaborating with Butchart. But for now, Sam planned to continue his relaxed relationship with his first officer.

"Rhett, my report concerning the prisoner will be sent to the admiral in the morning as usual. You have command of the *Nonnah* until zero-six-hundred hours tomorrow. This evening, I'm going to be occupied picking the prisoner's brain." Then he set the baited trap. "She's promised to reveal information concerning Captain Butchart. Apparently, they have a history. I don't want to be interrupted unless there's an emergency."

If Moon was truly collaborating with Butchart, Sam would soon know.

"Captain, are you saying Captain Butchart is under suspicion? Should I expect anything unusual, sir?"

"You and the officers are to focus only on getting the *Nonnah* to Pearl Harbor. Do you have any other concerns, Rhett?"

Moon shifted in his chair. "No, sir. Permission to resume my duties, sir?"

"Permission granted, Commander. I'll see you tomorrow morning."

By the time Bridges returned to Sidney's cell to deliver her to Sam's office, she'd bathed and freshened up the clothes Lorna had bought for her. She'd brushed her hair until it glowed, and its waves danced freely over her shoulders. All that remained was to find a way to quiet the butterflies in her stomach.

Following Bridges to Sam's office, her heart raced. Her mind was filled with a cascade of questions: What was he going to ask her? Would she have the courage to tell all her secrets as she'd promised? What would he be like without his uniform? Would he touch her face the way he had this morning?

16. Revealing the Crystal's Power

Afternoon, July 10, En Route to Pearl Harbor, Hawaii

W hen Sidney stepped into Sam's office, she was pleased to see he had on a short-sleeved white shirt and khaki trousers. Even casual, though, he was still meticulously starched and neatly pressed. She wondered if he could he ever relax and be just Sam.

"*Buenas noches*, Sam." She winked, testing his resolve to remain the starched naval officer.

He smiled briefly. "Good evening, Sidney. Let's go through my quarters and sit on the veranda."

Sam opened the door to his private quarters and stood to the side. Sidney's heart quickened its pace again as she stepped into his personal space. It contained a minimal amount of furniture, and what was there was simple but of fine quality. She wanted to see more, but he'd placed his hand on the small of her back and urged her to continue out onto the veranda through French doors.

The veranda was grand—it was originally intended to host private parties for cruise ship officers and wealthy guests. It extended thirty feet to the ship's railing and was enclosed on both sides by a high wall. A roof extended twelve feet out from the French doors to partially cover the veranda. It was a very private place. Sidney was pleased to see potted flowering plants and evergreen shrubs scattered about, giving the terrace the appearance of a garden. The floor even had artificial turf to resemble a lawn. It almost fooled her except for the feel of it on her bare feet.

She watched Sam as he busied himself with pouring a drink for her.

"This is a special blend of teas, lemon, and spice. My own concoction. Do you like it?"

Sidney sipped her drink and expressed her delight. "Mmm, I might want another. But we need to fix something. Your shoes and socks have to go."

Sam hesitated, then nodded and tossed off his shoes and socks.

"Do you ever go for a swim in the ocean, Sam?"

"Not unless the ship is anchored, and that's not in the plans tonight. So how does this Sidney picnic go?"

"Picture this, Sam. You're in a meadow carpeted with wild flowers. Beside us is a river rushing toward the ocean a few miles away. Mountains surround you, as do tall cedars and birch trees. Evergreen scent perfumes the air. The meadow is filled with the music of birds and humming bees. Great place for a picnic. Now, there are two levels of Sidney picnics. One is the 'feast or famine' picnic where you find a rock to sit on and try to down the cheese and crackers before the critters do."

"Critters?"

"Yes. A very hungry lot and no manners. Then, there's the 'share with nature' picnic. It's understood that ten percent of all the food will be placed outside the perimeter of the blanket. Critters are not allowed on the blanket."

Sam grinned. "Well, I doubt we'll be bothered by critters here."

"That's what you think. Have you checked for ladybugs under those bushes lately? And a wee mouse peeked out from under that azalea while you were mixing this drink." Sidney leaned toward Sam's ear and whispered, "We're not alone."

Sam laughed. "Damn. This was supposed to a private party. Now, since I'm supplying the critters, blanket, and food, would you mind supplying the meadow, mountains, and all the rest?"

"No problem. Just imagine you're at my home."

"What's this place called?"

"It's an island. We refer to it as Hawk's Island. A red-tailed hawk claims it as her territory."

"We? Perhaps you should start at the beginning."

Sidney stood up and placed her empty glass on the bar counter.

"Would you like more tea?" Sam asked.

"Not just yet, thanks. This isn't easy for me. I've never talked about my people to anyone before. It's a little frightening. I've vowed to always protect them—at least, never put them in any danger."

"Are your people similar to a religious group? Are they in trouble with—"

Sidney put up her hands to stop Sam. "No, no. Not religious—more spiritual. And not in trouble." Sidney paced, searching for the right words and where to begin. She put a hand to her chest to comfort the ache building in her heart. The recollection of the meadow made her homesick, and she was having doubts this was the right thing to do.

Sam stood up and placed a hand on her arm. "Are you all right?"

The doubts vanished. Somewhere in her soul, she believed she could trust him. "Yes. You better sit down. This is going to be a bit of a stretch."

Sam sat down, and Sidney returned to the chair beside him.

"Sam, I'm what's called a Guardian."

Sam grinned. "I know."

"What? You know?"

"Uh huh. Just wanted to hear you say it."

"Where did you, I mean, how … "

"Relax, Sidney. It's okay. I understand. A few days ago, actually in Acapulco, a man told me about the Guardians. Didn't believe him at the time, or at least had some doubts. It seemed such bizarre story. Then I realized there was no other explanation for all the odd things that've happened since you landed on my ship."

"Like what?"

"Oh, little things. Like the storm that rocked all the other ships except the *Nonnah* the first night after your arrival. Like the visions, the feather, the—"

"The feather?"

"Yes. I'll show it to you." Sam got up and disappeared into his private quarters. A few minutes later he returned with an envelope in his hand. "Here it is. The medical staff found it by your bed."

Sidney pulled out the feather. Sam was surprised at her reaction.

"You look shocked," Sam said

Sidney breathed the name. "Celeste."

"Who?"

"Oh, sorry. Her name is Celeste. She's the hawk the island is named after." Sidney hesitated. Turning to Sam, she became solemn "She's no ordinary hawk. And she wouldn't bring this gift to you unless, unless you and she were connected."

"Uh huh. Well, our scanners confused us a great deal. The report indicated the bird is thousands of years old. How do you know this is from your hawk?"

"Whenever I'm in trouble, Celeste shows up. Helps me get through life's challenges. She's more spirit than a physical bird. She's always been a great source of strength for me. It's hard to explain. I know her energy." She handed the feather back to Sam. "It's your feather. She brought it to you."

"Don't think so. Wasn't beside *my* bed."

"If she left it by your bed, your staff would probably have just thought it was garbage and disposed of it. She placed it so you'd take more notice of it. She knows I didn't need her feather. We communicate on a different level."

Sam took the feather and admired it again. "Why would the hawk want me to have this?"

"Probably to help you see things more clearly. Sort of like from her viewpoint when she's flying above the cliffs. She sees everything from a higher perspective. Does that make sense?"

"You mean the feather could cause me to see things through a vision?"

"Possibly. Visions are very powerful messages. But you'll only receive a vision if you're open to that experience." Sidney studied Sam for a moment. "Actually, I believe you're a waking Guardian, Sam. You've just been side tracked for a while. It happens."

Sam smiled. "A *what* Guardian?"

"A waking Guardian. Most of humanity are sleeping Guardians, moving unconsciously throughout their lives unaware of their Guardian nature. You, in spite of that rule book of yours, have begun to tune in to your inner wisdom. Do you understand?"

Sam placed the feather back into its protective envelope and abruptly changed the subject. "I'm hungry. How about you?"

"Famished." Sidney let the subject drop.

"All right. I'll get the food and bring the blanket out."

After a few minutes, Sam returned and uncovered the dishes of food. To Sidney's delight, he'd selected an array of exotic appetizers and finger food. Several small saucers contained a variety of dipping sauces, pickles, cheeses, and an assortment of breads.

"This is wonderful, Sam! All this could keep me satisfied for a week."

"Glad you approve. The dessert tray is still in the fridge — a special treat. I'll get the wine ready."

Sidney laid the blanket down in the shaded part of the veranda, and they sat down across from each other. For a moment Sam simply watched Sidney. Seated in her lotus position, she'd closed her eyes and tilted her face up toward the blue evening sky. He realized she was giving thanks to the universe for the bounty before them. Quietly, he followed suit.

During their meal, Sam quizzed Sidney on her home and lifestyle on the island. He was fascinated. More and more, he was certain Hawk's Island was the same place that had refused him safe passage to its shore. He told her of the many times he'd sailed to a particular island but had been unable to find a safe entry past the surrounding reef.

An easy silence fell between them. They had the realization that the island, and perhaps, more, connected them.

"Sam, I believe Hawk's Island could become your home."

Home, he thought. The word conjured up visions of people laughing, children playing. "Well, that may depend on how successful I am over the next week." He leaned toward her and in the voice of a Hollywood criminal, "If ya got an extra bunk, babe, I might hafta hide out in yer neck of the woods until the heat's off."

Sidney was momentarily speechless. She never expected Sam to be playful. She giggled, and then crossed her arms as though carefully considering his request. "I don't know. Will you be the captain still, or Samaru?"

Sam grinned and continued the charade. "Just Sam, babe. And I'll be traveling light. Just me and my boys, see."

"Good!" She chuckled. "Just what are you planning?"

Sam stiffened. He suddenly felt odd playing the part of a shady old-fashioned TV character. He returned to being the starched captain. "How about dessert first?"

"Later. I'm too full for dessert. I'd rather hear about your situation."

"How about a walk?" He stood and offered his hand to help her up.

Sidney accepted his offer, and together they walked along the veranda's railing. As they stood looking at the ocean's horizon, Sam knew he had to make a leap of faith, to finally trust Sidney. If she was ever going to reveal all her secrets, she had to believe Sam had come clean with his. So he told her about Joy's death and that his boys were living with Admiral Garland because Sam was under suspicion of participating with the underground.

"I'm not sure if I understand." Sidney said. "You're saying that Admiral Garland is holding your sons as hostages? How can he do that?"

"It's kind of a trade off. I get to see my boys once in a while and stay out of prison. Or I can refuse to follow orders and go to prison and probably never see them again."

"Sam. I can't believe you'd do anything illegal. You're so ... "

"So what?"

"Well, so by the book. What did you do to make the admiral suspicious?"

"It's the implications that I probably at least knew about what Joy was doing. You see, she came across one of the admiral's confidential files. She'd retrieved only a small portion of it but enough to discover he was mining crystals. These crystals were thought to be special, I guess, a potential source of energy."

Sidney felt a constriction in her throat and moved away from Sam.

"I believe you and my wife were both seduced by Badger. I believe you went after that *Thy Kingdom Come* file. The one concerning crystals."

Sidney placed her hand against her chest and turned away from Sam again.

"You look frightened. For Christ's sake's, Sidney, we're talking about a crystal. Not a weapon of mass destruction."

"You're right. I did go in to retrieve the crystal file. Badger needed to know who was controlling the crystals. In the wrong hands, this particular crystal can be a lethal weapon on a scale you can't even imagine."

"You can't convince me a crystal has that much power."

"Sun crystals do. And you, my friend, have one."

"God, you're giving me a headache. Where?"

"On your desk. You have it on a pedestal."

"Oh, that one. Darn thing keeps moving every … " Sam eyed her suspiciously.

"Every what?" She grinned.

"Never mind. Look, it's got a certain beauty, even some mystery, but a lethal weapon? Lorna's more lethal than that crystal."

"Would you like a demonstration?"

"Don't move." In a flash Sam ran into his office and returned with the sun crystal. "There! There's your killer crystal."

Sam was about to hand it to Sidney, but he reconsidered. Swiftly, he pulled his hand back and covered the crystal with his other hand.

"Just exactly how do you plan to give a demonstration — lethal or otherwise?"

"Why, Sam, it sounds like you might be a believer."

"You know, Miss Sidney, before you arrived I'd have tossed this piece of glass in a drawer and forgotten about it. Now, well, I'm not so sure."

"That's why the sun crystal has been safe for thousands of years. The vast majority of people believe only in the physical world. Universal energy and the forces of other dimensions are talked of and experienced only on a superficial level — more like a game or toy. But once humanity evolves, using energy and other dimensions will be a way of life. The sun crystal is a tool to access and magnify our limited ability to access the universal energy and higher dimensions."

"Uh huh. Now the translation please."

"The short version—universal life force energy surrounds you and empowers you to create what you need or desire for yourself. It's what I access to heal or to guide people to the higher dimensions."

Sam nodded. "Like with Marcus Darby."

"Right. The sun crystal is a tool to amplify this energy when more power is required. However, the sun crystal doesn't determine whether the energy will he used for the higher good or to cause misery."

"Uh huh. Just how powerful is it?"

"Depends on your ability to quiet your mind, connect with the crystal's energy, and focus on the desired outcome."

"Doesn't sound easy. Not just anyone can do that."

Sidney nodded. "True enough. And, fortunately, people dominated by their ego and filled with fear and hatred will have extreme difficulty in getting the crystal to work for them—but it's not impossible."

Sidney looked sadly out toward the horizon. She knew Frank Butchart was a lethal risk.

"There is one who can," she continued as she turned back to Sam. "Frank Butchart. He is, or was, a Guardian. He was once very powerful and has been able to retain a lot of his power. But using the powers for evil has backfired on Frank. Whatever energy you create, returns to you, Sam. Frank has become weaker, but he's still dangerous."

"Butchart?" Sam shuddered and shook his head. "This all sounds just a bit too hocus pocus. It's time for a demonstration."

"Okay. Have you learned the art of meditation?"

"Yes. Used to meditate at least once every day. It did reveal a depth of knowledge that couldn't be explained rationally."

She gazed over Sam's aura and noticed a thin, translucent golden light shimmering above his head. It blinked like a light bulb not secured tightly in its socket. Sam was on the threshold of waking. It was a dangerous time for him. The shift in consciousness frightened many waking Guardians. They put up blocks, clung to old habits and beliefs. Others grasped at the knowledge gained and used the power to serve their ego rather than the Light, the higher good, only to later find that Dark power turned on them in the end. This was Butchart's gradual undoing, and the cause of the illness Sidney had noted in him.

In the span of time it took for her to inhale, Sidney became aware that her role in the past year had nothing to do with crystals or saving the planet from madness. She was here for Sam. There was nothing more profound or sacred than guiding a waking Guardian. For when a waking Guardian negotiated the pitfalls and fully awoke, the universe celebrated.

Sidney smiled. She straightened her posture, focused on Sam's dark brown eyes, and stepped forward in her heart.

"All right. Sam, you'll bring this crystal to life."

"Yeah, right. Come on, I'm serious."

"So am I. I know you have the power to do it. It's waiting for you. Now, sit down on the blanket and set the crystal a couple of feet in front of you."

Reluctantly, Sam sat in front of the picnic plates and leftover food. He placed the sun crystal as Sidney had instructed.

"Good," Sidney said. "I'll sit beside you and guide you, but I won't connect with the crystal."

Sam rolled his eyes, still believing this would end up as a futile experiment.

"What am I supposed to get the crystal to do?" he asked.

"That's entirely up to you, and I don't want you to tell me what you're thinking of asking the crystal to do. All I ask is that your request to the crystal doesn't involve me or any other living thing. Start with something simple, like moving it to another spot, but don't tell me where. Agreed?"

Sam shrugged his shoulders. "Sure."

"Now, begin by whatever means you use to meditate. I'll continue to talk quietly to you. You may ignore me if you wish and follow your own intuition. You do have this ability, Sam. More than most, I believe."

"Okay. I'll proceed on that positive note." Sam closed his eyes and began a rhythmic slow and deep breathing. Sidney guided him to a peaceful place. She watched his expression and body soften and become relaxed. After five minutes, she led him on another task—a journey of connecting with the crystal.

"See the crystal in your mind, Sam. It's there, waiting, sleeping like a child just before the morning sun stirs the sleep away. If this was your child, think of how you might gently wake him. Feel that affection. Feel throughout your body the unconditional love you have for your child. Imagine a stream of pure golden light leaving your body and going to the child, the crystal. See the light lovingly surround the crystal. See the crystal rise and become filled with light, filled with your light."

Sidney let Sam continue on his own for a while. She gave him time to become acquainted with the energy she sensed he'd discovered. Gradually, she again guided him further.

"Remember, Sam, that you're safe. You're in full control and can end this at any time you choose. You are the captain at all times, my friend." She detected a smile on Sam's face. It gave her great joy to see that he wasn't only bravely pursuing this new experience, but seemed to be letting go and allowing himself to enjoy it.

"Now, Sam, from now on you're on your own. You and the crystal are in a partnership. The crystal is receiving your energy. Your thoughts are transferred to its energy source. Be clear on your intent and what you want the crystal to do. Focus on what's to be achieved, how it is to be achieved and the end result. See it in your mind as already having been completed."

Sidney sat back and relaxed, careful not to interfere with Sam's energy connection with the crystal. She cleared her mind of chatter and focused on enjoying only the present moment. A moment with Sam at her side, a moment that she knew would likely never happen again. Once he was free of the admiral, Sam would most certainly rebuild his life with his sons doing what he loved to do. Sailing ships. When she at last opened her eyes, Sam was smiling at her.

"What are you so pleased about?"

"Take a look." He gestured toward the blanket. Sidney was surprised. He'd done more than she'd thought possible for his first attempt. Not only were all the picnic plates now on the food cart, but they were clean and neatly stacked.

"I'm a neatness freak, and the mess on the blanket was irksome." Sam looked both pleased and shaken. "I guess I owe you an apology."

"Uh huh."

"Okay. You were right. Sorry I didn't trust you. I shall try to not doubt you again. Fair?"

"Actually, I hope you go on questioning. Intelligent people don't blindly accept another's point of view or values. I have a lot of respect for you, Sam, mostly because you're open to investigating something new. You're awesome! Totally, unequivocally, undeniably awesome!"

He shrugged his shoulders. The overt praise was too foreign. Sam changed the subject.

"How about a demonstration from you? And I'm not talking about moving something from here to there. You've been doing that with my crystal, I figure. I want to see something big. Something that might convince me the crystal in the admiral's hands would be terrible for the rest of us."

"Okay, I get the picture. You want to see an indication of the crystal's full potential. I can't really do that. The Elders discourage use of the crystals except for the protection of our people. But I can provide you with a small example."

Sidney closed her eyes and went into a deep meditative state. Ten minutes later she opened her eyes and planted a big grin on her face.

"You lose. Nothing happened," Sam said.

"That's what you think."

"Really? What did you do?"

"Not saying. You'll find out soon enough. Now, I'm ready for some dessert."

"You did something with the dessert, didn't you? Changed it into something else."

"Sam Waterhouse. You wanted something big, and you got it—at least as far as I was willing to go. Now, could I please have my dessert?"

Sam trotted back to his refrigerator and brought back two plates of cake with strawberries and ice cream. It was a rare treat indeed.

"Oh Sam, all of this has been more delicious and fantastic than I thought it could have been. You've been so wonderful."

"Now don't start that again."

"Okay. You're wearing your comlink, aren't you?"

"Yes, why?"

"You may need it in a few minutes. Could I have some more Waterhouse Tea?"

"Sidney?"

"Yes?"

"How can someone be so guilty and look so innocent?"

As he poured another glass of tea, he became aware of a change in the ship. Instead of the low hum of engines, he heard the sounds of the ocean. The comlink on the waistband of his shorts sounded an alarm. Sam placed the earpiece to his ear and listened.

"Rhett, did you say the ship's engines have stopped?"

"Everything was fine, according to Robert," Moon reported. "Then, without warning, it was like someone flicked a switch and they stopped."

Sidney wore a look of pure satisfaction as she innocently continued to eat her dessert.

"Rhett, see what you and Robert can do to get them running again."

"They won't," murmured Sidney, still munching on her cake.

"Standby, Rhett." Sam switched off his comlink's send signal and turned to Sidney. "And why not, Sidney?" asked Sam.

"The crystal won't allow it for another hour."

Sam's mouth was opened wide in shock. "What?"

"You wanted something big, right?" Sidney washed down the last forkful of cake with her tea. "Was that big enough?" She smiled back at him and lifted her brows.

He glanced at his watch and activated the send signal. "Do a thorough investigation, Rhett. Be on the alert for attack. Send a dive team down to get a visual of possible damage below the water line, and give me a report at eighteen-hundred hours." Sam disconnected the comlink and sat down in front of Sidney.

"Here's your cake. Better eat it before the ice cream melts," she said.

Sam was silent for a while, and Sidney let him think. She rolled over onto her stomach and continued to enjoy sharing the same time and space with him. It was blissful. When he'd finished his dessert, he set their plates on the food cart and asked Sidney to walk with him. Together they walked the pathways between the shrubs and garden plots to the ship's railing. Sam still didn't speak, and Sidney worried that she'd pushed him too far.

"Sam, perhaps this has been too much to swallow all at once. I grew up knowing this stuff. I even thought everyone else knew it too until I was old enough to know different. It was natural for those of us on the island."

"No, Sidney, that's not the problem. If it weren't for the fact that I practiced meditation when I was younger, I guess this would be more shocking. No, I'm more concerned about what Admiral Garland has up his sleeve. Now that you've shown me the potential of these crystals, I finally know what the top secret cargo is that the *Nonnah's* been hauling. Do you have any idea how many crates I've delivered to him?"

He couldn't hide the guilt he felt from Sidney.

"You didn't know, and even if you had, you weren't given any other choice," she said.

Sam shrugged off her attempt to soothe him. "He wasn't always this...this power hungry. He had political ambitions, certainly, but I'd respected him as a wise and trustworthy man. It wasn't until recent years that he seemed to change. I hadn't realized how fully gone he was until I stood in his office that day and he took my sons away."

"There's always hope. He could return to the man he was."

"I don't see how. But even if he did, we've still got to worry about Butchart. And how many others with his abilities?"

Sidney shook her head. "Those who use their gifts to do harm work solo. They can't trust or be trusted. No, Frank is on his own as far as Guardians are concerned."

Sam frowned. "Your Elders, can't they do something?"

"No. They've always maintained that it isn't their place to interfere. Their way is to cast a Light into the shadows, as they put it, and hope that those who walk in Darkness may one day choose to follow the Light."

"That's quite a mouthful."

"It's something I support and believe in as well. I could have helped the underground by using the crystal. It isn't the way. I used my own personal skills that I was born with like telekinesis and telepathy and such—but that's all."

"You can read my thoughts?"

"Only what you choose to send to me and only if I were to turn on my receiver, so to speak. Mostly over the years, I've learned to shut it off. One can receive so many conflicting messages. I found it better not to receive. But, yes, I can receive messages, mostly from my fellow Guardians."

Sam shook his head. "You're too much, Sidney. How can I help with this crystal problem?"

Sidney studied Sam's face. She wasn't ready to tell him about the memory rod.

"Later. How about a swim?" she suggested impulsively.

"Now?"

"Sure. You said that if the ship wasn't moving, or something to that effect, you'd go for a swim."

"That's not what I said."

"Maybe. But I'm ready." Without another word, she peeled off her blouse and shorts revealing in her blue lace panties and bra.

"What the hell do you think you're doing?"

"Going for a swim." In the next second, she hoisted herself up onto the railing and checked the view below. The ocean was directly below her and relatively calm. The warmth of the sun still held its early evening warmth. It was too good to pass up.

"Come on." She swung her legs over the railing and disappeared over the edge, plunging feet first into the ocean.

"Damn it all," Sam cursed. Striking his comlink he connected with Moon and told him to lower a raft into the ocean and have someone meet him on the port side of the ship. Without explaining any further, Sam jumped over the railing and landed not far from Sidney in the ocean.

As Sam began to swim toward her, she paddled away and soon disappeared under the waves. He waited for her to come to the surface. When she did, she was several yards away from him. Again he swam toward her and she disappeared under the waves. He waited. Suddenly, he felt her grab his legs and pull him under the surface. He tried to grab her as she continued to dive deeper, but she evaded his every move.

He gave up trying to pursue her and simply began to enjoy the water. Sam swam with the fierceness of an Olympian charging through the waves. He discovered Sidney was trying to follow. Although agile, she didn't have the power to keep up. He slowed his pace.

As she came closer, he dived under the waves and turned back until he was underneath her. He pushed himself up and grabbed her as he rose up out of the water, making her shriek before they fell back under the waves. Sidney laughed excitedly as she returned to the surface.

For the first time, she heard Sam laugh without the usual reserve. In a moment of exhilaration, he reached for her waist and held her tightly to him, only for a moment before quickly releasing her as the raft approached. Sidney was grateful for the moment, brief as it was. It had been long enough for her to finally embrace him as passionately as she dared.

Sidney and Sam pulled themselves into the raft and headed back to the ship. Sam took off his shirt and offered it to Sidney, telling her she was a little too exposed. She put it on. At the starboard side of the ship, the three climbed up a scramble net. Moon was waiting on the deck, frowning and with his fists clenched. He grabbed onto her arm as she swung her legs over the railing and landed on the deck.

"Was she causing trouble again?" he asked.

"No, and you can let go of her. Any change with the engines?" asked Sam.

Moon glared at Sidney before he released her. "No. Still don't know what the problem is."

No sooner had Sam spoken when Moon's comlink sounded. "Yes, Robert." The commander stood with his mouth open for a moment, his brows knitted together. "You're sure?" he asked. "The engines are working, no problem?"

When Moon turned back to Sam, he discovered the captain was already heading back to his office with the prisoner, both leaving a trail of water on the deck.

17. The Betrayal and the Kiss

Evening, July 10, En Route to Pearl Harbor, Hawaii

Sam grabbed a towel and told Sidney she could use his shower while he made a phone call.

"Computer, place comlink to Admiral Garland's residence. Scramble code."

While the connection was being made, Sam dried himself off and sat in front of the monitor. His long hair had come loose and hung wet on his bare shoulders. *This is the moment. The beginning of the end.* His freedom would be won by feeding the admiral's paranoia. If Moon had communicated with Butchart in the last hour, Butchart would be putting severe pressure on the admiral to ensure the prisoner was eliminated. Now Sam had to convince the admiral that Butchart couldn't be trusted.

The comlink sounded and Admiral Garland's sneering face appeared on Sam's monitor.

"Well, Sam," he growled. "I've been advised you didn't follow my orders to execute the prisoner. I demand an explanation!"

Sam was almost disappointed his suspicions about Commander Moon were founded.

"Admiral, there's been a significant change in her willingness to cooperate."

"Goddamn it, Waterhouse. I'm not interested in her cooperation. I want her miserable hide fed to the sharks."

"Admiral, I'm looking out for your best interest. Suppose you could put an end to the underground for good. Wipe out the nest. What then?"

The admiral reined in his impatience. "I'm listening."

Sam had cast the bait. It meant throwing the lamb into the path of the lion, but his lamb had powers beyond anything he understood. Sidney could survive.

"I know all about our prisoner and her underground group," Sam said, twisting the truth. "I know the where, who, and how many. And, I know what and who they're after. And … " Sam hesitated. "Admiral, are you alone?"

"Yes, of course. Get on with it."

"Sidney has declared she's something called a Guardian. They have a hidden colony, and Captain Butchart is one of them."

Admiral Garland sprang from his chair. "Just a goddamn minute. Are you suggesting Captain Butchart is that woman's accomplice?"

"Sir, Captain Butchart has powers he's kept secret from you. The Guardians have unusual powers. I've already reported to you that our prisoner can easily unlock doors. I've witnessed it."

"You're delusional." The admiral smirked.

"Admiral, listen carefully. Captain Butchart recognized Sidney as a Guardian. He couldn't afford the risk that she might reveal his true identity. He first tried to kill her using the truth serum. That didn't work, so he convinced you to have her executed. Normally, for trespassing and interfering with weapons, you'd only have her locked up for a long time. Is that not so, sir?"

"Waterhouse, Captain Butchart has never failed to ensure the safety of our operations. I trust his decisions. Completely! And he's certainly not involved with any witchcraft, if that's what you're suggesting."

"Sir, it was your decision to receive information regarding the prisoner directly from me. How did you discover that the execution had been delayed? From Captain Butchart? Sir, is he usurping your authority over this investigation?" Sam watched the admiral's eyes dart back and forth. "Sir, would you describe Captain Butchart's response to the execution's delay as bordering on significant agitation? Or was he only concerned with my apparent dereliction of duty?"

Sam knew he'd successfully planted a seed of doubt in the admiral's mind. That seed would take root over the next few days. When he arrived on the base and had a face-to-face meeting with the admiral, that doubt would escalate and become the admiral's undoing.

"Captain Waterhouse, you're making a serious allegation."

Sam sat forward toward the monitor. "Admiral, I know you're skilled in detecting lies. I suggest you ask Captain Butchart if he knows about these Guardians. He'll deny it, but you'll know if he's lying. Sir, only a Guardian knows about Guardians."

"Captain Waterhouse, as soon as you arrive in New Seattle, report to my office."

The connection was terminated, and Sam was elated. It was the first time in a long while he'd felt in control of his life.

He realized the cost of his plans. He was surrendering to the impulse to do whatever it took to get his life back and putting at risk the lives of Sidney and her people. Sam also knew, without any doubt, his career as a naval officer was coming to an end. From this day on, his life would never be the same. There would be no military rule book to fall back on. Fear and doubt flashed through his chest. He went into his private quarters and found Sidney in his bathroom, drying her hair. She'd changed into her blouse and shorts and left her underwear hanging on a hook to dry.

She doesn't need my protection. She has powers.

She made him uncomfortable. He felt it when she was close. He felt it in her words, as if something within him was listening and understood their meaning. Was he a truly Guardian? The thought made his head swim. Sam continued on to his deck's railing and waited. Sidney arrived at his side, but before she could make any comment about their play in the ocean, Sam quickly returned to the business of the day.

"I'm still curious. How can I help you stop the admiral's project with the crystals?"

"I'm not sure you can or, more precisely, if you should. Besides, getting involved with another problem will only complicate your situation."

"I appreciate your concern, but I'll be the best judge about whether or not I should get involved. Besides, you said the admiral has plans to do live demonstrations within a week. There's no telling how soon disaster may follow. We'd better be prepared, maybe even warn others if he can't be stopped in time."

Sidney could see that if she wasn't careful, a nasty argument would erupt, transforming the most wonderful evening she'd ever experienced into a lifetime of regret.

"You're right, Sam." She took his hands into hers. "You know what's best for you. Please understand why I'm reluctant to pass over these troubles to you."

Sam pulled her closer to him. In spite of his skin being saturated with the ocean's salt-water smell, she could still smell his scent. His dark eyes looked softly into hers. She felt the brief caress of his hand on her cheek. *If only…* she thought.

She considered confessing that she loved him, but reconsidered. It would only give him doubts about her rationality. Determined to end the picnic on a positive note, Sidney walked back to the blanket and picked up the crystal. It was sleeping again, still beautiful as it received the setting sun's energy and reflected its brightness and power. She thanked the crystal for its service and placed it on a table before she folded up the blanket, hoping he'd take her actions as a hint that their time together had come to a close.

"You're ready to return to your cell?" he asked.

"I'm ready to return to my *room*," she said, emphasizing that she didn't think of herself as a prisoner. She picked up the crystal and handed it back to him.

Sam called for the guards on his comlink, and then told Sidney, "I'll accompany you back to your room. I guess it's really never been your cell since you can leave any time you wish."

"Well, at least it keeps out the riff raff." She grinned.

They returned to Sam's office where he placed the crystal back onto its pedestal.

"It wouldn't hurt to thank your crystal for its service to you," Sidney said. "A crystal tends to work better for those who express their gratitude."

"Uh huh. And shall I give it a name and feed it too?"

Sam's remark reminded Sidney of Danik's casual approach to the Guardian's sacred truths. She cocked her head.

"You remind me of someone. He tends to be rather nonchalant about the forces of energy. It's nipped him in the butt a few times."

"Who's this someone? Someone special?" asked Sam casually.

She'd told Sam everything else about her Guardian people and community, but she hadn't revealed her brother. Danik was off limits for now, especially since he was too involved in helping her.

"You could say that," she answered. "Anyway, crystals do become tuned in, so to speak."

"Holding something back, Sidney?"

"What do you mean?"

"God, sometimes you're impossible! Who do I remind you of?"

"Oh, mostly Greystone."

"I doubt a Guardian Elder is nonchalant, as you put it, about crystals."

The guards arrived and escorted Sidney and Sam to the cell. Sam entered the code and pulled the door open.

"Remain near this door," he ordered the guards before following Sidney in.

Sidney hoped Sam would drop the subject of Danik.

"Will I continue to have my breakfast in your boardroom and all that other stuff afterward?"

"Yes. There are still some unanswered questions." Sam partially closed the door behind him. "How much more are you not telling me, Sidney?"

"Outside the Guardian community, I'd say you know more about me than anyone else ever has. As far as my assignment goes, you know the how, where, when, why, and that I failed."

Sam walked back and forth in front of her for a while. Finally, he stopped.

"I doubt you fail at anything. At the very least, the assignment, as you call it, isn't finished. Either you intend to finish it or someone else will." He smiled at her. "Perhaps this someone is the man who I remind you of, no?"

Sidney focused on producing a poker face. She'd learned that if she said nothing, he'd take her silence as admission of guilt.

Casually, she replied, "The underground has plans that I was never privy to, and frankly, I wasn't interested in getting any deeper."

"Nice try."

"What do you mean? That's the truth!"

"I don't think you've lied to me. But you're really good at diversion tactics." He lowered his voice. "I have come to the conclusion that there are things still in play, and since the base is under strict security protocol, one of your Guardian friends, not the underground, will finish what you started." He whispered in her ear, "I have an idea who that is, actually."

Sidney was startled. "What do you mean?"

Sam put his index finger to his lips. "Shh. Let's discuss that over breakfast."

"But you don't—"

Sam interrupted. "This discussion is over. How does Greystone end a discussion with a stubborn Wild Child?"

Hands on her hips, she sheepishly replied, "You really don't want to know."

"Yes, I do."

Sidney hesitated and felt the color of her face blossom to crimson. "He gives me a kiss."

"A kiss?" Sam moved closer to her and tilted her face to his. "Like this?" Tenderly, he kissed her forehead. He held her face in his hands briefly before letting her go. "How's that?"

Sidney's heart raced. The floor seemed to move this way and that. She heard him, smelled his skin, and felt the imprint of his lips on her forehead. But no words would serve her.

"My god, it works. That kiss was for trusting me. Good night, Sidney."

In the next moment, Sam was gone. As the door closed with a thud, she murmured, "Good night," as she stood still and focused only on the spot on her forehead.

She was embarrassed at having become so bowled over by her emotions. The tenderness of the kiss had taken her by surprise. She reminded herself that Sam was doing his job, and she had to admit, maybe even manipulating her. She trusted him enough to reveal certain secrets, but in case she was wrong, she wouldn't put Danik at risk.

Sidney prepared for bed, but as flustered as she was, she wasn't the least bit tired. She decided to put a blanket on the floor and simply focused on her breathing. In time, she reached for Danik and barely got a wink and a grin. He was busy, or so it appeared. She reached for Greystone. He sleepily conveyed that he was pleased she'd finally followed his advice. She reached for Seamus. He was there. Surprisingly, he was seated on the floor not far from her with a rather smug look on his face.

"Got yourself in a pickle, haven't you?" he said.

Tired of the male perspective, she waved him away. The sole remaining guide available to her was Celeste. Celeste acknowledged her without passing judgment, or any comment whatsoever. Sidney simply felt Celeste's huge wings wrap around her shoulders and lift her above their valley. Gracefully, they floated as one out toward the ocean with the sailboats rocking in the waves.

18. The Missing Prisoner

Thursday Morning, July 11, En Route to Pearl Harbor, Hawaii

In the early dawn Sam quietly entered Sidney's cell. He opened the door just wide enough to enter and let the light from the hallway sift into her room. She was asleep on her bed, lying naked on her left side facing the wall. A sheet loosely covered her legs up to her hips. She hugged the pillow underneath her shoulders. The light from the hallway delicately traced the contours of her body revealing only her back, shapely and long.

Carefully, he placed the blue lace bra and panties, rolled up tightly in his hand, onto the chair beside her bed. He inched closer to see her face. She was indeed asleep and making the soft noises one does when in the depths of slumber. Her arm and pillow hid the remaining secret parts of her body. The warm glow of her skin and the softness of her curves begged to be touched. He breathed a sigh and left, closing the door quietly behind him.

Sidney entered Sam's office for the routine breakfast interrogation. "Good morning, Captain. Thanks for returning my undies."

"Morning, Sidney. Don't mention it." He barely looked in her direction, preoccupied with reports on his computer. "We have a celebration today."

"Really?"

Glancing at her, he said with just a trace of a smile, "It's our anniversary."

He returned to some documents on his desk and placed them in a neat order. Sidney decided to play the game with him.

"Anniversary? Oh, I'm so embarrassed! Here I am with no gift to mark the occasion. Golly, how time flies when you're having fun. Let's see, this must be our what?"

Sam rolled his eyes. "Very amusing. The fact is it's been one week to the day since you arrived on my ship. You haven't escaped, you're still alive, and the admiral hasn't called for my arrest for delaying your execution—yet."

"Uh huh. And are you planning to celebrate all by yourself, or will there be invitations to this grand occasion?"

Sam smiled briefly. "Go have your breakfast, and we'll talk when you're done."

Sidney quickly ate and returned to his office. He asked her to sit down while he finished up with something at his computer, after which he turned to her.

"Enjoy breakfast?"

Sidney wanted to believe Sam's jovial mood was real and not a performance. The tone of his voice was deep and mellow. His face had softened. She noted the way he allowed his body to relax into the contours of the chair rather than fighting its comforts.

Yesterday's picnic had created a wave of confusion within her. Her emotions were doing a dance, shifting from being rigidly focused on her assignment and Danik, to seeing Captain Waterhouse in a new light—as a waking Guardian, and as someone with whom she was hopelessly, deeply, breathlessly in love.

"Yes, thank you. Breakfast was great. What's up?" She sat down.

"Why, Sidney," he teased. "You of all people know the value of not revealing all your secrets at once. Some should remain, ah *under cover* until the right time,"

She maintained a straight face as if his remark meant nothing more than a reference to her stonewalling of his questions. Still she felt her face become warm and rosy at the thought of him watching her sleep in her nakedness when he'd returned her underwear.

Sam stood up and went to his credenza to pick up the photo of his family. "You're a lot like Joy, headstrong and with high ideals." He placed the photo back on the credenza. "You picked up where Joy left off. Do you deny getting the file from the admiral's computer?"

Sidney could no longer evade telling the truth. "Yes, I did copy that file, but the copy's still on the base and will probably never be found."

"Can you be certain that copy won't fall into the wrong hands?"

"No."

"Then tell me where it is."

"Captain, as powerful as the Guardians are, there are others who fall equally on the Dark side of power, lethal beyond description. If you become involved, you'll be killed. Anyone who has had anything to do with the crystal's file has died or disappeared. I'd regret it for the rest of my life if you died as a result of that file. I just couldn't live with that."

"Sidney, I've been involved for the last year with that file."

"But not directly. You've been kept in the dark about the meaning of the contents."

"If you have friends planning an attempt to retrieve that copy, they'll fail. The admiral is ready and willing to hang anybody who threatens his security. I can get in and out of the Naval Base as easy as a bird. Perhaps Badger did have a reasonable concern. Perhaps people with wiser council need to know what the admiral is planning. Can you not see that?"

"Sam, if you're caught with that copy, you're as good as dead."

Sam placed a chair beside Sidney and sat down. He took hold of one of her hands. "Without any doubt, I'd rather regret the things I did, than the things I didn't."

Sidney swallowed. She looked away from his tender, dark eyes. The hand she'd normally bring to her chest to seek guidance was tucked snugly in Sam's.

"Sam, please understand that if I reveal everything to you, others who are involved—especially someone I care deeply about—may get hurt. If you go charging in, they may get caught in the crossfire."

Sam quickly withdrew his hand and stood up. Her reference to this someone, obviously a lover, pierced through his chest unexpectedly.

"I want you to think about regrets for the rest of the day, regrets about things you should have done," he said. "You have the rest of the day to yourself. I'll see you tomorrow morning. Dismissed."

Sidney was escorted back to her cell. She found the darkness soothing. It wrapped her in its calming shell and allowed her to be quiet. The clarity of her mind elevated her awareness to see with more than her eyes. In her meditation, she was shaken by a revelation. Sam had hinted that he was conspiring to deliver a fatal blow to his imprisonment, and now she saw the blow could destroy his path to returning to his Guardian nature.

As Sam made his plans, Dark forces were rising within him. Sidney had to divert them. She raised her consciousness to a higher realm and called upon Sam's higher self. Drumming sounds throbbed in the distance in tune with her heartbeat. She asked the Light to guide her words.

"Sam, you have the wisdom to choose your Guardian path, and the courage to see it through. You have clarity of your life purpose. You're aware of the infinite source of knowledge that guides you to seek the higher good. The universe showers you with an abundance of well-being and strength. You're an eternal being, loved unconditionally. You're a child of the one most high, Sam Waterhouse. You're a perfect being. And so it is."

In the late evening, sirens shattered the silence. Moon had been notified by the New Seattle Naval Base that the *Nonnah*'s primary source of defense, the submarine, was being relocated to higher priority operations. The risk of attack on the *Nonnah* was suddenly high. Though no enemy vessels had been spotted, Moon knew pirates wouldn't hesitate to attack a naval merchant ship carrying a supply of weapons and ammo at any opportunity. With minimal defenses, the *Nonnah* could be easily overtaken if the crew wasn't prepared.

"Red Alert! All hands report to your station!" screamed the ship's communication system.

Armed seamen scurried about while Sam and Lieutenant Commander Moon assessed the situation.

"Where do you think we're the most vulnerable, Rhett?"

"Well, they wouldn't sink the *Nonnah*. It's our cargo they'd be after. So they'd have to get on board, kill the crew. Their armed speedboats would keep most of crew busy on the gun turrets. Casualties would be heavy."

Sam had learned that in battle, rules were replaced with one's keen sense of ingenuity, anticipating moves and countermoves, studying the opponent's character, evaluating their desperation or courage, and accurately measuring their resources and capabilities. Most battles, Sam believed, weren't won by the might of the machinery, but by the courage and cunning of the one who wielded the sword.

"Rhett, you're in charge. There's nothing to indicate the *Nonnah* is under any immediate threat. But if the little devils start climbing aboard my ship, wake me. Until then, I'm getting some sleep. Any questions?"

"No, sir."

Friday, July 12, 0300 hours

"It's oh-three-hundred hours," remarked Carla. "Something would've happened by now if they were going to attack, don't you think, Rhett?"

Carla had her eyes fixed to her navigation equipment. Looking up to see if Commander Moon had heard her, she saw that he was engrossed in the radar unit. He and the radar operator frowned and stared into the green glare of the radar's screen.

"Commander?" she called.

"There's the bastards!" he growled. "Eight attack vessels. Carla, steady as she goes. Don't so much as make a twitch in our heading. They're moving directly toward our bow, still out of their firing range."

The commander switched the port and starboard lights off. Surveying the deck below, he saw the crew ready their firearms and heard the whine of the chopper's motor start up. Five minutes later, Buzz had the chopper airborne and out of sight. The ship's lights flicked on again. When the attack vessels were within visual range, the *Nonnah* appeared quietly en route to Honolulu. The boats slowly circled, creating a wide arc around the ship, like a wolf pack sizing up its victim. The commander waited. He could barely hear their engines.

His enemy was less cautious. The lights from the bridges of the small fifty-foot boats were dim but illuminated the gun turrets on their bows. Five hundred yards out from the *Nonnah*'s starboard side, the attack vessels spread out in a wide "V" formation and dropped motorized rafts into the water.

The commander tensed. He considered his enemy's next move. He was almost certain of what they'd do. If he was right, the *Nonnah*'s crew was prepared.

"Carla, alert the captain," said Moon.

Carla sounded the captain's comlink and double-checked to make sure her service pistol was armed. Once the rafts were within fifty yards of the *Nonnah*, the commander activated vibration mode on all personnel's comlinks. As the rafts edged up to the *Nonnah*'s starboard side, the attack vessels slowly moved into firing range. Moon left the navigation room and stood with his remaining officers, concealed on the bridge. He readied his handgun.

The unmistakable thud and scraping of grappling hooks sounded on the ship's starboard side. The commander waited. Like rats climbing up a rope, the enemy shimmied up their lines to the ship's railing. Dressed in black from head to toe with their faces painted black, the eighteen pirates were barely discernible from the backdrop of the dark sea. Flashes of light reflected off the knife blades grasped by their mouths and automatic firearms slung over their shoulders.

They paused, ready to retreat and drop to the ocean. Still hanging on the ocean side of the railing, they scanned up and down the ship's decks. They strained their eyes for any movement, listened for sounds of weapons being maneuvered, and sniffed for the scent of a seaman's nervous sweat.

Satisfied the element of surprise was on their side, they swung over the railing and crouched low on the deck. As one gave signals to the rest, a loud command came from the *Nonnah*'s bridge.

"Fire!"

Gunfire erupted from the *Nonnah*'s crew. The enemy scrambled to find cover. Three managed to jump overboard the second they heard the order to fire. Five bodies lay motionless on the deck. The remaining pirates returned fire, fiercely surging ahead to the ship's walls and finding cover behind crates.

The battle raged on for a long thirty-five minutes. The *Nonnah*'s crew lived up to its reputation for being well trained and fearless. Pirates dropped and cried in agony as the seamen fired mercilessly upon them. The pirates' boats exploded and blazed in the night sky.

Sam stood in the shadows watching his officers and naval crew handle the situation. He was pleased to see his first officer had the battle well under control.

"Captain," hollered Moon. "We sunk two of their boats. Buzz in the chopper got one. Third one is disabled. The rest have given up and left."

Sam looked with pride at his first officer, who was wild eyed and thrilled with his victory. The battle, brief as it was, had been well executed. Moon had waited to make his move on his terms. He ordered Buzz to return to the ship and a team to lower a lifeboat and pick up any surviving pirates. Crews were dispatched to survey the damage to the *Nonnah*'s hull and remove the bodies from the deck.

"Any casualties, Rhett?"

"A few of our men have been wounded. Doc's about ready with his report on numbers."

Sam nodded his approval. "I'll be in my office. When you're ready, give me a report on the casualties and damage. Well done, Number One!"

When he received the details of the damage, Sam turned on his computer and prepared a message to the admiral's office about the attack.

Encountered brief attack by unknown enemy at zero-three-thirty-five hours. No U.S. naval personnel deaths; two with serious wounds; six with minor wounds. Some damage to cargo. Extensive damage to the ship's decks but seaworthy. Two enemy surface vessels sunk, one disabled. Fifteen enemy casualties; eight wounded being treated by medical staff. Successful tactical defense operations under command of Commander Everett Moon.

Sam knew the attack on the *Nonnah* would scarcely raise anyone's eyebrows. Pirate attacks were as routine as engine problems. It was nearly 0500 hours. Believing Sidney might be worried about the battle, he activated his comlink to her cell.

"Sidney, are you awake?"

She didn't reply.

He called out a little louder, "Sidney, are you up?"

No response. Sam tensed. He connected to Bridges comlink and directed him to check on Sidney's cell immediately. A few minutes later, Bridges called Sam and advised him that Sidney wasn't in her cell and that her door was found ajar. Sam's comlink sounded and his monitor screen lit up. Admiral Garland was calling.

"Good morning, Admiral. You've received my initial report?"

"Yes. Any idea who the culprits were?"

"Not at this time. Lieutenant Bridges will interrogate the prisoners. Do you have any leads, sir?"

"No. Make doubly sure my packages are accounted for."

"Yes, sir. Admiral, we're fairly vulnerable right now. I want the Hawaiian Coast Guard out here."

"Fine. I'll alert Pearl Harbor."

The call was disconnected.

Sam found the commander inspecting the damage on the main deck.

"Rhett, Sidney is missing."

"Again?"

"Initiate a search. And, I want our ETA to Pearl Harbor. Also, make sure the officers are ready for our morning meeting."

"Yes, sir."

"At a gut level, what do you think those pirates were after?"

"The shipment stores of ammo and the explosive devices, of course. What else?"

Sam took a deep breath. "Has it occurred to you that the underground may try to rescue or kill the prisoner?"

"Actually, no. Such a high risk for one person. Even the military wouldn't do it unless—"

Sam interrupted. "Unless it was extremely important. Is it possible any one of the pirates could have gotten past the deck, grabbed her, and slipped over the side?"

Moon thought for a moment. "It's possible. Not likely, but possible."

"Find her, Rhett."

Sam contacted Buzz. "How's the chopper?"

"She's got a flesh wound, sir, but able to fly."

"See if you can pick up the scent of the pirate's escape. Just take note of where they're heading or anchored and report back."

"Aye, aye, Captain," replied Buzz. "There'll be enough sunlight soon that it shouldn't be a problem to spot them."

Sam checked his private quarters and his veranda. Cropley and his search team reported back twenty minutes later. There was no sign of her, not even where she'd been found the first time she went missing. They inspected all the places one would seek cover from gunfire, but from the engine room to the upper most deck, there was no trace of Sidney. All they found was a brief trail of blood from the main deck down to the lower inside decks near Sidney's cell.

19. The Slow Dance

Sam could think of only one way to get answers regarding Sidney's disappearance—the injured prisoners. He went to the infirmary to meet with Bridges. Stepping into the room, Sam noticed the smell of burned flesh. Dr. Duncan's medical staff was busy attending to five victims. One had already died and was placed on the floor in a black body bag.

Bridges was trying his best to extract information from an injured prisoner. Sam motioned to him to come into Dr. Duncan's office.

"What have they told you so far, Lieutenant?"

"Not a thing, sir. They're not saying who they are or where they're from. All they do is cuss and threaten. The one I'm talking to now was found hiding in the lower corridors, but he won't tell me why he was down there."

"All right. I'll have a go with him."

Sam and Bridges returned to the prisoner, who was lying on the examining table in the main room of the infirmary. The nurse attending to the man told Sam the patient had moderately severe burns and several fractures. He'd been given adequate analgesic, but was capable of talking.

"Good morning," barked Sam to the prisoner. "I'm Captain Waterhouse of the USS *Nonnah*. What's your name?"

The prisoner ignored Sam.

Sam eased his manner. "Your attack on the *Nonnah* was bold. What is it you were hoping to get?"

"Fuck you!"

Sam smiled. "Sorry, we don't have any of that on this ship. I really would like to get to the bottom of this before we reach Honolulu. Once we're there, you'll be turned over to the base authorities. I doubt you'll ever be a free man again — unless, of course … "

The prisoner snarled back, "Of course what?"

"You help me; I'll help you."

"Like shit if I'd believe that fucking line."

"I'm quite serious. On this ship there's only one authority higher than me. You know who that is?"

"Yeah, the fucking Admiral."

"No." Sam pointed to the ceiling. In a reverent whisper, he said, "God. You tell me who ordered this attack and what you were after. That's all. Think about it for a minute."

Sam stood back and ignored the prisoner. He surveyed the room, noting the bloody and burned clothes on the floor. They gave no clues as to the pirates' identity. He noticed the most critically injured seaman was in the intensive care room. Dr. Duncan and three assistants were working on him.

Sam nodded and returned his attention to the prisoner in front of him. He began to ask him if he'd changed his mind when he realized something had been odd in the intensive care room.

The prisoner asked, "Just what kind a deal are we talkin'?"

"A reduced sentence in return for information. That's the most I can offer you."

"Yeah? How much reduced? A year or two off eternity ain't much!"

Sam returned his gaze to the intensive care room.

"Are we talkin' just a couple of years or more like twenty?"

Sam ignored him and slowly made his way toward the intensive care room.

"Hey, Captain. We're talkin' deal here. Where the hell are you going?" The prisoner settled down when three armed guards approached him.

Sam stood in front of the window separating the ICR from the main medical ward. Dr. Duncan was intensely occupied with administering pharmaceuticals to the patient. Lorna and two other assistants administered to the man's wounds and monitored the scanners. Sam entered the room.

"How's he doing?," he asked.

"He needs major surgery," the doctor answered. "He'll need to be airlifted to Honolulu."

"Good morning, Captain," said one of the assistants.

Sam turned to her and saw what his gut had been trying to tell him. The white lab coat over her blouse and shorts had misled the search party.

Her long brown hair was tied back in a French braid, and except for her bare feet, she looked the part of a professional medical assistant.

"Sidney, why are you here?"

Lorna butted in. "Oh, she came here last night when we went on full alert. Kept me company and helped set up for casualties. Didn't the guard who brought her here let you know?"

"Did you see a guard bring her here, Lorna?"

"Come to think of it, no. But how else would she get here? Figured he'd have told you her whereabouts."

Sam glared at Sidney. "Well, he didn't."

"You're not going to take her, are you? Got so busy, I really could use an extra pair of hands. Besides, she seems to be able to help with her *Reiki* thing."

"Lieutenant Paddles!" barked Sam.

Lorna placed a stubborn hand on her hip, but seeing Sam's anger, she changed her mind about confronting him.

"My apologies, Captain."

Sam was angry and relieved at the same time. He struck his comlink and connected to Moon.

"Rhett, tell Buzz to cancel the search and return to the ship. Our missing prisoner is in the infirmary, and we've got a patient to evacuate." Sam turned back to Lorna. "Lieutenant Paddles, you're responsible for her now. You can have her until this prisoner is airlifted out. Then I want you to personally bring her to my office. Any questions?"

"No, sir," replied Lorna.

"Doctor, will you have time to join us at the breakfast meeting?" Sam asked.

"Yes, just a few minutes though."

Sam marched out of the room, and Sidney and Lorna grimaced at each other as if to say "Uh oh!"

A few minutes later, Lorna took Sidney aside to gather up more supplies. "You know, I'm almost certain he was more worried than mad that you were gone."

"No, he was just mad."

"Well, if you didn't matter to him, he wouldn't have got so worked up over it. You matter, girl."

"Yes. And I know why, and it's not what you're thinking."

"Uh huh. You got a man back home?"

"You promise not to tell anyone, especially Captain Waterhouse? Absolutely no one?"

"Hey, I know your bra size. Never told a soul. We're friends."

"Well, actually, I've never had a boyfriend."

"Uh huh. I don't believe a word. A pretty gal like you? And I can see you're all sweet over Sam."

Dr. Duncan called to Lorna.

"We'll get back to this later." Lorna shook her finger at Sidney.

Following close beside, Sidney whispered, "You're crazy. I just admire the man, respect him. He's been good to me. That's all."

"Don't you tell no fibs to Lorna Paddles."

Soon came the time when they had to prepare the seaman for evacuation. When the medical staff were loaded onto Buzz's chopper, Lorna delivered Sidney to Sam as ordered. Exhausted from being on duty more than twenty-four hours, the medical assistant planned to go straight to her quarters after receiving the blast she fully expected from Sam.

Just before entering Sam's reception room, she said, "You better tell him how you feel."

Sidney shook her head. "He's got bigger problems. Doesn't need to be bothered by some love-sick puppy. Anyway, he'd probably think it was a joke."

"Well, I know he wouldn't laugh. God only knows he's forgotten how."

"Oh no, he hasn't. We were playing in the ocean yesterday and he—"

Lorna grabbed Sidney's arm. "You were what?"

"Oh, well, I kind of forced him to go swimming and we, that is, he—"

"Playing? Swimming?"

Sidney nodded. "Uh huh."

"We're talking about this Sam, right?" Lorna pointed to Sam's office door.

"Yes."

"Sidney, if you don't tell him, I will."

Sidney gasped and shook her head. "Oh, god no. You mustn't say anything. You promised you wouldn't say a word to him, Lorna."

"Wouldn't tell who what?" barked Sam, standing at his now open office door.

The two women jumped.

"Oh, nothing important." Sidney smiled nervously. "Just girl talk."

Sam continued to scowl. "I doubt it. Lorna, step into the boardroom. Sidney, you sit here and don't move. I mean it!"

Sidney zipped over to her usual interrogation chair while Lorna and Sam walked into the boardroom and shut the door.

"Sit down, Lorna. You look like a wreck."

"Oh? You hinting that perhaps I should be scuttled?"

"Relax. I mostly just want Sidney to take my orders seriously. She tends to disregard rules."

"I see. She holds you in quite high regard, Sam."

"What did she mean about you not saying anything?"

Lorna waved her hand in the air. "Oh that. We were talking about her love life."

Sam nodded and stood up.

"Lorna, I'm counting on you to keep an eye on Sidney over the next few days. I'm flying to New Seattle as soon as we dock in Pearl Harbor. And please play nice with Commander Moon, okay? No pushing his buttons."

"Captain, a girl has to have some fun. But try not to worry about anything while you're away. Visiting your boys?"

"Yeah. You go get some rest."

He returned to his office to find Sidney still firmly seated. He sat down in his chair behind his desk and leaned back. Suddenly, he started chuckling as if he'd just remembered the punch line to a joke.

Sidney blushed. "Something on my nose?"

"No," he said, still chuckling. "It's incredible. You continually manage to turn this ship and its crew inside out. You better pick up your breakfast. Get what you want from the buffet and bring your tray out to the veranda. You can eat there while I have my meeting with the officers. Once you're done, Bridges will take you back to your room, er, cell."

She picked out a few things for her breakfast and went with Sam onto his veranda. She was fatigued from lack of sleep. The morning air was cool, and Sidney shivered in her blouse and shorts. Sam retrieved their picnic blanket and gave it to her.

"Could I stay out here this morning? I'd like to sleep in your hammock."

Sam thought for a moment, studying her eyes. He shook his head.

"I've almost lost you too many times. Not going to take any more chances than absolutely necessary. Understood?"

Sidney no longer felt tired or hungry. Sam's response had lifted her beyond those mere annoyances. She looked into the dark brown eyes that held her heart captive.

Resisting the urge to reach for him, she obediently responded, "Yes, Captain."

Exhausted, Sidney slept the rest of the morning in her cell. She woke shortly before lunch and began her usual daily routine of washing and tidying. She laughed at herself. In the past, her routine was a far cry from the meticulous efforts she'd now adopted. Sam's influence was strong. His order and discipline had given her a sense of security.

Sidney sat down on her bed and surveyed her room. It was spotless and tidy. It was definitely *not* her room. Her bedroom in her small, modest home on the island was in the loft. Her bed and furniture were made out of willow. The walls, made of straw bales and stucco, held in the warmth and protected her from the winter storms. By now the dust bunnies on the storage shelves and rafters had probably given birth to countless offspring. The sun would be shining through the small window in her bedroom that overlooked the forest. Chickadees and pine siskins would be upset with her not having refilled their feeding station with their favorite seeds. She could hear their chatter and see the fluttering of their wings as they hovered over empty trays.

Bridges entered her cell and escorted her to Sam's office. The captain wasn't there. She continued on to eat her lunch in the boardroom. From the opened window, she heard the crew working to repair the ship. She felt distant and removed from the lives of the people around her. When she'd finished her lunch she returned to where Bridges always waited for her in the reception room. As ever, the lieutenant remained detached and avoided any unnecessary conversation.

"The captain's orders are that you're to remain in your cell until this evening." He motioned for her to proceed to the hallway.

"No exercise on the deck today?"

"No."

"Why?"

"It's too dangerous right now."

As they approached a doorway that led to the deck, Sidney turned toward it instead of continuing down the hallway. Through its window she saw Sam standing with Moon, surveying the deck's damage and monitoring the temporary repairs. Large gaping holes were being cornered off. Shattered crates were being dismantled and the contents examined.

Bridges ordered, "Keep moving."

Sidney thought about spending another five or six hours in the dark cell. It was unbearable. "Mr. Bridges. I think I should go to the infirmary."

She placed her hand over her mouth as though trying to restrain vomiting. Bridges eyed her suspiciously and stepped back. Activating his comlink, he called to the captain, "Sir, the prisoner has requested to be taken to the infirmary, sir. I have her at the door on the midship starboard side."

Sidney glanced back at Sam. She couldn't tell if he was more alarmed or annoyed. He walked quickly over and burst through the door.

"What's the matter? You look fine to me," he said.

"I am fine. Just want to help. Seems to me there are quite a number of casualties that still need medical attention, and I'd like to help Dr. Duncan. That's all."

"No. It's too dangerous."

"What do you mean dangerous? Everyone else is working overtime. I can help."

"Sidney, you're not trained. You're just a civilian. The prisoners in the infirmary are savage killers. When they're turned over to the authorities at Pearl Harbor, you can dance on the deck if you like. Now go back to your cell."

Sidney stood up to Sam and placed her hands on her hips. "What do you mean *just* a civilian? I can help those people in ways your trained military personnel can't. Furthermore, I've survived Admiral Garland and Captain Butchart. If you think I can't handle a few disabled, burned, broken, dilapidated, militant carbon copies of Captain Butchart, you're terribly mistaken, *sir!*"

Sam stood erect, unmovable. "You won't go anywhere other than to my office or your cell, escorted by Lieutenant Bridges. Is that clear?"

"Yes, sir." Sidney saw there was no point in arguing.

"Bridges, deliver the prisoner to her cell."

"Aye, Captain."

On the way, Bridges surprised Sidney by initiating conversation.

"You sure got guts." At first Sidney thought he was angry; then she heard him chuckle. "Never saw anybody, except maybe Lorna, talk like that to the captain without a severe reprimand."

Sidney smiled. "Pays to be just a civilian, sometimes."

"Uh huh. Better watch your step, miss. You get too far away from the captain's eyes and you could be in trouble."

Sidney stopped and faced him. "Trouble? What kind of trouble?"

"Someone wants you dead real bad and is willing to pay big."

During the breakfast meeting, Sam received the full report from Lieutenant Bridges concerning the pirates' objective. The patient he'd been interrogating eventually talked. Someone had made a reckless attempt to eliminate Sidney. And the only madman that came to Sam's mind was Captain Butchart. But he knew someone else must also be involved, someone with money to burn. Wealthy as the admiral was, he'd use only official channels to protect his political ambitions. It was time to have another chat with New Seattle's Police Detective, Clay Flanders.

As the *Nonnah* approached Pearl Harbor, Sam asked Bridges to bring Sidney back to his office.

"Everything okay?" Sidney asked once she and Sam were alone.

Sam observed her delicate features and realized that when he'd thought of Joy in the last week, the familiar pain was gone.

"Someone desperately wants you eliminated, Sidney. We have to tighten security. Your access to the deck for exercise may be severely restricted until the *Nonnah* reaches New Seattle." Sam shut down his computer and electronic systems, tossing his comlink aside.

"Let's have dinner," he said.

Sidney saw that two trays had been delivered to Sam's boardroom.

As they ate, Sam asked, "Have you given more thought to telling me where you placed the copy of the file?"

She thought for a moment. "Someone will find you and give you guidance. You'll know that you can trust him. If you're meant to find that file, you'll find it without my help."

"Uh huh. Can you clarify that?"

She shook her head. "You know how to touch the higher dimensions for help. Anything you need to know is available to you."

She remembered how Greystone had guided her during her early years on the island. There was so much Sam needed to learn, to experience in order to develop a trust in his higher wisdom. But they didn't have time, so the best she could do was instruct him in the way of the Guardians throughout their meal.

Sam was receptive to her coaching and nodded when he understood and asked for clarification when he didn't. He was an easy student, as though he'd traveled the path before and only needed to be reminded of the pitfalls and traps. Sidney reached for his hand.

"You're in a very vulnerable state. Be wary of being deceived by a Dark path. It may appear to be for the higher good. People of fear will attempt to draw you back to old ways. Always ask yourself, 'Why am I doing this?'"

He nodded. "Come into my stateroom. I need to do some packing."

Sidney followed. "Packing? Why?"

He led her into his bedroom and went to his closet to pull out uniform shirts.

"I meant to tell you earlier. I'll be flying to New Seattle tomorrow morning."

He continued packing, but Sidney jumped and grabbed his arms. She pleaded with her eyes.

"Not to worry, Sidney. Bridges and Lorna will take care of you."

"I'm not worried about that. I … "

Sam pulled away from her and returned to his closet. He grabbed his uniform pants.

"No need to worry about anything, at least until the *Nonnah* arrives in New Seattle. Understood?"

He waited for her response. She stood like a frightened child, her hands drawn up to her chest. Tears brimmed in her eyes. He moved close to her.

"What's the matter, Sidney?"

She stepped away from him, again and again. "I should have known I couldn't handle this," she muttered to herself. Finally, she took a deep breath and approached him. She reached for his hands and held them in hers.

"Sam, I can't imagine going through a whole day without you." She touched his face.

"Sidney … "

"It's okay, Sam. I know you don't have the same feelings for me."

He caressed her arms. "You shouldn't go making such assumptions. I've shut down my feelings for so long, I'm not sure if I'm capable of feeling much of anything for anyone except for my boys. And, well … look, Sidney, I'll get you back to Dan. So far, you haven't done anything that—"

Sidney gasped. "You know about Danik?"

Sam folded his arms across his chest. "Actually, I've known about him since the first day. You called for him a couple of times in your delirium. Sounds like he's pretty special to you." Sam returned to his packing.

Sidney frowned. "You never mentioned that you knew about him."

"There wasn't any evidence to show that he participated in the espionage, other than to deliver you to the base." Sam grabbed extra pairs of socks and shorts. "Wasn't all that important." Sam disappeared into his bathroom to find his travel shaving kit. He hollered from the bathroom. "Anyway, I'm sure he's going to be relieved to get you back, right?"

Sidney didn't answer. Sam returned to the bedroom.

"Right?" he repeated.

Sidney smiled. "Uh huh."

Sam tossed the kits into the suitcase. "So, there's no problem. You'll forget about the miserable S.O.B. who kept you locked up and threatened to carry out your execution, right?" Sam straightened up from his suitcase and saw her still grinning at him. "What?" he asked.

She moved close to him. "You're right about one thing, Sam. Dan is special. I love him."

Sam turned back to his suitcase. "So everyone gets what they want."

Sidney grabbed Sam's arm and pulled him back toward her. "There's something you should know about Dan."

Sam pulled away and opened his dresser drawer. "Think I have a pretty good idea already except maybe why he let you go off on some damn suicidal mission." He slammed his dresser drawer shut. "How the hell could he do that?"

Sidney stepped between him and his dresser. "Because he knows that even in death, we can't be separated." She paused and looked into his eyes. "Sam, Danik is my brother." Sidney placed a brief kiss below his ear, and pulled back slightly with her lips lingering near his mouth. "There's no one else. There never has been anyone that I love … the way I love you."

Sam couldn't speak for the moment. The discovery that Sidney wasn't involved with someone else had opened up a flood of emotions he'd struggled to hold in check. He wanted to hold her, touch her. His need rose to the surface. It had been a year since he'd felt the burning passion of wanting to be with a woman.

"Sidney, you're quite, well, special." He caressed her face. Returning to his suitcase, he went through the motions of checking everything. "Got to admit you've flicked a switch in my life. I'd pretty well given up. Somehow, because of you, I've found hope. I'm grateful to you."

He closed the suitcase and placed it on the floor. He had to keep focused on the fact that he was leaving her, would probably never see her again. There was no way to predict how the struggle with the admiral would play out, but he was certain Sidney would never trust him again after this. He had to remain objective.

"I have one request," Sidney teased.

"Name it."

"Take me sailing some day, Sam, if we get out of this."

The request touched Sam. He recalled the vision in which he and Sidney were trying to find a safe place to anchor their sailing ship near the island's shore beyond the reef.

"Any place special?" he asked.

Sidney gazed into his eyes. "No. Just some place where there's the sea, the ship, and you and me. No one else, no rule book."

"Sidney…"

Sidney walked close to put her arms around his waist and rested her head against his shoulder. "If you had a choice, Sam, where would you like to be right now?"

What would it hurt? he wondered. He wanted her to feel safe. He owed her that much and more. But he couldn't surrender his heart. Not now when his sons' future depended upon him being clear headed. He held her tightly to his chest and whispered in her ear.

"I'd like to take you dancing—a nice slow waltz around the dance floor."

He lifted her face to his and kissed her passionately. In a single breath, all the barriers, all the rules, all the fears slipped aside. Sam unfastened the buttons of her shirt and eased the garment over her shoulders. It slipped to the floor around her ankles. Soon his uniform fell to the floor and became lost in the folds of her clothes as Sam and Sidney began their intimate dance.

20. Drowning an Admiral

Saturday, July 13, Pearl Harbor, Hawaii

As the first rays of the morning sun swept into Sam's bedroom, he woke to find Sidney sitting in her lotus position at the foot of the bed. She was deep in her meditation. The kiss of the sunrise touched her hair and graced the soft curves of her naked body. He saw the glow on her face and thought to himself that she was indeed a goddess—full of magic and mystery.

He shifted abruptly, hoping to get her attention. She slowly opened her eyes. All too soon, it was nearing time for Sam to disembark the *Nonnah*. Quietly they showered together, gently touching, softly kissing, scarcely breathing.

While Sidney dried her hair, Sam prepared a small breakfast. The tropical breeze washed away his anxiety, but it wouldn't be easy to say goodbye. He briefly considered taking Sidney off the ship and releasing her into the Hawaiian mists, although he knew he couldn't. If Admiral Garland discovered he'd set her free, Simon and Nathan would disappear before he reached New Seattle.

By the time Sidney joined him on his veranda, the sunrise was casting a rosy tone on the white walls of the veranda. She sat down on the deck in front of him and quietly began her ritual of giving thanks while Sam poured her a cup of coffee.

"What are you particularly grateful for today, Sidney?" he asked when she opened her eyes.

She patted his knee. "For the love and guidance of the Guardians, for all the trials and tribulations that taught me tolerance and courage, and for all the events that led me to you."

Sam nodded. "It's easy to be grateful for the good things in plain view. It takes a higher soul like yours to be grateful for your troubles, the gifts hidden in the darkness."

Sidney smiled. "Spoken like a true Guardian."

Sidney became quiet as she nibbled at her toast and cheese. Sam waited for her to speak, but he became concerned that her silence was born of worry.

He touched her hair lightly and asked, "What's on your mind?"

She hesitated, struggling with an internal conflict. She stood up and walked toward the ship's railing, and Sam followed her. He tried to be patient until he glanced at his watch.

"We don't have much time. I have to put you back in safekeeping and head to the airport."

Sidney appeared lost in the distant Hawaiian mountains. She nodded as if receiving advice from the island's spirits. Her eyes filled with tears.

"Sam, you can't come back to the ship."

"Explain."

She replied as if still in her trance. "Once you've taken your boys from the admiral, he'll have no advantage over you. The admiral's paranoia runs deep. And there are others, a woman, who considers you a great risk away from the admiral's control. You know too much. You may suffer the same fate as Joy. Take your boys and disappear with them. Please don't come back to this ship."

"Do you see some prediction?"

"Only a basic sketch. More of a feeling than a clear picture of the future. Admiral Garland isn't the real threat. And I believe there are those who are not worthy of your trust."

Sam shook his head. He knew that his life hung on a precipice and every step must be carefully placed.

"My son's lives are all that matter. You don't know how they've changed since living under a strictly regimented household. I'll do whatever it takes to get them out of there. And I'll be coming back. End of discussion."

"I can get off this ship myself. I have other resources. Once the *Nonnah* is docked in New Seattle, I—"

He kissed her forehead and led her toward his office. The kiss had been effective before at distracting her. His motives for coming back to the ship were clear in his mind. If necessary, he'd be paying for his freedom with the transfer of Sidney to Admiral Garland—not as a prisoner, but as a powerful ally—or so the admiral would be led to believe.

Sidney stepped away from Sam. The kiss had been mechanical. She recognized his manipulation and refused to be swayed. She brushed aside her annoyance and centered herself.

Finding her center in her Guardian soul, she said, "Whatever you're planning, don't forget the higher good. Whatever action you create in the universe will return to you, and you'll suffer the consequences of any harm done to others."

"Right." He was only half listening to her. With each passing minute he felt the shackles of the past year slip away. Nothing would get in his way now.

"Sam, you're not listening!"

Sam smiled at her and stepped into his office.

Sidney trailed along behind him. "They're going to kill you!"

"I've never run from a fight." He went to his desk and activated his computer and security systems.

"You need to think of your boys. They need you more than ever."

Sam's guilt about his failure in not being a better dad exploded to the surface. "Don't start telling me what a lousy father I've been!"

"That isn't what I meant."

There was a knock at Sam's door.

"Come in!" he shouted.

Commander Moon entered. "Everything okay, Captain?"

Sam straightened into his officer's posture. "Yes. How are the repairs coming along?"

"The engine's purring like a grouchy old lion, and the deck's temporary repairs are done, at least as much as we can do here. Got sheets of plywood covering the bigger holes. I've advised New Seattle Naval Base that more permanent deck repairs need to be scheduled when we arrive. You're ready to disembark, sir?"

"Not quite. I'll be off in twenty minutes. I'll see you at the gangplank.

Just before the commander left, he set a bright yellow shopping bag on Sam's desk.

"This just arrived for you, sir."

Sam checked his E-mail. The officers had returned to the ship and were reporting all systems ready for return to sea.

"The *Nonnah* is ready and so am I. Let's go." Sam firmly displayed military conduct. He was brisk and in control.

"Sam, I'm sorry. I don't believe you're a lousy father."

Sam studied Sidney momentarily. "You see something in your crystal ball?"

"Not a crystal ball. My intuition … and other ways." She moved close to him. "Have you packed all your things? Your crystal and Celeste's feather?"

"No. Just going to use my wits and a dab of gun powder, if necessary."

"No, Sam!"

"Don't worry. I'll just put a little dent in the admiral's armor. Nothing fatal." Sam paused, and then went to his desk and retrieved the feather and the crystal.

"Here, you take my crystal, and I'll bring the feather. Feel better?"

"No, you'll need the crystal more than me."

Sam tossed his crystal and the envelope with the feather into his suitcase. Picking up his luggage and the bag Moon had delivered, he led her out to the main deck.

"We have to take a bit of a detour. Watch your step," he said as he pointed to sheets of wood lying on the deck.

"Sam, will the routine stay the same? Will I have my meals in the boardroom?"

Sam led Sidney to a stairway, and they descended.

"I've advised Rhett to ensure a guard is with you at all times. It's his call about the meals. He may decide to modify things. I've asked Lorna to keep track of you. I mean … "

"I know."

They reached Sidney's cell and greeted the guard. Sam opened the door and led her into her room, flicking on the ceiling light before shutting the door behind him.

"Commander Moon will be the only one who can open this door. By the way, he knows about your ability to unlock things. All the officers know. It was necessary to ensure they were diligent."

"Uh huh. What else do they know about me?"

Her eyes conveyed the love she had for him, and it softened his resolve. Sam pulled her close.

"That you're a very, very strange woman." He kissed her lips softly and stepped away. "Sidney, will you tell me anything more about your activity on the base or how I can help?"

"No, Sam."

"Didn't figure you would. Had to ask one more time, just in case. Here's a small gift." He handed the yellow bag to her.

"This is for me?" she asked, her eyes wide.

Sam's comlink sounded. "Captain, your driver's here."

"I'll be there in fifteen minutes."

Sidney put her nose close to the inside of the bag. "It has a wonderful, light fragrance."

"It's frangipani blossoms, temple tree. Hawaiians call it plumeria. Often used in weddings, I guess. Supposed to have special significance."

"Oh, Sam," she whispered. As she pulled the pale green, fragrant, pillar candle out of the bag, petals of fresh yellow blossoms tumbled out and fell at her feet. She set the candle in its crystal base, shaped like the plumeria blossoms, on her side table. She scooped up the fragrant petals from the floor and placed them around the candle.

"Here, I'll light it for you. You can keep the lighter. Just don't burn down my ship, okay?" He tried to sound serious, but failed.

Sidney's smile touched him deeply. There was no escaping her allure and the way his rule book vanished at the mere thought of kissing her. He shut off the ceiling light.

"Thank you, Sam. It's so beautiful."

He grinned. "So I don't have to take it back?"

She shook her head, wiping away a tear. "I love you, Samaru Waterhouse."

He paused momentarily. "I know." In the soft candlelight, he kissed her one more time—a long, passionate kiss. Then he released her.

Sidney stepped back and looked intently into his face. She assumed the role of a sage Guardian, wise and powerful.

"Trust your intuition. Know that you have guides who will help you. All you have to do is ask. Open yourself to their messages. You have access to far more power than you're conscious of right now."

He grinned. "What, more feathers under my bed?"

She remained steadfast. "Celeste and others—they will be there for you, always. Above all else, trust your intuition." She lightly tapped his chest over his heart. "It will lead you to the higher good."

Opening the cell door, he glanced back to see her standing in the candlelight. Its warm glow shimmered on the gray walls and onto Sidney's warm brown hair and silhouette. He burned the image into his memory.

"I'll be back, Sidney."

She hesitated to respond. She was holding on to every last moment and putting it away for safekeeping. She stood tall. Softly, she whispered, "I'll be here, Sam."

He shut the door, activated the locking mechanism, and reassured himself that Sidney would remain safe during his absence. She was invincible. Every time someone tried to destroy her, she survived through her powerful connection with her legion of gods.

Sam rented a car when he arrived at the New Seattle airport early Saturday afternoon and drove to the Naval Base. He dashed through the rain into the base administration building. Inside, the security staff met him.

"Check in here, sir," said the guard.

Sam offered his hand to the scanner. He left his luggage behind the security desk and ensured his pistol was secure in its shoulder harness. He had a meeting with the admiral in half an hour. In the meantime, he wanted to retrace Sidney's path. He stood where she hid under the steps at the subbasement and thought it strange no one had seen her. On the basement level he found the storage room.

Searching the room for anything out of the ordinary, he discovered an old desk and tried to open the drawers. One was stuck. He worked at the drawer to see why it was jammed and eventually freed a piece of cardboard that had been wedged along its side. Inside he found Sidney's shoes and gloves. *So this is where you left your shoes,* he thought. He noted the grease on the gloves and wondered where she'd been. He put the shoes and gloves back in the drawer and made his way to the stairwell.

As he headed up to the admiral's office, he felt in control. The admiral was going to have to swim for his life, drowning in his paranoia. A few suggestions implicating Butchart, and the admiral would be his. Sam felt anger well up. He'd get his revenge and his life back.

As he stepped into the admiral's office, his heart beat rapidly. He took a deep breath, held it for a moment, and let it go. Quickly, he stepped up to Admiral Garland's desk and stood at attention.

"Captain Waterhouse reporting, sir."

"At ease."

Admiral Garland remained seated at his desk. From the position of his military throne, he looked Sam over. He tapped the desk with a pen and did his best to sneer and thrust the weight of his authority in Sam's direction. Sam had the impression that the man had shrunk and aged since the last time he'd seen him, only a couple months earlier.

"Let's get down to business, Waterhouse. It appears you may have found a connection between Captain Butchart and the prisoner. He did become agitated when I asked about these so-called Guardians. However, it doesn't prove any disloyalty."

Sam swallowed his hostility. "Admiral, Butchart is a Guardian. I know this without any doubt. How do you know he's never used his unusual abilities to manipulate you? Perhaps I wasn't clear in my reports about just how powerful these people are."

"Oh, for Christ's sake. Butchart has yet to display any unusual tricks other than getting the truth out of liars."

"Not tricks, Admiral. I assure you. You won't find these people in a carnival. They live in secret, isolated from government controls. If he hasn't told you about his past, you can't trust him, sir."

Admiral Garland burst out of his chair, sending it skidding back against the wall. "Captain Butchart is far more loyal and trustworthy than you."

Sam leaped out of his chair.

"Would you bet your career or your life on it, Admiral?" Sam paused to let the remark strike its mark. "If you had special powers, if you could manipulate energy and move things, could you resist using it to gain wealth and power?" Sam lowered his voice. "Admiral, has there ever been an incident when you wondered how something happened, something connected with Captain Butchart?"

Admiral Garland hesitated. He moved away from his desk. Sam stepped forward, pressing for an answer.

"Anything, Admiral. It would've appeared sudden, without any known cause—perhaps thought of as an odd coincidence at the time, simply a random occurrence."

Admiral Garland waved his hand in the air. "Hell, things like that happen all the time. Doesn't mean shit."

Sam could see the admiral was trying to shrug off something. Something bothered him. It was time to let his doubts fester on their own and change tactics.

"Admiral, there's something else you need to know. Your secret project is in jeopardy."

"What secret project?"

Sam lowered his voice. "A certain file you call *Thy Kingdom Come*. The file my wife discovered, the one that ultimately caused her death. I never knew the significance behind that file until I got our prisoner to talk."

The admiral eyed him suspiciously. "And what does she have to do with this so-called file?"

"She found it in your computer!"

The admiral smirked. "Now I know you've gone over the edge, Waterhouse."

"Sir, just listen, please. That file refers to a proposed new energy source, sun crystals." Sam watched the admiral's reaction. His eyes had lit up at the words *sun crystal*. "According to our prisoner, some people believe these sun crystals are powerful."

"Captain Waterhouse, I'm beginning to believe either you've become mentally deranged or soft headed over that prisoner, or both!"

"Do you recall when I reported that the prisoner gave a demonstration on how she was able to unlock doors?"

The admiral glowered. "Go on!"

"Sir, she did that without any crystal. She doesn't need it. Both she and Captain Butchart have a paranormal ability to perform magic. It's not sleight of hand or some illusion, sir." Sam began his tactic to lead the admiral down the wrong path. "Sir, those crystals I've been transporting to you are little more than circus props."

Sam noted that the admiral was making every effort to appear not affected. He restrained himself from pacing as he normally did when agitated.

"Waterhouse, the military has been supporting a variety of research activities. I assure you we're not spending valuable resources on 'circus props.'"

"Admiral, cults and gypsies having been toting crystals around since the dawn of time. Are you sure you haven't been misled to support a hocus pocus operation? I know your scientists have been studying these crystals and may have had some success. Is that not so?"

Admiral Garland became flushed at the insinuation of being duped.

"Captain, we, er, I am preparing to demonstrate a new energy source that will revolutionize the entire planet. I wouldn't risk appearing the fool if I wasn't certain the government will be impressed. And if it happens to include an unusual form of energy, what of it?"

Sam wondered just who "we" was. "And will Frank Butchart play a part in that demonstration?"

"The what, who, and how are classified, Waterhouse."

"Sir, I'm betting the scientists have experienced success only when Captain Butchart is present during the experiments. He's a Guardian, Admiral. He has powers like Sidney. Your scientists' claims regarding the crystals are bogus. It's Butchart, sir. When a Guardian stokes up his mystical fires, it appears as if the crystal is doing the work. They glow, but that's the trick, sir. The real power is coming from the Guardian, not that rock."

Sam was sure he was creating doubt in the admiral's mind, perhaps to the point of postponing the demonstration. He had no doubt the admiral was going to go a few rounds with Butchart before the weekend was over.

The admiral's comlink sounded, announcing an incoming call. He took a breath and slowly released the tension from his face.

"Waterhouse, we'll continue this talk at another time. You're coming by the house to pick up the boys, correct? Perkins will accompany them, as you know."

"Yes, fine. Taking my boys out for supper tonight and then to the sailing races tomorrow."

After being dismissed, Sam returned to the storage room to retrieve the gloves and running shoes he'd found earlier. He stuffed the gloves into a pocket in his blazer and folded the jacket around the shoes, making sure they were concealed.

21. Savannah's Gift

Late Afternoon, Saturday, July 13

As soon as he arrived at his hotel, Sam placed a call to the police station. Once he was connected to Clay's comlink, the two men agreed to meet for coffee.

At first Sam said little to Clay about Sidney or his role as the admiral's executioner. He had to test the waters to see if he could still trust the detective. He talked about ports, the ship, his crew, and his boys. After a while, Sam sat back in his chair.

"You were right, Clay. Should have taken my boys and disappeared. Never thought the admiral would've been so desperate."

"Uh huh." Clay leaned forward. "Sam, I got this niggling feeling in my gut."

"Like what?"

"You're not here just to spend a few days with your boys."

Sam remained quiet and waited for the detective to continue with his theory. Clay also sat quietly, staring at Sam.

Sam grinned. "You know, this coffee's a hell of a lot better than the last one you bought me."

"Sam!"

"Yes?"

Clay groaned. "Oh, you military sorts."

Sam leaned forward and whispered. "I know. We clam up tighter than a bull frog's ass."

The two laughed, but Clay didn't drop it. "Sam, what have you got up your sleeve?"

"Relax, Clay. Left my gun at the hotel."

Clay shook his head. "Thank God."

"There's one favor I'd like to ask of you." Sam grabbed the bag he'd brought with him and handed it to Clay. "What's the chance of getting your lab people to go over these items? See if they can tell where they've been, what's on them, that kind of stuff."

Clay peered into the bag. "Running shoes and gloves. Where'd you find these?"

"They're part of an investigation. I received a prisoner almost two weeks ago. During interrogation I discovered she'd been sent to the base for the purpose of accessing the same confidential file Joy had opened. She was apprehended and charged with spying and sabotage."

"Who sent her?"

"Badger."

"Really? Now, what are the chances you knew about Badger when I was investigating Joy's murder? You know he's dead?"

Sam shifted in his chair. It was time to come clean. "Yes, I know he's dead, and yes, I should've told you about Joy's involvement with him."

Clay waved his finger at Sam. "You didn't trust me, sailor. Go on."

"While on my ship, some pirates tried to capture her for execution."

Clay sat back and smiled. "God, you have an interesting life! This prisoner have a name?"

"Sidney Davenport. And there's someone else who's anxious to shut her up—Captain Butchart."

"Ah, yes. Frank. He and I didn't see eye to eye as I recall."

"She's confessed to all said crimes but she refuses to reveal where she hid the copy she made of that damn file. According to the prisoner, Admiral Garland's gearing up for a demonstration involving the file. She's convinced that the whole planet will be thrown into chaos as a result. If you can identify where these clothes have been, I might be able to find that file and learn why so many people are ending up dead or missing over it."

Clay raised his eyebrows. "You after my job, Sam?"

"Someone went to a lot of expense and risk to eliminate this prisoner. Just a guess, but would that someone be the Madame you mentioned last year?"

"Difficult to say. Some good police officers have disappeared while doing research on her activities. No evidence, no known address, no nothing."

"I think you're a smart cop. And with me poking around for that file, you might find your life is going to get a lot more interesting in the next day or so."

He pushed the bag of clothes toward the detective.

"So why don't you take this stuff to *your* lab?" Clay asked.

Sam thought carefully over his response. "I'm still under suspicion among some of the brass. Your staff would have a more objective approach."

Clay leaned forward. "This Sidney Davenport have some redeeming qualities?"

Sam hesitated and cleared his throat. "Some might think so. Anyway, she's different, a bit weird. One of a kind, you might say. How about it?"

Clay leaned back. "I should be able to get it by the legal beagles."

He folded the top of the bag down and agreed to call Sam when he got the lab results. The rain had nearly stopped by the time they parted, and as Sam walked back to his hotel, he focused only on the next step ahead. As people brushed by him, their sounds and their motion barely entered his consciousness. Pools of water reflected the city lights, but as bright and dazzling as the scene was, it faded behind the candle glow in a small cell on his ship.

Once he'd showered and changed into civvies, he drove his rented car to the admiral's mansion. His sons were waiting for him at the top of the front steps. As Sam was about to get out to greet them, they ran down the stairs and jumped into another vehicle. Perkins, the admiral's private guard, waved at Sam and instructed him to follow. Disappointed, Sam returned to his car and followed Perkins. They arrived at an upscale Japanese dining room and were seated, with Perkins at a separate table nearby.

The evening started off with awkward silence on the part of both Simon and Nathan. This was getting to be typical, but the tension was more pronounced than the last time Sam had been to visit.

Simon, twelve years old, was much like Sam. Things had to be in their right place and work perfectly. He had no patience for sloppiness and was intolerant of lies and devious people. Nathan, ten, was a hugger and hated anyone being mad at him, especially his mom. He wore his emotions on his sleeve, and it annoyed Simon immensely.

Both boys sat nervously at the dinner table, carrying on polite conversation in between long gaps of silence. They fidgeted in their seats and toyed with their food. When Sam suggested they attend a sailing tournament the next day, the boys half-heartedly agreed to the plan. The vague distance Sam had come to expect between him and his sons had become a gulf of solemn indifference.

He watched his boys. They avoided eye contact with him, but he saw hopelessness in their faces. It was the same look that had been on his face for the past year. He wondered what it would take to wake them up. He wasn't a Sidney, but he wondered if some of her diversion tactics would work on them. Perhaps, if his behavior was bizarre enough, it might work.

He let out a short, almost imperceptible chuckle and glanced at them. No reaction They continued to play with their chopsticks. He tried again, deeper and louder. Still no reaction. He escalated to a brief laugh.

Simon looked up. "What?"

"Oh, sorry. Nothing. Just a thought." Sam laughed more vigorously, placing his hand over his mouth as if to abate his merriment.

Nathan glanced at him sideways, and Sam made exaggerated moves as if attempting to contain his laughter. His shoulders convulsed, holding back the contractions of a snicker that wanted to be released.

"All right!" exclaimed Simon. "What's going on? Did I miss some stupid joke?"

Sam waved his hand in the air. "No, son. It's nothing. Really. Enjoying your dinner?" Sam choked back another chuckle.

"Fine!" retorted Simon.

Sam let out a long laugh as though he couldn't contain it any longer. He eventually regained his composure and wiped tears that had escaped his eyes. Both of his sons eyed him suspiciously.

"Sorry," he whispered. "Anyone for dessert?"

Again he placed his hand over his mouth to restrain a snort that found its way out through his nose.

Nathan frowned. "Dad! Christ, you on something?"

Simon gave Nathan a swat, barely grazing his shoulder. "Keep your voice down and watch your language, Boozebrain."

Nathan gave Simon a shove back. "Mind your own business, Fuzzballs." The shoving continued until Sam interjected.

"Boys, hey, hey, let's keep it down." Then switching to a dignified manner and a snobbish tone of voice, he said, "We're family. We don't treat each other that way. Fuzzballs, you apologize to Boozebrain, and Boozebrain you apologize to Fuzzballs."

The shock on his sons' faces was more than he could stand. He burst out into a full-scale, genuine belly laugh. His hand hit the table, which sent a plate flying to the floor and a glass of water spilling onto Sam's pants. He bolted upright, which sent his chair tumbling back into another patron's elbow, knocking the food from his chopsticks high into the air and over into the next table's soup, splashing its owner.

Simon and Nathan, bewildered by their dad's unusual behavior, stood up in stunned amazement. It wasn't long before a familiar seed began to sprout within them. At first, they did their best to try to look disgusted. But Nathan was the first to let out a giggle.

"Hey, Fuzzballs, you gonna tell the admiral about this?" he asked.

Simon grinned. "Nope."

The cascade of mishaps dissolved the tension and transformed the strained bonds into a river of love that between father and son and brother and brother was unlike anything else. Underneath the pain of separation and loss, the river danced and sang a joyous song within Sam's chest.

When they parted for the evening, the boys happily agreed to get together the next day for the sailing tournament finals.

Sidney sat on the edge of her bed and tried to connect with Danik. He seemed to be involved in an intense group discussion. He sent her a brief wash of love and indicated he'd check in with her later.

For the moment, she simply sat in her lotus position, freeing her mind to the universe. A fragrance entered her space. It wasn't the yellow plumeria blossoms still brightly gracing the base of her candle. The fragrance was softer, lighter. It came and went like musical notes rising and falling. It was a spirit, knocking on Sidney's inner door and ever so gently caressing her face with its fragrant form. Touching, and then not touching. Tentatively seeking, and then receding.

Sidney sat quietly, allowing the being to express itself in its own way and time. She saw nothing at first. Gradually, subtle messages began to radiate from the visitor. They weren't formed in words or thoughts. Instead, the messages came in the form of visions, feelings, musical notes that translated into a knowing within Sidney's flesh.

At first, the messages were clear and beautiful. They were of the being's love and passion — a profound hope and aching desire to become a part of some desired change. There were moments when Sidney experienced an urgency, a breathless anticipation of great transformations.

Then Dark visions, hollow and without the touch of the Creator's breath, surfaced. It produced such terror within Sidney that she gasped and asked the entity to not take her there. The visions ceased immediately, but she knew the entity continued to carry that focus in some part of its reality.

Never before had Sidney been in contact with such a powerful spirit. And yet, as strong as it was, it also had a gentleness and innocence only found in small children. As she had this realization, Sidney saw the spirit take shape. Tentatively, the form stepped from the ethereal dimensions and shyly approached. Sidney recognized her instantly. She'd seen her before, but the child spirit had always kept her distance, always remained aloof but curious.

When she'd told Greystone about the child spirit, who appeared about the size of a four-year-old, he'd nodded and advised Sidney to send loving energy to it.

"Her name is Savannah," he'd told her. "She waits."

"Waits for what?" the eleven-year-old Sidney had asked.

Greystone had never answered. It remained a mystery. Sidney saw the child spirit only every two or three years. Each time she tried to connect with Savannah, the child would withdraw and disappear.

As Sidney sat on the bed, watching Savannah approach, she remembered seeing the child spirit briefly only a few months earlier. It seemed odd that the child would reappear so soon. Perhaps she had a special message this time. Sidney was determined to not give the spirit any reason to withdraw. It was difficult. Every fiber of her being wanted to reach for the child and hold her.

Savannah was small and appeared delicate. Curly, dark hair framed her small, chubby face. Savannah brushed away the curls that had fallen in front of her eyes. The girl wore blue denim coveralls over a bright red print shirt. She was barefoot. When the child was within arm's length, Sidney saw beneath long lashes, brown eyes that revealed a soul of unfathomable knowing.

"Hello, Savannah," Sidney said ever so softly. "I'm happy you've come to visit me."

For the first time Sidney could recall, Savannah smiled. Her eyes nearly disappeared as the plump cheeks became more round and rosy. The child took another step closer. Sidney ached to reach out and caress her face. She breathed deeply and touched her only in the way Greystone had advised — a glowing, pure white light containing tiny droplets of the colors of the rainbow traveled from Sidney's entire body and showered over Savannah.

Savannah twirled under the light as it cascaded over her form. She giggled as she lifted her arms toward the ceiling and danced in a circle. When the shower of love had been completely received, Savannah revealed something she held tightly in her small hands.

They were red rose petals. As her fingers unfolded, the petals lifted and joined to form a large red rose. Gradually, the petals closed in to form a rose bud.

Sidney was in awe of the miracle. Savannah looked at her with a mischievous expression and motioned with her finger for Sidney to lean forward. Sidney did so, nearly touching Savannah's forehead with her lips. As she considered planting a brief kiss, Savannah raised the rose bud to her lips and blew. The bud dissolved into a glowing red mist. Surprised, Sidney gasped in wonder. In so doing, she inhaled the mist.

A warm sensation unlike any other traveled throughout her body. Before she could utter a word of gratitude, the child spirit spoke. Her voice had a musical tone, like the sound of children laughing and being completely at peace with their connection to their higher selves. It surprised Sidney into silence.

It wasn't so much that it was the first time Savannah had spoken; it was what Savannah had said that shocked her. The moment before Savannah had slipped back into her world, she'd tenderly caressed Sidney's face with her tiny fingers and softly said, "Mommy."

Sidney inhaled and held it. It was the only method she knew of to keep herself centered in a crisis.

"Breathe deeply," her beloved mentor had always told her on the days when her world turned upside down. "Step outside the trouble. See it as being separate from you. See it from the perspective of your higher self. Then make your choices."

It had always worked when she remembered to do it, but this time was different. It seemed impossible to step outside the trouble. Sidney was flooded with emotions ranging from sheer delight and exhilaration to utter turmoil. She calmed enough to notice Danik was waiting for her.

"Shall I make an appointment, miss," he said in a mocking tone. "You seem to be rather occupied."

Sidney was never so grateful for his humor. "You should talk, Mr. Busybody. What's up?"

"Got some irons in the fire. Waiting for your ship to come in, if you'll excuse the expression. Tried getting into the base but —"

"Danik, you didn't!"

"Easy, girl. No, not me. Somebody else. Anyway, no one but the military is allowed in there now. That memory rod with the file will likely remain in that elevator shaft till the building falls down. Where's Mr. Wonderful?"

Sidney smiled and fidgeted. "Last I heard he was flying to New Seattle."

"Don't play coy with me, little sister. You know exactly where he is. Maybe he can help us get that file."

Sidney glared at her brother and shook her finger at him. "He's got enough trouble."

Danik chuckled. "Yeah, like what!"

"He wants to get his boys away from Admiral Garland. The admiral will do whatever it takes to stop him. I'm worried that Sam, I mean Captain Waterhouse, will do anything to get them back."

"Yes, Sidney, I understand Sam's situation."

"No you don't. Danik, he's a waking Guardian. He's in a very vulnerable state right now. We could lose him again."

"Again?"

"Yes, he found his way to the island. Then his wife was killed and he got off course."

"Are his powers manifesting yet?"

"Yes, and he's very powerful when focused. But Danik, he's extremely desperate to get his sons back and to get out from under the admiral's control. If he allows his anger to rule his actions, if he causes harm, he could slip further into the Dark sleep, perhaps beyond our reach."

"But don't you see, if he helps us get that file, the information on it may be enough for the underground to take down the admiral. If the admiral's out of action, our problems are solved, including Sam's."

"The admiral's not the problem, Danik. And, I'm not sure taking him down, as you put it, is the right way to go. He hasn't always been ruthless. He once was a very wise man. Just like Frank Butchart."

"Yeah, well, I've got some plans for good old Frank, too."

Sidney turned her back to Danik. It was frightening to hear him talk like that.

"Sorry, Sidney. Didn't mean that the way it sounded. Greystone wants me to bring him back home. Remember? Come and sit with me."

The siblings sat down on the floor facing each other. Danik got up on his knees and held out his hands, palms up. Sidney did the same and laid her palms onto his.

"You seem rather tense. Is something else wrong?" he asked.

Sidney released the essence of her energy into her hands and let her secrets flow along with her love for her brother. Her experience with Savannah rose to the surface.

"Yes, I remember Savy. She's quite a ... Sidney!" His eyes were wide. "Oh my God, Sidney, you're pregnant!"

"Thank you for announcing that in such a sensitive manner. Been in too much of a state of shock to sense anything but terror and joy, all at the same time."

Danik held her and rocked her in his arms. "My baby sister's going to have a baby—Savannah. Uncle Danik. That sounds nice. You think Savy will like me?" Danik paused. "Does he love you, Sid? Sam, I mean."

"Hard to tell. He's spent the last year shut down, and he's very good at hiding his feelings, physically *and* energetically."

All too soon Danik released her. "Got to be going, Sid."

"Don't say anything if you see him. Okay?"

"Uh huh. Love you."

22. Madame's Spy

Early Morning, Sunday, July 14, New Seattle

Admiral Garland arrived at the naval base early Sunday morning. He hurried to his office without acknowledging the security personnel when they greeted him. Slamming the door shut, he flicked on his computer and entered codes to bring up the secret files.

"Computer, open file *Thy Kingdom Come*."

He searched through the document's subfolders, hungrily looking for the research reports. Entering more codes, he opened the file he was certain had proven the crystals were capable of transforming matter. He'd tried to dismiss Sam's outrageous claims, but all night the captain's words echoed through his mind. The only way he was going to silence them was with solid evidence against his crazy theory.

Glancing over the report, he retraced the scientist's data. There were inconsistencies in the crystals' response to manipulation. Sometimes the crystals obeyed the energy stimulus. Other times, the crystal remained lifeless. He searched for a pattern. Finally, he found it. There it was—so obvious now that he was searching for it. The only times the crystals appeared to function were when Butchart was present.

"Damn!" Activating his comlink, he shouted, "Captain Butchart, report to my office!"

In the minutes before Butchart arrived, the admiral devised a plan. He calmed down and sat casually behind his desk. He wanted to see how much of a fight Butchart would put up if he was told he'd not be present during the upcoming demonstration. When Butchart arrived, the admiral directed him to sit.

"Frank, I've been advised that the East American Naval Port requires a temporary placement of someone with your skills. You've been selected. I'll need you to advise who can perform your duties in your absence."

Butchart was briefly stunned. "Sir, we're busy setting up security for the government leaders' visit to our base next week for the demonstration. Our most influential leaders will be present, and they demand a high level of security. Surely another security officer is capable of filling the East American position, sir."

"No, Frank. I know in your efficient hands security has already been planned and details addressed. All that's needed is for your staff to carry out your instructions. You'll leave in the morning."

Butchart began to almost convulse in his chair and stood up. "Admiral, I must be present during the demonstration."

"Sit!" For a while, the admiral simply sent daggers of rage in Butchart's direction. Butchart had become his military confidant and his personal advisor. Now, like all others, he'd been proven unworthy.

Butchart did his best to regain his composure. He'd been through countless moments over the years when the admiral had appeared to be on the verge of personally conducting a beheading. He lowered back down into the chair, shifting his position only once.

The admiral stood and unlocked a drawer in his desk. He pulled out a crystal. As the sunlight caught the facets, jagged rays of light swirled throughout the office and into Butchart's eyes. He winced. The admiral placed the crystal gingerly on his desk as though it was important that it sat just so.

"I know why you believe it's urgent that you be on this base during the demonstration. You!" He thrust his finger toward the captain. "You're responsible for the success of the scientists' work. You turned the water to wine. You, and not the scientists, made the chairs disappear. You, Frank!"

"Sir?" Butchart placed a look of puzzlement on his face.

"You heard me. Activate this, this rock. Make it dance, lower the temperature in this room, blow up this whole goddamn desk, if you like. Hey, how about making it rain. That's it." He waved his hand in the air. "Make it rain, Frank."

"Sir, the scientists—"

"Forget the scientists. Unless you're some cult voodoo headhunter, this is just a damn rock. Isn't it?"

Butchart was sweating and becoming flushed. "I don't believe that's true, sir."

"Don't you lie to me. The only times the so-called sun crystals worked were when you were present. *You* made the crystals work, not the scientists. You're part of some damn cult!"

Butchart leaped out of his chair. "And who gave you that line of bullshit?"

"As a matter of fact, it was Captain Waterhouse."

The muscles in Butchart's face flexed with the clenching of his teeth. He shook his head. "That's interesting, Admiral. Why would he have any knowledge of the crystals?"

"Apparently our prisoner told him."

"Goddamn it, Admiral. Why the hell are we even considering what she's telling Waterhouse? Just because his brain has probably shifted a bit south of his head doesn't mean we have to give any credit to a prisoner's lies. She'll say anything to save her skin."

The admiral moved around his desk to stand directly in front of Butchart.

"In every lie, I've discovered there's a hint of truth."

He went to his door and opened it to see if anyone was eavesdropping. All was quiet. He closed the door and returned to Butchart.

"How successful is the demonstration going to be if you're several thousand miles away?"

Butchart looked away and remained silent.

"Damn you, Frank, you have unique powers, and you kept that valuable information from me." He stepped close to Butchart. "Why?" he shouted, thrusting his fist up to Butchart's face.

Butchart flinched. "Sir, if I'd told you ten years ago that I could move objects from one place to another location, or that I could transform water to wine, I know exactly what you would've done. You'd have fired me on the spot. You'd have never even asked for a demonstration. I even tested that ground with you. Do you remember me telling you that some people have unique powers? You laughed so hard you nearly choked!"

"Never mind that for now. If Madame finds out we've deceived her, *we are dead!* She believes our scientists are capable of unlocking secret methods that'll allow her to command these damn rocks herself. Will she be able to do that?"

Butchart hesitated. "It's possible, sir. But not without considerable training."

The admiral slumped into his chair. "Well, how do you suggest we give her that good news?"

"We don't, sir. As long as I'm present during the demonstration next week, she'll be reasonably satisfied with her scientists. With me always accompanying you, you'll never fail."

"I need to know more about just who the hell you are." The revelations were hitting the admiral too fast. He didn't know who to trust. "Finish your immediate business then stay off the base until we can discuss this at my home office tomorrow night. Now get out!"

Butchart nearly ran to his office. He swung into his chair and focused on slowing his breathing. Activating his computer and initiating the voice scramble codes, he placed the call.

"Yes?" said the voice on the other end.

It always amazed Butchart that Madame, with all her power and wealth, answered her own calls. No go-betweens, no messengers, no second in command, no mistakes.

"Frank here. You may be receiving a call from the admiral soon. He may shut down the project. Waterhouse got him agitated."

"And how did that happen, my dear?"

Butchart tensed. Madame was most lethal when she was being nice. "That damn prisoner on the *Nonnah* has knowledge about the crystals."

"Our dear Miss Davenport, yes?"

Butchart swallowed. He hoped Madame hadn't discovered the link between him and the prisoner. "Yes, Madame."

"Frank, you assured me she would be executed. She has knowledge of the file and probably its contents. Therefore, she must be terminated. It's unfortunate the pirates were unable to capture her and complete the execution. Contact Commander Moon and direct him to ensure Miss Davenport remains in solitary confinement. You're certain he'll refuse to carry out the execution?"

"Yes, Madame. His authority doesn't allow it. However, Commander Moon will ensure the prisoner won't be allowed out of her cell."

"No problem. I'll destroy that creature once the *Nonnah* arrives in New Seattle. And now Waterhouse is about to be eliminated. You keep Admiral Garland in line. Don't disappointment me, Frank!"

Butchart mustered his courage. "Madame, perhaps we should postpone the demonstration. The scientists have had some success, but—"

"We'll continue as planned. Even a minor demonstration will start the process of shifting power from the global energy giants. The crystals will work for me."

"Madame, the shift of power will be phenomenal and quick. We need to consider whether we're prepared for the hostility that will surely erupt."

Madame laughed. "Yes, there will bloodshed. Quite a lot I expect." After a brief silence, she asked, "Frank, are you keeping something from me?"

Butchart's hands perspired. His face twitched as pain descended upon his eyes. "Just concerned for your safety, Madame."

The comlink connection was broken.

Although Sam's navy blue T-shirt and shorts had a small navy logo on them, he hoped to be able to melt into the crowd and be just a dad for the day. The boys and Perkins jumped into Sam's vehicle, and sped away from the mansion to the wharf.

When the sailing tournament neared the final competitions, they looked for a better vantage point from which to view their favorite, the *Storm Blazer*. Grabbing their hotdogs and drinks, they found a row of seats in the dome covered bleachers and sat down. They spread themselves out, taking all available room and forcing Perkins to sit a few rows higher. To their dismay, two other men climbed up to their row and asked if they could sit beside them. Reluctantly, they shifted to make extra space and allowed the two strangers to sit down. At least it was better than having Perkins right there.

"Great day, isn't it?" one of the men asked Sam.

Sam simply nodded, trying to discourage any further conversation.

Undaunted, the stranger continued. "Yep, great day for sailing or doing just about anything except mountain climbing—too hot. Tomorrow should be better for that. Ever try mountain climbing?"

Sam shook his head. "No." He tried to look preoccupied with the race brochure.

"Didn't figure so. Don't look like the mountain climbing type. These your boys?"

Sam once again tried to discourage the talkative stranger and only replied with, "Uh huh." He glanced back at Perkins to see if he was taking any special interest in the stranger. He was. It presented an opportunity to rankle the guard.

Sam turned his attention to the stranger. He appeared to be perhaps in his late twenties and handsome in a boyish way. Brown curly hair rested on his shoulders. His brown eyes were bright, and his direct gaze was kind yet intense.

Sam turned to his boys. "You boys like to go mountain climbing tomorrow?"

"Can't, Dad. School tomorrow."

"Oh yes, sorry. I forgot." He looked back at the stranger. "Well, I tried. So you climb mountains, Mr...?"

"Danik Davenport." Danik presented his right hand to shake. Sam hesitated momentarily before grasping it. Danik gripped slightly longer than necessary, peering not just into Sam's eyes, but beyond. After completing his scan, Danik grinned and shifted his hand in Sam's, creating a friendly clutch as brothers might.

"This is my friend Ryan. And you?" Danik asked.

"Sam Waterhouse." For the first time since joining the American Naval Academy, Sam omitted his rank. He was now, and forever more would be, only Samaru Waterhouse. "It would seem we have a mutual friend."

"Uh huh. About that mountain climbing, I do quite a bit. But then, you probably know that by now. Some sailing, flying..."

Sam felt drawn in to Danik's easy manner. He glanced back to Perkins who was eyeing him suspiciously. Sam lowered his voice. "Better not provoke him." He half-turned his head to indicate the guard. Keeping his voice down and his head pointed forward he continued talking with Danik.

"Flying? You're a pilot?"

"Both Ryan and I fly helicopters. Rescue sailors off mountains," he said chuckling and nudging Sam in the ribs. "We've got plans to go over with you later. Not to worry, Sam, I'll find you. Have a nice day."

Danik and Ryan got up and descended the bleachers before Sam could respond.

Aboard the *Nonnah* that same Sunday morning, Moon opened the door to Sidney's cell and stepped in. She stood up immediately, sensing something was wrong.

Moon studied her face and smiled. "Remember when I told you that you were a fool not to have followed through with your escape attempt?"

Sidney frowned. "Seems to me, sir, that you said I was naïve."

"Sidney, Sidney, I'm wondering if perhaps I've misjudged you." He reached to touch her hair. She stepped back. "It's unfortunate the captain dug so deeply into your secrets. It appears you're about to become the hottest thing up for grabs."

Sidney stood tall. "Can you be more precise, Commander?"

"No. Suffice it to say that you won't be allowed to leave this room under any circumstances and no one will be allowed to enter—except for me, of course."

She nodded. "I see. Business as usual."

Moon scowled. "Business is about to conclude, miss."

After getting a late morning call from Clay on Monday morning, Sam went to the café to meet him. The detective pushed the bag containing Sidney's gloves and shoes toward him.

"Discover anything?" Sam asked.

"Interesting. Actually, fascinating, Sam. Any guesses what we found, just for the fun of it?"

"Okay, the grease on the gloves is a lubricant. Close?"

"Dead on, Sam. The shoes have a variety of material on the soles and canvas tops. Scuff marks on the side of one shoe indicates something, perhaps metal, banged away at it for a while. Can't tell exactly what, though."

"That's not exactly fascinating, Clay. You got more?"

"Uh huh. Lab took a few samples from the inside of the gloves, traces of cells that had been sloughed off from the skin of the wearer. You know what they found?"

Sam sat back and considered the answer to Clay's question. He grinned. "Pixie dust?"

"Damn near. Turned the whole lab into frenzy. Damn it all, Sam, people started asking questions about where I got the gloves. Damn scientists are all worked up and want some kind of explanation. The boss is now on my case. What the hell have you gotten yourself into?"

Sam looked off into the distance. "Ever watch tugboats, Clay?"

"No. Sam, focus. What's this all about?"

"Tugboats are little boats that get big boats out of trouble. Suppose you first tell me what the lab found?"

"I think you know what the lab found. You first, sailor."

"Okay, Clay. The lab probably found that the cells were unusually healthy and resilient, for one. For another, they're able to maintain their integrity longer than usual without physical or environmental support. And, perhaps, they're the most genetically perfect cells they've ever seen. Have I covered it?"

"Pretty much." Clay drummed the table with his fingers. "You said her name is Sidney Davenport. Are you gonna tell me exactly who this pixie is?"

Sam laughed. "Actually, she's no sweet little pixie. She stubborn as hell, manipulative, has little respect for authority, doesn't live by any code of conduct that I've heard of. And *rule*, now, there's a four letter word. And did I mention she has a temper? If you accuse her of lying—look out! Furthermore, she has this thing for picnics."

"Picnics?"

"Yes. Two kinds."

Clay's eyebrows were raised. "Two kinds?"

Sam was about to respond when he became conscious that he'd just opened up a space in his heart. A space reserved for only one. A space that was now occupied by a tall slender woman with long brown hair framing a beautiful face. Pale green eyes that sparkled with vitality and an uncommon wisdom. Her smile tipped his boat over each and every time. Her power was soft yet apparently stronger than his determination to shut her out.

Clay waved his hands in front of Sam. "Hello. Anybody home?"

"Sorry, Clay. Got lost there for a second." Sam smiled. "How can I help you straighten out this business with the lab?"

"Hell, don't you worry about that. Been around long enough to know how to *fix* things. Just wanted to know who or what this creature is. Are you in any trouble—I mean, more than usual?"

Sam chuckled. "Better keep on the alert for an admiral gone over the edge."

"Serious?"

"Don't go getting your gun greased up. Nothing should involve you or the police force directly. But I do intend to get full custody of my boys."

"How?"

Sam looked at his watch. "Gotta run." He gulped down the last of his coffee and gave Clay a thumbs up before dashing out of the café.

Once Sam was out of sight, Clay activated his comlink and waited for the response.

"Hello?" replied the man.

"Perkins, can you talk?"

"Yeah, Clay. Thought you wouldn't call unless it was urgent."

"Listen, Perkins, Sam's got something up his sleeve. Looks like he's making a move to get his kids back. Just stick close to the kids until Butchart's ready to make his move. Clear?"

"Yes, sir. Have you seen Double D?"

"No, but no doubt he's around. Keep your radar up, Perk."

"Yes, sir."

Clay left the café hopeful that Sam would call later and reveal more of his plans.

23. Madness and Clarity

Afternoon, July 15, New Seattle

Sam signed in at the base and went immediately to the elevator. He didn't have much time before he had to pick up his boys at school. He descended to the basement level, and the doors opened and he stepped out. He looked down the corridors toward the direction of the storage room and decided there was no need to follow that path again. The doors were about to close, so he stuck his foot into their path, and they reversed. The knock on his shoes jolted him mentally.

That's it, he thought. *That's how the marks got on her shoes.* But the marks indicated the doors must have banged on her shoe repeatedly, as though she needed time. Time for ... *Time to hide the memory rod.* Instinctively, he looked up to the elevator's ceiling. *And that's where her gloves got the grease.* Lubrication from the cables. The ceiling panels were high, but Sidney could've sprung off the hand-hold bar to toss the panel aside and then lift herself above the ceiling.

He did as Sidney had done — took off one of his shoes and placed it in the path of the open elevator doors and climbed up to the roof of the elevator.

"Well, hello there. I see you've been waiting. Sorry, but I've been detained by one very stubborn Guardian."

He untied the rod from the elevator shaft housing and placed it into the barrel of his handgun. Then he went to pick up his sons.

Always under the watchful eyes of Perkins, Sam and his boys went horseback riding in the mountains outside of New Seattle. All too soon they had to return to the admiral's home. The boys ran upstairs to change for dinner while Sam stood as tall as he could in front of his seething superior officer in the admiral's home office.

"Good evening, sir." Sam turned slightly away from the admiral, took a breath, and found a calm center within. "Admiral, you've been good to my boys, generous. But they need something different now. Something that will lead them to become men of sound character. We got to our rank not because someone handed it to us. It was earned. Every victory was gratifying because we'd proven to be worthy."

"You forget that you proved to be unworthy of my trust."

"Perhaps you're right. The wisest choices weren't made by Joy or myself."

The admiral straightened his posture and went to his desk. "What exactly are you getting at?"

"Tomorrow I'll pick Nathan and Simon up after school and bring them here. They'll be packed by then. They'll express their gratitude to you, your family, and staff and ... then we'll be out of your hair. All of us."

"You're assuming an awful lot, Captain Waterhouse. I don't believe they'll willingly give up the good life they've had, even to follow you. And you're still assigned to the *Nonnah*. You'll return to your ship tomorrow evening. I've no intention of changing anything. Is that clear?"

"Quite clear, but unacceptable, sir."

"That's too bad. You may pick up Nathan and Simon at school observed by my security to ensure you return here."

The head housekeeper knocked on the door and announced the dinner was ready.

The admiral glared at Sam. "We'll continue this after dinner."

Sam sat across from his boys in the dining room. They were joined by the admiral's daughter, Marianne, and her son, Chad. Silence prevailed over the stiffly seated diners. All were dressed as for a formal occasion. Sam and the admiral were in naval uniform, and Sam's sons had changed into black dinner suits and combed their hair neatly against their heads. They looked impeccably clean — and like dogs about to bolt from their chains, Sam noted.

Everyone waited for the admiral to begin. As he spooned soup from his bowl, Sam spoke up. "Aren't we forgetting something, sir? Perhaps grace would be nice. Doesn't hurt to thank the big guy for all our blessings today." He pointed to the ceiling.

"Thank whomever you like for whatever blessings you deem were bestowed upon you, Captain."

The admiral returned to his soup, blowing on it. Nathan and Simon studied their dad. Nathan was grinning, eager to see the next move his dad was to make. Simon tentatively reached for his soup spoon. With his eyes closed, Sam sat quiet for a moment. Then clearly but reverently, he addressed God.

"Great Spirit, we give thanks for the fellowship and love of friends and family at this table. We give thanks for your unconditional love that sustains our spirits and for the abundance of food that nourishes our bodies. We give thanks for each new day so that we may have another opportunity to plant the seeds of your Light among those who live in Darkness. We ask for guidance in striving for the higher good in our thoughts and deeds. We thank you for these many blessings, gifts in both the Light and those hidden in the Darkness. For in both the Light and the Darkness, your love is ever present. Amen."

"That was beautiful, Captain," Marianne said. "We used to, that is, when mama—"

"Can we have a little less noise at this table!" the admiral shouted.

"Oh, pardon me, Father," said Marianne submissively.

The remainder of the meal continued mostly in silence. Sam watched his boys. They sat like little gentlemen in their suits. It was nice to see they had acquired good manners at the table, but Sam thought a little more fun and chatting about the previous day's adventures was in order. As dessert was being served, he brought up the subject of Nathan's interaction with a certain green lizard at the sailing tournament.

"So, where do you think Lizzy is now, Nathan?" asked Sam.

Nathan shook his head, indicating this wasn't the time to bring up the subject.

Sam snickered. "Bet he's still running. The look on your face when he dropped into your lap." He turned to his oldest son. "Who do you figure was more scared, Simon? Nathan or poor little lizard? How big was this terrible beast?"

Simon grinned. "Geez, it was only maybe five inches long, including its tail."

"That's not true. It was at least a foot long," said Nathan. "That thing attacked me."

Sam laughed. "Well, if it wasn't for your agility and speed, it could've been a lizard saying grace over a juicy meal tonight—your big toe." Sam was still laughing. "Guess you're more of a seaman than a nature buff."

Marianne spoke up. "Actually, Simon is the one who handles the outdoors without any complaint."

"Oh, yes. That's right, Marianne. You took them camping last weekend. How did that go? Any lunatic lizards after Nathan?" Sam asked.

"Things were pretty tame, at least probably by your standards, Captain. But come to think of it, on the first night, or was it the second? Anyway, Simon was in one tent and Nathan was with Chad in another. An hour or so after we were in our sleeping bags, there was this sound. Like some animal in pain. It was just awful. Woke me with a start, felt like it was right outside my tent. I scrambled to find my flashlight. Couldn't find the silly thing at first. When I finally got it I ran outside ready to smack whatever was out there."

Simon shook his head and smirked.

"I first noticed Chad and Nathan's tent," Marianne continued. "It looked like something had grabbed it or had been thrashing at it. The boys were nowhere to be seen. I called for Simon and, bless his heart, he came running right away to my side, such a brave young man. I called and called, and so did Simon. Chad and Nathan finally shimmied down from a tree not too far from our camp. Never did see the animal, don't even know what it was. It was awful, Captain. You can be very proud of Simon. And, Nathan, well he had the skin scraped off the inside of his legs when he slid down that tree trunk, but oh, can he climb trees!"

Simon's shoulders trembled with the laughter he was trying to contain. He let out a loud growl that ended as a painful scream.

"*You*. It was you!" shouted Nathan, grabbing onto Simon's shoulders. "You lousy—"

The admiral banged on the table. "If you don't all mind, I'd like to enjoy my dessert. Quiet!"

The snickering continued unabated. Simon and Nathan jostled with each other as much as they dared. When the admiral could no longer take the informality at his table, he told the three boys to go to their rooms. Simon and Nathan hesitated.

"Go on. I'll check in with you before I leave," Sam assured them, and they ran off.

Sam sat back in his chair and sipped his coffee. He held the cup in his hand, receiving its warmth and letting the delicious flavor linger in his mouth. The adults were again quiet, and Sam's thoughts drifted to nowhere in particular. He found himself more relaxed than he would've thought possible at the table of his nemesis.

He looked beyond the room's double archway into the hallway, which glowed softly from candle light. It reminded him of the last time he'd seen Sidney. The terra cotta tile floor was warm in contrast to the blue shadows in the darkening garden beyond the large French doors. He noticed a shadow on the hallway floor, the maid perhaps coming to clear the dishes. He savored another mouthful of his coffee and looked back to the floor.

The bare feet made him almost choke. Sidney stood in the hallway, as perfect and clear as the pillars beside her.

"What's wrong, Captain? Is it too hot?" asked Marianne.

Marianne looked in the direction Sam had been staring and said, "Yes, the terra cotta is beautiful. Shipped all the way from Italy, wasn't it, Dad?"

The admiral simply grunted. Sam returned his focus to Sidney, standing plainly on the Italian tile. Obviously, no one else could see her. She softly smiled and beckoned with her eyes. She went to the French doors behind her, opened them and stepped through, disappearing into the garden.

"Excuse me." Sam rushed toward the doors. "Going for a walk."

Before anyone could respond, he was through the hallway and outside the French doors. Sam followed the garden path among trees and hedges, catching a glimpse of Sidney several yards ahead at each turn.

He called to her, "Sidney, wait!"

She didn't respond. He ran to catch up to her. Just when he thought she should be within reach, he discovered he was at the perimeter of the admiral's property. Danik and Ryan stood on the other side of a tall iron fence.

"Hello, Sam."

Sam was stunned. "What the hell is going on? Where's Sidney?"

"Danik grinned. "She's on your ship, Captain." Danik raised his right hand toward the fence. A lock clicked and a section of the fence swung open. "That's what we need to talk about. We need to get her off that ship as soon as it arrives in harbor, if not before."

Sam walked through the opening. He was still trying to sort out what he'd just seen.

"Sam?"

"First I need to get my sons out of here. My boys come first. Sidney knows that."

"Sam, she's powerful. But she's flesh and blood too."

"You have any suggestions?" Sam asked.

"Glad you asked. What are the chances of Ryan and me landing our chopper on the *Nonnah*?"

Sam shook his head. "That would be daring to say the least, even suicidal. Any attempt would result in an immediate defensive action against an intruder. Commander Moon is currently acting captain and will follow orders from only naval command or Captain Butchart. He won't abide by orders from me."

Danik's eyebrows lifted. "Why not?"

"Even if I were to talk to him from a monitor-equipped comlink, he'd be concerned I was being coerced into a request like that. And there's something you don't know about Commander Moon. I believe he's been influenced by Captain Butchart concerning Sidney. He won't kill her, but he won't help her either."

Danik crossed his arms and frowned. "And you're not returning to the *Nonnah*, are you?"

"Once my boys are safe, I'll…"

"They're safe now, Sam."

"I make one wrong move and the admiral will make sure they disappear. I can't risk that!"

Danik was deep in thought and walked in a close perimeter around Sam. Sam became uneasy with the tension. He loosened the grip of his tie at his throat.

"I'd better get back to the admiral," he said and stepped toward the open gate.

"Not so fast." With a wave of Danik's hand, the gate slammed shut. "You plan to bargain for your sons' release with Sidney's life. Perhaps mine, Ryan's, and those of the rest of my people. Am I correct?"

Sam felt the heat from Danik's glare. "It's not my intention to involve anyone beyond Sidney."

Danik shook his head. "Not acceptable. What do you think, Ryan? Plan B?"

Ryan groaned. "Hey man, we said we wouldn't. Too risky."

"Might as well be hanged for a sheep as a lamb!" Danik said. "We'd better let 'em know right away we're on board." He waved his hand and the gate swung open. "Be seeing you, Sam."

Danik seemed far too at ease for someone planning something risky. Sam was confident he was bluffing. And so he watched the duo disappear into the night shadows, and then headed back to the admiral's home.

Soon after Sam had left the dining room, Butchart arrived. He was directed to wait in the admiral's office.

"Frank, sit down," the admiral said when he came in.

Butchart was prepared. He'd taken special effort to subdue the tumor pressing down on his brain with pain medication. His training as a Guardian had provided him with the tools to manage it, shrink its size to nearly nothing, but with the stress of Madame's arrival on the base a year earlier, the cancer had returned with a vengeance.

He reached into his briefcase and pulled out a large sun crystal.

"Admiral, you have yet to understand the potential of this crystal. Allow me to demonstrate."

Butchart stepped back and closed his eyes, breathing deeply. After a few minutes, the crystal began to glow. Its brilliance lit up the room. In another second, the only light in the room was from the crystal.

"I've just turned off all the power on your property. Good for a start, sir?" Butchart asked, obviously pleased with himself.

The admiral raised his eyebrows and gasped. He was in shock. "Everything is off?"

"Even your security system, which would normally seal off rooms, shut gates, and sound off a siren with a power failure. Absolutely nothing will work in this house except by manual labor."

Marianne rushed into the room. "Dad, we have a problem. There's no power."

"Never mind, my dear. It'll be all right shortly. Just keep the servants quiet for now." When Marianne had left, the admiral turned back to Butchart.

"Okay, that's impressive, but you'd better be able to reverse that."

Butchart again connected with his crystal, and the power resumed. "Have someone shut down your power source. The crystal will provide all the power you need to run this house."

The admiral ordered his staff to turn off the main power source and was elated to find that the crystal performed as promised. The entire house—lights, appliances, security—functioned at optimum levels through the sun crystal's energy.

"How long will it continue supporting this house, Frank?"

"I'd have to give it a booster every hour. It'll gradually lose its connection with me. But as you can see, it takes little time or effort on my part."

"Don't believe a word of it, Admiral," Sam said, bursting into the room. "He's just making sure you'll keep busy hoarding these little rocks while he gains more control. It's his Guardian sacred teachings that put on this show. Nicely done, Frank. But I'll show you that I can do even better with what Sidney has taught me. And Admiral, I'll achieve more without Frank's paperweight."

Butchart lunged at Sam. "You miserable piece of shit. Get out of here. Get back to your rotting ship."

Sam quickly sidestepped the attack and remained unruffled.

"Calm down, Frank," demanded the admiral. "I've purposely invited you both here tonight so we can get to the bottom of this." He turned to Sam. "You're up, Waterhouse."

Sam swallowed. He'd expected a face-to-face confrontation with Butchart at some point, but not so soon.

"Let's see, Admiral. How about something of more military strategic implications?" Sam thought for a moment. "How about your chopper out on the helipad? If I were to get it airborne and maneuver it?"

The admiral was intrigued. "Move my helicopter off its pad, and turn it in another direction. But don't fire the guns."

Sam was nervous. He'd only moved small objects before. But if he wanted to keep the admiral's attention, he had to do something big—without using that crystal on the table. Focus was the key. He stood at the side of the window and spotted the garage to his right a short distance from the mansion. He began his meditation technique. Standing erect with his hands lifted slightly away from his sides, he created a faint rainbow-colored arch extending from one hand, over his head, and down into the opposite hand.

In a few more seconds, the men heard the whine of the chopper's engine. The chopper soon came into view as it hovered above the treetops. The admiral looked back at the sun crystal on his desk. It showed not a glimmer, no rays of energy emitting from its facets as it had when Butchart had given his demonstration. It sat just like a paperweight, lifeless. As far as he could tell, the source of power Sam accessed to perform this amazing task came from within him.

Gradually, the chopper shifted its position toward the garage. It flew over the driveway where both Sam's and Butchart's vehicles were parked.

The admiral was speechless, his eyes wide with amazement. Sam remained silent and in a meditative state. His hands were motionless. The admiral grabbed Sam's shoulder.

"Well done!" he shouted above the roar of the chopper's engine.

Suddenly, the chopper switched positions and fired toward the window.

Butchart and the admiral dove away from the window but not before bullets shattered it. Flying debris struck Butchart's shoulder and arm. The admiral crawled on the floor under the flying bullets to his desk. He reached into a drawer and grabbed his gun, aiming it square at Sam's head.

"Stop it or I'll blow your head off!" he shouted.

The firing stopped, and Sam returned the chopper to the helipad.

"God, that was too damn close," Sam said, feeling rather stunned. "Are you all right, Admiral?"

The admiral kept his aim on Sam. "What the hell were you trying to do?"

"Kill us," Butchart said. "You're under arrest, Waterhouse!" He was trying to brace his bloody right arm and hold his gun with his good hand.

"Hang on a minute, Frank," cautioned the admiral.

"Admiral, for Christ sake, this traitor—"

"Frank, if I intended to commit murder, you'd both be dead right now. Actually, it would've been the ideal opportunity. Doubt the police would suspect me since I was in the room when the chopper attacked. Admiral, when you grabbed my arm, it changed my focus to this room. At least that's what it felt like."

The admiral lowered his gun and surveyed the damage to his office.

"Shit. Look what he did. And with no pilot. Just think what this could mean to operations, Frank."

"And," Sam interjected, "no crystal." It was a lie. He'd accessed the crystal hidden in his shoe. "But do you see what can happen when you're an amateur … we could all be dead. I'm sorry about the damage, sir. We'd better make sure no one else is hurt in the house."

Sam moved toward the door and heard people outside the room. Perkins, with his gun drawn, opened the door just as Sam pulled on the door handle. He was followed by everyone else in the house, including Simon and Nathan.

"Wow, Dad. Who attacked us?" asked Simon.

Sam grabbed his sons. "Are you both all right?"

The boys shook off their father's concern.

"Hey, look at the wall. It's Swiss cheese!" Nathan shouted.

Marianne noticed Butchart's wound and sent the maid to get the first aid supplies.

"Better go to the hospital, sir," she said.

"Marianne, make sure no one else is hurt. I'll get someone to fix the damage first thing in the morning. Everyone out," demanded the admiral. He allowed the maid to quickly dress Butchart's wounds and then sent her away as well.

The admiral, pale and agitated, approached Butchart. The admiral's energy was fading. His voice trembled and had lost its fire.

"The only thing that can save your ass now is to explain Sam's performance."

Butchart, physically weak and baffled, tried to come up with a plausible explanation "He … he had to have used a crystal … or an accomplice."

Sam continued to deliberately confuse the admiral. "Do I have a crystal, Admiral?

"You're a goddamn Guardian!" Butchart shouted. He thrust his fist at Sam's face and winced in pain from the exertion.

Sam shrugged. "Sidney tells me I'm what's called a waking Guardian, but this is all brand new to me. I haven't kept secrets from the admiral. But you've never told him of your powers for all these years. Who's the real traitor here?"

"Your interference is over, Waterhouse!"

Butchart directed his gun toward Sam's head. Sam stood close enough that with a swift step in Butchart's direction and a blow from Sam's hand, the gun flew across the room. Butchart's rage was beyond the pain in his arm. His fists flew and zoned in on Sam's body. Sam fought back with the intensity of his disgust for the man. They rolled in the broken glass, pounding their fists at each other. Butchart was weakened and failed to do any harm to Sam. Sam took the advantage and thrust him against the wall hard enough that the room shuddered with the impact. Sam's rage escalated, like that of an animal anxious to kill.

The admiral reached for his gun and struggled to grasp it with his trembling hands. Standing back from Butchart and Sam, he hesitated to act, no longer sure of himself.

"Stand back, or I'll have my guards arrest the both of you." He fired the pistol at the ceiling. The skirmish ceased. "Sam, don't push me. What you don't know is that Madame is—"

Butchart lunged toward the admiral. "Shut up, Admiral. Just shut the hell up!"

"You forget yourself, Captain Butchart," the admiral warned angrily.

Sam raised his eyebrows. "Madame? Who's Madame?"

The admiral gritted his teeth. "Someone you're better off not knowing. She owns the crystals, and perhaps some of my staff." He glared at Butchart.

Butchart's face became pale and slightly twisted. "Sir, I've given the better part of my life protecting you and your goals. Whatever I've done was to keep your hands clean."

The admiral's eyes opened wide in alarm. "Just what precisely have you done using this Guardian power of yours?"

Sam jumped in. "You can't trust him. Just think. When you have the demonstration, it'll be him controlling the show. Your rank will have no effect when Butchart turns on you with his Guardian powers. You can see that, can't you?"

Butchart leaped between Sam and the admiral. "Admiral, this is absolutely the most ridiculous—"

Sam struck Butchart squarely on his jaw and knocked him to the floor. Butchart was dazed and unable to move. Sam continued to feed the admiral's paranoia. Once the admiral was no longer thinking clearly, he could take over.

"Sir, just think of the chaos worldwide. If you don't stop good old Frank here, what'll be the consequences of the damage he's capable of? And you'll be held responsible. Lose your commission, dishonorable discharge, perhaps prison."

Butchart was regaining consciousness. He stood up and attempted to grab onto Sam. He stumbled.

"Admiral, don't listen to him," he said weakly.

Butchart grabbed a chair and slumped down. His energy was spent. The admiral stared blankly at Sam. Sam had him.

"Admiral, you saw what I did with almost no training. Think of the devastation Butchart—an experienced Guardian—can cause."

The admiral lifted the gun that had been loosely dangling at his side. He slowly brought it up higher and higher, first aiming at Sam, then at Butchart. The gun shook violently. He aimed again at Sam, taking a deep breath through his clenched teeth. Sam was turning the admiral's orderly life upside down.

The admiral switched his aim to Butchart. Butchart had kept the truth about his past secret. A Guardian. *Two* Guardians. Whatever the hell they were. *Does Waterhouse have more power than Butchart?* Neither could be trusted. Madame would destroy his life. He needed the truth, but the truth was buried, elusive. Gone.

Sam saw the impending mental collapse on the admiral's face. The plan was working. Just a little nudge and the man would plunge into an abyss of darkness, lost from reality, perhaps even unloading his gun's ammunition into Butchart's face.

Sam reeled with the realization that his battle was nearly won. At last, he could destroy both the admiral and Butchart. The sensation of being free from his duty to the admiral and the loathing of Butchart was exhilarating. Nothing else mattered. He was about to deal his final blow when Sidney's voice echoed the phrase "For the higher good." Clearly his plan wasn't for the higher good. He shook her words off and approached the admiral, taking the gun from his hand. Butchart was nearly passed out.

"Sir," he began, "there's more to Butchart's devious plan. If he teams up with other Guardians ... " Sam placed his hand over his eyes and shuddered in a mock display. "They could shut down our country's energy sources, with just a thought. A whole city would go down in hours, then the state in a few days, then total collapse of this country. Think about it, Admiral. The country won't need you when Butchart and his Madame are at the controls. You'll go down in history as the one who caused the collapse of America. You know that, don't you?"

The admiral was no longer focused on Sam's face or anything else in the room. His mouth moved, but no words came forth. It was done. Sam produced papers from his blazer—papers that would free him—and set them on the admiral's desk. All he needed now was Admiral Garland's signature.

"Dad," a child's voice called out. "Are you going to see us tomorrow?"

Sam spun around. Nathan was standing in the doorway.

"Get out of here!" Sam shouted. His fire still burned and continued to spill its wrath.

Nathan's mouth dropped open and tears welled in his eyes. "I'm sorry, Dad. Really. Just was scared 'n all. You mad at me, Dad?"

Sam was dumfounded. *How could I have shouted at him? What's happening to me?* He hardly recognized the man he'd become. But he still felt the gut-wrenching need to complete what he'd started. And yet, if he did, he could see with certainty that he'd become twisted like Butchart. He'd never be free of the Dark forces that would follow him. Nausea swelled in his belly, the floor swayed, and he was chilled to the bone. He saw madness overtaking his life, the worst kind of prison.

He hoped he could undo the damage he'd caused. He knelt down on his knee in front of Nathan.

"I'll never leave you again," he said, wrapping his arms around his son's slender shoulders. "I love you and Simon very much. Now go back upstairs. I'll see you before I go back to the hotel. Tomorrow, I'll pick you guys up from school. Okay?"

Nathan hugged his dad back and nodded. "Okay, Dad." He dashed out of the room.

Sam went to the Admiral and put him in his chair behind the desk. He called for the servant and gave orders to get water for the Admiral and called for Perkins. He placed Butchart on the floor and checked the shoulder wound. It was already healing, but Butchart was still weak. He laid a blanket over the injured man. When Perkins arrived, the servants helped walk Butchart out to Perkin's vehicle with orders to deliver him to his home.

The admiral was still trembling, but regaining his control. Sam stood in front of the admiral's desk.

"Sir, I apologize. My behavior toward you was insubordinate and cruel. My actions were dishonorable to my rank and my heritage as a Guardian."

The admiral eyed him suspiciously. "Fine," he barked. "But I demand one more thing from you right now. Explain how you got that chopper to fly and fire its guns without the crystal."

Sam sat down. He smiled and spoke softly. "You see, Admiral, that explanation comes with a price tag."

The admiral straightened his posture. "Figured so."

The admiral leaned down to a desk drawer and pulled out a bottle of aged scotch whiskey and two glasses.

Detective Clay Flanders' comlink buzzed. "Flanders speaking."

"Perkins. The heat's been turned up. Waterhouse nearly killed the admiral and Frank. Trashed part of the mansion with the admiral's chopper. Got a piece of Frank."

"Christ! Is tomorrow still on?"

"Yeah. Frank hasn't changed the plans, but the timing's still up in the air. Better not talk to him tonight. He's like a wounded animal."

"Well, we better find out what Waterhouse is up to."

"That's the problem. Hook had the hotel staked out, but Waterhouse never showed."

"Jesus! We better be ready when Frank wants to make his move. Has he picked the spot?"

"Yeah, that old photography place on Seventh. Going to use the dark room. Figures no one will hear any hollerin' from there."

"Good. Sure be a lot easier if we knew what Waterhouse was up to. Might have a bunch of that underground helping him. He said he'd call tonight. Must be busy. Can't call him or he'd get even more suspicious. Keep me posted, Perkins."

Sam sat down on the bed. He felt off kilter. On his drive to his hotel, he'd had the most incredible urge to pull off the freeway. Clearly, a voice had said, "Get out now!" He'd abandoned the vehicle and, just as he reached a safe distance, it had exploded. Sam had disappeared into the darkness and found a different motel, the one he was currently at.

He fished out the memory rod from his gun and inserted it into a laptop provided by the hotel. In spite of his exhaustion, he was anxious to open the file that Joy had felt worth the risk. He went through the folders and pages and read document after document. Shortly after 0200 hours, he placed a call to the *Nonnah.*

"Commander Moon speaking."

"Good evening, Rhett. Sam here. Long day for you?"

"Yes, sir. Where are you?"

"Hotel. Patch me through to Bridges."

"Is this about the prisoner, sir?"

"Yes, why?"

"I have orders from HQ that there's to be no further contact with her. She remains in her cell in isolation."

Sam blinked. "From who at HQ, Commander?"

"Head of Security, Captain Butchart, sir."

Sam hesitated. "At what time, Commander?"

Moon touched a few keys on his computer keyboard and read the report. "Received direct order at oh nine thirty-eight today, sir."

"Anything else you wish to report?"

Moon shifted in the captain's chair. "No, sir. All systems and personnel normal."

Sam searched for insight into what was happening on his ship. "Rhett, be careful. Good night."

24. Admiral Garland's Awakening

Morning, Tuesday, July 16, New Seattle

It was only 0634 hours when Sam woke with an ache which had begun in his chest, but now threatened to spread to the rest of his body. It had nothing to do with his muscles. This was deeper, a vacant feeling which could only be filled with the sound of her voice and her company. With voice communication no longer an option, Sam wondered if another connection was possible.

He sat on his bed, hands relaxed on his thighs, and breathed slowly. Soon he was able to hush the chatter of his mind. At one point he thought about grabbing the crystal and accessing its power, but his intuition told him he didn't need it. He continued his meditation in silence.

The sense of being in his hotel room faded. His body became as fluid as his breath, without shape or limitation. He sensed moving through light. Her beautiful pale green eyes, smiling and teasing, beckoned him. He remained centered. Currents of energy surrounded her, and as he shifted to connect, they were enveloped in a swirl of dancing rays. He briefly whispered her name, her Guardian name—Wild Child. Then he sent the energy of his heart to her, immersing her entire being in his love.

"Hello, Sam. Everything okay?" She conveyed a deep, abiding love through the touch of her ethereal fingers in his hair.

"Yep. Everything okay there?"

She nodded. "Uh huh."

With a boyish grin on his face, Sam inhaled, and the connection was gone.

At 1500 hours, Sam waited by his sons' school. He was half an hour early, anxious to finally have them back, completely and wholly under his care and guidance. The late afternoon sun shone down on the vacant schoolyard. Finding a bench under a solitary tree, he sat and contemplated what was to come in the next few hours.

He wondered who'd been behind the previous night's attempt to kill him. He glanced around the school grounds. The morning paper had reported the incident, saying the owner of the vehicle hadn't been identified, but that police forensics discovered the remnants of a bomb that had been detonated from a remote transmitter. The name Madame echoed in Sam's head. Again he looked around, trying to spot odd shadows among the buildings, shapes that didn't belong in the trees. It bothered him that Perkins was nowhere in sight. Sam hadn't seen Frank Butchart or heard from Admiral Garland all day, a fact that made him nervous.

The admiral and he had tried to come to an agreement, or at least the framework of an agreement. He would get his sons and his freedom in exchange for Sidney's cooperation to work for the navy. But he knew Sidney wouldn't agree, and a feeling of doom alternated with a sense of release. Even if he and his boys got free of the admiral, they'd have Butchart and Madame to worry about.

Sam's hand still bore the bruises from his fight with Butchart the previous night. He massaged the soreness and let go of the dark feelings he had for the desperate man. He discovered it was a matter of choice, and the gut wrenching desire to strangle the man was gradually being replaced with a vague sense of pity.

Gazing down at his hands, he noticed two tiny bare feet standing beside him. He looked up to the child's face. The little girl was dressed in coveralls. She smiled sheepishly at Sam as she twined fingers in her curly, long, dark brown hair.

"Hi, sweetheart. Where's your mommy?" Sam asked.

"Over there." She pointed in a westerly direction.

Sam looked about but saw no one. He became concerned that she may be lost.

"What's your name, little one?"

The child playfully ran around the bench, giggling and kicking up dust. She began singing a song. Sam couldn't make out the words other than something that sounded like "Savy anna, savy anna is coming, coming."

"Is your name Anna?" he asked when she finally stopped in front of him.

The child put her hands on her hips and indignantly declared, "No. Savannah."

"Oh, Savannah. I get it. Are you lost, Savannah?"

The child giggled again. "No." She looked at Sam's bruised hand and touched it lightly. She looked into his eyes. "Daddy."

"Dirty? No, just a bruise. It's okay. I think we'd better find your mother."

"Okay." She reached up to him, indicating that she wanted to be picked up. Sam lifted her and walked into the school. Inside, he set her down and held onto her hand.

"Can I help you sir?" a young woman asked.

Sam hadn't heard her approach and was startled. "Oh, yes. Are you a teacher or parent here?"

"I'm a teacher. What's your problem?" she said rather stiffly.

"This little girl. I was hoping her mother might be here."

"What little girl, sir?"

"This … " The child was nowhere in sight. "Sorry, she must've found her mother. I'll just wait here for my boys."

How bizarre, he thought. *Is this the life of a Guardian? Mystery upon mystery?*

Soon the children began to race out of the school. Sam stood and watched for his boys. He thought it was odd that Perkins hadn't shown up yet. It took some time for the chattering students to exit the school, so Sam went outside to stand along with the other parents. He was becoming concerned. Once all the students seemed to be out of the school and his boys were nowhere to be seen, he went into the school and found the same teacher he'd spoken to earlier.

"Yes?" she questioned, annoyed. "What child's parent are you looking for, now?"

"Actually, it's my boys. They, that is, I was to pick them up after school. Are all the classes out?"

"Yes, all classes are finished. Perhaps you should check with the school's principal, Dorothy Gray, right over there in that office at the end of the hall."

"Thank you, miss." Sam hurried down the hall. Once he found Dorothy Gray, he introduced himself.

"Oh, how nice to meet you, Captain. In for just a few days, are you?"

"Yes. Can you tell me where my sons are?"

"Certainly, Captain. Two of your fine naval officers came and picked them up a couple of hours ago."

"What? They're gone?"

"Why, yes. Must admit, their teachers weren't too happy about the unscheduled interruption, but the men insisted. They told the teachers that there was some urgent family business and the boys were needed right away. I'm surprised you don't know anything about this, Captain."

Sam grabbed onto the principal's arms. "Ms. Gray, did the men give their names?"

The principal's friendly demeanor dropped at Sam's rough contact. She yanked her arms out of his grip.

"I understand there are nuances with your custody arrangement, so before I tell you anything more, I'll have to check the files to see what information you're authorized to receive. You may have a seat while I locate your file."

Sam didn't waste any more time. He rushed out of the school and back to his rented car. On his way, he connected to his boys' comlink. They didn't reply. Upon reaching his car, he contacted the Admiral's office.

"Admiral Garland's office. Celine speaking."

"Celine! I've got to speak to the admiral right away."

"Is that you, Captain Waterhouse?"

"Yes. Now, the admiral, now!" he demanded.

"I'm sorry, Captain. The admiral isn't in, and we don't expect him back today. He said he had personal business to attend to and would be at his home office by sixteen-hundred hours."

Sam's heart pounded in his chest. It raced along, robbing him of his breath. His whole body felt heavy and unwilling to move as fast as he needed it to. He cut off his conversation with Celine and visually scanned the school grounds. Nothing appeared out of place. In an act of desperation, he called out his sons' names and held his breath. He only heard the sound of his heartbeat in his ears.

It was almost 1555 hours. He called the admiral's home office. Only the answering unit responded. He clicked off the call and connected with the admiral's house staff who also advised him that the admiral wasn't expected home until for perhaps another hour.

"Is Perkins, there?" he asked.

"No, sir."

"The second the admiral gets home, tell him to call me. Understand? It's urgent. And if the boys show up there, make sure they call me immediately. Is that clear?" He was almost shouting.

"Yes, Captain."

Sam considered calling Clay. He initiated a call to the detective's comlink twice and canceled both times. He had a gut feeling this either wasn't the right time or, perhaps, it was best to keep the civilian forces out of this. He wished he knew how to get in touch with Danik. He called Commander Moon.

"USS *Nonnah*, Commander Moon."

"Rhett, have you received any orders from the admiral's office this afternoon?"

"Hello, Sam. Yes, and rather odd. Just got it, about an hour ago. The *Nonnah* is to remain off shore from New Seattle. My orders are to anchor out at sea one hundred nautical miles southwest of the base. What's going on, Sam?"

"Oh Christ," he muttered.

"Sounds like there's trouble."

"Could be, Rhett. Is there anything else going on that's out of the ordinary?"

"Butchart has ordered that for the next twenty-four hours no helicopters are to approach the *Nonnah* unless approved by him personally."

Sam clenched his teeth and breathed forcefully through his nose. The orders had a devastating effect on his plans. He wouldn't be able to reach Sidney and get her off the ship. He paced feverishly around his car.

"Captain?" called out Moon.

Sam closed his eyes and tried to regain control of his thoughts. "Rhett, at this point you and the *Nonnah* are in no danger. But my boys have disappeared. I can't let them take my boys, Rhett."

"Who? Captain, surely the admiral has—"

"Rhett, the admiral isn't necessarily in control anymore. Waterhouse out."

Sam placed a call again to the admiral's home office. Admiral Garland answered.

Sam struggled to control his anger. "Sir, I'm at the school, but my boys are gone. Perkins never showed. I was told two naval officers took them out of school early. Where the hell are they?"

The admiral paused before responding and cleared his throat.

"Just hold on, Waterhouse. Every few weeks Perkins has to take the boys to some sports tournament, or to a dentist's appointment, or out for any number of reasons. I'm sure they're fine."

Sam's suspicions wouldn't let go. He made his way directly to the admiral's home.

Butchart checked his watch. It was 1600 hours. He hoped everything went well at the school. By now he figured that Sam was crawling the walls, a thought that gave him pleasure. He drove to the admiral's home. On his way, he contacted Perkins.

"Got the two screaming Waterhouse brats locked up in the lab's dark room," Perkins reported. "Everything's under control. A video link is ready so Sam can see we're damn serious, sir."

"Excellent. Stand by. I'll call from the admiral's home in about an hour and half." Butchart was eager to exercise his superiority over both Sam and the admiral.

Sam met the admiral in his office. Though temporary repairs had been made, it was obvious a skirmish had taken place in the admiral's domain.

"I spoke with Perkins," the admiral said. "It's as I thought — the boys are at a basketball tournament. They'll be back by seventeen-hundred hours."

"They never mentioned it yesterday. My boys better be here within the hour." Sam could see the admiral was nervous, fidgeting with a pen. He avoided eye contact with Sam. "Admiral, within the hour," he repeated.

"Oh, hell, why are you making a fuss? Perkins has always treated the boys well, buys them ice cream, takes them shopping. Like an uncle, he is."

Sam wanted to relax, but his instincts wouldn't let go of the feeling of imminent danger.

"I've given more thought to your offer." Sam sat in front of the admiral and consciously focused on his breathing. *Remain calm.* "Sidney won't agree to working for the U.S. Naval Forces."

"That's unfortunate. Our deal was for you to give me Sidney and you'll get your freedom. You talk to that woman and make her know the consequences if she doesn't cooperate."

"I can't do that, sir."

"Then you'd better get ready to board the *Nonnah*. She's anchored just beyond New Seattle's naval harbor."

Sam gritted his teeth. "All right, just let Sidney go."

"No. In fact, I plan take her off the ship and deal with her personally. If she's who you say she is, then I need Butchart to handle her. It'll be a while before I can trust her."

"He'll kill her."

"Not unless I order him to."

Sam abandoned his endeavor to remain calm. "Are you so arrogant that you think Captain Butchart follows your orders and disregards his own agenda?"

The two men cursed each other without reservation for rank or military conduct. The outpouring contained the old wounds and suspicions. It was with great effort that both refrained from physical violence. After ten minutes of shooting verbal daggers at one another, the two men became silent.

The admiral stood silent, surveying the room that only yesterday had been shattered by bullets. He believed his life was also becoming a disaster, surrounded by villains and the inept. He was constantly on the defensive, guessing at who might be waiting to impale him with a knife into his back. It was exhausting to be constantly on the alert. Lately he felt older than his fifty-two years, lacking his usual sharp mind and energetic body. He feared for his sanity.

As Sam observed him, he saw a lonely man struggling to maintain what he believed in as good and enduring. He saw a man lost without the loving guidance of his wife and adrift from the quiet within that brings peace, clarity, and joy. Sam felt a surprising connection to the man he'd despised.

Ever so carefully, Sam withdrew a long, narrow envelope from his inside breast pocket. He hesitated. What was in the envelope was considered a sacred gift.

Does one share such things? Will its magic be enough to calm the paranoia in the admiral, enough to open his eyes to see the truth of the destruction he's wielding with Madame? Will its Light help him see clearly and set him free from his fears?"

Sam reached into the envelope and took out the feather, the red-tailed hawk's feather that had driven him to near insanity only a few days ago. He stepped toward the admiral and slowly offered the feather to him.

"What the hell is that?" the admiral scowled and stepped away.

Sam slowed his breathing. It was vital for him to make a connection with his nemesis. Time was running out. To obtain his freedom and get Sidney off the *Nonnah*, he needed the admiral as an ally.

"Admiral, you of all people know that what appears to be fact, isn't all there is to know. This appears to be a feather, but it isn't. See for yourself."

Sam realized he needed to use his Guardian nature. With that conscious thought, he felt a surge of energy. In seconds he shifted from Captain Samaru Waterhouse to Sam, the Guardian. Even his voice changed slightly. As he spoke, he hoped the admiral would give in to trust.

"Please take the gift." He offered the feather with an open palm. "I know you're a wise man and fear nothing. This gift will show you that though something may appear fragile, it has great strength and endurance, like you, John."

The admiral was taken aback. Very few people called him John. It made him feel like the man he'd been many years ago. Before he was an admiral. Before his wife died. Gingerly, he took the feather into his trembling hand. He looked at its colorful markings and studied the delicate edges. Sam moved quickly to place a chair behind the admiral as he slumped backward, still focused on the feather as it spoke to him in a language known only to his higher self.

The trembling of his hand became worse, and the feather fell to the floor. His entire body shook, and his eyes were wide with fear.

"No!" he screamed. "No! Run!"

The admiral leaped from his chair and darted about the room. Then he found a corner and pressed himself into it. Clawing at the walls, panting and mumbling nonsense, he collapsed to the floor.

Sam knelt down and reached for the admiral's chest. Touching the space near his heart, he said, "John, you're free."

Instantly, the vision that was revealing the truth to the Admiral was terminated. He was confused and embarrassed to find himself huddled on the floor. Slowly, he rose to standing and touched a severely damaged section of wall.

"How, why?" he stammered. He looked over to Sam, standing calm beside him. "I saw … things. Terrible things, Sam. A world gone mad, and *I* was making it happen. Like I was mad myself." He grabbed Sam's arm. "What have I done?"

Sam held the admiral's shoulder and motioned for him to have a seat. He retrieved the feather, placed it back into its envelope and into his coat pocket.

"You'll feel better in a few minutes," Sam said, offering the man a glass of water.

"I never meant for any of this to happen," the admiral said in complete surrender.

Sam waited for the man to regain his composure. "Admiral, what's your vision for this planet's future?"

"The future? My vision? God, it better not be what I just saw." He gazed out through the clear plastic that was now stretched over the window opening. Soon he began to paint a picture. "I see children playing in clean, clear water. I see boreal forests filled with birds. Nations without borders. I see peace, Sam." He appeared calmer than Sam could ever remember. "I see peace," he repeated.

Sam sat down across from the admiral. "Sounds like you and I have similar visions. We may only disagree on how to arrive there."

The admiral looked forlorn. "You know, Sam, once you start keeping company with the insane, visions become twisted."

"I know all about what company you've been keeping."

The admiral studied Sam's face. "How could you? No one knows, aside from Butchart."

"*Thy Kingdom Come*. And Madame. I found a copy of the complete file."

The admiral stiffened.

"Relax. No one but me has read the complete file. I have a copy, thanks to Sidney."

The admiral rolled his eyes. "Her again! Why thanks to her?"

"Sidney copied it from your computer and then hid it. She seems to believe that the file causes anyone who touches it nothing but grief and death. Seems pretty accurate, so far."

The admiral frowned. "Perhaps that's why Frank Butchart appears ill at times. He's become fanatical over the crystal project security. Chances are he's now one of Madame's spies."

Sam moved close to the admiral's ear. Barely speaking above a whisper he asked, "Admiral, if, and only *if* the crystal were powerful, who would you think should have access to that power? Someone like Butchart? Madame? Me, you … who?"

The admiral's eyes were wide with shock "Are you saying those crystals do have power? They can be used to destroy, like what happened yesterday?"

Sam nodded. "They have no power on their own. The crystal only amplifies the intent of the one accessing the crystal, making the power last longer and become stronger. But they can't be activated unless the user is able to be calm and focused. Someone like Butchart. The crystal doesn't differentiate between what's for the higher good and what's for harm."

The admiral starred at Sam. "Did you use a crystal yesterday? Where is it?"

"It's hidden in my shoe."

The admiral shook his head. "Damn, what have I done? I don't know what possessed me to agree to Madame's plan. No one should be trusted with that much power. No one." He looked away, again deep in thought. "I'm going lock up those crystals, Sam."

The admiral placed a call to the Naval Base science lab. He ordered the scientists to shut down the lab and leave immediately. He then ordered his head of security to ensure the lab was locked and to prevent anyone from entering it. They were to use lethal force if necessary.

He turned to Sam. "I was skeptical about the crystals in the beginning but was motivated by Madame to participate in her project. I figured that if the crystal were proven to be powerful, I'd be viewed as a hero, saving the world from these dark times. I figured a person like her wouldn't bother with crystals unless she knew for a fact they had power. Over this past year I began to have doubts about her, particularly because she watched my every move. At first, I thought perhaps she was just overly zealous in her work, but then the threats started, and Sam, she has the wealth and manpower to back those up."

The admiral's comlink sounded, and the security staff at his gate announced that Captain Butchart had arrived.

25. Guardians of Light and Dark Duel

July 16, 1735 Hours, New Seattle

"Let Captain Butchart pass," the admiral commanded his front gate security. "And let me know the second there's any indication of Madame or her troops approaching." He turned back to Sam. "You realize both of us are going to have to fight for our lives before the day is done! Madame isn't going to let you walk away."

"She appears to have already made an attempt on mine," Sam murmured. "Had a little car trouble last night."

The admiral grimaced. "She always knows my every move. She's probably gathering up her forces as we speak."

"Sir, I have to get my boys out of here. We're going to have to come up with a strategy."

"Give Frank the feather. Perhaps it'll bring him back to his senses too."

"He'd recognize it and stay clear of its influence. No, and I don't dare use any Guardian powers. Look what happened the last time. I can't risk any lives, especially those of my sons."

Frank entered the room. The three men faced each other in a triangle formation, each with his arms crossed over his chest. Sam had no respect for Butchart and no trust, yet made an effort to start the conversation without hostility.

"I want apologize to you for yesterday's incident. As I told Admiral Garland, it was totally accidental. I had no intention of doing any damage or harming anyone. How are your wounds?"

Butchart glared at Sam. "Never mind my wounds." Then Butchart smiled. He was in his element. He'd taken more of his medication, and his arm was free of pain. "By the way, your boys are fine ... for now. They'll be released unharmed the second you admit the truth about the crystals. It's that simple."

The admiral was shocked. His eyes were wide and his mouth opened, but no sounds were emitted. He took a breath.

"Frank, you've lost your mind!" the admiral shouted.

Sam glared at Butchart. His uneasy feeling about his sons' absence was founded after all.

"I've nothing more to say about those rocks!" Sam stood firm, his shoulders square with Butchart's. His hands remained clenched at his side as he resisted grabbing the man's throat. "Where are my boys?"

Butchart wasn't intimidated. "Perhaps you'll change your mind once you see your kids suffering from your poor judgment."

Admiral Garland approached Butchart. "I forbid you to harm those boys. You have no business putting innocent children at risk. I order you to release them. Right now, Frank!"

Butchart was surprised at the admiral's show of concern for the boys.

"Admiral, this has to be done. It'll answer any doubts you've had about the crystals. You'll see that all the money and struggle was worth it. You're destined to lead this country, breathe new life into this whole damn planet. They'll call you the most heroic leader of all time."

Sam noticed the admiral's reaction to the idea of being the chosen one. For a moment, he was drawn back into the lust for power. His chin inched a bit higher, and his shoulders shifted back. It lasted only briefly, then the admiral stepped out of the mold. He put his hand on Butchart's shoulder.

"This isn't the time, Frank . . . or the way. Let the boys go. We'll solve this between men."

Butchart stood back. "You'll see, sir. You'll see that this man has been lying to you. He and his wife committed treasonous acts against you and this country. We must eliminate anyone who interferes with the project. Nothing must get in our way. Madame demands absolute loyalty."

Butchart switched on the admiral's comlink monitor and connected with a dimly lit room at the photo lab. Sam saw both Simon and Nathan handcuffed and lying in long, shallow lab sinks that years ago had been used for custom development of photographs. Large jugs sat on a nearby table.

Perkins and some other men came into view in the background. A man near Perkins kept his back to the video camera. There was something familiar about him, and it nagged at Sam.

"What the hell are you doing, Perkins?" the admiral roared.

"Say hi to your dad, boys," said Perkins with a smirk. "Waterhouse, these jugs contain acid, in case you were wondering."

"You're just as sick as this maniac, Perkins," said Sam, pointing to Butchart. "If you harm my boys, I'll make sure you live just long enough to regret it." He thought about using his crystal, but knew it would be useless to even try. His heart pounded, and his mouth was dry. There was no chance of him calming enough to access the crystal's energy.

Butchart stepped in front of the monitor. The man with his back to the camera disappeared out of view.

"Now, Waterhouse, the admiral is waiting. Sidney told you about the crystals. All you need to do right now is to admit that the sun crystals are the source of limitless power."

Sam leaned into Frank's face. "Go to hell!"

"Wrong answer, Waterhouse. Perkins, get the acid!"

"The admiral already knows about the crystals' power. And he's promised to lock them up."

Butchart's attention snapped to the admiral. "Is this true?"

The admiral raised his hands as if to push Butchart back. "Just for the time being, Frank. There's too much at stake. Take a look at this room. I've got to be certain this is the right time to bring the crystals to the government."

Butchart stepped up close to the admiral. "She'll kill us."

"She'll be mad as hell, but she needs me, Frank. I'm her access to the government. I've already shut down the lab, just minutes ago. The crystals will be moved to a vault somewhere safe until I am satisfied there's no risk to the stability of America. Or the rest of the world, for that matter. No doubt she is just finding out now that I've interfered with her plans."

Butchart grabbed the admiral's arm. "Don't give up, Admiral. This is your time to be known as a hero, the man who saved the world from these dark times."

The admiral studied Butchart's face. Finally he could see the desperation in the eyes, the hardness of the mouth, and hear the fear in his voice. The emptiness of his character was now so obvious. Butchart was barely human.

"You're a sick man, Frank. Return the boys and we'll forget this business. The Base has doctors. You need help."

Butchart's face twitched, and he briefly winced. "I don't need your help." He pointed to Sam. "I need you to not cave in to this turncoat."

Simon and Nathan began to squirm and whimper. A jug was brought over to the sinks, and their eyes became wide with fear.

"No, no!" they cried out. "Dad, make them stop. Please, Dad!"

Sam was becoming frantic. "Boys, relax. Frank isn't the sort to spend the rest of his miserable life in prison. He's just scaring you. Nothing's going to happen to you, I promise."

Admiral Garland approached Butchart once more. "How much, Frank. Name your price to let those boys go."

Butchart's rage escalated to insanity. "You'll pay for your interference, Waterhouse," he seethed through clenched teeth. "Pour the acid, Perkins."

Perkins nodded to the man beside him with his back still facing the video camera. The man raised a small glass container just above Simon's chest. Simon glanced at the man. There was a moment in which Sam caught the expression on his son's face. It was a moment of trust, as if the man with the glass was a friend. The liquid dropped onto Simon's chest. He screamed in agony, and misty fumes obliterated the view.

Sam grabbed Butchart by his uniform and pushed him against a wall. "Stop it!" he screamed. "For God's sake, stop!" He could still hear Simon screaming. "I'll tear you to pieces!" He reached for Butchart's neck.

Butchart wrestled free and screamed, "I'll destroy them like I destroyed that bitch wife of yours!" He dodged Sam and stood in front of the monitor, his eyes like a wild man. "Kill them, Perkins! Kill them both."

"You bastard! You killed Joy!" Sam shouted.

"Yeah, I killed your traitorous wife, Waterhouse. And it was almost as much fun to hear her screams as I ran her down as it is to hear your son's now."

Sam slammed his fist into Butchart's face. Dazed, Butchart sank to the floor.

A voice on the comlink shouted out, "Got that, Clay?"

"Yep, sure did, Danik. And I'll add it to the list of all the other charges he's accumulated with this little scheme of his." Detective Clay Flanders turned around and came into view on the monitor.

"Hi, sailor. Told you I'd get the bastard that killed Joy. Admiral Garland, I'd appreciate it if you'd hang on to Captain Butchart, and please instruct your security to let my men in — they're stationed around your property."

The admiral nodded. "We'll take care of him."

"My boys! They're okay?" Sam shouted, finally grasping what had just happened.

"Sit up, Simon, show your dad you're okay," Clay said. Simon grinned and waved at the monitor just before the connection clicked off.

Butchart forced himself to standing and lunged toward the door. He met a wall in the form of Sam Waterhouse.

"You're finished, Butchart," said Sam. "I *am* a Guardian." It sounded like a declaration, something he now firmly believed in.

He grabbed Butchart with such vengeance that he was airborne for a few moments before slamming into the floor. The two men wrestled until Sam's fist again connected with Butchart's jaw, sending him into a semi-conscious stupor from which he wouldn't soon recover. The officers stationed around the perimeter entered the room and placed handcuffs on Butchart's wrists.

Few words were spoken. Sam felt like he'd arrived at the conclusion of what had been a nightmare video running in an endless loop. He felt relief. Relief that finally justice would be served for the murder of his wife.

The admiral paced.

"What's on your mind, sir?" Sam asked quietly.

"The usual," he murmured.

"Let me guess—the implications of Butchart's activities being made public in a trial may not be in your best interest. It could ruin your future in the navy."

The admiral snorted. "Can't let him testify, Sam."

"Well, sir, you can't kill him either."

The admiral had a look on his face as if to say, "Oh, yeah?" Then he smiled and shook his head. "What have you done to me, Sam?"

Sam smiled back. "This is your new life, John."

A commotion was heard from outside the admiral's office door. Clay had arrived with Sam's boys, Danik, and Perkins.

The boys were hollering and burst into the office. "Dad, Dad, did you see us? That was so cool. We played a trick on that old buzzard, didn't we!"

Sam was overjoyed. He embraced them both, unable to say the words of how he felt. "Yes, we did, boys. Now, I want you to go to your rooms and pack your backpacks."

"We're going camping, Dad?" asked Simon.

"For a while, maybe. Just pack as if you are. Just the essentials. Okay?" He looked them over. "You're both fine. No problems?"

"Heck no, Dad," replied Nathan.

"Stay in your rooms until I call for you." He winked at Nathan. "Promise?" They were delighted, grinning and wrestling with each other as they headed out of the office.

"Gonna take your teddy, Nathan?" Simon teased.

"That's dumb, but I bet you're taking Beth's photo with you." Nathan laughed.

"Sorry about putting you through that, gentlemen," Clay said after the boys had run upstairs. "Perkins and I knew that if either of you knew about the set up, it might not work. We had to push your panic buttons to make sure Frank was pushed to the edge. Not sure how good an actor you are." Clay gave a fake slow motion blow to Sam's chin. "With everyone at a fever pitch, I knew Frank would fess up."

Sam eyed Perkins, who thrust his hand forward for a handshake. "No hard feelings, Sam?"

Sam hesitated. Clay explained that Perkins was a special agent and had been collecting information for him since Joy's death, working undercover. Sam relented and shook Perkins' hand.

"Actually, come to think of it, you've been watching over my boys the whole time. I owe you a lot. Thanks," Sam said.

Danik stepped in and interrupted. "Gentlemen, this may appear totally out of protocol, but I'm taking Frank back to where he belongs." Tension filled the room as the officers frowned at Danik. "Look, I know he's committed criminal acts and you're probably planning to see him rot in jail."

The admiral interrupted. "Just where is this place, Mr. ah ... ?"

"Danik is the name. Just Danik. Can't say exactly where this place is, but once I get him there, he won't be coming back unless he's become an Olympic swimmer."

The admiral was puzzled. "Just why do *you* want him?"

"Oh, don't get me wrong, sir. I'd just as soon leave him with you."

Sam interjected. "Danik, the admiral has been told about the Guardians. He knows the basics."

Danik went on to explain that the Guardian Elders wanted Frank returned to Hawk's Island. They hoped that one day he'd return to make amends for what he'd done. Even so, Clay was unwilling to release his prisoner.

Sam motioned for Clay and the admiral to meet with him away from the group. After a few minutes of discussion, Clay told the police officers they were dismissed and that Butchart was remaining on scene for the time being.

Clay shook his head. "As far as the books are concerned, Joy's murder is still not solved. Sam pointed out that if I tried to explain this business about Guardians, the police chief might have me admitted into a mental ward. You keep Frank out of my hair, and I keep my job and credibility. Agreed?"

The admiral turned to Danik. "All right, Danik, get this trash off my property. I'd better not ever see or hear from him again. Is that clear?"

Danik saluted. "Right away, sir. My partner is arriving with our chopper. Should be landing here any minute. Sam, can you give me a hand with our sick puppy?"

Danik started to lift Butchart from the floor and then let him drop as he slapped his forehead.

"Oh, Admiral, I'm terribly sorry but I completely forgot to mention there's a fee for this," Danik said rather sheepishly. "Completely slipped my mind." He turned to Sam and waved his hand in circles around his head. "The brain's just not what it used to be."

"What are you talking about?" asked the admiral.

"You see, we're quite willing to take Frank off your hands, especially given all the damage he could do to your plans, you know, political ambitions and all that."

"Get on with it!" shouted the admiral.

Danik winced and turned to Sam. "Is he always this cranky?"

Sam smiled. "Better be quick, Danik. He's not a patient man."

Danik nodded. "This is how it goes, sir. We take care of your problem in return for giving Sidney back to us. You really are getting the better part of the deal, sir. I mean, you know what Frank is like, and well, Sidney's a handful too. You won't have any more interference from either of them, I promise. It's a really great trade. Trust me, things sure aren't going to be peaceful around the campfire anymore with those two around. Do we have a deal, sir?"

The admiral turned to Sam. "I suppose you're going to pack up your kids and leave with this character?"

"You don't need me or the *Nonnah* now that you're shutting down the crystal project. The deal is Danik will take Frank, my boys, and me to the *Nonnah*, pick up Sidney, and —"

"Just hold on a minute Waterhouse. As happy as I am to be rid of Butchart, we both have Madame about to descend upon us."

"Danik, go get Simon and Nathan and bring them down while I negotiate with the admiral."

Danik didn't have to get the boys. They were waiting at the bottom of the stairs and had heard the conversation. They bolted into the office ecstatically clutching their backpacks.

"Wow, Dad. Just like the movies," exclaimed Nathan. "Come on, Simon. Let's get out to the chopper."

"Just a minute, boys. We're not going anywhere until the admiral agrees to release Sidney." Sam turned back to the admiral. "Let her go, sir."

The admiral was tense. He was being backed into a corner, a place he wasn't acquainted with. The sound of an approaching chopper could be heard. The admiral went to the window and observed a huge helicopter landing in his parking lot.

"What on Earth is that!" he called out above the noise of the chopper's rotary engines.

"Ain't she a beauty?" said Danik with boyish pride. "She does rescue work, mostly in the mountains. She's as powerful as you can get, not as fast as your little Spitfire there, sir, but there's no place she can't go."

The chopper's engine slowed to an idle. "Well, let's go get Sidney," said Danik hopefully.

The admiral gritted his teeth. "Just step back, mister. Don't move anyone anywhere just yet." He was trying to restrain his indignation with Danik's insolence.

Sam caught Danik's eye and motioned for him to ease up, then he told his sons to wait with their backpacks at the front door. They scurried out giggling with excitement. Sam turned to the admiral.

"Admiral, if I might have a word with you in private, sir?"

They walked across the hall and stepped through the French doors.

"Leave the door ajar, Sam. Want to keep an eye on that…character."

The admiral's view remained on Danik, who sat on the floor beside Butchart, who'd lapsed into withdrawal, oblivious to people and noise.

"Sam, I can't release Sidney. I shouldn't release you either, but I'm going to. I owe you that much. But Sidney, as powerful as she is, would be a phenomenal asset to our military strategies. And she knows too much."

"Admiral, what would you rather have—one little trout or a whole lake filled endlessly with every kind of fish you'd like on your dinner plate?"

The admiral was now focused intently at Sam. "Keep talking."

"Suppose Sidney were to show you the way to find that lake?"

"Sam, speak plainly!"

"What I mean is that with this Madame set on destroying whatever or whoever gets in her way, it might be prudent to seek the assistance of not just one person but an entire community. The Guardians have ways that…suffice it to say you have the same vision as they do. And I'd stake my life they'd provide you with support and not ask for anything in return."

"And what's the catch?"

"Seeking only the higher good. Sidney can probably explain it to you better than I can."

The admiral thought for a while, watching Danik and Butchart. Sam let him have his space and time. The admiral at last turned to Sam.

"This is what's going to take place, Sam. You, the boys, and I will take my chopper. Danik and Butchart will go in theirs. We'll all go to the *Nonnah*. Once I've met with Sidney, I'll make my decision. Is that clear?"

"Yes, sir."

"There's one problem though. We're going to have to be fast. If Madame gets wind of this, and she always does somehow, we'll all end up dead. Is that clear? We must act very quickly to get you and your boys off the *Nonnah* as soon as possible."

Sam quickly relayed the information to Danik, who shrugged his shoulders as if it was a minor glitch in his plans. Sam and Danik hoisted Frank up into the old chopper. The Admiral, Sam, and the two boys went to the admiral's chopper and soon were heading to the *Nonnah*, listless in the quiet Pacific.

26. The Admiral's Guardian

July 16, 1845 Hours

Their reception at the *Nonnah* was far different than they'd expected. The crew was armed and ready for a major confrontation. The admiral watched from inside his chopper as sailors stood or crouched in fighting position on the ship's decks. The large cannons were armed and manned.

"What the hell?" said the admiral, puzzled by the aggressive stance. "Don't they recognize my chopper?"

"Commander Moon is following Frank's orders," Sam explained.

"Russell," said the admiral to his pilot, "keep the engine running. We may have to leave quickly. Let's go, Sam. You boys stay here with Russell."

Sam nodded in agreement but motioned for his boys to keep their comlink line open. Sam and the admiral stepped down from the chopper as Moon approached them with two armed sailors by his side. Moon stopped several feet away, carefully observing who exited the chopper. Suddenly, a ruckus was heard coming from the stern.

Guns were drawn and aimed at someone running toward the admiral. It was Danik, dodging around and vaulting over anything in his way. A soldier fired directly at Danik but to everyone's surprise, the Guardian remained steadfast in his pace toward the admiral.

Sam hollered, "Let him through, Rhett!"

Moon gave the order to stand down, and the sailors stepped back and stood at ease. When he reached the admiral and Sam, his salute was almost hesitant. It was briskly returned by the admiral and Sam.

"Welcome aboard the USS *Nonnah*, Admiral Garland and Captain Waterhouse."

Sam waited for a response from the admiral, and held his breath. Protocol interfered with his intense need to get Sidney. His old rule book had become a torment, rather than a security. He waited for the admiral to make his move.

"Lieutenant Commander Moon, we'll meet in the boardroom to discuss an urgent matter. Get the prisoner and have her delivered to the boardroom as well."

The admiral spotted Danik tossing a bullet back forth between his hands as though it was too hot to hold.

He shook his head. "This is Danik. He'll accompany us."

Sam headed for the ship's hallway. "I'll get Sidney."

Moon held up his hand. "That's not possible, sir. The code has been changed. Only I can open her door."

"Rhett, escort the admiral to the boardroom. Sidney and I'll be there shortly. Danik, follow the admiral."

Sam left and swiftly followed the corridors and stairways down to Sidney's cell. Once he reached her door, Bridges stood at attention.

"At ease," Sam said. "How've things been?"

"All I can say, sir, is that I'm real glad you're back. Things got … a bit weird."

Sam held up his hand. "No need to say any more. Go on deck and provide assistance to the pilot of the chopper on the stern in case things get more weird."

"Aye, aye, sir."

Bridges left and Sam turned to Sidney's door. He placed his hand on it and closed his eyes, calling to her from within in a voice stronger than the steel that separated them.

Sidney, sitting on her bed and aware of the excitement on the ship during the past few minutes, was drawn to stand next to the door. She placed her hand on its surface. In her mind's eye, saw Sam on the other side. She breathed slowly and deeply, accessing the locking mechanism's energy. In seconds, the door was unlocked, and she pushed gently. Sam grabbed the handle and pulled it open.

Sidney stepped through the doorway and stood in front of Sam. Slowly she brought her hands up along his arms. He gazed into her eyes and smiled. Wrapping his arms around her shoulders, he pulled her close. No words were spoken. The feelings of love forbade any utterance that could come close to expressing their passion for each other. He kissed her lips, caressed her, wove his fingers into her hair and down her back. She teased him with her kisses and held her body close to his.

Finally, Sam spoke. "Tonight I'll hold you in my arms, my precious witch. I love you, Sidney. Right now we must hurry. We have a little business to take care of—the admiral's here, and he's quite interested in talking with you."

Sidney smiled. "Talking's a nice change. Last time we were together all he could do was scream at me."

"He's going to let you go but will be asking for something in return. He's hoping for an ally. Is it possible your Guardian friends would help him protect the crystals from Madame?"

"The Guardians have always been willing and ready to help."

"Sidney, we're talking about going up against the insane, the unconscionable."

"Uh huh. Perhaps like Frank?"

"Speaking of whom, he isn't well and is tied up in your brother's chopper, which is sitting on the stern of this ship."

Sidney's went wide. "Danik's here?"

"Yes. He and his pilot are determined to not leave without you. Let's go."

They hurried to Sam's office. As soon as they stepped into the reception room, he directed his staff to fill out his resignation papers.

"I'll need the admiral's signature on them immediately."

Sam led Sidney into his office and motioned for her to wait. He stepped into the boardroom and told the admiral he'd be just another two minutes. He went back to Sidney and pulled her into his private quarters.

"If things in there start to look as if the admiral isn't going to release you, I'll give Danik a signal to get off this ship. You and he do whatever you can to get to his chopper. *Whatever*, Sidney. Just get off this ship as fast as you can."

Sidney's eyes welled up with tears. "Sam, I can't leave you."

"Not another word. I'll find you later. Whatever it takes, I'll find you." Sam kissed her on her forehead. "I love you."

Sidney smiled. "I know."

He kissed her again. "We don't have much time. The admiral believes Madame is on her way to put an end to all of us."

"What's the signal?"

"Danik seems to be in the habit of reading my mind. He'll know."

"Sam…"

"Yes?"

Sidney shook her head. "Later. It's going to be okay, Sam. I'm ready."

Sam and Sidney entered the boardroom. She first greeted the admiral, walking up to him and extending her hand.

"Admiral Garland, I'm sincerely pleased to see you, sir."

The admiral quickly thrust out his hand and shook hers.

"Sit down," he commanded.

"Yes, sir. In just one moment. There's someone else I'd like to say hello to, if you don't mind. My brother."

The admiral nodded. She trotted over to Danik and grabbed him by the shoulders and hugged him tightly. He hugged her back and was reluctant to release her. She buried her face in his neck and whispered instructions regarding the signal that Sam had spoken of. Danik nodded and released her.

The admiral sat down and motioned for Sidney to sit beside him. Sam sat next to her. Moon and Danik took chairs on the other side of the table.

The admiral spoke to Commander Moon. "Captain Waterhouse is resigning from his commission and the United States Naval Force. As a result, you'll be required to continue as the acting captain of the *Nonnah* until formal papers are completed. Do you have any problem with that?"

Moon sat up straight in his chair. "No, sir. I recommend Lieutenant Bridges as my first officer, sir."

"Fine. Thank you. On to my other problem. Captain Waterhouse, you know my predicament. Lieutenant Commander Moon, the details are confidential, but I'll summarize. There are those putting pressure on me to comply with demands that could cause serious risk to freedoms enjoyed by our country, if not the well-being of humanity across the entire planet."

Moon was unmoved.

"Initially I was led into a project with the belief that honorable people were behind the quest to deliver great power into the hands of our leaders. Now, I find such isn't the case. In fact, some who've been in close alliance with me on this project have become tainted with the poison of this group. With help from Sam, I now see this business will lead us into nothing but a dark hole, mass destruction, and suffering. This is where you come in, Sidney."

Sidney tried to maintain the proper reserve and decorum when addressing an admiral. Between thoughts of returning home and being with Sam she could barely sit still and remain calm. And yet, there was a nagging feeling that there was to be a great loss. She grabbed tightly onto Sam's hand which was resting on her thigh.

The admiral turned to Moon. "I want to talk to Sidney in private. You and Sam can spend some time finalizing the turnover of command. Danik, make sure Sam's boys are okay."

Moon had a hard look in his eyes as he studied Sam. When Sam turned toward him and nodded, Moon stood and sneered. "You're turning your back on your career, abandoning your loyalty to defend America. For what! That?" he said, thrusting a finger in Sidney's direction. .

Sam still wore the uniform of his rank but felt no attachment to it. He was now a Guardian and had no need for the external symbols of power. His authentic power was within and more potent that the guns on the *Nonnah*. There was so much he wanted to say to his first officer, but it was clear that Everett Moon was not in a listening frame of mind. "You're an excellent naval officer. Take good care of the *Nonnah* and her crew." Sam glanced at Sidney. "We don't have much time." He headed toward his office. "Rhett, let's get the Admiral's documents ready."

Alone with Sidney, the admiral got up and stood at the windows. He was searching for a way to ask for help and convey just how desperately it was needed.

"Sidney, I understand you have some unique talents."

Sidney approached the admiral. "You're referring to my Guardian gifts, I suppose. Please understand I'm pretty much a novice. I haven't mastered the true Guardian capacity nor have I attained the wisdom of the Guardian Elders."

"Wisdom is something gained only through time. You're young, but you appear to have risen adequately to the challenge you were sent for."

"Adequately, perhaps. But this black hole you're referring to, it's enough to frighten me down to my toenails. Fear is a poor ally, sir."

The admiral smiled. "Fear—it's been something I eat and sleep, day in and day out."

"Is that not what those who oppose freedom are counting on? While we're focused on fear, we're disabled and unable see with clarity a resolution to the conflict."

"Do the Guardians have an antidote to fear?"

"Wisdom and, believe it or not, unconditional love."

The admiral shook his head. "Okay, suppose I'm in the market for ally who has these qualities. Will you help?"

"I believe, Admiral, that my people would be willing to support you in your efforts to prevent a disaster."

"That's a generous offer. However, I have doubts your people, isolated and spiritual as they are, are going to agree to get their hands bloody."

"It's true the Guardians won't involve themselves in any combat or cause harm to anyone, including those with whom you're in opposition. However, they've always worked with those who have a vision for the higher good."

"How do I know I can trust you, truly trust you?"

Sidney stepped up close to the admiral. "Sir, I'll give you proof. Are you willing to put yourself in my hands for a few minutes?"

"What exactly do you mean?"

"Come and sit down in front of me." The admiral and Sidney sat down in chairs facing each other. Sidney placed her hands in front of the admiral with her palms facing the ceiling.

"Place your palms on mine." The admiral did as she instructed. "Are you okay with this so far?"

"Yes, but what does this prove?"

"I need you to become completely calm. Breathe for a while. Slow and deep."

The admiral pulled his hands away. "If you think you're going to put me into a trance and ... "

"Admiral, if you want an ally, you're going to have to trust that ally. Yes?"

The admiral frowned. "Just what are we doing?"

"In a nutshell, Admiral, I'm going to let you into my mind. You'll know everything about me from the day I was born until now. You'll know my strengths and weaknesses. You'll see my Light and my Shadow side. You'll know if what I'm saying is truth. Are you ready for that much proof?"

The admiral was nervous. "I can't do that."

"Admiral John Garland, trust yourself first. You're a powerful being with great internal wisdom. Look into your heart. You know you can do this."

The admiral slowly put his hands back on Sidney's palms and began his breathing exercise as instructed. He felt the warmth of her hands and gazed into her eyes. In time, a calmness swept over him.

He murmured, "I'm impressed. This is nice."

"I want you to know that you're safe. You're in full control and can stop this exercise anytime you choose. Are you ready to go further and deeper?"

He nodded.

"I want you to close your eyes. When you feel you're being drawn to something, go with it. You're safe."

The admiral relaxed. He only briefly uttered "This is ... " and in the next moment he was in another dimension. When he returned from the journey five minutes later, he sat back and stared at Sidney in awe. Once he got his bearings again, he stood up and returned to the view of the ocean through the windows.

"I very nearly killed you," he said mostly to himself. He turned to Sidney. "It seems odd. A moment ago I knew everything about you, but it seems to be fading like a dream. But it wasn't a dream. What was the man's name?"

"His name is Aaron. His intention is to see you in your office. In about a week, I believe."

The admiral nodded his approval. "Is he good?"

"He's my father, Admiral. He's the one you need."

The admiral stood gazing into Sidney's eyes. He touched her face. "You're free to go home, Sidney. I release you. I'll wait for Aaron."

"Thank you, Admiral." Her eyes sparkled with tears.

"I do remember one thing quite clearly," the admiral said. "Does Sam know?"

"No, not yet. He's got enough on his plate right now."

He smiled. "Good luck, Sidney."

The admiral and Sidney stepped into Sam's office. The documents were completed. Moon and the admiral signed the documents.

"Lieutenant Commander Moon, you're now the USS *Nonnah*'s Captain."

Moon continued to show no emotion. It was as though he'd expected the appointment all along. But when the admiral told Sam that he, his sons, and Sidney were free to disembark, Moon reacted.

"You can't be serious! You're letting her go?"

Sidney quickly moved to stand beside Sam, who confronted Moon.

"You've taken a special interest in the business with Sidney beyond your responsibility, particularly since collaborating with Captain Butchart. Explain your involvement with Butchart."

Moon looked away momentarily and turned back with a smile.

The admiral interjected. "Collaborated with Butchart? Explain now."

"Just a misunderstanding, sir. I thought the captain's approach to interrogating the prisoner was unusual. I was concerned that she may be manipulating him, so I decided to do some investigation of my own. Captain Butchart seemed the logical place to get more information. Just had the navy's best interest in mind, sir."

"Keep in mind, Rhett, that any further insubordination on your part will be dealt with severely. Is that understood?"

Moon straightened his posture. "Yes. My apologies, sir."

Sam took off his naval hat and coat. He laid them on a chair in what had been his office. He walked up to the admiral and shook his hand. "Goodbye, Admiral. Good luck."

Without further ceremony, he and Sidney left the office and headed toward the admiral's helicopter to retrieve his sons. Before they reached the upper deck, the sky became shadowed.

27. Madame's Revenge

July 16, 1915 Hours, Aboard the Nonnah

Quiet rotors of stealth helicopters descended from the blue sky. Eight in number, with guns directed toward the *Nonnah*, the helicopters swirled around the ship's decks in a menacing fashion. They bore no identifying markers nor did they send any signal of greeting or demands. Sam held Sidney close.

The admiral knew instantly that the choppers were Madame's advance guard. "Moon," he hollered "Red Alert!" The ship's loud siren pierced the calm evening sky. Seamen scurried to man the gun turrets and took defensive positions along the decks. Sam and Sidney climbed a stairway to the uppermost deck where the admiral's chopper sat waiting. Fifty feet away, Russell sat in the pilot's seat gearing up the engine. A burst of gunfire cut Sam and Sidney off from their approach.

Sam motioned for Sidney to take cover in a corner out of view of the attackers, and he sprang forward. He took only two steps before the enemy fired upon the admiral's chopper. It instantly burst into a fireball. Sam screamed in horror, his hands reaching out toward the burning bits on the deck as if to pull his sons from the wreckage. In seconds, little remained but the shell of the small craft. Sam scrambled along with seamen toward the flames. Carrying firefighting equipment, the men smothered the inferno.

Sam crumbled down to his knees as though in agony. Sidney grabbed hold of his shoulders as he screamed the names of his sons into the billowing black smoke.

The admiral watched the attack from the ship's bridge. Moon gave orders for the seamen to fire warning shots toward the chopper. Carla announced, "There's a call for you, sir. Says it's 'Madame.'"

"Admiral Garland here!" he shouted into the comlink to Madame's chopper.

Madame's voice was calm and detached. "Cease fire, Admiral. I can destroy your little ship in seconds."

The admiral nodded to Moon. "Stand down."

"John, you disappoint me. Just when we're within days of resolving the energy crisis, you're having second thoughts, and now it appears you're letting two individuals go who know far more than they should and could be very useful to us. This isn't acceptable."

The admiral gritted his teeth. He'd been horrified to see the chopper carrying the Waterhouse boys explode into flames.

Bridges was suddenly at the admiral's side. "Sir, the Waterhouse boys were transferred to Ryan's chopper. They're safe. I suggest we get them out of here quick."

The admiral nodded. With his helicopter destroyed, it would impossible to get Sam and Sidney off his ship – unless they were able to commandeer another chopper.

"Madame, we'll get nothing from Captain Waterhouse or the woman. You have no idea what I've been able to negotiate—I have something far better than those damn rocks," he said.

"Not interested in your diversion tactics. I'm here to emphasize why you must comply with *my* plan. You've been misbehaving, Admiral. Once I've landed, I'll reveal my demands to you. And you're not leaving this ship until the scientists return to their labors. Is that clear?"

"Fine. One more thing. I have a medivac chopper on the stern ready to transport a critically ill sailor to the hospital. Let him go!"

"First show me that Captain Waterhouse and the woman are still on the ship."

"Sam, do exactly as I say," ordered the admiral into Sam's earpiece. "Stand with Sidney out on the main deck. Do you copy?"

Sam struggled to his feet. "Copy, sir." He trembled with rage and horror. Sidney stood beside him and grasped his hand.

They carried out the admiral's instructions and stood beneath the helicopters circling just above them. They watched Ryan's chopper climb from the ship's stern and rush toward the northern horizon. At a command from the admiral, they made their way to the conference room where the admiral and Moon waited with six security men.

Bridges approached as Sam entered the room.

"Captain, your boys are fine. They're in the other chopper heading north."

Sam was trembling. He grabbed onto Bridges' shoulders and shook him. "You're sure? You transferred them to Ryan's chopper?"

Bridges nodded and braced himself to suppress his emotions of having saved the life of the boys. "Danik and me, well we had a feeling that ... "

"Thank God!" the admiral and Sam responded. "By the way, where is Danik?" asked Sam.

"Right here" said Danik as he entered the room.

"All right," the admiral said. "Looks like we're going to have some difficulty getting all of you off the ship." He turned to Moon, who had been simmering behind the scenes. "Commander, er, Captain Moon, I leave the tactical operations to you. Do whatever is necessary to save the *Nonnah* and her crew. I will deal with Sam and his team."

Moon saluted, "Yes, sir." As soon as his back was turned, he began barking orders to his officers and headed to the bridge.

"All right, this is what's happening," the admiral said, eying the security staff. "Madame is about to land on this ship. She's aware of my defection from the crystal project. She's against letting the two of you go. Figures you know too much. She'll kill this entire ship's crew to get Sidney, and you too, Sam. Now, I need some of those Guardian tricks. Can you defuse this situation? Danik, got any ideas? We don't have much time."

"Sir," called out Lieutenant Bridges, "another helicopter is approaching and positioning to land on the stern helipad."

"Fine. Captain Moon," he called into his comlink, "allow only Madame's chopper to land on the stern's helipad. Make sure no others board this ship."

Sidney looked to her brother. "Danik, you figure Sam and I could take on the choppers?"

"Piece of cake. We'll let the Madame of Darkness land, and once she's left her chopper, you and Sam give those flying evil raptors a piece of Guardian hospitality. Got your crystal, Sam?"

"Yes, right here," Sam said, pulling it out of his pants pocket.

Danik grinned. "Good. Sidney will explain what to do with it. I'll stay here with the admiral, make sure his uniform doesn't even get wrinkled. I'll meet up with you later at the stern helipad."

Sam and Sidney slipped unnoticed to the main deck and vanished among the crates while the admiral watched Madame's helicopter land. She jumped down onto the deck, along with six security personnel all armed with automatic weapons. Upon being greeted by a dozen sailors with side arms, Madame's guards quickly disarmed the sailors who accompanied them to the conference room. The admiral's security men received instructions from the admiral to wait outside the conference room. Madame and her men surrounded the admiral and Danik. The admiral greeted them coldly. "You owe me one chopper and one pilot."

Madame approached the admiral. "Quit your whining. Where are the captain and Miss Davenport? And who's this?" She motioned toward Danik.

The admiral remained firm in his stance. "My security."

The woman chuckled. "Just one? You're rather confident for an old man." She stood in front of Danik. Staring into his eyes, she simultaneously ran one of her hands slowly over his body. "What, no weapons?" she asked with a sultry smile.

Danik leaned in close to her ear. "Sweetness, you haven't checked in all the right places." He winked at her.

She smiled. "Oh, you're precious! We need to talk later." She turned back to the admiral. "Okay, show time. You have five minutes to bring those two … misguided people in here. Clear?"

"Take a look out the window," said Danik. "Your helicopters appear to be having trouble staying airborne. Gee, I wonder what could be causing that. Oops." He barely managed to restrain a chuckle. "There goes another one."

One by one the helicopters were losing power and slowly descending onto the surface of the ocean, just managing to stay upright in the waves. The woman watched out the window in disbelief. Only two helicopters remained airborne.

"Start firing, you idiots!" demanded the woman. The chopper pilots were occupied trying to avoiding crashing into the ocean. Some gunfire went wild, scattering bullets into the ocean or the steel wall of the ship.

The admiral heard Moon on his comlink, "Gunners, fire! Engine room, I want full power, now! Navigation room, head into port. Commander Bridges, call for air and naval support."

The woman, seething with rage, turned to the admiral. "I'm through with you!" She pulled out her weapon from inside her blazer.

The admiral stepped back, fear written on his face. Madame's security forces drew their guns and waited for orders. "Danik?" the admiral hollered, his voice trembling.

Danik patted the admiral on his shoulder. "Stay calm, admiral."

"I'll replace you by tomorrow morning." She thrust her gun between the admiral's eyes and pulled the trigger. Nothing happened. "Shoot! Kill them!" she ordered. Her men attempted to fire their guns at the admiral and Danik. Again and again, their guns failed to fire.

"Security," hollered the admiral. The sailors rushed into the room with their weapons drawn and began to muscle Madame's men down onto the floor and place restraints on them.

Danik took the trembling admiral by the arm. "There's more company coming." He motioned toward the distant horizon at more of Madame's approaching helicopters.

Madame's look of shock was quickly replaced by rage. "You bastard!" she shouted and attempted to slap Danik's face. His hand shot up in an instant and held onto her wrist. Her anger abruptly vanished. A look of surprise transformed her face. "The only way you could have disarmed our guns was with a crystal. You know how to make it work." She was almost laughing. "Name your price, my dear. Whatever, it's yours." She attempted to wriggle free from Danik's grasp.

"Some other time, my dear." He turned her over to one of the seamen and turned to the admiral. "We'll be in touch. You'll be okay now."

Danik darted out of the room to help Sam and Sidney. Once he reached them, the trio headed for Madame's helicopter. The chopper's armed guards attempted to fire their weapons, but found them useless. Bullets rained down onto the *Nonnah*, now traveling at almost full speed toward the New Seattle Harbor. The gunners of the *Nonnah* were firing back in a futile attempt to defend the ship from the more heavily armed choppers. One of the *Nonnah*'s guns exploded and three seamen lay bloody and lifeless on the deck.

Danik saw that they had a long distance to run out in the open to get to the helicopter. Their focus and energy was now entirely on getting to the chopper and away from the *Nonnah*. They had no time to disable the approaching enemy. Sam doubted this was Madame's entire complement of attack choppers. The longer the three of them were on the *Nonnah*, the greater the risk to the rest of the crew. They had to get out of there fast.

Bullets were now being blasted into the ship from six more helicopters. Sam knew the airborne enemy wouldn't disable their chopper on the helipad. It was the only means of escape for Madame's group. If they could just get across that thirty-foot expanse, they'd have a chance. Sidney continued to focus on deactivating the weapons of the chopper's two guards who were still trying to fire on them.

Danik watched the helicopters closely. His experience as a chopper pilot gave him some understanding of when their firing accuracy would be minimal. As long as they moved quickly across their path, they had a chance. Two aircraft came in, and not being able to get the targets clearly in their sights, fired blindly, creating gaping holes in the deck.

Danik yelled, "Now! Run!"

Danik, the faster runner, got to the first guard and threw him to the ground hard enough that he was stunned and slow to get up. The other surrendered when he saw Sam's gun pointed in his direction. Sidney was just in front of Sam when the two guards hit the deck. Another group of helicopters flew overhead firing mercilessly in their direction. They were still several feet from the helicopter.

Danik yelled, "Sidney, run!"

From higher up on the ship, a lone man lay with his rifle to his shoulder. In his crosshairs was Sam's head. He squeezed the trigger. Avoiding a spray of gunfire coming from the helicopters to his left, Sam tumbled to the deck, his gun falling from his hand and skidding across the deck. Sidney fell.

Danik grabbed her hand and hoisted her up into the chopper. So frantic to get Sam aboard, he failed to notice the blood stain on her shirt. He went back to Sam.

"Come on, buddy!"

Danik grabbed his arm and very nearly flung him toward the chopper's open door. He looked up at Sidney's face. It was wild with excitement, and her hair whipped around her face with the force the wind currents created by the choppers rotors.

"Let's go home," she called out.

Sam hoisted himself into the chopper and sat down in the seat beside the pilot. Danik closed the door and jumped into the pilot's seat and revved up the engines.

The modern chopper was quick to respond to Danik's touch on the joystick. Almost instantly, the craft lifted off the deck.

"Sam, you know anything about chopper guns?" Danik asked.

"Some. Give me the cook's tour."

"Hell, I was hoping you'd know. Just see if you can scare these boys off. I think that thing over there … yes, that. Grab hold and see if it has any juice. Sidney, are you strapped in? We're going to fly like a bat out of hell!"

Sidney, feeling weak, assured him she was firmly strapped in her seat. Danik maneuvered the chopper like it was a toy, making it climb and dip in quick succession, twirling this way and that. The other choppers approached with their guns firing. Just as they were within range, Danik veered and dipped, fast. Sam, unable to calm himself to affect the attacking choppers' engines, grabbed onto the gun trigger and fired warning shots. Closer and closer they came, bullets just off to one side, then the attack broke off.

U.S. naval fighters, in the air and on the sea, had arrived. Madame's band of killers dispersed and quickly vanished. Sam and Danik cheered. It was almost too good to be true. They had escaped unharmed.

Once they were sure the danger was past, Sam relaxed. "How long to the island?"

"Let's see, it should be about another hour at this rate of speed. Lot faster than the chopper we use. Probably get there about the same time as Ryan and your boys."

Sam was relieved. Soon they could all return to some sort of a normal life. He turned to look back at Sidney. She had fainted. He suddenly noticed the blood stain on her shirt.

"Oh, my God, Sidney." He got up and lifted her shirt to find a bullet wound near her left breast, nearly sealed over. "Sidney!"

She opened her eyes and tried to sit up. She was weak. "I'm cold, Sam."

"Danik, she's been shot. You've got to help her."

Sam went to the controls while Danik checked Sidney. He sat beside his sister and put his hand over her wound while he breathed deeply and closed his eyes. After a few moments, a tear rolled down his check. He opened up his eyes and saw she was gazing back at him.

"Sidney, no. Please, not now."

She nodded. "Just get me home, Dan."

Danik put his arm around her shoulders to support her. He took her hands and held them firmly to his chest.

"You're going to be always in here," he said, pressing her hand over his heart.

"I know, Danik. Me too." She was nearly breathless. "Much farther?"

"Another half an hour and you're home."

Danik wiped the tears from his eyes.

"Danik, what? For Christ's sake, tell me she's okay!" Sam shouted.

"You have to come back here, Sam."

He switched places with Sam, who immediately took Sidney into his arms. Danik checked the chopper's controls and ensured the aircraft's heading was true before he swallowed and tried to find the words that were too painful to utter.

"Sam, Sidney has a bullet in her heart muscle."

"Oh my God. Danik, do something. Help her."

"Sam, I could telepathically move the bullet into the heart sac but that would cause almost instant death. There's nothing I can do. If there was anything, I'd give my life for her. I'm going to have to fly this chopper. You stay with her and do what you can. When we get home, maybe Greystone can help her."

Sam heard the words but they seemed distant. A numbness permeated his mind and body. It was impossible to take a breath. The walls of the chopper vanished into a gray abyss.

Sidney shifted in his arms. "Sam, take a breath," she said in a commanding tone of voice. "Don't go back there, please." She gasped for air and reached to touch his face. "This isn't over. I love you, Sam."

Sam looked into her face. Love reflected back onto him as it had when he'd opened her cell door earlier that day.

"That's right. It isn't over. Greystone will help you."

"No, Sam. Greystone can't help me now, but he can help her."

"Sidney, you've survived worse. Don't give up, damn it!"

Sidney ushered up what little reserve she had and tried to hold her head up. "Sam, we're not over."

Sam began to tremble and weep.

"Listen. You and I are so strongly connected, death can't separate us. When you've given up your anger and sorrow, you'll find me. I'll be standing there, right in front of you, waiting for you to see me. I promise you, Sam. It's that simple." She stopped to catch her breath.

Sam gently brought her to his chest and caressed her face while tears flowed down his face. "Simple but impossible, my love. If you die, so do I."

"Sam, put your hand on my chest over my heart."

He didn't hesitate to follow her request. "Now close your eyes and ... take several slow ... deep breaths."

"Sidney, I ... "

"Slow ... deep breaths. I want you ... to know ... that I'm ... not afraid. I'll ... take you ... to where I ... will be waiting."

Sam reluctantly closed his eyes and breathed. Time and space faded as did the torment. He felt himself become more than a physical being. His physical nature became lost in the spiritual ecstasy of merging into a higher dimension. His old limiting emotions slipped away, revealing joy and love as being his true nature. He discovered the essence of his soul, complete and glowing with abundance and Light. In fact, he became aware of the Light shimmering and dancing in, around, and within all he perceived as being near him. As his clarity increased, so did his understanding of where he was.

"What do you think, so far, Sam?" said the voice from behind him. He turned around. Her face was no longer pale. The glow of love on her face radiated as brightly as morning mist.

"Sidney, this is ... "

"My home. Your home too, when it's time. But you need to take care of her first."

She softly touched his face, smoothing over the lines showing his confusion, and waved her other hand toward the curtain of golden haze.

It melted away. Before them was a sailboat, rocking on the gentle waves of an endless sea. "I'll be here, Sam. And when you call for me, I'll be there with you. I'm only a thought away. I love you so."

He looked tenderly into her eyes. In spite of the realization that they'd be separated in the physical world, while in this place, he felt that time span was nothing more than a brief interlude. He was aware, though, that he'd have to endure the painful transition once he returned to the world of time and space. Sam then noticed a small pair of hands grasping onto Sidney's shorts. A small child peeked out from behind Sidney's legs. He recognized the little girl. She was exactly the same child he'd encountered at the school grounds. "Savannah?" he asked.

She grinned sheepishly. "That's me," she said, glancing up at Sidney. Then the grin was quickly gone and replaced by disappointment.

Sam looked back at Sidney with a startled look on his face. "She's ours?"

Sidney nodded. "But unless Greystone can perform one of his rare miracles, her physical life will have been little more than a few days."

Sam embraced Sidney.

"I love you more than words can express, Sidney. I always will."

He heard her reply, "I know," as the sound of the chopper returned to his consciousness. The motor was winding down. They had landed. Danik tugged at him to release Sidney.

"Sam, this is Greystone." Danik pointed to a man in the chopper's opened doorway.

"Bring her into the cabin, my friend."

Sam picked up Sidney, whose body was completely limp. He barely detected any breathing from her. Danik jumped out and Sam handed Sidney over to him. Quickly, she was carried to a nearby cabin and placed on a bed. Greystone and the Elders surrounded Sidney and placed their hands on her body. They looked at each other and shook their heads. Their hands had provided some support, and her breathing became somewhat stronger.

Sam called out to her, "Sidney, you're home now. Sidney! Sidney!"

Excruciating pain returned with its horrible, strangling grip on his heart. He tried to steady himself, to remember the place he'd been, to be strong for her. He hung onto the belief that the Guardian Elders would perform their magic and keep her alive.

Greystone approached Sam and put his arms around him. Sam stiffened. The soft touch made him want to completely surrender to the grief. But he believed that if he let the overwhelming sorrow overtake his heart, his sanity would come to an end.

Greystone spoke softly and yet with a sense of urgency. "Sam, we must act fast to save Savy."

All he heard were the words of encouragement, not the name. He was elated to hear that there was hope for Sidney.

"Yes, yes, I understand. Whatever it takes. Save her. I'd give my life. Just do it."

"You're sure? This won't be easy for you."

"Please, save her. Nothing else matters."

Greystone nodded. "Come over here, Sam. Sit down on the bed." Greystone patted Sam's shoulders. He looked into Sam's eyes with affection. "You're truly a courageous man. I understand why Sidney loves you so much."

Greystone placed his fingertips on Sam's forehead. The world around him fell away.

EPILOGUE

Four Years Later

S am tried to recall exactly how long it had been since Sidney's transformation to the spirit world. Sitting on her ledge above the valley, he had to think hard about whether it had already been almost four years. Time had little meaning on Hawk's Island. The Guardians didn't track time in measures of hours, days, or years. Their lives carried on in a sequence of moments, treasured and then released to the universe.

Sam's daughter squirmed to be released from his lap.

"Savannah, sit still. Just a few more minutes, please Savy."

She lay back in his arms and gazed up at him. Without expressing any words, she conveyed to him that he was pushing the limits with her patience.

"Two minutes." He tweaked her small nose.

She grinned and closed her eyes.

Sam recalled how difficult that first year had been. The grief of Sidney's loss, the abrupt change in his identity from that of a man of the sea to Guardian—not to mention acting as host for his unborn daughter for eight months.

Sam now remembered how the Elders had gathered around Sidney's mortally wounded body. Greystone's hand had rested lightly on Sidney's chest, sharing his energy with her body. Sidney's wound was fatal and her healing was beyond even the Elders' powers, but her baby could likely be saved. She would only continue to breathe for a few minutes, so a solution had to be found quickly. A vision of a kangaroo and the way it could carry its developing embryo "joey" in a pouch struck Greystone. He shouted, "Sam has to become like a kangaroo!"

Livingstone had frowned. "Greystone, what … " He paused and then understood. "Yes, we can make a pouch on Sam's belly. It will take more than a simple transfer of the embryo, though. Sam has no womb to provide the environment necessary for a human baby to develop."

"The answer," Greystone had said, "is the Holy Membrane. It will surround the baby's body and will be the conduit through which the baby receives the Universal Life Force."

Birthstone's eyes lit up. "Yes," she said. "But it is empowered by and responds to the intent and thoughts of the being it surrounds. Until Savannah takes her first breath, we would have to be in continuous contact with Savannah's Holy Membrane. Through our intent we can empower it to convert energy to nutrients and cleanse her body."

Greystone placed his hand on Sidney's abdomen. With great tenderness, his index finger traced a line and the tissues parted, exposing the nearly invisible embryo in her sac. Combining their powerful mystical energies, the Elders created a bond with the embryo. Still within Sidney, an energy field developed that separated her from her mother. The energy field swirled around the tiny body that had been growing weak from being starved of blood. In seconds, the energy field became a transparent membrane. It shimmered with iridescent colors, and the fluids within bathed Savannah's cells until they glowed with new life.

At that moment, Sidney took her last breath.

Birthstone went to Sam, still unconscious on the adjacent cot. She connected with Sam's Universal Life Force energy and asked, "Samaru Waterhouse, do you accept responsibility for the hosting of your daughter?"

Sam opened his eyes in shock, trying to understand what he was being asked. Host his daughter? In his stupor, the request made no sense to him, and he frowned in confusion and disbelief.

Birthstone continued to explain. "You recall that Sidney was with child—your child. You will only be carrying your child for the next eight months, and you will not be harmed or changed in any way. The Elders will help make it work. There is no other way to save Savannah."

Sam tried to sit up, and swayed back onto his cot as though he had been drugged. "Sidney?" he whispered.

Birthstone placed a reassuring hand on Sam's shoulder. "Sidney can no longer carry Savannah. The burden falls to you."

Sam thought about his sons when they were infants. He had carried them protectively. He then recalled the small child he had met at the school grounds and suddenly knew that she had been his daughter, Savannah. She needed him now. Even in his half-awake state, he realized that Savannah was all that was left of Sidney and he needed her even more. Needed to keep her alive, at any cost to himself.

Danik's face came into his view as he knelt down beside Sam. "Hey, sailor, we can do this. Piece of cake. We'll all look after your sons while you're laid up." Danik grabbed onto Sam's hand and squeezed. "It's gonna take some fortitude, but I know you can handle it."

Sam nodded. "Okay, let's get on with it." Quickly, with Greystone's touch, Sam was again unconscious.

Birthstone traced a line on Sam's belly. The tissues parted to reveal the muscular abdominal wall. Birthstone's left hand hovered above his exposed abdomen, and the muscles there began to quiver. Quickly they began to shape a small hollow bowl, with the opening toward Sam's heart. "Sam is ready," Birthstone announced.

Instantly, the membrane housing Savannah was nestled in the bowl. Birthstone touched the edges of the retracted skin. Gently, the skin returned to its former state, intact and without any mark to show it had been separated. The transfer was complete. To protect Savannah, the Elders had kept Sam in a dormant state most of the time. Twenty-four hours a day, an Elder was with Sam. Energy was transferred to Savannah, which then became all that she needed, as easily as they turn water to wine.

He remembered little of being in the dormant state, other than Danik at his side any time he was briefly awake. He knew he was carrying his daughter, but in his foggy mind, it didn't seem to matter. He also came to understand that Sidney had died. It was a crushing realization, but over the next thirty weeks, the pain of the blow softened.

His body had quickly returned to its normal physique once the Elders removed a fully developed Savannah from the pouch. After Sam returned to full consciousness, his boys had given him focus. Simon and Nathan were rebels and at first had been resistant to remaining on the island. But together, they worked at becoming a family again, adjusting to the changes in their lives and in each other. Their family bonds held firm, and aside from a few threats and fistfights between the boys, the Waterhouse family had slowly merged into the Guardian's lifestyle.

Greystone and Danik had hovered over Sam that first year. Waking up in the middle of the night, he'd feel the terrible loss of Sidney. Somehow, Greystone had always known when to be there at his side. He'd arrive, saying nothing and carrying a bowl of warm soup or tea. Greystone was the most powerful, yet loving man Sam had ever met.

Danik persisted in instructing him on ways to become aware of the presence of Sidney's spirit. But Sam's sorrow continued to simmer just under the surface, and his grief prevented him from shifting into the place where Sidney waited. His efforts to open the doorway to Sidney continued to be excruciatingly frustrating. It seemed impenetrable. If Sidney was standing there on the other side, he'd never know it—except for one glimmer of hope.

Each evening, as he slept in Sidney's old bed, he'd carefully place his crystal on the bedside table. In the morning, the crystal would be gone. At first, Sam thought he was losing his mind. Then he remembered the game Sidney had played with him when they'd first met, moving the crystal in his office from one location to another.

Before doing anything else in the morning, he'd have to find where she'd hid the crystal. It was a connection, tenuous at best, but still a connection with her. It was almost enough.

Sam snickered to himself, recalling the incident less than two months earlier. He'd been searching his small house for a missing sock. Having only two pairs, he was becoming alarmed that some rodent might have whisked it off and he'd be left with only three socks. His search became frantic.

In a moment of desperation and without giving any thought, he blurted, "Sidney, where's that damned sock!"

"Right where you left it last night, Sam."

Sam had heard her and the teasing smile in her voice. He stood there, waiting for more. He ached for more. He closed his eyes tightly, and yet the tears still made their way down his face.

"I love you," he called out to the empty room.

There had been no reply.

"Hi, Dad," called out Simon, approaching him from the trail and bringing Sam back into the moment.

Nathan was with him, panting from the exertion of climbing the rocky trail. Beads of sweat formed on their foreheads.

"Hey, Savy. Dad still not letting you sit by yourself up here?" Simon chided his sister.

Savannah frowned. "No!" she said with a note of irritation.

"Come sit down, boys," Sam called out to his sons. "What's happening? Thought you were still in class."

"All done. It's five already. You comin' down for supper?"

"I've been here that long?" asked Sam. "Didn't realize it was getting so late. You go ahead and take Savy with you. I'll meet you down there. Save a spot for me beside you brats in the lodge."

"Oh no. We're not sitting with you old folks," his youngest son said, teasing him.

Nathan grabbed Savannah's hand and led her back to the trail and down the mountain. Sam continued to sit on the ledge, looking out toward the ocean.

He thought of Admiral Garland and the file. It was only a brief thought. Once he'd turned the memory rod over to Danik, he'd made it clear to everyone that he wanted nothing more to do with that business. Recently, he'd overheard that Danik's father, Aaron, continued to work with the admiral, but little progress had been made in defusing the Dark forces. Madame had escaped and remained elusive. She was hunting for Danik, having discovered that he wielded great power using the sun crystals. Frank Butchart had died. The *Nonnah* had been decommissioned, the crew scattered throughout the naval forces.

Upon inspection of the crystals, Aaron found that most of them had been damaged by the scientists and were now useless. The eight remaining intact crystals were with the Guardians, safe — for the time being.

The admiral had been granted a few visits to the island. On each occasion, Sam briefly greeted the man and then returned to his chores or his sanctuary on the ledge. Today, he felt the past had no more power over him. Today, there was only the moment — free of pain and sorrow.

The ocean called to him. He could just barely see his sailboat anchored in the bay, gently rocking with the waves. Never before today had the island's spell infused him with such pure ecstasy — the complete and utter miracle of being alive, to be one with all. To feel immersed in healing energy. To be simply in the moment. He closed his eyes.

The sun, hovering just over the mountain across the valley, held its warmth and caressed Sam's face. He welcomed it into his being and thanked the universe for all the blessings of the day. He inhaled deeply, held his breath for a moment, and then released it. He emptied his mind, inviting wholly and unconditionally all that had a need to be one with him. In doing so, he felt a sudden snap within his chest, as if a shell surrounding him had become too small. In the center of his forehead a slight pain pushed through and eased with the opening of his third eye.

The fragrance of plumeria blossoms arrived first, just moments before he felt the touch of her hand on his face. He opened his eyes and saw pale green eyes smiling back at him. Sidney was seated in front of him with an inquiring look on her face.

"I'm wondering, Sam, if this is a good time to go sailing."

He reached for her.

The Guardians gathered inside the lodge for their supper. The Waterhouse boys had saved a seat for their dad and were wrestling with Savannah to get her to sit still.

Greystone approached the small child. "Savy, listen to your brothers. By the way, boys, I think your dad might not be joining us for dinner tonight. I noticed his sailboat heading out to sea. Remember to keep some food aside for him. He'll be hungry when he gets back."

ACKNOWLEDGMENTS

How does a ship thank the ocean? The relationship is fraught with dangers of sinking or being shredded over a reef. And yet, the ship, if guided by wisdom and dogged determination, discovers its journey exceeds the joy in arriving at the destination. And so it is with the writing of this story. The experience was an intense journey of self-discovery.

This story would not have begun if it were not for a vision that shook me so deeply that I resorted to writing about the experience to free myself from its constant nagging. What I thought would be a few pages became a thousand pages. Over ten years I was an instrument of a force that instructed me on what to say and how to say it. Anytime my ego determined a story line, the "voice" became silent, and the story came to a halt without an ending. Thankfully, on computers there is the "delete" key. I would go back and obediently allow the storyteller within to direct the writing.

Writers must suffer the risks of exposing their soul to the critical eye of the public and rejection from publishers. And so it is with great respect that I bow to my publisher, Omnific Publishing, for accepting this jewel in its raw and unpolished form. In particular, I am forever grateful for the editor, Beverly Nickleson, whose incredible talent was instrumental to glean out the purest clarity of every scene and to bring into focus the soul of each character.

Candace Jane Dorsey is an author and instructor in my first writing class at the University of Alberta Extension. Because of her, I began to see hope that this story may be worth doing very well. Candace continued to be a source of inspiration and knowledge that guided me throughout this challenging and loved project.

Friends with experience in the naval forces advised me on military protocol and life aboard a ship. In particular, I am grateful to my friend, Bill Stevenson, Leading Torpedoman Operator, who served in WWII aboard the famous HMCS Haida, a Tribal class destroyer.

My first editor, Elizabeth Medwid, had patience matched by insistence on excellence. Elizabeth had a gift of telling me what precious pages had to be deleted, and managed to accomplish that with my ego still intact.

Since childhood, my mother, Margaret Woodroffe Cropley, nurtured my paranormal experiences. There were no chantings to gods or goddesses. But each time I told her of my visions or visitation of guides, she would quietly acknowledge and smile.

I am most grateful for my loving husband, Ralph Weir. Throughout the writing of this story he was my most critical advisor and greatest fan.

And dear reader, as Sidney said, "I am grateful for the love and guidance of the Guardians, for all the trials and tribulations that taught me tolerance and courage, and for all the events that led me to you."

ABOUT THE AUTHOR

As a Canadian, Feather Stone was allowed the freedom to explore a kaleidoscope of infinite ways of being human. The only restrictions imposed by her parents were that racism was not acceptable and deliberately causing harm to any other being or creature for any reason was not tolerated. Upon meeting her spirit guide when she was a child, Feather's life became a journey of experiencing the paranormal. Through her practice of meditation and Reiki and study of Shamanism, she's been able to shift to dimensions that defy description.

On February 15, 2002, Feather was honored to receive the Exemplary Service Medal from Lieutenant Governor Lois Hole (representative of HRH Queen Elizabeth II) for her service as a paramedic with Edmonton's Emergency Response Department. She and her husband are now enjoying retirement and loving their sheltie, Jasper, and two cats, Smokey and Leo. Her motto? Change your thinking, change your life.

Young Adult

Shades of Atlantis and *Ember* by Carol Oates
Breaking Point by Jess Bowen
Life, Liberty, and Pursuit by Susan Kaye Quinn

Anthologies

A Valentine Anthology including short stories by Alice Clayton, Jennifer DeLucy, Nicki Elson, Jessica McQuinn, Victoria Michaels, and Alison Oburia

Summer Lovin' Anthology: Summer Breeze including short stories by Hannah Downing, Nicki Elson, Sarah M. Glover, Jennifer Lane, Killian McRae, Carol Oates, and Susan Kaye Quinn

Summer Lovin' Anthology: Heat Wave including short stories by Kasi Alexander, Debra Anastasia, Robin DeJarnett, Jessica McQuinn, Lisa Sanchez, and BJ Thornton

Alternative Romance

Becoming sage by Kasi Alexander